All the Time in the World

All the Time in the World

A NOVEL

Caroline Angell

A HOLT PAPERBACK HENRY HOLT AND COMPANY NEW YORK

Holt Paperbacks
Henry Holt and Company, LLC
Publishers since 1866
175 Fifth Avenue
New York, New York 10010
www.henryholt.com

Distributed in Canada by H. B. Fenn and Company Ltd.

Library of Congress Cataloging-in-Publication Data

Angell, Caroline.
All the Time in the World : a novel / Caroline Angell.
pages cm
ISBN 978-1-62779-401-5 (paperback)—ISBN 978-1-62779-402-2
(electronic book) 1. Nannies—Fiction. 2. Women musicians—
Fiction. 3. Grief—Fiction. 4. Families—Fiction. I. Title.
PS3601.N55435T55 2016
813'.6—dc23 2015026379

Henry Holt books are available for special promotions and premiums.
For details contact: Director, Special Markets.

First Edition 2016

Designed by Meryl Sussman Levavi

Printed in the United States of America

1 3 5 7 9 10 8 6 4 2

For my grandmother, the original Charlotte

PART ONE

Gretchen

The day she died was not beautiful. There have been a few world disasters in my lifetime, generation-defining events, and the ones I remember most clearly were marked with the hideous irony of a perfect blue sky. But the day Gretchen McLean died was miserable and drizzly, with periods of that nasty, keening wind that blows your raincoat hood straight back from your head and whips the garbage on Lexington Avenue into your face. It was appropriate, almost righteous. Towers fall, and the sun should not warm your skin; buses explode, and the breeze should not trace gentle ripples across the reservoir. But on the day that Gretchen died, even the weather seemed to understand its role. Because on the day that the mother of two little boys dies without warning, the wind should absolutely howl.

February, the day before

"I left the juice box on the counter. You might want to take a paper towel too. He squeezes them when he puts the straw in,"

Gretchen tells me. "Right, George?" She pokes little George in the belly.

"All over me when I put the traw in," he confirms. I'm pretty good at deciphering George-speak now, but it took me six or seven months to catch on. Gretchen understood it from the moment it started, which I'd prefer to chalk up to her intuitive mommy-skills, rather than to my slow-babysitter syndrome.

I walked in the door exactly seven minutes late today, which is an unusual occurrence. Of course, today is the day that Gretchen is in a hurry to leave, and now her meticulousness, which I normally laugh at, is giving me a complex. I'd love to give her an acceptable excuse for my lateness, but the wrong comment could lead to revelations I'm not willing to share. I don't want to risk it, even though we've known each other for two years and, in some ways, are as close as family. The less you know about someone, the easier it is to make up the details, which is exactly what you want to do when it comes to the person who will help raise your children.

Gretchen hands George his shoes and then tears off a paper towel, folds it up, and puts it under the juice box on the counter. "Or would you rather I put it in the stroller, Charlotte?"

"The counter is fine."

"Hey, I meant to text you," she says, "and then I think I forgot—do you have plans tonight?"

"Do you need me to stay late?"

"We thought we might go out," says Gretchen. "But no big deal if you can't stay. We'll do it another night." I wonder if she means that, or if she made the reservation a while ago and took it for granted that I would be able to stay. I rarely say no to her, and I know I'm not the only one.

"I think it will be fine." I calculate the extra hours in my head and console myself with the thought. "You should go out. I'll stay."

"Thank you! That's great. Oh, before I forget, one of the

stroller wheels keeps turning sideways. Makes it drag a little, just fyi . . ." She is back to business, and I pull out my phone to text Everett, who is probably still in my bed.

"Have to work late. Go back to New Haven if you want to. Will feel bad if you stay an extra day. Don't be mad." I send the text and then regret that last insecure sentence.

Everett, my good friend from grad school, had shown up unannounced at my door at 9:30 last night with two things on his mind, both of which kept me tossing and turning longer than preferable. I'm not used to having another person in my space all night, so at 6:37 a.m. I was wide awake and spinning, despite having slept for only a couple of hours. Mornings with Gretchen and the boys are more difficult if I make less-than-stellar choices the night before, but on the whole, I like my employment situation and would like it to stay as it is. I have no family in New York, and barely any of my friends from school have relocated here. Gretchen's family has become somewhat of a refuge for me in this city, where everyone is in such a hurry not to look each other in the eye. Babysitting in Manhattan is a decent living, and since keeping a roof over my head is a priority for me, working for Gretchen has been ideal. But that isn't a thing you can say to someone like Everett—someone who proclaims he would rather eat chickpeas out of a tin can in a basement in Bay Ridge than sacrifice one minute where he could be Making Art. Luckily, his trust fund and his acceptance to Yale's doctoral program have kept him from such a fate thus far.

"Me riding in the troller, Tahr-lette?" George asks, bringing me back to the present.

"Yes, bug, you're riding in the stroller."

"And we go get Matt?"

"Yes, we're picking up Matt," I say. Impatience won't do; the day is just starting, and it's a marathon, not a sprint. George is at that toddler stage of communication where I have to repeat everything he says back to him, so he can be sure his objectives are understood and will be met. "Can you fasten those shoes, pal? Do you need a little help?"

"Me do it," he says, with great authority.

"Good job, Georgie," Gretchen says, leaning down to kiss him. "Mommy has to go and run a few errands, and I'll see you in a little bit.

"Grocery tore, Mommy?"

"Yes, and the drug store, and the library. And maybe Banana Republic," she says to me with mock apology. "I'm a sucker for the forty-percent-off signs."

"Me too," I say.

"You and Matt are going to play on the playground with Charlotte," Gretchen says to George.

"Me go down that widdle side, Mommy?"

"Which little slide?"

"That widdle twisty side?"

"Sure, you can show Charlotte that little twisty slide."

"That sounds like fun, Georgie," I say.

Gretchen slings her bag over her shoulder, not Marc Jacobs, not Chanel, even though I know she can afford it. "Okay, you guys," she says. "Have fun. See you later."

"Bye, Mommy!"

"Bye-bye, honey."

I start to gather up our things for an outing, but the stroller-packing process is sluggish for many reasons, none of which I can attribute to Georgie.

"We're gonna need to stop for something caffeinated," I say. "I'm as slow as a baby in a lead diaper today." George laughs so hard he falls over sideways. He loves to be in on jokes about babies.

"The Philharmonic is playing my first solo piece in the next concert series," Everett had said last night when I, already in my pajamas, had opened my door to him. "At Carnegie Hall." He said it casually, like it was no big deal, even though we both knew it was. At the same time, he was holding up a bottle of really nice bourbon as if we were celebrating, and the juxtaposition confused me. How did he want me to react?

After we'd finished our master's program, Everett had taken a year off to see what kind of work he might be interested in pursuing, and then applied to Yale the following year to become a doctor of musical arts. He'd had minor projects come and go, but nothing on this scale, which is how I'd justified not being in attendance for any of them in the past few years. This was a big one. I should have been going crazy, and he should have been going crazy. Instead, we acted like we were sitting around the poker table, waiting for the other one to give up a tell.

"You should come with me to hear it," he said, while I was busy not saying anything, like an asshole. "I'll take you to the after-party. And we can sit in the audience together and be elitist. Or mock other people for being elitist. Your choice."

"Only if you promise not to crush all the tiny bones in my hand if the first violin goes sharp," I said.

"So, you'll come?"

"Ah . . . when is it?"

"Six weeks."

"Are you frantically rewriting?"

"More constantly than frantically."

I squeezed my fingers together to relieve the tension in them as I stared at Everett, still just outside the door to my apartment, and I tried to think of something to say. Indecision overwhelmed me, but it wasn't an unfamiliar feeling, particularly in my recent history. Three years ago, my life had been as linear as a road map, the progression so natural that sometimes it took me a while to notice the milestones. I could draw a straight line from Yamaha preschool to the beloved record player my parents kept in our upstairs hallway, where I would sit and fixate for hours as a kid; from the evolution of my high school passions, Joni Mitchell to Vivaldi to Sondheim to the Clash; from conservatory in the

Midwest, to graduate school in New York, to scholarships and recitals and being chosen over and over and over.

It's surprising and, at times, miraculous that original music can still be made when you think about how little we have to work with, melodically. There are only twelve notes on our Western musical scale. The difference between the me standing there last night, not offering any kind of enthusiastic welcome to Everett, and the me that existed three years ago has everything to do with that scale. Until three years ago, I had spent an absurd portion of my time putting those notes together, stacking them against each other, stretching them out, and manipulating them into the shape of things I heard in my head. In an oblivion born of constant, lifelong validation, I had thought that those things would be mine forever, the melodies I constructed, and that it would always be my choice when and how and with whom to share them.

But that was not the case, and in hindsight, maybe it was naive of me to think that I would have all the time in the world to make those choices. You never know how important the things in your own mind are, that specific pattern of neuron firing that only *your* brain does, until someone takes them away from you.

The realization came upon me so quickly that there was barely time for acceptance; there was nothing to do but stay put. It hadn't made sense to move to a different city, because everything would still be the same. There would still be a part of me that had been borne away without my consent, and there would still be the risk that it would happen again. I might as well be in New York City, where there were plenty of meanwhile jobs, places that I could enjoy predictability and a bit of financial security until I figured out what to do next.

Meanwhile had lasted until now. And there was Everett, on my doorstep. I stepped back to let him in, feeling the unbalance of being thrown back three years in time. He was with me, but we weren't in the same place. *The Philharmonic. Carnegie Hall.*

Two miles and a whole solar system away from my apartment by the East River.

"It sounds great," I said. "It's hard for me to take time off from work though, unless it's an emergency."

"What, you can't afford it?" He retrieved a pack of cigarettes from the pocket of his jeans and stuck one behind his ear. Add that to the sweater he wore draped over his shoulders, and you had a portrait of old-money Delaware. Everett, as drawn by a caricature artist.

"That's part of it. It's also hard on the family that I work for when I'm not around."

"I thought the mother only worked part-time."

"She does, but the boys have opposite schedules. A lot of their stuff overlaps," I said. "Anyway, I'll do my best. I really will." I walked into the bathroom and shut the door, turning on the water and letting it run while I stood in front of the sink, alone, in the only place inside my small apartment that he couldn't invade. He doesn't know anything about life with kids, I reminded myself. No one does, unless they actually *have kids* to deal with.

"Think these are getting too widdle," says George, in the present. I'm not sure what he means. I've packed the juice box and paper towel in the bottom of the stroller, along with my wallet, keys, and phone. I add two extra pairs of mittens and then do a check. Hand sanitizer: check. "Too widdle on my feet." Tissues: check. Bag of superheroes: check. "Too sah-mall, too sah-mall," says George, and at the last minute I decide that Matt will probably want a snack, so I put in a granola bar and some veggie straws. I finish loading just as I hear a quiet thump-thump from the other room, and when I come back to the living room to check on George's progress, I find him rolling a tiny Corvette along the floor and over two mountains fashioned from his shoes, which are no longer on his feet.

"Well, okay," I say, reaching for his hand. "Let's go find some different ones." He follows me, happy not to have to repeat himself until the end of time.

Everett's reply to my text comes in as I'm heading out the door with Georgie, but it's a little too explicit for me to answer while I'm wheeling a stroller down the sidewalk.

February, two years before

"Come on in," Gretchen says, smiling, as she holds the door open. She is blonde, and she looks like a catalogue model. "Matthew isn't feeling very well today, so he's been on the couch for a while. George doesn't walk yet, but he's a really fast crawler, so watch your step!"

Gretchen and her husband, Scotty, found me on an Internet babysitting service. I'm not sure what it was I wrote that caught their attention, but if I had to guess, I'd say it was probably the lines about my musical background. I'd decided to leave out the part about my master's in composition in order to make myself sound less educated and therefore within a reasonable price range, or so I told myself. I suppose it's also possible that I wanted to make babysitting sound less like a job that I was hoping to fill in the gap with while I figured out how to use that master's in composition to take the next steps in my career. Whatever the reason, the sentence had boiled down to something like "Coming from a family with strong creative values, I frequently use music and singing to engage the children." I'm glad that Gretchen and Scotty decided to overlook the questionable grammatical structure—creative values? Like maybe my family takes liberties with traditional values? Or perhaps my family made up their own values, creatively?—and instead chose to pay attention to how I might teach their children the "Itsy Bitsy Spider."

"It's awesome to meet you guys," I say. "Do you mind if I wash my hands really quick? I've been on the bus."

As I wash my hands with the orange-creamsicle-scented

foaming soap, I repeat their names to myself. George, Matthew. I'm relieved not to have to summon an earnest inquiry as to which of her family members she named little Fieldston after.

"Your apartment is lovely," I say, once I've found my way back to the foyer, and it's the understatement of the millennium. Her apartment is unbelievable. I can't see to the end of it on any one side.

"Thank you," she says, leading me to the kitchen table. The kids are visible through the archway to the living room. "It's an old building, so it has its quirks, but we really love it here."

When she's ascertained the requisite information (I live about a mile away; my schedule is somewhat flexible; there's no evidence that I'm a serial killer), the conversation turns to music, confirming my suspicions that she likes the idea of that influence around her kids.

"You'll have to forgive my ignorance. I know nothing about it, obviously, but you said you're a composer, right? Or that you went to school for composition?"

"Yes," I say, without elaborating. I don't want anything we discuss to give her an idea of how temporary this job might be for me.

"And what's the difference between a composer and a songwriter? Or *is* there a difference?"

"Not really," I say. "You might call yourself a songwriter if what you really wanted to do is write pop music or songs that people would hear on the radio. But a songwriter is just a specific kind of composer, that's all."

"But that isn't what you want to do?" she asks. "Be on the radio? Write songs for Justin Bieber?"

"Alas, I'm pretty sure the Biebs writes his own stuff," I say.

"Bummer," she says, and we both laugh.

"I used to love writing with other people, or for them. Back when I was in school, I mean," I add, hoping she won't notice or question the "used to."

"All I remember from my music classes as a kid are mnemonic devices for the notes, and trying to figure out what key something is in using tiny number signs," says Gretchen.

"Right, and lowercase b's," I say. "There was a fair amount of theory, for sure. I took a bunch of seminars, and my favorite was on collaborative composition. I really loved writing with a group on a specific project because there was something about it that let me communicate in a different way than when I was just hanging out, being regular Charlotte. I'm not cut out for performing, but I did my internship with an orchestrator for musical theater, and I had a great time with that."

"That sounds wonderful. Scotty and I love to see theater, if we're ever in town at the same time," says Gretchen. "He gets really excited about it and does all this research. He'd deny it, but I can't tell you how many times I've ended up at some downtown hole with thirty seats, watching something experimental that Scotty read about in the *Times* magazine. Especially before we had kids. So do you think that's the way you'll go, writing music collaboratively?"

"I think I will go down whatever road presents itself," I say, and a feeling rolls through me that I tell myself is anticipation but might be fear. Vague answers are not the way to connect with her, but I can't seem to stop myself from giving them.

"Well, if you ever feel like you're getting rusty, I know a couple of little kids who'd love to collaborate with you. They have a whole bucket of instruments waiting to be used for their intended purpose," she says.

"Sounds great," I say.

"Speaking of the monkeys, are you ready to meet them?" She leads the way to the living room, where we ignore all the super nice furniture and sit down on the floor.

She introduces me to the boys, who don't have much to say. After Gretchen and I have chatted for a while longer about allergies, likes and dislikes, schedules, and the satanic roots of gluten, she gives me the list of specific family obstacles.

"Scotty is away for work a lot of the time—sometimes for a while, sometimes just overnight. I work part-time as a nutritionist, but most of my clients are in the neighborhood."

"Okay." Little George is sidestepping his way around the coffee table. His hand grazes a little wooden nesting doll, causing it to wobble. I reach out automatically to steady it.

"Matthew can be stubborn."

I consider telling her that I once babysat for a family who only wore underwear at home—Mom, both kids, *and* Dad—what's a little stubbornness compared to the house where pants go to die? I decide to reserve this anecdote for the future, as pants-less households aren't always considered an agreeable topic for polite conversation. "Okay. What's your normal policy for handling that?"

"I try to talk him out of it. And if that doesn't work, a little bribery goes a long way."

I'm surprised at this—not surprised that she employs this age-old and incredibly effective tactic—but surprised that she'll admit it with no apparent shame. "Okay, ha, that's awesome. I'll follow your lead," I say.

"And we're a little bit afraid that George will never speak." She is perfectly pleasant, but I decide that she is not joking. Indeed, George has continued to crawl around us on the floor, picking things up, getting into other things, playing with toys, and pulling himself up to sidle along the furniture, but I haven't heard even a squawk out of him.

"He cries, so we know he can use his voice, but other than that, he doesn't make noise, vocally. No chatting or laughing or anything. Matt was chatting up a storm when he was George's age."

"How old is he?" I ask.

"He's thirteen months, and Matt is almost four."

"When do you turn four, pal?" I address the question to Matthew, who is lying on the chaise lounge with both feet up on the wall behind it. He frowns at me and doesn't answer. How dare you interrupt my *Spiderman* cartoon, stranger.

"Matty, can you please answer Charlotte's question?"

He sort of harrumphs and stares even harder at the flickering screen. Peter Parker is getting romantic with a girl from another galaxy. Racy.

"Sweetheart, if you're going to be impolite, we'll have to turn off the TV."

"June sixth," he grumbles.

"Hey," I say to him. "That looks like a bed pillow you're holding, not a couch pillow." He narrows his eyes at me, trying to assess what I'm all about. "When I was a kid, I always tried to trick my mom into letting me have a bed pillow on the couch. Did you trick your mom too? Or did she make an exception because you're not feeling too well?" He gives me a small smile, then turns his attention back to galaxy-girl's invisible aircraft.

"So we're going ahead with Georgie as if everything is fine," says Gretchen. "The pediatrician thinks a year and a month is too young to have him evaluated, and Scotty and I agree." She catches George as he passes by on one of his laps, adjusting one of the tabs on the side of his diaper and then releasing him again, all in one fluid motion. "Scotty, Matty, Georgie. Everyone has an 'ee.' Except for me. I'll have to be called Mommy to fit in. I told Scotty he could start a thing with 'Gretchy' over my dead body. You'll have to watch out. Charlie, Lottie, I'm sure they could think of one."

"The options are grim," I say.

George turns from the glass end table he is holding on to and faces where we sit on the floor. He takes four tottering steps in our direction, becomes unstable and squats, then stands back up and staggers all the way to Gretchen's outstretched arms.

"Scratch what I said earlier. I guess he walks now," she says, and I look at her expression and George's expression, and I am hooked.

February, the day before

"Do the pie-der on the floor." George is bored in the stroller while I stand on line, waiting for my iced coffee. After two years of singing this song, the kids are still entertained by it, but I'm having trouble coming up with new material.

"There's a spider on the floor, on the floor . . ." I sing.

"No! Do a glass of milk on your head!"

"There's a glass of milk on my head, on my head." He laughs. "There's a glass of milk on my head, on my head. Oh I wish I had something inSTEAD of this glass of milk on my HEAD, like maybe orange juice or ginger ale—"

"That not how it goes!"

"How does it go?" But he refuses to sing it himself. "Hey, what else could we drink besides orange juice and ginger ale and milk?"

"Chalk-lit milk?"

"Yeah, definitely. Or maybe water?"

"Fuzzy water. Die-ah Coke."

"Who likes Diet Coke?"

"Tahr-lette." After two years and four months of not speaking, just as speech therapy and autism evaluations were being contemplated, George had decided that he had plenty to say, in full sentences, no less. Now that he's three, he rarely runs out of things to talk about.

"Who likes coffee?"

"Daddy."

"Just Daddy? Doesn't someone else like coffee? Someone whose name rhymes with Par-lette?"

"Tahr-lette?"

"Ding ding ding! Right on, little dude. What does Mommy like?"

"Milk-sakes!"

"Milkshakes? Dream on! Anything else?"

"Iced tea. Wine."

"Wine? Mommy likes wine?"

"Yes, and me like wine."

"You like wine? Really? Georgie likes wine? Does Matty like wine?"

"No. Me and Mommy and Daddy like wine. Matt like apple juice."

"That's true; he does like apple juice."

"And Matt not like white milk."

"Do we have to put chocolate in it to get him to drink it?"

"Yes."

Once we're out of Starbucks, I secure my coffee and jog the last block up to school, tilting the stroller back so that George will laugh and feel like he's flying. When we arrive, I park the stroller amid a sea of similar vehicles in the school lobby and set him free from his constraints. "You want to get out, bug?"

"No."

"But we have to go up and get Matt in a minute."

"Me tay in the troller," he says. "You carry me?"

"I'll carry you up the stairs, but you have to walk down, okay?"

"You hold me?" he says.

"On the way up."

"On the way down?"

"Maybe," I say, but I don't look him in the face while I say it, because he can always tell when I'm avoiding the truth, which reminds me again of Everett.

Last night, after leaving him to fend for himself in my kitchen, I put my head close to the hot water running out of the bathroom sink, inhaling the steam. I could tell that Everett was struggling to understand my response, or lack of it, to his news, but I couldn't tell him any of the things that were going through my mind, the things from our past that his news had brought forth. There were only two people other than me who knew anything about it, and I wasn't ready to let him into that group. I locked the door to the bathroom, sat down on the floor, and pulled out my phone to text them.

"S.O.S."

"Where are you?" came the reply from my sister Jane.

"On the bathroom floor."

"Very Elizabeth Gilbert of you," said our other sister, Claudia.

"Why??" said Jane.

"Having a rough day. Will explain soon. Everett is here. I'm hiding."

"I love you and you can get through anything!!!!" said Jane.

"Use your body to distract him, then make a run for it," said Claudia.

"I love both of your kitten-faces," I typed back. "Okay, I'm going back out there."

I changed out of my pajamas and opened the door to the bathroom, preparing an elaborate mea culpa about the lateness of the hour and my relative crankiness, but Everett didn't seem in a hurry to demand an explanation. "It was pretty pointless of you to get dressed just for me," he says. I should have known that the order of his priorities would work to my advantage.

"Tahr-lette, these not for inside," says George, pulling on my pant leg. He holds up his mittened hands, and I feel bad for letting my thoughts slide elsewhere. He's right; it's abnormally hot in here, as a glut of mommies and nannies deck the lobby. Among the Puerto Rican nannies and the Caribbean nannies and the Dominican nannies are the occasional French au pairs and grad-student babysitters. I count myself among the latter category, as there isn't really a slot for women in their late twenties with two advanced degrees and no current plans to use either one of them.

Also present today are both of the Class Mommies. Jillian, mother of Aaron and Ainsley (twins), is the alpha mommy. She is, without a doubt, the queen bee, a fairy princess among mortals. She has long, perfectly layered hair, walks miles in heeled boots every day, and dons a Carolina Herrera coat that makes me long to win the Powerball. It's possible the word *vivacious* was invented to describe her. The worst part is, there is no evidence to suggest even a hint of insincerity in her demeanor. She is the quintessential woman.

Ellerie, mother of Ellerie (whom the rest of us refer to as Little L), is the beta mommy. Naming her daughter after herself might have been an indicator into the true depth of her insecurity, or maybe she imagines she has created another generation of herself, in order to correct any imperfections in the current version. Possibly both are true. But whatever the case, she wears her negative, grasping heart on her sleeve, and even her Chloé handbag can't seem to make her feel better about her life.

As I am liberating Georgie's fingers from his mittens, I can hear her perpetually defensive voice lodging a complaint to the mommy contingent (the nannies and mommies rarely cross-pollinate in this environment). The edges of that voice never seem to dull down, and for a moment I wonder if age will ever soften it, or if it will just quit one day, abruptly, having reached its capacity for abuse.

I read in the newspaper this morning that the White House has released some unclassified documents outlining their recent policy on targeted drone strikes on terrorist leaders, even those born in America. I'm oddly excited by the topic—not that I have a passionate opinion one way or the other—but simply that this has been reported and is bound to whip up a controversy. Do we have the right to execute American citizens without due process? Or is national security a greater issue? Do we need to trust our leaders to gather an appropriate amount of evidence before they carry out the strike? If I were a high school teacher, I would drop my lesson plan for the day and hold a great debate. This is an issue I would love to hear argued, supported, even complained about.

But that isn't what I hear in the lobby of North Madison Primary and Preschool (affectionately known as North-Mad). ". . . needs to put her foot down about it. It's not just the sugar; it's the dyes! And, poor things, they don't know better. They want the sweet things, and they want to be able to do what all their friends are doing! I mean I don't want to be the one to throw the word *discrimination* into the mix . . ."

I'd venture a guess that Ellerie hasn't seen the news today. Drone strikes probably didn't come up on *Good Morning America*, either.

The two other mommies look a little dazed, but Jillian nods as if she's considering the information seriously. "Is it happening often enough that you think the headmistress ought to know? Maybe we could speak to the lead teacher and see if she can do something? Ainsley loves fruit roll-ups. She was delighted. But Aaron said he didn't eat it; he had a cheese stick instead. At least we know they have options."

"Well, Ellerie came home crying, and if it's going to be such an affective issue, then I say we need to all come together and ask that something be done . . ."

Perhaps George senses that I'm about to commit a huge faux pas and make a face at another nanny, because he chooses that moment to lurch forward in the stroller. As the straps are unbuckled, he is no longer properly restrained, and I throw my arm out to catch him about a second before his nose hits the ground.

I hoist him up onto my hip. He has that look in his eyes, that look that says things could go either way. To sob with terror or to laugh with adventure? I know that I alone will be the deciding factor, so I say to him, in a voice that doesn't project relief or fear or any other negative emotional cues, "Whoops! Got to be careful there, crazy-pants," and kiss him on the cheek.

The kindergarten doors open then, and as George and I

march up the stairs with the tide of grown-ups, Jillian smiles at me and says, "Good catch!" I think she looks relieved to have been distracted from Ellerie's rant.

One of Matt's classmates, Sahina, has a nanny whose English I can never understand, which has made for many an awkward exchange of pleasantries. She approaches me as I am adjusting the ear flaps on Matt's tiny hat, moving them out of his eyes. I'm pretty sure she's German, and her name is either Bridget or Digit—I could swear she says Digit, but Bridget makes more sense. "You want Sahina playdate?"

I'm not sure what she's asking me, so I say, "We're going to the playground inside the park at Seventy-Sixth. Would you like to come with us?"

"Okay," she says. "We play with Ellerie too."

"I really appreciate this, Gidget," says Ellerie Senior. (Gidget, really?) "Oh, are you guys going with Matt and George? Great! Charlotte, is it okay if I pick up Ellerie at your house around five? It's much closer than Sahina's on the West Side."

"I should probably talk to Gretchen," I say.

"Oh, would you? Thanks so much! Have fun, baby!" Ellerie leaves Little L half-zipped, clutching a lunch box and a baggie of carrots, not knowing which adult is responsible for her.

I manage to hold Georgie and the hands of both Little L and Matt on the way down the stairs. If I trip, we're all done for. When we get downstairs, I look for G/D/Bridget and find her strapping Sahina into a stroller. She is way too big for a stroller, and Little L and Matt are exchanging glances.

Before either of them can make this judgment call out loud, I say, "Who wants a snack?"

"Me," says Matt. George is silent. He never wants a snack. Little L looks like she wishes she could say "me," but instead she purses her lips and digs her tiny fingers into her carrot bag.

"Elle," I say. "I brought some veggie straws for Matt and George, but the only problem is, I brought too many. Would you like to help them eat some of their snack?" Little L nods. We all start down the street, and while Little L will not yet direct any of her questions to either me or Sahina's nanny, at least she is chattering to the other kids. It's cold out, but the sky is a brilliant blue, and I need my sunglasses. When we get to the playground, Matt and Little L go tearing off for the tallest slide, with Sahina not far behind. Georgie is slower to start. He digs around in the bottom of the stroller until he finds a different pair of mittens, then proceeds with the painstaking process of taking off his current mittens and replacing them with the new ones. G/D/Bridget is watching his progress with interest.

"I want them on the playground," she says.

"Oh yeah? Okay."

"Tomorrow is not nice out," she continues. I take that to mean she's glad they can play outside today, because tomorrow the weather will be crappy.

"I'm happy they like this playground because it's small, and you can see the whole thing from one vantage point—from one place," I say and then wonder what other innocuous things I can come up with to discuss. Little L, Sahina, and Matt have run by me at least ten times since we got here, back and forth and over and under and around again.

George and his little legs have done about three laps, and he keeps calling "MATT!" and then realizing that his brother is on the opposite side of the playground. I stand up. I'm pretty sure he's headed for a meltdown. Just as I reach him, he pauses by the gate. There's a cocker spaniel off his leash wandering by, and as he and George spot each other, they both amble to a slow halt. The dog waits while George approaches and squats down in front of him, staring into his eyes, communicating in silence. After about thirty seconds, George reaches out slowly and pets the dog around his ears. The dog licks his chin, and George stands up while the dog trots back to his owner, who is sitting on a bench chatting to her girlfriend.

"What wonderful dog manners he has," the lady calls to me. "You've taught him very well." It looked to me more like dog *whispering*, but it's not worth correcting her, or even correcting her assumption that he's my kid.

"Thanks," I call back and turn my attention to George just in time to see him take a deep breath and holler "MAAAAATTTT!" louder than I would have thought possible.

Matt, Sahina, Little L, and every other kid on the playground stop what they are doing and look for the source of this primal sound, and Georgie takes the opportunity to run to Matt's side as if nothing happened. After a moment, things get back to normal, and Matt seems to be including his brother in whatever chase game they're playing.

"They work together; they figure how to make it work," says G/D/Bridget, and this time I know what she means, and for a moment I'm overwhelmed with curiosity about the woman, where she's from, what makes her tick, what her life is like away from Sahina and the world of wobbly bridges and patterned, reusable Ziploc bags. And I wonder what she'd think of mine, if I told her that right now I'm feeling ill at ease and distracted, and not just because of sibling dynamics or having an extra kid foisted off on me.

Everett had opened his eyes this morning to find me watching him, like a creepy stalker or like someone with feelings for him that were stronger than my own. I had been thinking of all the times we had fallen into this routine of spending the night together, and of the reasons I had never allowed myself to try to make us into something else. The night I had premiered my silly first-year midterm, Five Concertos for Ukulele, was the first time, and after that, going home together seemed to make sense if neither of us was significantly attached. Our involvement had come and gone in waves since then, a pattern that had seemed more inconvenient to break than to let run its course.

"Hi," Everett had said, kicking the sheets down around our

feet and stretching out. I sat up and grabbed a T-shirt from the floor, not sure if it was mine or his, and pulled it over my head.

"Hi," I said. "I know it's early. The younger boy I babysit doesn't have preschool today, and his mom has a bunch of stuff to do, so I told her I'd come over early."

"How old is the younger one?"

"He's three," I said, walking over to the crappy, impossible-to-tune-or-part-with upright piano that sits in front of my window.

"New York City," he said. "Their preschools are like my third grade."

I sat down at the piano like I was staking out territory at a Vietnam protest. "Everett, you're so full of shit. I know you went to prep school."

"But I didn't go to preschool for three years before kindergarten," he said, getting up to join me at the piano. He didn't bother with clothes. He lit a cigarette, and I took it from him and inhaled, something I never do unless he's around. "And I didn't have a nanny," he went on. "My mother made it work, and I have three sisters." He sat down next to me, not touching me, even though it felt like he was.

"That must be where you learned how to sweet-talk the ladies," I said, handing back his cigarette.

Everett put his hands on the keys and traveled up and down between two octaves, wandering for a minute, like a lady jazz singer. Then he really started to play, not bothering to ask me to move but playing around me.

"Play something from your piece," I said, and he merged into something new, something that churned with angst. Classic Everett.

"This is the solo viola," he said. "And here's where she's joined by a bassoon—"

"Viola and bassoon?" I listened for a minute. "But that harmony is wide. Those two instruments are so *middle*. It should be, like, violin and French horn or something."

He took his hands off the keyboard and got up. "Good idea. I'm going to write that down."

"Aren't you going to play any more of it?"

"No," he said, getting back in bed. "I'm not giving you a way to rationalize not showing up for the actual concert. It's here in the city and everything. You probably won't have to miss work at all."

"Sometimes I work late," I said, which sounded even stupider out loud than I had feared it would.

"You can take one night off. Colleen and Roger are driving down from Boston." Colleen and Roger, our old grad school buddies, had moved to Boston independently of each other, gotten themselves prestigious positions, he with the opera and she with a large cathedral, and then married each other, with very little warning.

"That's nice of them."

"And Snyder is coming too."

"Snyder lives in New York. He has no excuse." I tried to cover the tops of my bare legs with the T-shirt I was wearing, but I couldn't pull it down far enough, which still didn't give me a clue as to whether it was mine or his.

"Aha. You admit you have no excuse."

"Well, I guess if he has a job with weird hours, I'll give him a pass."

"He doesn't have a job at all. He's living off the money he made on that Japanese commercial he scored for Peter Jackson. He's not in New York anymore, because—I'm quoting—'you have to be in L.A. to write for the pictures.'"

"The *pictures*," I said. "Ew."

"I knew you'd like that one." Everett leaned back against the headboard.

"He's flying in from L.A.?"

"My point is that everyone will be here. I even heard from Jess," said Everett. "She's in London, but she said she would try to come."

The moment he said "Jess," I reached for the keyboard, automatically, but I couldn't think of anything to play from memory. My hands rested there, idle. "Out of all those people, I have the least important work to do, so I should drop everything to be there?"

"Charlotte, of course not. I didn't mean it like that."

"I have a job, Everett. I help raise kids. I think of it as kind of important. Maybe that's just my opinion?" I struck a chord on the piano, so low you could barely tell the difference between the pitches. "Not everyone has family money to fall back on while they figure things out." I found another chord, lower and more dissonant than the first.

"Stop," he said and came back to the piano. Piano benches are never meant for two people, but Everett thinks all space belongs to him. He sat down and put his right hand over my left hand, lifting it off the piano. He put it between his two hands, working his thumbs into my tendons. "I want you to come. Call me nostalgic. Most of our old friends will be here in one place, and since you live here, it would be a nice opportunity for us all to be together. That's all. End of begging." There it is, I thought. There is our relationship. Neither one of us is willing to be responsible for the other's feelings, so we will never take it down to true intimacy, and that is fine with me.

I took my hand away, got up, and retrieved my pants from the floor.

"When did you hear from Jess?" Turned out upon closer inspection that it was Everett's shirt I was wearing, so I took it off and exchanged it for one of my own.

"We're not really in touch," Everett said. "But I keep track of her. Don't you?"

"Sometimes, I guess."

"I e-mailed her to let her know. She was so excited, so effusive about it. Just like always. Her feelings are so huge," he said. "She told me she would try to make it."

I didn't trust myself to say anything in reply. Jess Fairchild is a composer, famous to the extent that composers can be famous, and she had been our teacher in grad school for one life-changing semester in our final year. Jess and her field of collaborative composition seduced us; she was only a few years older than we were, but to me, to Everett, to the eight other students lucky enough to be accepted into the seminar, the way she taught about making music with a team was enough to convert us into disciples. That semester had culminated in an individual session with her as our final project; a morning or afternoon of one-on-one time to see what you could make together, and it was there that I did the best work of my life thus far. We had looked at each other, Jess and I, and we both knew it. We were flushed and giddy and clapping like excited kindergartners, understanding without having to articulate it that what we had come up with was special. I had gotten an A in the course, but that was nothing new. My whole life had been As.

After that semester ended, no one in the seminar heard from her, which in all honesty was okay with us at the time. It added to her brand of charisma; she had come in and out like an apparition, leaving nothing but a feeling in the guts of ten students, a feeling that we were on our way. Eventually, we heard *of* her. We heard of her in Vienna directing a festival, in L.A. scoring an action movie, in Tel Aviv conducting a symphony. And a few months later, one of us—I can't remember who, although at times it has seemed almost painfully important that I do so—had heard she had written the opening title theme to a new dramatic television series. I had gathered with the classmates from my seminar to watch the premiere, so proud of her, proud that I had known her, proud that I had worked with her and that she had chosen me as her student.

Forty-five seconds later, the euphoria had fled. I felt suspended, as though something had passed through and emptied me of *me*.

The word *maybe* is a great debate between possibility and reality. As I sat on the arm of a recliner, passing a bag of Chex Mix back and forth with my classmate Colleen, listening to my best recollection of what Jess and I had written during my final exam fifteen weeks earlier, I thought *maybe*. Maybe I'm remembering it wrong. Maybe she only used the precise pieces that she was responsible for. Maybe she wants to surprise me; she could be dialing my number right now, dropping a check in the mail, waiting until I see my name on the closing credits in tiny white letters to get in touch.

A few hours later, though, there was no more possibility. There was only reality. The best work of my life was out in the world. And my name wasn't on it.

What could I say? There had been no witness, no recording. No one wants to say the word *plagiarism* out loud, because it's ugly, and because it's nearly impossible to prove in music. Twelve notes on a scale are not very many. Similarity is inevitable. No one wants to be Salieri or Kit Marlowe, a less celebrated talent, whining, "I did that first!"

As far as I knew, none of us had seen Jess after our sessions or in the years since that semester had ended, though apparently, there had been some communication, with some of us. At least one of us.

"You're getting dressed now?" Everett walked naked over to the kitchen cupboard to find a mug to use as an ashtray.

"I have to get to work." I was buttoning up my pants. "I don't think I can handle another round."

He lit another cigarette. "Ooh baby."

"Don't get a big head about it."

"Dirty."

"Everett, ew. Go home."

"You're mad at me? You sound mad. I can try to make you feel better, if you can wait seven or eight minutes—"

"I'm not mad," I said. "I'm late. I have to work, like I said."

"Maybe I'll stay another day."

"Sure," I said. "Spare keys are hanging by the door."

"I really want you to try and come to the concert," he said. "Will you? Try, at least?"

"Yes, of course. I was always going to try."

"You know, tomorrow is Valentine's Day," he said.

"I have to get going," I said, doing my best to zip up my overstuffed backpack with one hand while I unlocked the front door. Everett watched me go. He made no move to get up and send me off.

"Tahr-lette, you bring your oo-lay-lee?" George is leaning against the back of the bench. He has been done playing for twenty minutes, and he'd really like to go home, but I would like to stretch our playground time a little longer, to keep Little L and Matt outdoors until it's time for her to get picked up.

"My *ukulele*." I'm impressed that he has graduated from calling it "that widdle guitar." "No, babe. I left it at your house when we went to pick up Matt. I'm sorry. But we can still sing, if you want to." G/D/Bridget smiles at me over some kind of sewing project. It looks like a cross-stitch. Is that what adults do for entertainment in Germany?

"What we sing?"

"I don't know. The Thomas the Train theme song?"

"Nooooo."

"I thought that was your favorite!"

"That NOT my favorite."

"Oh, okay. Peter Rabbit?"

"No." He proceeds to veto "Winnie-the-Pooh," "Baa Baa Black Sheep," and every Bob Dylan song I can think of.

"Bug, I'm at the end of my list, here. Do you want to make something up?" He nods and looks at me expectantly. He wants *me* to make something up.

I pick a generic melody and sing about the kids on the playground, letting him fill in the rhymes where he can. Rhyming is definitely on this kid's list of favorite activities. G/D/Bridget even joins in once or twice, and after a while, Sahina has come over to join us, completing our makeshift campfire circle. Just as I'm about to announce my ingenious rhyme for twisty slide (misty-eyed), I notice Matt, standing on his own at the edge of the playground. At first, I think he might be trying to take a covert leak between the bars of the fence, but I can see his pants are fully buttoned, and he's looking down at something. I tell George I'm going to get Matt so we can head home, and I saunter over to where he is standing, like I just needed to stretch my legs.

"Oh, hey, pal," I say. "Is there a squirrel over there or something?"

"A rat," he says and points. Actually, that's a kind description of the thing that lies before us. It's more carcass than rat. I can see most of its ribs, where the flesh has been picked away, and I don't think either of us would have been able to recognize what type of rodent it was if it weren't for the tail, which is pretty much the only part of the creature that's fully intact.

"That's really disgusting, Matty. Sorry you saw that."

"But what do you think happened to him?" he asks, not moving away from it, which is unfortunate, as flies are starting to collect in the vicinity.

"Well, I guess it died, love."

"But how did it get died?"

"I'm not sure," I say, and I steer him away from the pile formerly known as rat. "Maybe it was really old."

"It looked small to me."

"Maybe a hawk got it."

Matt stops in his tracks. "What hawk? A hawk made the rat die?"

"Maybe," I say, cursing myself for introducing murder into the conversation. "Hawks eat smaller animals, honey. That's what they do for food."

"Do you think Pale Male ate him?"

"I hope not," I say.

"But what's going to happen to him now?"

"I guess he'll just . . . stay put." I don't want to tell him what the flies are going to do to the rat's unfortunate body.

"When you die, you just stay put?"

"Maybe it will go to rat heaven."

"Where's that?"

"Somewhere where there aren't any hawks."

"But where *is* that? Is it in the American States?"

"Hey, we were just about to sing another song. Want to sing with us? You know this one."

"What is it?"

" 'Somewhere Over the Rainbow.' "

He looks solemn for a minute, and I'm worried that I'll be bringing a psychologically damaged child home to Gretchen. "Can we change the words?" he asks, and I'm relieved when I see a smile poking at the corners of his mouth, however smirk-like it may be.

"Sure. What do you want them to be?"

"Somewhere over the hawk's nest."

"Weird, weird, you weirdo," I say, and as we approach George, he plops himself into the stroller and starts trying to fasten the straps with his little mittened paws.

"And it can be all about that rat. And his little fly friends," says Matt.

"Gross, you're gross!" I say, and he runs over to the slide and starts walking backward up the silvery slope. "We're going in one minute!" I call.

"What Matt looking at?" asks George.

"Oh, just something gross," I say, but that's not enough for George. He hops back out of the stroller and marches over to the fence, trailed by Sahina.

I start to go with them, but I feel a hand on my arm. "What they look at?" asks G/D/Bridget.

"A dead rat," I say. She tightens her grip on my arm.

"It's okay, they see it," she says. "Better to see it. Better to understand."

"Maybe," I say. "But I don't want George to have nightmares."

"Nightmares okay," she says. "Nightmares happening."

"*I* might have nightmares," I tell her. "It's pretty gross."

"I should see this gross thing," she says walking over with me to retrieve the kids. "If Sahina has nightmare, I should have it too."

WHEN I GET back to the McLeans' apartment with the boys and Little L, it's about five minutes until five. I decide to stick the kids on a bench in the lobby to wait for Ellerie instead of taking them upstairs.

I text Gretchen. "Hey. We're here but in the lobby, waiting for L's mom. Ok?"

"Cool. Have fun!!!!" says her answering text.

"Matt's babysitter?" says Little L.

"Yes, love?"

"Do you have any more snacks?"

"I do," I tell her. "But it's almost time for dinner, so I can't give you any snacks unless your mommy says okay."

"Can you call her?"

"I don't have her number, sweetie." As I say it, I realize the true absurdity of that statement. "We can ask her when she gets here. She'll be here soon."

She pouts but doesn't say anything. I am distracted by a squirming Georgie, so I collect the hats and mittens from the boys. I turn around just in time to see Little L tear into Matt's granola bar and take a bite.

Matt and George can't quite believe it. They heard me say no, and they know Little L heard me too. She is staring at me while she chews, daring me to say something to her, and I'm amazed at her audacity. Somehow I know that Matt and George, while they might sometimes defy me or their parents, would never disobey an adult they barely knew. My heart has gone out to Little L in the past. She has clearly never had mutual respect modeled for her. I use this to calm me down in the present as I hold out my hand for the granola bar. "Ellerie, I'm going to need you to give that back to me, sweetheart. We need to get Mommy's permission before we eat anything so close to dinner."

Little L looks at me and takes another bite. I want to grab it right out of her hands and make her sit in the corner, but instead I squat down and get in her face. "I'm going to count to three." She avoids my eyes. "One . . . two—"

"Ellerie Maxwell Covington, what are you eating, young lady?" Ellerie Senior is standing in the doorway with several shopping bags from Ralph Lauren dangling off her wrists, which are resting on her hips.

"Matt's babysitter gave it to me because I was hungry," Little L replies without missing a beat.

I refuse to be outmaneuvered by a five-year-old, and so I say, "Elle, please tell your mother the whole story." Little L is silent, and Ellerie is waiting for an explanation so I say, "I thought we should probably wait and see what you thought, but I guess she must have been hungry—"

Matt has no patience for my diplomacy. "She grabbed it out of the stroller," he says, and the elder Ellerie gives him a look that can only be described as withering.

"Well, it doesn't really matter. I know what a nightmare she can be, of course, but her father lets her get away with it, so she thinks she's entitled." As her mother goes on, I'm doing my best not to look down at Little L, but I can't help feeling sorry for the wee swiper, who apparently lives in the middle of a loveless, competitive igloo. "In the future though, Charlotte, I really don't like her to have any snacks after three thirty." In the future? The implication of this statement snaps me back into the present. This is not my life forever, I say to myself. This is not my real life. In fact, this cannot be my life long enough to be sent on another playdate with the Elleries.

"I would have called to ask you," I say, "but I don't have your number. I should probably get that from you if you want them to play together in the future."

"Oh, it's okay. Gretchen has my number. She can call me if there's any need. Say thank you to Matt, Ellerie."

"Thank you, Matt," says Little L, and they both sort of half wave with their backs turned as they walk out the door.

As we head toward the elevator, Matt rolls his eyes and says, "What a WEIRDO." He presses the button for our floor.

"What a weirdo," Georgie echoes as the doors slide shut.

When we get into the apartment, Gretchen is cooking and video chatting with her sister. She waves to us and continues her conversation. I wipe the kids' hands and faces and unzip them. Once I free them, they start running around the living room, acting crazy. Gretchen points with her sauce spoon at a Banana Republic bag on the kitchen table and mouths, "For you!" at me.

I shake my head at her, and she mouths, "It was on sale!" and then throws the bag at me. I catch it and unwrap a beautiful off-white cashmere winter hat, which I know I'll knock off into a mud puddle the minute I get outside.

"Thank you," I mouth back, even though I know she probably bought it because she feels bad for assuming I could stay late without asking. "Bath?" I mouth, and she nods. I write, "You're the best. I loooooove presents" on a Post-it note and give it to her so she'll feel better, and she smiles as I exit the kitchen.

"Me hold it!" Georgie is screaming right in Matt's face as Matt holds a blue light saber out of his reach.

"I had it first!" Matt screams back.

"No, me, I did," I say. "*I* had it first. I've been keeping the Sith Lords down at heel all afternoon. Didn't you see me swinging it at them? I think maybe I got one."

"I had it first," Matt insists, but he's giving me that blinky look that says he's not so sure.

"It's the blue one, right? I'm pretty sure I cut one of those Darth guys to ribbons with it earlier. And left the pieces in the bathtub."

"No, you didn't," says Matt, uncertain as to whether he should fear me or follow me.

"See for yourself." I corral the two wild monkeys back through the hall and into the tub.

July, two years before

It's been a few months since I started working for Gretchen and Scotty. The boys and I tumble our exhausted, dirty selves through the door after an excursion in Central Park, during which I was convinced I had lost Georgie about five times. Playing hide-and-seek by the Delacorte Clock (at Gretchen's suggestion) shouldn't have been terribly stressful, as there are only, like, three possible hiding spots, but George is inexplicably the best hide-and-seeker I've ever met, and each time I was ready to notify the nearest park official, he would come tearing in from some unknown location. So it's with the slightly sick stomach of an adrenaline overdose that I'm herding the boys in the door, only to find Gretchen looking out the living room window with Matt's red Mickey Mouse binoculars. She whirls around, totally caught in the act, and dissolves into laughter because she knows that I know what she's doing.

"Did you see Pale Male, Mommy?" Matt is excited as he scoots over to join his mother next to the window.

"No sightings yet, honey. Here, do you want to try?" She sets him up with the binoculars, while mouthing to me, "He's in the kitchen!" A few weeks earlier, we had discovered, by way of preschool reconnaissance, that a certain A-list celebrity lived in the building across from theirs. Through a bit of stalking under the ruse "looking for Pale Male" (a hawk who lives on the edge of Central Park but serves us as a very effective code name), we had actually had a few sightings into the celebrity's kitchen. Gretchen loves celebrities and always seems to know more about them than anyone else, and it's hard not to get caught up in her hilarious enthusiasm.

Georgie has been patient in the stroller for a few moments, but now he is ready to get out. He squirms and points and bucks the stroller a little, which I'm having trouble convincing him is a bad idea. I let him out, and he is on his way to join Matt, but not before he displays his streak of methodical independence (or perhaps, Pavlovian impulse) in executing the "coming home" routine. He takes off his shoes and jacket and holds out his hands for me to wipe them with a wet towel. Matt is still wearing both his shoes and coat, and I will have to be clever about removing them without incurring what we like to call his "transitional wrath."

George tugs on Matt's hand to indicate that he would like to try the binoculars. Matt ignores him. George taps on the binoculars and points to himself. Nothing. George smacks Matt in the back of the knees, causing him to buckle and drop the binoculars, which George quickly retrieves. Matt wails, more of a loud whine really, and much more a noise you'd expect from a two-year-old than a four-year-old. I am both impressed with the effectiveness of Georgie's tactic and annoyed with Matt's helplessness, but I know I should ignore those instincts and give George a time-out for employing the use of force.

"Give me the binoculars, please," I say. I wish Gretchen had witnessed the incident and could therefore dole out the consequences, but she has moved to the kitchen to make something in the blender.

"Charlotte, Georgie hit me! He hit me in the—"

"I know, Matt, I saw him. George, please give me the binoculars."

Georgie points out the window and then puts the binoculars to his face.

"George, it's not nice to hit people. Please give them to me." I take them out of his hands, and he sits down on the floor and scream-cries in fury.

"I want to look for Pale Male!" Matt tries to grab the binoculars from me, but I hold them out of reach. "I had them first, Charlotte!"

"Why do you think George hit you, Matt? It's not nice to ignore people. You need to answer when people ask questions, love."

"He *didn't* ask, he never *asks*—"

"That's not really the point, honey—"

"But I HAD THEM FIRST!"

Gretchen appears. "Actually, I think *I* had them first. Come here, boys," she says, heading back to the window. "Look. See the building with the water tower that has red letters? That's where we saw his girlfriend-bird. You look first Matt, and Mommy will hold them. See it?"

"I see the red letters!"

"Now let George look." She stands behind George at the windowsill with her hands on either side of him so he won't fall. "See, George?"

Georgie points.

"Yes, that's it. You see it?" He nods.

"Okay, now look around at the other buildings and see if you can see Pale Male. Okay? Matt gets the binoculars until Mommy says switch, and then you switch, or the binoculars go away." I hand the binoculars to Matt, and Gretchen is laughing as we walk into the kitchen. "It's the cranky hour, huh?"

"Looks that way," I say. "So, you saw him? I'm so mad we weren't here! Was he cooking?"

"He was washing dishes! Can you believe it?"

"That is awesome."

"Scotty suggested I walk around naked to get his attention."

"That's so funny! You should do it."

"I'll be sure to give you the heads up so you can keep the kids out a little longer," she says. "Hey, speaking of naked, would you mind giving them a bath before you go? They didn't have one yesterday."

"And they've been rolling around in the dirt," I say. "We rolled down a hill."

"Switch!" Gretchen calls.

"We already switched," Matt calls back, and indeed, George is holding the binoculars, albeit the wrong way. At eighteen months, he hasn't quite grasped the concept of binoculars, but if Matt thinks something is important, Georgie insists on a turn as well. I'm about to correct his grip, but I see Matt rotate them gently in George's pudgy hands, and I decide to stay out of it.

"One more turn for each of you, and then Charlotte's going to give you a bath," Gretchen says. "Any requests for dinner?"

"Pancakes!"

"Not breakfast food."

"Tacos?"

"Great idea, Matty." She takes the binoculars and sends the kids off toward the bathroom. I follow them down the hall, and I know the minute we step outside the invisible Mommy-radius, because they are immediately at odds again.

February, the day before Valentine's Day

I am brushing Georgie's hair after the current bath while wearing my new Banana Republic hat, as I imagine this is the only opportunity I'll get to wear it in pristine condition before it meets its demise in the weather outside. He is sitting on the edge of his bed, holding his little stuffed golden retriever, Pup. George's Pup is the essence of joy itself. If George needs a way to express the true violence of love he's feeling in his little soul—for anything, for anyone—he simply beams a smile in a way his face can hardly contain and says "Pup!" It's been one of his communication standards since he began speaking nine and a half months ago, and I hope it never ends.

"Your teacher told me you flushed the potty on your own! I'm so proud of you."

"Pup!" (I am so happy that I made you so happy!)

"Want to watch Charlie Brown?"

"Pup!" (YES, immediately!)

"Mommy's home!"

"Mommy, my PUP!" (I've been dragging around this stuffed dog while you weren't home even though I know I'm not supposed to take him out of my bed and I kind of thought you'd never come back so now I'm confessing to you that I have this dog but it's all okay because you're here now so I don't need him except I still a little bit do and now I have BOTH OF YOU.)

George is calm, and after a fifteen-minute bout of transitional wrath when I dared to ask him to put on his own pajamas, Matt is relatively calm too.

"Me bring Pup out to the table. He watch me eat." Sometimes George thinks if he inserts the proper authority into his tone, I'll forget who's in charge and go right along with whatever he suggests.

"I think your Pup needs to stay here, bug. You don't want him to get all messy at the dinner table."

"We watch Diego while we eat?"

"George," says Matt, walking in the door and draping himself onto my back with his arms over my shoulders. "Wouldn't you rather watch that movie Mommy taped?"

I stand up with Matt on my back and George on my front, and we make our way down the hall, laughing. Gretchen has somehow transformed into trendy-restaurant attire without anyone noticing and is spooning homemade sauce onto stuffed shells. I'm wary that she's done something to those stuffed shells to make them more nutritious.

I lift Georgie up into his booster chair. "Mommy, you tape a movie for us? We watch it?"

"I did," Gretchen says. "And if you're good during dinner, you can watch it with Charlotte before bed."

"You going to eat dinner?" George asks.

"Yes, Daddy and I are going to eat dinner at a restaurant," she says. "But we'll come in and give you hugs and kisses when we get home."

"I will give no kisses. There's no one in this house I want to kiss," says Scotty, appearing in the doorway. He must have come straight from the airport; I think he's been in Abu Dhabi for most of the past week. I'm surprised that none of us heard his key in the latch, not even Georgie and his superhuman senses.

"You always want to kiss Mommy," Matt says, as a point of fact.

"That's true," he says. "Especially when she looks like this."

Gretchen slides her hands under his suit jacket and helps him off with it. "Take a load off," she tells him. "Our reservation is not until eight."

"Oh, Charlotte, I'll take over with that," Scotty says. I am cutting Georgie's shells into tiny pieces. "Do you think he'll fare better with a spoon or a fork?"

"A spoon, I think," I say as I vacate the seat. "But Gretchen put both out." I collect a few of the empty dishes sitting on the table and take them to the kitchen to rinse out.

"Did you eat yet?" Scotty calls to me as he sits down to monitor the spoon's continued back and forth progress in George's airspace.

"Not yet," I say.

"Would you like some shells? Or do you want to order in?" Gretchen asks, and I wish that I was not the focus of this conversation. I haven't begun to think about what I might want for dinner. Plus, the low-fat ricotta spilling out of the whole-wheat shells is laced with something green, probably spinach, maybe kale, and I'm not sure I can stomach it.

"I think I'll probably eat after these guys are in bed," I say.

"Well, I'll leave some cash on the counter. Please get whatever you want," says Gretchen.

"Or you can order from our Seamless account on the computer, if you'd rather," calls Scotty. They are determined to feed me.

"Thank you," I say, loading the dishes into the dishwasher.

"Do you have any Valentine's plans?" Gretchen asks me. I take my time deciding which sponge will better scrape the remains of George's collard greens out of his Sonic the Hedgehog bowl. This bowl is old-school, I note. It must have belonged to Scotty or Gretchen as a child. Even if I could put aside the boss aspects of Gretchen for a while and talk to her like a regular person, there are three other sets of ears in the vicinity that wouldn't necessarily appreciate the gospel truth about my Valentine's agenda, which will most likely involve an argument with Everett about the Philharmonic, sex I'm not proud of, and using the rest of that expensive bottle of liquor that he brought to distract me from my troubles instead of celebrate his victory.

"I have many plans," I say, making my way back to the table and sitting down next to Matt. "All of them involve some form of chocolate. It's going to be carnage. You won't want to be anywhere near it." Gretchen and Scotty laugh, and I tap the side of Matt's plate because he is staring off into space instead of eating.

"I don't want this," he says, indicating his full-minus-two-bites plate of shells and sauce. "I want avocado."

"I will give you half an avocado if you eat half of this plate," I say. The nightly dinner-bargain has begun. Georgie, on the other hand, is squirreling his food into his cheeks and refusing to swallow, causing him to choke every so often and Scotty to run open-mouth checks, like a nurse in a mental hospital distributing pills. Matt only wants to eat what he likes at the moment; George would rather not eat at all. Teaching these kids to be independent eaters is the best ongoing lesson in patience that I've ever experienced, and on days like today, I have to squash my natural impulses, which run along the lines of taking away their plates when they start their pint-sized negotiations and letting them learn not to complain by going to bed with empty bellies.

"Can I have a pickle?" asks Matt. Other little boys can be sent into spasms of joy by the prospect of eating an ice cream cone. For these little boys, a pickle does the trick.

"Take three bites of dinner, and I'll give you a pickle," I say, getting up again to see what else might be in the refrigerator.

"I didn't get a roll," he says.

"Matthew, I told you the other day that we're not eating rolls until after dinner. Otherwise, you get too full, remember?" Gretchen calls from the kitchen, where I see she has counted out sixty dollars and laid it on the counter next to her laptop, which is open to the Seamless page. What does she imagine I'll be ordering for dinner, I wonder, that will cost me that much money? "Please let Charlotte see you take some bites, and then we'll see about a pickle or some avocado."

"I don't feel like eating. I want someone to help me," Matt says, and this is enough to push Scotty over the edge.

"Matthew, you will eat what is in front of you, and you will eat it now, son. Otherwise, I am taking your plate to the kitchen, and you can go right to bed and not eat again until breakfast." I can see that Matt is regretting pushing his luck. Scotty is not to be bargained with. I sit back down next to the little sourpuss and try, without much success, to look sympathetic as we all finish dinner in relative silence.

"Do you want to watch the movie now and eat your special Valentine's cookies on the couch?" Gretchen asks.

"Valentine's Day is not until tomorrow," says tired, droopy Matt as he allows himself to be shepherded to the couch.

"I know. But Daddy and I are going to celebrate tonight with each other, and then we'll celebrate with you boys tomorrow."

"Valentine's Day is Daddy's favorite holiday," adds Scotty, lifting Georgie off his booster seat and dumping him next to Matt on the couch, where he promptly flops over and closes his eyes. Georgie will not see one frame of this movie. "So I try to make it go on for as many days as possible."

"Why is it your favorite holiday, Daddy?" asks Matt.

"Because Mommy always gives me a present that I really, really like," Scotty says, and I laugh and then try to pretend I wasn't laughing, I didn't get it. It's okay though, because Gretchen laughs too and whacks Scotty on the arm.

"What is it?" Matt persists, but he is losing steam as Gretchen cues up *A Charlie Brown Valentine.*

"It's a little different every year," says Scotty, sounding like Matt when he's trying to see how much he can get away with.

"He says, like he only gets a present *once a year*," says Gretchen. "Makes me want to keep the supercool skinny tie I got you at Banana Republic today and use it as a headband."

"Maybe George could use it as a leash for Pup," says Scotty.

"Are you ready to go?" she asks.

"Yes, immediately," Scotty says, kissing both boys.

"It won't be too long before this one drops, and then you can change the channel to C-span, turn off the sound, and analyze your boyfriend Jay Carney's microexpressions," Gretchen says to me, smoothing Matt's hair back.

"Exactly. That will keep me entertained for hours, so no need to hurry back, you two." Gretchen and Scotty head out the door and press the button for the elevator.

"If this restaurant is everything *The New York Times* promises," Gretchen calls back, "I'll make sure to bring you a foil swan."

"You know me so well. Seriously. Get out of my head." I shut the door behind them and head back to my couch of fallen comrades.

Valentine's Day

I wake up disoriented the next morning. The light through my window is coming in at an angle I don't recognize, and it's a gray, filtering light. I look at my phone, and it is almost 9:30. The night before, Gretchen told me that she and Scotty would get the kids off to school this morning since I was at their house so late. I never get to sleep in like this, except on Sunday.

There is a text from Gretchen, and for a moment I panic, thinking she changed her mind and I was too dead asleep to answer my phone. It's not the case though ("Good morning! I have a client uptown at 11:30—should be home by 1 or so. See if G will eat some peas with his sweet potato and chicken?"). I put the covers back over my head for another twenty minutes until I can summon the willpower to get up and grind some coffee beans.

I turn on NPR and grab the newspaper from the mat outside my apartment door. Out the window I can see streaks of rain hitting the glass, and I wonder how many Valentine plans will be reimagined because of nasty weather.

I open my e-mail, and there's one from my mother entitled "Perfect for you??" I scroll through the job listing from my hometown, a local car dealership looking for someone to write and produce a jingle for their upcoming TV and radio spots.

Another text comes in, this time from Everett. "I'm sorry."

I delete it and click over to WhiteHouse.gov on my laptop to watch the press briefing from yesterday while I drink my third cup of coffee. It's coming at me from all sides today.

When I'm done admiring Jay Carney's tenacious and charming ability to stay on message, I click back to my e-mail and drag my mom's most recent attempt into the folder with the rest of them. She knows better than to bombard me. The dozen or so job postings she's sent me in the past two years have been carefully selected, all from my hometown and the surrounding area, or Craigslist postings she found while searching under New York City. At the bottom of the folder is a grant application she sent me. I filled it out last year but stopped short of sending it when I realized that a professional recommendation was required to complete it. The deadline stands out to me, July 31, and I wonder if it's the same every year. I e-mail the website to myself, just as another text from Everett comes in.

"I shouldn't have hounded you like that." Delete.

I check the weather report before I attempt to figure out what I'm wearing. It's in the forties, but it's expected to rain all day, and the wind is apparently coming in from two directions in periodic gusts. I can hear it knocking the scaffolding around my building against itself. It's a trick to figure out what to wear for an entire day out of my own house in weather like this, especially when there's stroller hauling involved.

A third text. "I'm the worst. Judgy wudgy was a bear."

I text him back. "EW. STOP."

"I thought if I put it in kid terms you might talk to me."

"I'm not not-talking to you. Can't talk NOW. On my way to work."

"Okay. I'm coming for you later." I have no idea what that means.

I finally opt for yoga pants, several layers of thin sweaters, and a raincoat on the clothing front. An umbrella will be useless in the wind. Wellies are a given, so I pull on boot socks over my pants.

I grab the crosstown bus on Seventy-Ninth, but by the time I walk uptown from the bus stop and make it into the lobby at North-Mad, I may as well have jumped into the East River. As I am wringing myself out, I see through the large glass panels into the crazy obstacle course this school calls a gym, where they teach the kids karate, yoga, rock climbing, parkour, and general fearlessness. The kindergarteners are climbing up an unstable rope ladder onto a ten-foot pile of molded foam rocks then jumping into the soft-foam ravine below. Some kids are somersaulting into it. Matt is standing with Ainsley and another little girl named Samantha, waiting his turn to careen headlong through space. I wave to him and then point to George's classroom, where the kids are lined up and ready to go.

"Me wave to Matt," says George, and I leave him next to the window while I venture over to exhume our stroller from the gridlocked parking situation. A nice, out-of-place-looking dad who is on the verge of mangling his Gucci suit by offering to lift out each stroller hands me ours. I see that Gretchen has left me the plastic stroller cover to keep Georgie dry. She also left an umbrella in the bottom for me. It's Burberry. I hope I don't lose it.

By the time George and I are properly encased in our foul weather gear, it's a quarter after twelve. I sprint to their apartment with the stroller, thankful that it's so close, and when we arrive, I see that George has fallen asleep under the protection and warmth of the plastic. Apparently, we will be rearranging the order of things today. If I wake him up by 1:30, we'll have time to eat and run out to get Matt at 3:00. Or he can stay home with Gretchen while I run out by myself, which would be easiest.

I carry him back to his room to sleep it off. It occurs to me that Gretchen could come home at any minute. I should probably double-check to make sure she doesn't want me to wake him up, feed him, and put him back to bed. Unlikely, but still her call. I send her a text. There is no reply. So I make myself a grilled cheese sandwich with organic Jarlsberg and Ezekiel bread, and sit down on the couch. I open my laptop and glance through the website that I e-mailed to myself earlier. None of the requirements have changed. My application is pretty much still complete, since I have nothing to add in the résumé section. I stare at the last question on the form, and my four-line, quippy answer. The question asked me to describe the most meaningful professional experience of my life thus far, and I had written an anecdote about watching an actor fall into the orchestra pit while I was doing my internship.

I scroll through the saved addresses in my e-mail, looking for my internship supervisor, but I stop when I get to the Fs. Fairchild, Jess. Her name might as well be the only one there. I feel the prickle of nerves all through me. What would happen if I e-mailed Jess and asked for a recommendation? Before I can fuss over this idea for another minute, I chicken out, close my in-box, and click on the TV to whatever Gretchen was watching last. HGTV.

One thirty comes and goes, and still no word from Gretchen or sleeping George. I go back to his room, open the blinds, and rattle the toys in his toy bin until he wakes up. He eats, he sits on the potty, we build a shining city out of Duplos, and now it has to be time to start getting ready to pick up Matt since Gretchen is not home. I send her another text ("will take G with me to pick up M, see you later"), and we bundle up, hop into the elevator, and start our second sprint of the day to North-Mad.

TWO OF MY sweaters are in the dryer, along with all of the boys' clothes from earlier. They have bathed and are now eating cupcakes on beanbag chairs in front of the TV. I'm pretty sure I have a solid case for our Valentine's activity when Gretchen gets home, should she question it. It's almost 4:00. She hasn't yet told me if she would like me to start or order dinner. I decide to call her and see if I can get some quick answers.

I call her once and get her voice mail. I try her one more time before I leave a message. The second time I call, the phone is picked up after half a ring, and the voice on the other end of the line is not Gretchen's but that of a curt female I don't recognize.

"Who is this?" the woman clips.

"Ah, this is Charlotte. Who is *this*?"

"This is Rosie Ramsay in the Emergency department." Rosie Ramsay? Is she kidding with that name?

"This is Gretchen McLean's phone," I say, kind of dumbly.

"I know." The woman's voice is not at all gentle, as in hindsight I think it should have been. "What is your relationship to Ms. McLean?"

"It's Mrs.," I correct her, pointless and automatic and wary. "I'm her babysitter. I'm here with her two boys. Can I please talk to her?"

"Do you have a way to contact Mr. McLean?" Rosie Ramsay asks me.

"Isn't his number in her phone?" I ask.

"Her phone is locked with a passcode. You are the first phone call she's gotten since she got here. Texts came in, but we couldn't retrieve them because of the code."

"Why do you have Gretchen's phone?" I can't force my mind to wade through the nerves and come up with an explanation, and Rosie Ramsay doesn't seem in a hurry to fill me in.

"Mrs. McLean is here with us in Emergency. The surgeon has just gone in to start a procedure."

"Why? What happened?"

"I'm sorry," says the harpy on the other end, "but I can't give out information to anyone who isn't next of kin."

"Well. Okay. Would you like me to put her five-year-old son on the phone so that you can tell him what's happening?"

A brief moment of silence. "Mrs. McLean was hit by a taxi crossing Eighty-Sixth Street a few hours ago," she tells me.

"You mean, you mean, what do you mean? She was in a taxi?" I lower my voice. "And they got hit?"

"Mrs. McLean was on foot," says Rosie Ramsay. "And the driver of the taxi ran the red light." I don't say anything to this because all I can think of are curse words. She says, "If you have a way to contact Mr. McLean, you really ought to do so, and have him come down to the ER right away." She gives me an address and then hangs up.

I stand in the kitchen holding the silent phone to my ear, and it feels like that moment after all the warm water has drained out of the tub and you are paralyzed, shivering, unable to move since the extension of your limbs from your body will only make you colder.

Scotty. I snap out of it, and in the clarity of the snap, I realize that I don't have Scotty's phone number. Two years of working for them, and I've never had the need.

I look around for an emergency phone list, but I'm wasting time. I can't think of where it could be.

"Matt," I call. "Do you know your Daddy's cell phone number?"

"No," he calls back. Wall-E and Eve are dancing through time and space. Shit. I know the name of the firm he works for, so I grab my phone and Google the number for the switchboard.

The receptionist answers, and I interrupt her recitation of the firm's partners. "I need to speak to Scotty McLean. It's urgent."

She puts me through to Scotty's secretary, and I repeat the request.

"I'm sorry," she tells me in a melodious voice that has the perfect combination of gatekeeper and compassion, "Mr. McLean is on a conference call. May I take a message?"

"No! Please, I'm so sorry, but you have to interrupt him. This is his babysitter. It's an emergency."

She takes a beat and must decide I'm telling the truth. "Hold for a moment," she says, and then I hear Scotty's voice, and I am really starting to panic now, but trying not to. The kids. The kids, the kids.

"Charlotte?" he says. "Are you okay?"

"The boys are okay," I say. "It's Gretchen. I just called her phone and got some woman from the emergency room. Apparently, they brought her in earlier today and didn't know how to contact anyone."

"What happened to her?" he asks. I start to repeat what Rosie Ramsay told me, and then I worry that the boys will hear me. It's vitally important that my words come out at exactly the right volume, but my throat feels constricted. "Charlotte? Do you know what happened?"

"She was hit by a car, I think," I say. "They wouldn't tell me much."

In the other room, Wall-E is declaring his love for Eve, repeating her name over and over, and she is answering in a similar fashion. Matt thinks it's hilarious, and he is imitating their voices, making Georgie laugh. My entire capacity for thought is occupied by these sounds. I worry that Scotty might be fighting a similar distraction until I hear him speak again.

"Charlotte. Okay, Charlotte. I'm going to transfer you back to my assistant. Give her your cell phone number, then have the doorman call you a cab. I'll meet you at the hospital. You'll probably beat me, so I'll text you, and you can tell me where to meet you after you figure out where she is. Can you do that?"

"Yeah," I say. "I mean, yes. See you there." He clicks the phone over, and I give his secretary (who identifies herself as Eliza) my cell phone number. We hang up, and I grab a pad of paper. My mind is reeling, and something is going to slip through the cracks if I'm not meticulous. *Doorman call a cab*, I scribble. *Coats and hats. Water, juice, pretzels, bananas. Pup. Something for Matt to do? Locate Gretchen. Text Scotty back.* I throw the phone into my tote bag and move around the kitchen, burning through my list in a haze of unreality. The kids are oblivious to my actions until I pause the TV with no warning, and both their heads swivel to pin me with accusatory stares.

"I'm sorry," I say to them. "We need to do something quickly. We had a change of plans, and we need to get in a car and go meet your mom and dad. I have all your stuff, but Matt, I need you to put on your shoes and coat while I get George ready."

"Where are we going?"

"I need you to do it now, pal. I'll explain when we get downstairs." He must hear something urgent in my voice because he obeys me for once in his life. Roughly five minutes have elapsed since I hung up with Scotty. I pick up my backpack and a tote full of their stuff, take a kid by each hand, and lock the door on the way out.

The elevator stops twice on the way down, and each time, I want to scream with fury. Matt keeps looking at me with increasing anxiety as I stifle these impulses, and he asks again where we're going. Georgie's eyes have teared up, which he doesn't want me to see, so he buries his face in my side.

I put Matt in the car first, then George. It takes a few minutes for my adrenaline-riddled hands to function properly and buckle their belts, but I do it, and I tell the driver where we're headed while simultaneously trying to impart the gravity of the situation to him, silently with widened eyes. Either he gets it, or he's a maniac.

As we whip downtown along Park, I am shocked to see the state of the trees. Branches are down everywhere, and some are dangling precariously from the tree that spawned the fallen limbs. It's a five-minute ride. I hand the driver a twenty and tell him he should keep the change. I hustle the kids through the automatic doors. We are about ten feet from the information desk when Matt stops, stock-still in the middle of the body traffic, and looks at me.

"Why are we at the hospital?"

I squat down. He deserves to have someone look him in the eye and tell him the truth. I'm unequal to the task, but there isn't anyone else here. I set Georgie down next to Matt and put my hands on both of their shoulders, because it has to be me, and I want them to remember that the messenger tried her best.

"Mommy is here at the hospital. She was in an accident, and the doctors need to look at her and check her out, and it might take a little while. Daddy is coming from work to meet us."

Matt nods, and George indicates with his arms that he would like to be picked back up. I stand up, holding him, and we walk to the front desk.

"I'm looking for Gretchen McLean," I tell the receptionist.

"Which department?"

"Emergency, I think. Or she might be in surgery now. Is that different?"

"When did she come in?"

"I'm not sure? A few hours ago."

"Are you her next of kin?"

"These are her children, and I'm her babysitter."

"I don't have a Gretchen McAbe listed in the system."

"It's not—" I have to pause and swallow a shout. "The last name is McLean. If you could just point me toward emergency—"

"Could you spell that, Miss?"

"M-C-L-E-A-N." She is typing and clicking, and typing some more, and suddenly I am hit with inspiration.

"What department does Rosie Ramsay work in?"

WE HAVE FINALLY come to the waiting room at the end of the labyrinth that I was sure would never end, and I answer Scotty's text, telling him which entrance to use. A woman in scrubs walks over to greet us. She is tiny, and I know at once that this is her, Rosie, purveyor of horrifying news.

"Their father is on his way. Please, do you have anything that you can tell me?"

"She's still in surgery. Let one of the floor nurses know when

Mr. McLean arrives, and I'll send her doctor out to talk to him." She walks away, and I have a sudden urge to chuck a juice box at her head, which, for now, I squelch.

There are only five other people in the waiting room, and all of them seem to be alone. I set up Gretchen's iPad with a movie for the kids to watch and settle them into chairs, using their coats to cushion them. I give them each a juice box and open up the bag of pretzels, but neither of them even reaches for one. George is clutching his Pup, and Matt has his TV-trance face on. I wish I hadn't brought them here. Contemplation of mortality isn't a thing that happens frequently in the mind of a little kid, and here we are, bathing in the contemplation, Matt and I. George is too young to understand the implications of severity a hospital presents, but he does understand that his mother's body, while previously considered indestructible, must have been compromised in some way to land us here with all the doctors.

I can't sit down. If I sit down, do I accept that I have no power and can only wait? I can't sit down. I walk to the vending machine and get a Diet Coke.

I open it.

I drink it.

I read every bulletin board in the room.

I stand behind the boys and lose my mind in *The Lorax* for three minutes.

Then suddenly, Scotty is there, and he looks thunderous. Somehow, the normal mildness of his manner has escaped him. There is no iota of the silliness he usually displays for the kids, which is pretty much the only aspect of his personality I'm familiar with. Right now, he looks like he's made of deal breakers, held together by force and bringing it down the hall with him.

The minute he's inside I point him out to the head nurse, and she must see the same thing I do because she does not hesitate to pursue the immediate retrieval of Rosie Ramsay and the alleged doctor.

"She's going to get the doctor," I say when he is near enough to hear my voice, and I indicate the retreating nurse.

"Thank you, Charlotte." Scotty is holding his overcoat, and I wonder if he wore it here or carried it the whole way. He sets down his briefcase with the coat on top of it and buttons his suit jacket. "Hi, boys."

Matt continues to stare at the screen and does not respond. Georgie slides down off his chair, holding Pup, and comes over to greet his father.

"We see Mommy now?"

"That's the first time he's said anything since I told them we needed to come and meet you," I say, as casually as possible, hoping that Georgie won't be shamed into silence again. I can tell that Scotty is also relieved.

"I don't think we can see Mommy yet," he says to George, picking him up. "I need to speak to the doctor first. What is that Pup doing out of your bed?"

Georgie smiles, rather smugly, and shrugs his little shoulders. "Tahr-lette get him out of my bed and bring him," he says. His subtext: *I had nothing to do with this.* He knows when he is being funny. Scotty kisses him and kisses Pup and then sets George back down.

"You can watch your movie, buddy. I'll let you know when we can talk to Mommy."

Rosie Ramsay appears in the doorway accompanied by a white-haired man with square glasses and light-orange scrubs, and she points us out. She does not come over to greet Scotty, however; she disappears back through the doors like her tail's on fire. The man approaches and shakes Scotty's hand.

"I'm Doctor Russell. Are you Mrs. McLean's husband?"

Scotty nods once in a stony, deliberate silence. I want to attribute it to apprehension, but it isn't a huge stretch to imagine it as a strategy of intimidation. The doctor turns toward me, but I don't offer my name.

"Do you want me to go sit with the kids?" I ask Scotty.

"I think they're okay." Does that mean he wants me to listen? I should have asked that instead. But I assume he would have told me to bug off if that's what he wanted, and I stay.

"Mrs. McLean was hit from the right by a taxi that apparently had no intention of stopping for the red light. She sustained internal injuries, most critically to her liver, and so far, we have been unsuccessful in our attempts to stop the bleeding. She also has several broken ribs, a collapsed lung, and a bit of swelling in the brain. We've induced a coma to see if we can stop the swelling from progressing, but she will need to go back into surgery in a few hours to see if we can repair the affected organs."

Scotty nods as the doctor speaks, as if he is processing the information appropriately, but I am totally lost. Internal bleeding that they can't stop? They're going to let her bleed for a few hours while they wait to see if her brain stops swelling?

"That sounds like bullshit," Scotty says, startling both me and the doctor. I'm mostly startled because he has voiced the words in my head, and it's so surreal that I wonder a little bit if it is actually me who spoke. "I'm sorry, Doctor Russell. It just seems unbelievable to me that you're going to let her keep bleeding until you see what her brain's going to do. Doesn't that sound crazy to you when *I* say it?"

The doctor is much gentler than Rosie Ramsay. "I understand how difficult this must be to hear, Mr. McLean, but your wife's body is not in any condition to withstand another surgery until we can get a handle on her brain."

Scotty's face turns gray. I've never seen such a thing before, not ever, not from anyone. "I have two little boys," he says in a low, steady tone that I would fear if I were in a boardroom with him.

"We're doing everything we can for her, sir," Dr. Russell says. "I'll send my scrub nurse Rosie out with periodic updates, and I will talk to you whenever I get the chance."

"Thank you," Scotty says, and Dr. Russell disappears through the same double set of doors that Rosie Ramsay disappeared through earlier. Rosie, the scrub nurse. The mystery is solved.

I stand and Scotty stands. After a few minutes, Scotty sits down in the nearest chair, slowly, like you would if you were doing some thigh-strengthening exercise at the gym. He rubs his hands over his eyes and leaves them there long enough to make me nervous. It's not a posture I want the boys to see. But he seems much calmer and of a more normal color when he looks up at me.

"I think I'd better call her parents."

"Okay," I say. "Can I help? Phone calls, or anything? Do you want some coffee?"

"What's that you have?" he asks, indicating my half-empty Diet Coke.

I give it to him. "It's still cold. You can finish it."

"Gretchen hates it when I drink this shit. I'm surprised she hasn't broken you of the habit yet." He finishes my soda in two swallows.

"Many have tried," I say. "Gretchen equates it to shooting processed poison directly into my veins."

"She truly believes that. She's determined to save you from a life of addiction," he says.

"I don't have any of the family numbers," I say. "But I can use your phone if you need some help."

"You know what? Eliza has them. I hate to ask her to come over here after work, but it could be helpful," he says.

"I can call her," I say. I think my phone saved her number. "That way you can call Gretchen's parents."

He has none of the look of command he had moments ago. "I don't know what to say to them." He looks at the boys. "I don't really know what to say to anyone." He stands again. He shakes his head, like he is trying to physically move information into place within his brain. "Thank you, Charlotte. If you can call Eliza, that would be helpful."

I want to reassure him, to tell him that I believe if we keep moving, the doctors will keep moving, Gretchen will keep breathing, the world will keep turning. I want to tell him I'm sure she'll be all right.

I don't tell him that though, because to do so would be a trite way to voice the thing that has to happen for everyone in this room to be all right.

WE ARE ALL sitting. Scotty, Eliza, me, Matty (getting to the end of *The Lorax*), and Georgie, who is sitting astride me, facing me, with his head resting above my belly, sleeping. Matt is still watching his show, barely blinking, and has somehow usurped Pup from his sleeping brother. The doctor has informed us that Gretchen's brain is now a bit further toward the side of stable, and they will be prepping her for surgery in about a half hour.

Gretchen's parents are at the airport in Palm Beach, getting ready to board a plane. Her sister is driving in from Connecticut, and Scotty's parents and older brother are awaiting news in Maine. His younger brother lives here in New York, but Eliza hasn't been able to get ahold of him.

I'm supremely annoyed by this. I have encountered Uncle Patrick on several prior occasions. He's handsome, arrogant, and I feel almost certain that he won't answer the phone or listen to the messages because it's Eliza calling and not Scotty himself.

"I'm hungry," Matt says. The credits are rolling on the movie. I thought he would be asleep by now out of sheer boredom, but it's only about a quarter after seven. Of course he's hungry. Everyone here must be hungry.

"I know, buddy. Do you want a pretzel?" Scotty says.

"I hate pretzels," says Matt with a dark look at me, as if I am the creator of all pretzels on this earth.

"Yesterday you loved them," I say. "Do you want something out of the machine?"

"M&Ms," he says. I look at the vending machine across the room, considering it. I'm tempted to give him whatever he wants. I notice that only three of the five other people originally in this waiting room are still here. I hadn't registered the departure of the other two. I wonder where they went and whether their news was good or bad.

"Not chocolate, pal," I say to Matt, remembering that I still have the afternoon Valentine cupcakes to account for.

"I can run down to the cafeteria and see what I can find," Eliza offers. She doesn't look very old to me, certainly not old enough to be part of the same workforce as Scotty. Her dark-brown hair is shiny and perfectly arranged in a barrette. Her pencil skirt has no wrinkles, and her pressed white blouse with the tiny ruffles has no stains. I have never imagined Scotty as the kind of man who would screw around with someone like Eliza, but Patrick is a different story. I feel sure that the reason he won't answer her phone calls has something to do with their sordid past.

"Thank you, Eliza," says Scotty.

"What do you want me to look for, Matt?" Eliza asks.

Matt looks at me.

"Do you know what you want for dinner?" I ask him.

"Pizza," he says, and Eliza stands up, tall on her Ferragamo heels. I'm still wearing my wellies. Actually, I'm contemplating taking off my wellies and going around in my sock feet.

"Could you maybe use your manners?" I whisper to Matt. He shakes his head and then blanches at the look I give him.

"Please," he says, in kind of a singsong way, not at all nicely.

"Sure," she says and clicks off to find out where the cafeteria is. The more I think about it, the clearer my memory becomes on the history of Patrick and Eliza, and the surer I am that it's the reason he's not here. I feel filled with righteous, irrational anger toward Patrick. I shift Georgie onto the chair, laying him on his side, and tuck his jacket in behind him so he won't roll off.

"Can I have your phone, Scotty? I'll try Patrick again." He hands it over, and I dial out. This time Patrick picks up, as I knew he would.

"Hello," he says.

"Patrick, it's Charlotte," I say.

"Who?"

"Charlotte. Scotty and Gretchen's babysitter."

"Well, hey there, Charlotte," Patrick says. He speaks loudly, in order to be heard over a rush of background noise, and I hold the phone away from my ear. Scotty's iPhone case is made of some sort of black leather, which makes it massive and hard to hang on to. "It's been a while. What's going on? How are you?"

"Not great," I say. "I'm in the emergency room with Scotty and the boys. Eliza is here too, and she's been trying to reach you. Gretchen was in an accident, and she's about to go in for her second surgery."

The background noise on the other end lessens significantly. He must have stepped out of whatever dive he was slumming it in.

"What kind of accident?"

"She was hit by a car crossing Eighty-Sixth Street. We're in the waiting room at the hospital." I give him the cross streets, and he says he'll be there as soon as he can, which probably means as soon as he can close his tab and weasel his way out of whatever plans with whatever undergraduate.

Eliza comes back with Matt's food and with coffee for the adults. I haven't had coffee since around eleven this morning. Thus it's probable that I'm starting to exhibit the physical symptoms of withdrawal. I try to keep my hands from shaking—with withdrawal, with adrenaline, with fear—as I accept the coffee from pretty, pretty, well-kept Eliza. Scotty's coffee drips a little as he takes it from her, and she looks stricken.

"Oh, I'm so sorry, Mr. McLean! Let me get a damp paper towel—"

"It's fine, Eliza, really; don't worry about—"

"Oh, but your shirt . . ." They go on like this for a minute. I'm still hung up on the fact that she calls him Mr. McLean. I thought formality was dead. Apparently, I've been in the land of New York City progressive education for too long.

Eliza has hurried over to the drinking fountain, despite Scotty's protests, when there's a flurry of activity beyond the double doors. Scotty notices it too and stands up to get a better look. Four or five people in scrubs are rushing in the same direction, and through the sudden stillness in the waiting room, we can hear a faint whine coming from beyond the doors. Scotty looks around wildly for just a moment—the first involuntary thing I've seen him do since we got here—and then strides toward the doors, pushing his way through them with no regard for the "authorized personnel only" sign that forbids such an action.

"Where is he going?" Matt asks me, the sudden change in atmosphere fueling his panic.

"I don't know," I say. "Maybe . . . I don't know."

"DAD!" he hollers, before I can stop him. "WHERE ARE YOU GOING?"

At this, Georgie sits bolt upright and wails.

The day before

I try and make it a rule not to fall asleep when I'm sitting late, but the previous night's lack of sleep has caught me up. By 1:30 a.m., I have long since passed the point where I turned into a pumpkin and am well on my way to rotting in the patch. Gretchen's text ("in cab!!! coming back now!") startles me awake enough to turn off the TV, check on the sleeping boys, and start getting my stuff together. When I check my phone, there are four other texts, all from Everett, who apparently got increasingly pissed at me as I dozed on Gretchen and Scotty's couch.

"Any idea what time you'll be home?" at 8:15.

"Coming back soon??" at 9:47.

"Starving. Ordering food. Want anything?" at 9:53.

A long gap, and then, "Screw it, I obviously can't compete with your pretend-kids. Might go back to NH . . ." at 10:50.

My fingers stab at the touchscreen. I miss the satisfaction of pounding on an actual keyboard. "I told you earlier that you should go. Go!!" I send the text, then turn off my phone. I don't want to know if he replies. I scan the room. What needs to be done before Gretchen and Scotty get home? The dishes are done, the toys are picked up, my food containers are recycled, and I am looking for my other shoe (I think Georgie chucked it somewhere earlier) when they walk in the door. Scotty looks tired, like he hasn't yet gotten the canary, and Gretchen looks a little tipsy.

"You have to try this restaurant, Charlotte! We brought you some chocolate cake. I almost ate it in the cab," Gretchen says, handing me a mashed foil package.

"She asked the guy to wrap it into a swan for you," Scotty says, and he laughs and gives her the look, THAT LOOK, the two-seconds-too-long look I recognize as the let's-be-alone-together-so-I-can-go-crazy-on-you look. To which she seems oblivious. "And that guy had to find another guy—"

"But the second guy didn't know how to do it either!" she says.

"And then the guy at the next table offered to do it, but we were pretty sure—" Scotty goes on.

"—that you wouldn't want a stranger touching your food," Gretchen finishes. "So it's just wrapped in foil."

"I promise to eat it right away, so your efforts were not in vain," I say, squatting down to peer under the couch for the missing shoe.

"How were they?" Gretchen asks.

"I didn't speak a word to either of them from the time you left." I rescue Iron Man's helmet and two refrigerator magnets from underneath the couch. "They both fell asleep out here. I'm glad they got pj's on before dinner."

"I hope you didn't throw out your back carrying Matthew to bed," she says.

"I guess we'll see tomorrow when I wake up," I say, finally locating my shoe inside the Play-Doh bin. I put it on quickly and edge toward the door.

"Why don't you take the morning off? We can take them to school tomorrow, and then maybe you can sleep in and pick up George at noon, at North-Mad. Does that sound okay?" Gretchen is struggling to unwind a scarf from around her neck.

"Are you sure?" I say. "I don't mind taking them."

"No, you should stay home. Drink your four cups of coffee in bed, for a change," she says.

"You mock my caffeine intake now," I tell her. "But the boys know the truth about what happens when Charlotte has no coffee."

"Viola Swamp?" Scotty takes Gretchen's purse from her and sets it down. He puts his hands into the tangle of her scarf as she holds hers out to the side in a gesture of laughing surrender.

"More like the Hulk," I say. I pull my new hat down over my ears, zip up my jacket, and grab my backpack, which contains, among other things, three bottles of hand sanitizer, a library book I thought was lost but was magically found by George, and my ukulele. "Thank you again for my hat."

"You're so welcome," Gretchen says. "Oh! Babe, it's an infinity scarf." She takes it off over her head and stretches the circle of fabric between her hands, and we laugh at Scotty's baffled expression.

"I'm pretty sure there's a 'how many advanced degrees does it take' joke in there somewhere," I say. "Good night, you guys."

"Scotty will walk you down to get a cab," says Gretchen.

"It's really okay," I say. "It's only—"

"Nine blocks away, yeah, we know," she says. "It's almost two in the morning. Scotty will get you a cab. See you tomorrow." She walks into the kitchen, and Scotty watches her go, and the way he is watching her makes me uncomfortable, for a reason I can't put my finger on.

"I'll be out in a minute, all right?" he says. I step outside the front door to wait in the hall. This is so silly. I'd be fine on my own. I might even walk.

I can hear Scotty start to say something, right by the door which I didn't pull shut, thinking he'd be right out. I'm about to push it open and ask him to repeat himself when I hear, "But you know how much I fucking *love* you, right? You do know *that*." He definitely isn't talking to me.

"It's not about that. It's about you leaving me alone again. You don't even seem to care, you might as well have said it's *easy*—"

"That's *not* what I said—"

"Let me tell you something about complexity, Scotty," Gretchen says, sounding blurry, which I'd rather attribute to the half-open door than anything having to do with emotion or inebriation. "This morning some kid *pushed* Matthew on the playground while we were waiting for the doors to open—just pushed him, totally on purpose, with *aggression*, and he's looking at me like, 'I know I'm not supposed to hit back, Mom, but what do I do now?' and the look he was giving me was just so incredulous, like accusatory almost, like, how could I have let that happen and still have rules like 'no hitting?' "

I want to pull the door shut, but I'm afraid they'll notice the click, so I reach out to turn the knob, one tense millimeter at a time.

"And I'm trying to explain it to him, telling our *five-year-old* that things aren't always black and white. Things aren't always SIMPLE."

"I'm sorry, I'm sorry. Jesus, I picked the wrong word, obviously."

"But is that really what you think? God, Scotty. You always do this."

"Do what? I can't even follow your—"

"You leave me alone. I'm always alone!"

"Jesus Christ. Okay. I'm going to walk Charlotte out, and then we'll talk, okay?"

I let go of the door and scoot to the other side of the vestibule so I'll have an easier time pretending I didn't hear anything.

"You'd better not be in bed when I get back, or else I can't be held responsible for my actions. You hear me? Do *not* get in that bed," says Scotty. I hear Gretchen laughing at that, even in the midst of what is clearly an ongoing squabble, and I pull my phone out of my pocket and pretend to text, even though it's off, as Scotty opens the door.

As we ride the elevator down, Scotty asks me little innocuous questions relating to things he's heard about my life from Gretchen. It's much more common that I hear him referred to in the third person than see him in the flesh, but if he were the subject of a trivia question, I bet I'd know the answer. I'm pretty sure the same is true for him of me, which puts us squarely in the realm of people who know much more about each other than they have ascertained from actually talking to each other. End-of-the-night small talk is usually awkward, but Scotty is too well-bred to be awkward. I answer his questions about my sister's new apartment in Boston and my recent foray into the culture of espresso, and I feel very fond of him. When we get to the ground floor, he does not hand me over to the doorman, because he and Gretchen have made it clear that they are personally invested in getting me safely into a cab, always. Because they are also very fond of me.

Scotty raises his arm and gets the attention of a cab quickly, thank God, because I am ready to drop. There are two types of women who are shuttled into taxis while simultaneously being palmed a wad of cash: babysitters and prostitutes. I almost laugh at this thought but stop for fear I might have to explain the joke.

"Eighty-First, by the river," he tells the driver, and I glance at the money he's handed me.

"You guys can pay me at the end of the week like normal, if you want," I say through the open door as he is about to shut it. I roll down the window.

"She will. This is for tonight," he says.

"It's too much," I say.

"We really appreciate it, Charlotte. Happy Valentine's Day." He slaps the side of the cab, and the driver must understand this as some universal signal for "Step on it, pal," because he is off like a shot. I count again what's in my hand, and for a moment I feel a little thrill, like maybe my discretion has just been bought.

Valentine's Day

I'm momentarily inert, torn between moving to comfort Georgie and going to stop Matt from running after Scotty. I have to go for Matt though, because he's the more imminent threat, and Eliza is frozen by the water fountain, in a fit of supreme unhelpfulness.

I catch Matt around the waist and hang on to him. I don't know what to say, so I wrap my arms around him, pinning his arms to his sides and holding him until he stops struggling and sags against me, and I can lead him back over to the chair where George sits, half-asleep and sobbing. I haul Georgie down off his chair and sit on the floor with him in my lap, pulling Matt down beside us and letting them both soak my second-to-last sweater with their tears.

I can't see what's going on through the window, but Eliza can, and I use her face as a barometer. She puts her hands over her mouth, and I gesture forcefully at her and mouth, "What?"

"They're wheeling her bed down the hall," she says in a very low voice, and I appreciate her efforts not to alarm the boys. A moment later, Scotty is back through the doors, escorted by Rosie Ramsay and a comically burly orderly.

"I'm sorry, sir, but I need to go back in," Rosie is saying. "I'll come out as soon as we have an update."

The orderly posts himself in front of the double doors, and Scotty has nothing to do but stand in the middle of the room, unable to get where he wants to go.

"Daddy?" Matt scrambles up and pastes himself to Scotty's hip before I can catch him with my free arm. "Did you get to see Mommy?"

Scotty runs his hand through Matt's hair. Every so often, Matt will ask, "What's going on in there?" or simply, "Daddy?" Each time I watch Matt's face fall as he waits for an answer and doesn't get it is like a casual abrasion to my calm facade. It goes on this way for maybe ten minutes. I don't know if my composure can withstand much more, but every time I try to get up, Georgie tightens his grip on the front of my sweater.

The door to the outside opens then, and Patrick enters. His gait is almost identical to Scotty's, and the coloring is the same. He wears a similar suit. The first time I met Patrick, I thought they might be twins. Until Patrick opened his mouth, of course, and the four-year age gap bent over and showed its hindquarters.

The scene he encounters must throw him for a loop, because he stops to take it in for a moment, and that's not the Patrick I remember. We're a sight, I'm sure; me on the floor, George splayed out on my lap, Eliza cowering by the water fountain, and Matt and Scotty frozen like some pathetic statue in the middle of the room. Narnia.

"Hi," I say, because no one else is going to. "Thanks, it's good you, I mean, it's good you came."

"I'm glad you called, Charlotte," he says, as if no one else had thought to loop him in on the events of the day. "Hey, Eliza. Hi, kids."

"Mommy's in the hospital," Matt tells him.

"Is she with the doctor, buddy?"

"She's back there," he says, pointing to the double doors.

"Do we know what's happening?" Patrick addresses the question to Scotty, but Scotty seems preoccupied with Matt, looking down at him with vague recognition, as if his name and relation are just out of reach.

"You know what?" says Patrick, pulling Matt over by the arm to where I sit with Georgie, who is still whimpering but losing the battle against his drooping eyelids. "I think maybe your dad needs some air. I'm sure Charlotte brought something for you to do, right, Charlotte?"

Eliza's expression doesn't change, but I can feel her solidarity from across the room, and it saves me from either saying or doing something childish and aggressive, like maybe kicking Uncle Patrick.

"I want to see Mommy," says Matt.

"As soon as the doctor says it's okay, we'll see her," I say. "I'm sorry. Do you want to play *Angry Birds*?"

"Okay," says Matt.

Patrick puts his arm around his brother's shoulders and leads him outside. A moment later, he pokes his head back in. "Does either one of you have a lighter?" he asks, and Eliza and I stare at him. His ability to be inappropriate is so consistent. "Never mind. I'll ask someone out here," he says and disappears again.

Just as quickly, he is back inside without Scotty. Eliza and I are equally baffled. Who is smoking? But we don't have time to give the moment its due consideration because Patrick is motioning to me, and I have to get to my feet holding George, which adds about thirty awkward maneuvers to the process of getting up.

"I don't know that it's the best idea for you guys to be here," Patrick says.

"*Who* do you mean, Patrick?" I ask him.

"Don't you think it would make more sense for you to take the boys home? This can't be good for them," he clarifies.

"Scotty asked us to meet him here, so we came. If he wants us to go, we will. I don't think he has a clear idea of what's going on yet. Do you?"

"Do you think he knew how serious it was when he asked you to come?" he asks.

"No," I say. "We had no idea. But, I mean, I think he wants them to be able to see Gretchen, as soon as they can. Otherwise, they're going to be terrified, you know?"

Patrick gives me the most honest, sober look I've ever seen from him. He could almost be a decent guy with that look. "Well, whatever you think is best. You know the boys." I'm right on the verge of cutting him some slack when he adds, "What is Eliza still doing here? Scotty says she made a bunch of phone calls already. She doesn't need to hang around."

"I don't know, man. She's been pretty helpful. I guess she'll go when Scotty is sure he doesn't need her to do anything else."

"She and I have a bit of a past," says Patrick, as if he is confiding some delightful piece of intrigue to me, when in reality, all he is doing is confirming the accuracy of my recollection. "I guess it's a little awkward, but what the hell. It's not my call."

Scotty comes back in then, smelling like smoke (Eliza and I finally do get to widen our eyes at each other at this) but looking somewhat calmer. He sits down, and Patrick sits next to him, and Eliza abandons her post by the water fountain and sits. I lay Georgie down on a chair again and take the iPad out of Matt's hand before it can slide out on its own. He is about to drop, so I stand him up and then help him lie down on a few adjoining chairs with his head in my lap.

"They took her back into surgery a little early," Scotty says as soon as it's clear that Matt is sleeping. The sound of his voice is a surprising break in the ambient noise of the waiting room. "They didn't want to, but her liver is failing, and her organs were starting to shut down. That—that was what we could hear, the heart monitor—anyway, they need to try and stabilize the liver right away, and if they can do that, they'll try for the other organs."

I close my eyes then because I don't have a free hand to block my ears with.

June, two years before

I meet Patrick for the first time a few months after I started working for Gretchen and Scotty. I have only seen Scotty a handful of times before this, but they need an extra hand at Matt's fourth birthday party. There are twenty-five kids in attendance and twice as many adults.

Patrick's first words to me come as I'm refilling one of the ice buckets.

"I hear you're the new babysitter. Thank God! I was afraid we'd have a problem if you looked like the stereotypical au pair—you know, a tall, blonde Norwegian model—but you don't! So we're all good. I'm Uncle Patrick."

I don't know what he expects me to say to that, so I continue on with my task. He might be waiting for some witty banter, or at the very least for me to blush at his attentions. Instead, I pretend that the exchange has not taken place, that I have not, in fact, met perfect Gretchen's jackass younger brother-in-law. I don't want him to exist in a family as lovely as this one.

Apparently, though, he does exist, and we are having a conversation. He leans one Nautica-clad hip against the counter and points to Jillian, whose name I can't yet keep straight in my head.

"What's her deal? You know a lot of these women, right?"

"She has twins who go to school with Matthew," I say, slugging the bucket, heavy with new ice, up into my arms. "Excuse me."

"Need any help?" he asks, when I am most of the way out the door.

"I'm good," I call back. I take the bucket over to the drink table and start placing new cans and bottles inside. Adults must come to birthday parties on the Upper East Side for the booze.

Gretchen and Scotty have encouraged me multiple times to partake, but I can't bring myself to dip in.

Gretchen comes over to refill a bowl with tiny hot dog buns. She nudges my arm with hers.

"I see you've met Uncle Patrick," she says. "Charming, isn't he?"

"I'm sure there are many women who think so," I say, trying to squeeze the last two Perriers into the bucket.

"Just wait until he gets another beer or two in him. I'm sure he'll tell you the story of how Scotty and I met. He loves that story. Tells it at every family holiday dinner after the kids go to bed. Just remember, I came to my senses!" She hurries away to check on the next round of macaroni-and-cheese bites (which come out on kid-sized porcelain spoons) before I can get the story out of her.

Sure enough, Patrick ends up on the couch (with his third or seventh beer) toward the end of the party, with George asleep next to him. He watches me clean up wrapping paper and stuff it into a trash bag.

"What do you do, Charlotte? I mean, when you're not maintaining house and brood with Gretchen and my bro."

"Oh, you know. Not too much. Bet on the ponies, organize underground poker tournaments, that kind of thing."

Patrick fixes me with a look like I'm suddenly interesting and not merely the only one available for an idle chat.

"Really?"

"No. Not really."

"Gretchen said you were some kind of singer, or something." I'll take that as a testament to his listening skills. "So, what, you frequent the late-night lounges? The punk clubs?"

"If I did, we'd surely have met before now," I say, picking up shreds of gift wrap. Some little girl went bananas with the curling ribbon.

"Did Gretchen ever tell you that we used to go out?"

"Who did?" I ask.

"Me and Gretchen."

This is surprising, but I continue stuffing paper into the garbage bag.

"It was hot," he says, gunning for my reaction now. "Two dates. Two nights together." I look at him then, and he raises his eyebrows. Ew. "We pretty much set the room on fire wherever we went together."

"And then she married Scotty?" I say, as I pluck tiny bits of tissue paper out of the Persian rug.

"They met one morning at brunch. I had to leave a little early, and I guess he must have told some crazy stories. Next thing I knew, they were going steady." He finishes his beer and leans over to kiss George's cheek, which is a sweet moment. The many women who fall at his feet must cling to moments like that. I think he's going to get up, but he doesn't.

"Where were you going?" I ask him. "When you left brunch, I mean?"

"You've already heard this story," he accuses me.

"I don't think she has, but she can probably guess," says Scotty, carrying two additional trash bags out of the kitchen.

"Hey, we never said we were exclusive," says Patrick. "C'est la vie, I suppose."

"Charlotte, you didn't happen to see how many Shirley Temples Matthew had, did you?" Scotty asks. "He's back in our bathroom with his head in the toilet."

"No, I'm sorry," I say. "Oh gosh. He told me he was drinking apple juice. I'm so sorry."

"Yes, he does that. Don't worry. I think he's going to learn his lesson. He told Gretchen he was drinking apple juice too, but what's coming up looks suspiciously like grenadine." Scotty pulls on the strings of one of the trash bags, struggling to tie it off. The bag is so full that he doesn't have much to work with.

"He obviously has his father's constitution." Patrick sets his empty beer bottle down on the end table. I pick it up and take it over to the recycling bag that Scotty has stashed by the front door.

Gretchen comes into the living room, looking for George. "Our fledgling bartender is asleep on your side of the bed," she tells Scotty. "How'd you make that happen?" she asks Patrick, pointing to George's prone body.

"I just told him to chill out," Patrick says. I would dearly love to give him an afternoon all to himself with his nephews and then hear him say that again.

"Patrick has been regaling Charlotte with the tale of how we met," says Scotty to Gretchen. I love it that this is their favorite inside joke.

"The nights get hotter and hotter," Gretchen says. "We set more and more things on fire. I'm surprised we're not on some kind of FDNY watch list, the way he tells the story." No one laughs louder than Patrick.

"I can't believe you tell that story at family dinners," I say, tying up my garbage bag full of wrapping paper.

"Classy, right?" Scotty says, taking that last bag from me and putting it in the hall with the others ready to go out. "Gretchen, I have my wallet here. How much do we owe you, Charlotte?"

Gretchen speaks before I have a chance and says a number several hundred dollars higher than necessary.

"No," I say. "It was only three hours."

"Yes, but we didn't expect you to have to act like a caterer," says Gretchen. "I didn't realize how much work this would be. Seriously. I thought I might just have you posted at the door to make sure none of the monkeys escaped, but you had to run around like a maniac refilling ice buckets and cupcake trays."

"And using your body as a buffer between that toddler's head and the corner of the table—did anyone else see that? It was impressive," Scotty adds, handing me some cash.

"It was fun," I say. "Really—"

"Charlotte, don't argue," Gretchen says, propelling me to the door. "Scotty will get you a cab."

"It's only four o'clock—" I start to protest.

"Her mind is made up," says Scotty as Gretchen hands me off to him. I grab two of the garbage bags as she waves me toward the door, feeling like it's the least I can do.

As Scotty holds the door open to let me through with the huge bags of trash, I hear Patrick's voice from the other room.

"Jesus Christ, Gretch. That girl costs you more than my last prostitute."

Valentine's Day

I'm jolted awake by my phone, vibrating underneath my hip, and I look up to scan the waiting room. Not much has changed. I check my watch. I must have fallen asleep for a minute. Or maybe ten. Eliza is gathering her coat and purse, and Patrick is sitting next to Scotty with his hand on his brother's back. Scotty has his head in his hands again. The boys are still sleeping. It has been almost five hours since we arrived at the hospital, and to me it seems absurd that Gretchen is not in charge of what is happening. Gretchen is on her second surgery. In five hours? Can that possibly be right?

I look at my phone, and there's a text message from Everett.

"Are you home from work yet?" I turn the phone off. He'll never find me where I am right now, even if he tries. I wonder for a moment where he is, whether he would come if I asked him to, but I'm having trouble imagining that anyone in my life would understand the gravity of this situation, especially Everett and his snarky comments about my pretend kids.

Eliza comes to my side. "I think it might be better if I go before the rest of the family gets here. You won't need extra bodies once they start to arrive."

I have the fleeting thought that perhaps I should offer Scotty the same thing of myself, but I can't imagine going home and waiting for news or leaving the boys in the middle of such precariousness.

"Thank you for coming, Eliza. I'm sure Scotty really appreciates it, and I know, ah, I know that Gretchen would."

"You still have my number, right?" she says, hesitating for a moment as she puts on her coat. "Would you mind . . . I mean, I'm very concerned. I don't want to bother anyone, but . . ."

"I will text you and let you know what's happening," I say. "I definitely will."

"Thanks." She glances in the direction of the two men but doesn't say good-bye. As she heads off toward the door, I can see her put her cell phone to her ear, and I'd bet a million dollars that she's calling her mother. That's exactly what I feel like doing.

I can't though, because I might fall apart, and the last thing Scotty needs right now is to comfort someone else.

I roll up my damp sweater and get up, moving Matt's head carefully from my lap to the sweater pillow. That's it for the sweaters—there are no more to waste. I'm down to the last one. I need some caffeine posthaste. I move in the direction of the vending machine, weighing the merits of getting three Diet Cokes and downing them one after another versus trying to maintain the appearance of self-control and waiting fifteen minutes between each one. I am about to retrieve my wallet when I see the double doors start to swing open.

It's Dr. Russell, and he is alone. There is no Rosie Ramsay flanking him. Suddenly, I am desperate for her to appear. I stand on my toes and try my best to see down the hallway. She is not there.

Patrick sees me see the doctor, and he taps Scotty and stands up. Scotty looks at the doctor, and he stands up also.

The doctor approaches and shakes Patrick's hand, and he is

speaking in such a low voice that I can't hear a word he says. I could probably come up with a justification for moving closer, but I don't want to. I want to. I can't. I don't want to.

I can't see anyone's face except for the doctor's, and his is so neutral that I have no idea what he could possibly be saying. I wish that Eliza had stayed. Her face is so nakedly emotional that I might have been prepared for what is about to come.

The doctor puts his hand on Scotty's arm and squeezes for a brief moment, and then he turns around and walks back toward the double doors. Just before he reaches them, he turns to Scotty, who is not looking. Dr. Russell is forced to address Patrick.

"Rosie will be out in just a few moments to take you back."

Something leaps in my stomach, and for this brief space of time, I am thrown into a moment of total unknowing. I have no feeling one way or another. I know nothing. I hope, but I'm afraid. I am about to get an answer. But right in this moment, I know nothing.

And then Scotty turns to look at the boys, and the look in his eyes is the look of a person who is no longer a person, of a man whose soul has fled his body. No light comes off him in the normal human way. He is somehow duller than he has been, than everyone else in this room, than maybe anyone has ever been, ever. He looks at his children, and the thoughts he should be having are not there in his eyes. He is not thinking.

Because if he were thinking, his thoughts would have to be she's dead. She died. Gretchen is dead. My wife is dead. Their mother is dead.

LATER, WHILE I'M sitting alone with Patrick waiting for this day to be over, I will turn to him, and I will ask him how old Gretchen is. Is, not was, because I will not yet be able to stand that tense. He will comment that it's funny that I don't know their exact ages, and he will answer that she is thirty-six, and I will nod and leave the room as quickly as possible. Tears will come leaking out, even though what I really want to do is gasp and sob and be the worst mess, thinking of all the things she had left to do. I will be relentless in my thought cycle, and the bottom line will be this: what if Gretchen, like me, was still making excuses for why her *real life hadn't yet started* at the tail end of her twenties? If that were the case, she would have only really lived for a few years. My heart will beat fast to the rhythm of these thoughts all throughout the rest of the evening, and when I get home, I will fall into a shallow sleep on my tear-wet pillow, and I will dream of all the things that no one will say about me if I die tomorrow.

PART TWO

Matthew

April, six weeks after

The thermometer says you're not sick. See?" I show Matt the display on the side of the thermometer, even though I know he has no idea what he's looking at. "You don't have a fever."

"I really don't feel good. I'm tired. My head hurts," Matt says, giving me an exaggerated wince-face.

George is trying valiantly to scale the end of Matt's bed to join his brother, but Matt keeps pushing covers and animals in George's direction, causing minor avalanches that prevent any progress. If Matt stays home from school, George will try to stay home too. He will throw fits. He has declared his great distaste for going anywhere or doing anything without his brother. I've been contemplating moving his bed into Matt's room. For now, we've settled for a crude tin-can telephone system between their rooms that has been the cause of many a late-night close encounter with a string booby trap.

"Matt, I don't want you to stay home again." I pick up two

monogrammed throw pillows off the floor, then think better of it and put them back down, in case Georgie falls off the end of the bed. "I want you to try and go to school. I think you'll be okay once you're there with all your friends. If you still feel bad, you can ask Miss Leslie to call me, and I'll come get you." I pull open the closet door so he can contemplate his clothing options.

Matt flops over to face the other direction and doesn't say anything. I try not to sigh. It's a sound they hear too frequently from me since they started back to school three weeks ago. The three weeks before that were utter chaos in the land of a little kid, making it almost a month and a half since the world had order.

"Come on, baby, let's get dressed." I pick up George and carry him into his room. "Do you want to hold your Chickie while we get some clothes on?"

"I not a baby. I get big," he says, taking his little yellow chicken from me with great dignity. Chickie is a toy that I brought in as a ringer. Pup was never found after that night we left the hospital. At the time, it had seemed like the worst case of insult to injury I had ever encountered. I think I cried more for the loss of Pup than George did. In his mind, I think somehow he had equated Pup's departure with Gretchen's, that he had made it okay, thinking that Mommy and Pup had gone off together to the same place. But I had obsessed over it. I had called the New York City taxi authority. I had stalked the hospital lost and found. I had checked every tote bag and closet three times. Pup was nowhere. We don't speak of Pup in this house anymore.

I dress George and release him down the hall so he can play while he waits for me to retrieve Matt and toast his waffle. The TV is not on, so I think Scotty has probably left for work.

Matt is sitting up in bed. He's taken off his pajamas and is hanging out in his underwear, staring into space, as if he forgot what he was doing halfway through getting dressed.

"Do you want to wear this green shirt?" I ask. "George is wearing his orange one. You guys can match."

"No," he says.

"How about this one?" I go to his closet and pull out a blue plaid button-down. "Your mommy loved this shirt." I see no point in participating in the rampaging silence that everyone else maintains around the boys where Gretchen's existence is concerned.

"No," he says. "I hate that one." I can't wait until next year when North-Mad starts enforcing the uniforms.

"Would you like to pick?" I say, determined to hang on to my patience. Lately, it seems that not only does Matt want to turn everything into a fight but that he actually revels in it. The more the fight escalates, the more he enjoys it. The psychologist they've been seeing has some theory about the anger phase of grief, but I'm of the opinion that the more I engage with him, the more likely this will become the norm forever. I don't want him to spend his whole life fighting, simply for the energy in the drama.

He slinks out of bed and stands in front of his dresser, probably because I am in front of the closet, and I take that to mean that he will put on clothes and be out when he is ready.

"Don't forget to put on socks," I say and then want to scold myself for nagging.

I'm surprised when I enter the kitchen to find George sitting on Scotty's lap at the table. Scotty is drinking coffee and staring at the business section of the *Times*, and George appears to read it with him. It hurts my heart, because I know that Georgie must be counting the precious minutes he is having with his father right now. It won't be long before he is shut out again, forced on the other side of the invisible wall that separates Scotty from the rest of the world.

Scotty gestures to the coffeemaker. "The front page and the sports section are over there," he says. "Or you can have this one, if you want."

"Well, you know how I love the sports section." I pour coffee for myself and put two multigrain waffles into the toaster.

Scotty maneuvers Georgie off his lap and sets him on the floor.

"See you later," he says and kisses no one. There's no one in this house that he wants to kiss.

I lift George into the booster seat and set him up with his waffle, then walk back down the hall to check on Matt's progress. He is in his bed, with his pajamas back on and the covers pulled up over his head.

Valentine's Day

Once I realize that Gretchen has died, my first thought is that I need to text Eliza.

But what to text? She should know, of course. It's the responsible thing to do where Scotty's job is concerned; plus, I promised. But if I type the words, will it become more true? Will it be less true if fewer people know? And if I am able to force my fingers to acknowledge the truth, how will I phrase it? What words could I possibly use?

Scotty has shifted his frozen stare from the sleeping boys, to the doors the doctor has just walked back through. Maybe the doctor wasn't sure. Maybe he's gone back to double-check. It would be silly to text Eliza now. The doctor should make sure that this is indeed the truth before I start a widespread panic via text. Patrick is standing behind Scotty with his hands on his brother's shoulders, like a father might stand. I'm confused for a moment, wondering how Patrick can appear so much taller, until I realize that Scotty is hunched over and has been inching that way since the doctor walked away. What if he falls? I'm suddenly afraid he might, and I don't want that. But Patrick has him; Patrick is guiding him to a chair.

Scotty sits in that chair for a long time. Rosie Ramsay comes out once or twice. Do they want to take him back to identify the body? Did they use a stale phrase, like "see her one last time"? Patrick waves Rosie off. He is crying. Patrick is crying?

And then I realize that *I'm* crying. Of course, I'm crying too. I don't want the boys to wake up and see me crying. I don't want them to wake up until I hear from Scotty that he knows how he wants to handle this.

But Scotty is the only conscious person in the room who is not crying, so I'm not sure I'm going to hear anything at all from him.

Gretchen's sister and her teenage daughter walk in then. They are coming down the long, frustrating hallway, and I can see them approaching for what seems like a distorted amount of time before they arrive in our waiting room. I have a sudden flash of gratitude that Patrick is here and appearing to function. This is not my responsibility. I'm not part of this family, not really. This thought is disconcerting, and what's worse is that it's followed by a now-or-never moment. If I want to get out, now is the time to do it, the time to leave and not come back. Right now, no one I matter to is in a state of awareness; Gretchen is dead, Scotty is in limbo, and George and Matt are sleeping. Before I hear anyone ask for me or about me, there's still time to escape.

I don't. There's no weighing of pros and cons. I simply don't. I don't move. I don't go while I have the chance. I don't do anything.

Gretchen's sister's name is Lila, and the daughter's name is something innocuous. Mary? I think that's right. Patrick rises to greet Lila.

I am thinking, in a muted, panicky way, of all the roles that have been vacated by the loss of her, all the capacities that suddenly no longer exist. The mother of two particular little boys, the wife of a particular husband. Someone's daughter, someone's best friend, sister, ex-girlfriend, confidante. The object of someone's particular affection, jealousy, animosity, maybe? There's going to be competition, I think, in a flash of foreboding. There will be competition in this grief. Everyone will have memories, stories. Everyone will have had a unique experience of her, with her, and they will compete to prove who loved her the most. Thank God the boys are too young to understand that. I want to throw my body in between them and anyone who might lay that on them.

It seems Patrick has already taken on that role for Scotty. Even now, as Lila weeps into the arms of her fourteen-year-old, Patrick is on the other side of her, holding her up, guiding her to a chair as he did for Scotty. It's not helpful that through her sobs Lila keeps saying, "Oh Scotty, oh Scotty," over and over like some kind of morbid record skip. Patrick seems to understand that no one needs to hear that. He says, "Shh, shh," a few times, like you would to soothe a child, and she does stop eventually. No sooner has she quieted down than Patrick catches my attention over her slumped form and shakes his head. To me, it looks dismissive. I'm glad because now I can go back to hating him.

By taking no action, by my staying put here tonight, I have condemned myself to watching a horrifying parade. There will be more family to arrive and hear this news. There will be more people to call. There will be more tears, more wailing, more foreheads covered in ash and breasts beaten. And I will watch it all.

And then the boys will wake up, and that will be the absolute worst.

I text Eliza. I can't think of an appropriate way to say what's happened. I just type two words: "She died."

A little time passes, and I get her response. One word only: "No."

April, six weeks after

I have finally gotten both kids to school, employing a small amount of literal dragging. Georgie has a playdate today and will be picked up by another nanny. I explain this one more time to him, even though I know it won't make him any happier when it comes time for the playdate to actually start. After depositing George in his classroom and tricking him into surrendering Chickie, I am about to foist Matt into the hands of Miss Leslie, the head kindergarten teacher.

As she sends Matt over to put his things away in the designated cubby, I start to go, but she calls me back over.

"I've left a message with Mr. McLean's secretary, but I don't want to be a nag. We don't have another number for him. The cell phone number we have is—" She catches herself and recovers with grace. She has exactly the right temperament for a kindergarten teacher. "The number we have on file was Gretchen's."

"I can give you his cell number," I say. I am reluctant because I know that if Eliza took a message, then he had definitely received it and chosen not to call back, at least not yet. "Could you maybe, I mean, is there a way you could tell me what it was regarding? I can check again with him to make sure that he knows."

I understand her hesitation—I'm not the parent. She hasn't seen a parent's face in six weeks. She's only seen mine, and maybe Gramma Mae's once or twice.

"Well, we're having trouble getting Matt to follow directions, which isn't typical for him," Miss Leslie finally says. "We know he hears what we say. We know that he knows what we mean but chooses to do what he'd rather do instead. It's completely understandable, and we're prepared to deal with it in a way that's conducive to grieving, but . . ." She isn't looking me in the eye, like she's casting around for the right way to phrase it. "There's been a recurring incident with Ainsley, and we need to make sure that the other kids are okay and feel safe."

"Of course," I say. "What's been happening?"

"We thought it was silly at first, but now Ainsley winds up crying at the end of every recess, maybe three or four times now," Miss Leslie says, more gently than I would have.

"Oh, wow. I don't know what to say," I tell her. "I'm so sorry. Is he hurting her?"

"Not initially," she says, looking uncomfortable. "He keeps asking her if she wants to get married, and she'll laugh, and sometimes she says yes and sometimes no. It's pretty much no, though. When she says yes, he'll say things like, 'You're my wife now forever, we have to live together, you can move into my house, and Georgie will go live at yours,' stuff like that. And then when she wants to stop pretending, he'll grab her arms and drag or push her into their corner 'house.' Or, like the other day, he kind of shook her a little."

"Stop, stop," I say, and I don't know why I say that, although it's probably what I would say if Matt could hear me. "I'm so sorry. I can't believe he did that. Is she okay? Does Jillian—I mean, is she mad? Oh, no, I'm so sorry."

"Everyone is fine." Miss Leslie is comforting me. "It didn't escalate that far, and we've been keeping them apart at recess. But I need to tell Jillian about it, just to make her aware, and I wanted to be able to tell her that Mr. McLean is also aware."

"Of course," I say. "I'll make sure he hears the message. Let me also give you my cell phone number so that you can reach someone right away if you need to during the day."

"Are you the only one who's there with them, besides their dad?" she asks. I'm annoyed by the implications in this question, but I try not to let on. Miss Leslie is either my exact same age or a few years younger, from the looks of her, which somehow makes her sympathy worse.

"Their grandmother, Gretchen's mom, was here for about a month. She left two weeks ago, and since then, it's mostly me with the boys, until they figure out what they want to do more permanently." The last part of that is of my own invention. I suspect Scotty hasn't gotten around to entertaining what's next for the boys' future. "They go out to visit their aunt on the weekends."

"It must be very hard for you," says Miss Leslie.

"It's very hard for everyone," I say.

Valentine's Day

By the time Gretchen's parents arrive at the hospital, Lila and Mary have collected themselves enough to go with Rosie Ramsay and do whatever it is that needs to be done back there. Patrick, in a fit of wisdom, has opted not to leave the waiting room and therefore not let Scotty out of his sight. However often I will it not to, my heart is starting to bleed for Patrick. I am dreading the moment that the boys will have to learn that the central figure in their lives is no more; it's an equally unfathomable task to have to deliver the news that a daughter has not outlived her parents—that they have not made it in time to even say good-bye—and Patrick will have to be the one to take on those tasks when Gretchen's parents arrive.

Simon and Mae Edgerly have a Midwestern charm combined with a suburban reserve that I've always found endearing. They live outside of Chicago near Northwestern University, where Gretchen grew up and went to college before she moved to New York and met Scotty. Now that they're in their sixties, they spend the coldest three months of the year in Palm Beach and would have been on the last two weeks of that trip had it not been so direly interrupted.

Simon weeps openly. I can't watch it for very long, but when I decide to look at something else, I find the image burned onto my retina. Mae asks if she can join Lila and Mary, and when the three return to the waiting room, where everything is hushed so as not to wake the boys, she looks sad but composed, a direct juxtaposition to the pile of destruction that is Gretchen's father.

I wish that I could hear what she says next, but I am sitting down at Georgie's feet, and no one will let their voice travel far enough to be heard in my corner. What I see is Mae, squatting down so she is level with Scotty's face and physically lifting his head out of his hands. She looks at Patrick, nodding and smiling a little, and he gets up then and leaves the room. She is speaking intensely, with an occasional tear running down her face, which she does nothing to impede. She is holding on to Scotty's hands and grips them more tightly every so often. It goes on for a long time, so long that most of the other activity in the room stops, and all that can be heard are the background hospital functions and the low murmur of her voice.

She clasps her own hands together around Scotty's then and touches her forehead to them, closing her eyes. She whispers, and the sound has a specific cadence, though I can't make out the words. Prayer? I have no idea what the family's background is, but if I had to paint a picture of prayer, it would probably look something like that. But what kind of a god can be prayed to tonight? This night is by far the most successful argument against God that I have ever witnessed.

After a moment she opens her eyes, lifts Scotty's chin with one hand, and says something brief. He stands up, and Mae puts her arm around him. They both walk to the double doors and disappear into the hallway beyond. I have no idea what kind of man will return when he comes back to us.

Patrick reappears then, maybe from the men's room. It looks like he has splashed some water on his face. He sits down next to me.

"Charlotte, are you okay?"

I shake my head, but I don't do it because I want him to comfort me. I do it because thinking about George and Matt and the countdown until they are forced out of Eden is like a wrecking ball to my brain. He puts his arm around me, loosely, and I'm too tired to shrug him off.

"I don't know what to do about these guys," I say, and he nods his agreement. He doesn't know what to do either.

When Scotty comes back out with Gramma Mae, his eyes are still dry. But he is composed and appears to be thinking more clearly. I hear her voice then.

"The one thing you can do is get your house in order. We'll have to work together to make plans, but there are things that must be done at home first." Her gaze rolls over Patrick, over me, and lands on the boys. Scotty's glance follows hers, and I wish that Patrick would get his arm off me.

I stand up, and I offer no words of comfort to Scotty, because I have none. I don't want to tell him how sorry I am. It will mean nothing.

"Would you like me to help you get them home?" I ask, and he nods.

"Charlotte, I wish you could have known how much Gretchen valued you," says Mae, and my stomach turns over because she has moved so quickly into a memory tense. "She told me once that she had no idea what she should pay you because how could she put a price on someone helping to raise her children? She was thankful to have found such a wonderful person to be part of their lives." It sounds like I'm in the memory tense now too, and my heart is beating very fast with mixed emotions. I appreciate how coherent and in control she is. I know she's trying to help me feel better. But I can't accept a secondhand affirmation. There were two people who knew, truly, what my role was, and now there is only one. And he can barely stand.

"Thank you," I say. Then I catch Patrick's attention as I turn around to pick up Georgie and wrap him in his coat. "Can you carry Matt and help me get a cab?" I ask him, and without waiting for a response, I pick up our bags and walk past Scotty. "I'll see you back at the apartment," I say and walk outside to wait.

Patrick helps me buckle Matt and George into the backseat. I get in next to them, and he gets up front with the driver. I give the driver the address, and as we start off up Park, I hear a muffled laugh from the front seat.

"What?"

He turns around to look at me with irony. "I'm thinking that we probably ought to call Eliza and get her back. She's really good at making plans."

April, six weeks after

After I extract myself from North-Mad and the empathetic eyes of Miss Leslie, I head over to Fifth Avenue and decide that instead of rattling around in the house, going stir-crazy until it's time to catch a cab, I will walk downtown, all the way into lower Manhattan, to meet Scotty for lunch near his office. Miss Leslie's commentary has hastened my courage; today will be the day that we decide what we're going to do. I called Scotty and asked him if we could go to lunch and make some decisions. He agreed because there was nothing else he could do, really. The future is descending.

Halfway down the requisite stretch of Fifth Avenue, my phone rings. The area code is 646, and I pick up quickly, terrified that Matt has been expelled from kindergarten sometime in the last hour.

"Hello?"

"May I speak with Charlotte?" A man's voice. I try to remember if the head of North-Mad is a man or a woman.

"Speaking," I say.

"I'm calling to confirm your reservation for the postshow reception following the performance on Friday evening at eight p.m. . . ." He drones on for at least twenty seconds while I sift through the sand in my brain. Everett. The Philharmonic. Carnegie Hall. Jess.

I want to interrupt the voice on the other end of the line to point out the absolute absurdity of the suggestion that I will be attending Everett's concert. I want this stranger to know that the hampers in my place of employment are completely stuffed, due to the ridiculous amounts of laundry that little boys create. I want to tell him that if I'm doing anything on Friday, it will involve relieving those hampers of their burden; there will not even be enough time for spot treating the bits of spinach and applesauce out of my clothing after all the meals of the day have concluded, let alone showers, or figuring out what to wear to an event that doesn't involve plastic tablecloths.

Before I can clue the unknown man in on the reality of my situation, he varies his speech pattern slightly, like he's asking a question. I have to ask him to repeat it.

"Will the reservation be only for one?"

"Um. I guess so?"

"How many tickets to the show do you have reserved for your party?"

"I don't know. I think the composer reserved them—it—for me. I hope. Do you have that information there? Can you check?"

"You'll have to call the box office for that, ma'am." He monotones the number at me, but I don't have anything to write it down with.

"Thank you," I say. "And I think it's just one for the reception. Just me, I mean."

"Very good," he says. We hang up, and I call my older sister in Portland; I need to speak to someone who's not flailing around in emotional sludge.

She picks up right away. "Hello?"

"Hi, Jane."

"Hello, my little spring chicken," she says. "I'm at Home Depot. Can I call you back after I talk to the tile guy?"

"Everett's playing a concert at Carnegie Hall."

"Wow. Everett. There's a name I haven't heard in a while."

"He showed up at my door a few weeks ago. That night I texted you, remember? It was. Lord. It was the day before she died. I was obsessing about Everett and his concert, feeling jealous, thinking all these petty thoughts while she was—I don't know—in an ambulance. Lying on the pavement. Maybe while the surgeon was trying to—"

"Stop that. Stop it right now," says Jane.

"I almost e-mailed Jess that day too. She's going to be at this concert, did I mention that?"

"Wow."

"I can't go. How could I go? I'm super busy with George and Matt. They need—"

"You mean, how could you possibly do anything fun, that doesn't involve guilt or tribute, so soon after Gretchen died?" The element of truth in Jane's mild sarcasm feels like a crochet hook to the ribs.

"I'm not sure I would call it fun, exactly, but yes. They're miserable, Janie. Their life is so terrible. Going out, celebrating—it feels like jumping ship. And holy shit, it's been so long since I was in that world. It would be a lot for me."

"I know," she says. "I think they're lucky that you worry about those things."

"Well. I loved her too." My eyes and nose are running, but I had used my last tissue wiping syrup off George's forehead.

"I know you did." Jane stays on the line. I am near the entrance to the zoo, and I stop walking, considering taking one of the wandering paths inside Central Park down to Fifty-Ninth Street instead of continuing along Fifth. "I have to get off the phone," she says gently. "I hope you'll think about this for a while before you make any concrete decisions. Shutting everyone out of your life apart from those kids won't end well for anyone, especially you."

"How are you at Home Depot? Isn't it like six in the morning?"

"We have a twenty-four-hour Home Depot," she says. "Don't tell Dad. He'll get jealous and try to move out here, and then Mom will have my hide."

"You're so down-home," I say. "Using expressions like 'have

my hide' and installing your own tile. Gramma would be so proud of you."

"She sure would," she says. "I'm next in line! Don't want to miss my shot with Walter the tile man."

"Sounds like a sexy dude," I say.

"Want to say hi to him?"

"Yeah."

"Hold on," she says.

A few seconds later, I hear a voice that could be my grandfather's say, "Hullo, Walter here."

"Hi, Walter," I say. "This is Jane's sister. Please don't let her leave there with purple tile. Her husband will throw her out. She'll try to make a case for it, and it's your job to talk her out of it."

"Will do ya, ma'am," says Walter, and I can hear Jane laughing as she gets back on the phone.

"I'm calling Claudia next," I say. "So never mind about calling me back. She can have the title of benevolent sister, and you'll just be the girl who whored it up with Walter for a backsplash."

"It's going to be a beautiful backsplash," Jane says. We hang up, and I decide against walking through the park. I'm not in the mood for that kind of beauty. I continue along Fifth, stepping carefully on the uneven stones that make up the Park side of the street, and call our little sister, Claudia. She lives in Boston for no good reason, and it's my endless quest to try and get her to move to New York. She refuses and keeps moving to different apartments in Boston every time a lease runs out.

"Claud-hopper," I say, after she says hello like maybe she's still sleeping. "Are you sleeping?"

"I'm a bartender," she says irritably. "I went to bed, like, three hours ago."

"I wasn't judging, just asking," I say.

"Well, I'm awake now," she grumbles. "What's going on?"

"I'm walking downtown," I say.

"Did you call me because you got bored walking a long distance?"

"Would you be mad?"

"Yes."

"I would never do that," I say, even though I totally would. "I'm on my way to lunch with Scotty. I have to ask him about a lot of uncomfortable logistical things."

"Why do you have to go to lunch with him? Can't you talk to him—" Her voice is drowned out by a sudden whirring noise.

"What is that? The blender?"

"Coffee grinder."

"I missed what you said."

"I said, why can't you talk to him when he gets home from work?"

"He comes home from work at, like, ten or eleven every night," I say. "No one wants to talk then, least of all me. I have to be back at their apartment at six thirty in the morning."

"Oh Lord," Claudia says, and I know that if my flower child, turn-with-the-tide sister thinks something is a little bit crazy, it's not a sign that the river is flowing in the right direction.

"Why are you out of bed?" I ask.

"What?"

"Why are you making coffee? Aren't you going back to sleep when we hang up?"

"Mind your own business."

"It's the absolute worst time to discuss employment stuff with Scotty, you know?" I say.

"You need to take care of yourself," says Claudia. "I know they've been really good to you, and you care about them. But you're not a member of their family."

"I feel kind of guilty for making him deal with yet another thing," I say.

"He has to," she says. "He has to function."

"I guess," I say. "What's reasonable, do you think?"

"I think it would be reasonable of you to drop into the conversation that you have a huge amount of student loan debt and that he should probably take it off your hands for you."

"Be serious."

"I am serious. That's what Mom would say."

"I called *you* for exactly that reason." I step to the curb for a second, letting a Hispanic man with a huge pack of random, mismatched dogs go by me. The smallest of the group, a spotted dachshund, leads the way, and he is followed by a golden retriever, a boxer, two midsize labs, and three fluffy white hypoallergenic dogs of varying breeds. It must be time for the midday walk at one of the neighborhood doggy day cares.

"Ha. Well, what are you making now?" Claudia asks, and I give her the weekly number.

"It used to be for about thirty-six hours, but recently it's been more like ninety," I say. "They've been spending weekends in Connecticut with their aunt, and that's pretty much the only time I'm not with them." I stop for a second to pull the zipper of my jacket up to my chin. It's colder outside than I think it should be in April. "I don't want to have to talk about this with him. He should realize on his own that it's not a sustainable situation."

"I know you don't want to talk about it. You never do. Probably because you always start crying and never get to make the points you want to make."

"You are the meanest girl I know." I pause in front of the entrance to the NQR trains but decide to keep walking. I'm starting to regret initiating this conversation.

"It sounds really complex, and I don't blame you for being sensitive. I blame Mom and Dad, of course. We all have too many feelings. But you need to make an effort not to let the feelings hold you hostage the way they have your entire life."

"I don't know what you mean by that."

"Like, remember how you were with those ducks?"

"What ducks?"

"The ducks we would see, in the spring. A mom duck would come by with her babies, and you would count them to make sure they were all there. And if you saw one go by on its own, well, forget it," says Claudia. "You'd stand out on the dock, holding a stick. Maybe you were going to poke anything that came by that looked threatening, get it away from the orphan duck."

"Or maybe I was going to whack the duckling with the stick, put it out of its misery, but never worked up the nerve," I say.

"Maybe you were," says Claudia. "We never knew. You never wanted to talk about it. You just stood out there, determined to be the silent duck hero. For, like, hours and hours."

"I'm not trying to be a hero," I say, but I can't say anything else because maybe I am. Not in the way she means it, though, not in the way that earns glory or accolades. I don't know how to convince my sister of this, let alone anyone else, because an adequate explanation of what I *am* doing seems just out of reach. "Hey, speaking of ducks. You know where there are ducks? In the ponds of Central Park. You miss ducks, don't you? Of course you do. That's why you brought them up. You should move here."

"You know where there are also ducks?" Claudia is clinking dishes around. I'm guessing all her mugs are dirty, and she has to take one out of the full dishwasher and wash it by hand in order to drink her coffee. "In the public garden, right here in Boston. There are millions of ducks. Sometimes we even see them in the street."

"That's a myth perpetuated by a children's book. Don't be fooled. The man who wrote that book was living in New York City, studying ducklings he kept in his bathtub. You need to move to New York to see some real ducks."

"I actually don't miss ducks at all."

"Come on. You're pining for them."

"See, now I can tell that you're keeping me on the line because you're bored with walking. How long before you get to the restaurant and I can go back to bed?"

"I'm still in Midtown. About to pass Saint Patrick's."

"You should go in and light a candle. Make a wish."

"I don't think that's how it works." I look up at the massive building. It's been surrounded by scaffolding, under construction since I first moved to the city. There are no signs that they'll be finished with it anytime soon. The amount of time that they spend on renovations must somehow be worth it, proportional to how long they're hoping the building will stand.

"We're not Catholic," says Claudia. "Maybe wishing will work, this one time. Maybe that's how they convert you. You're granted one wish from the candle-genie."

"Maybe." I climb the steps but turn around before I reach the doors, imagining the look on Scotty's face if I were to tell him I was late because I stopped into a church to light a candle on my way. "Everything feels so high stakes. What can I do, Claudia?"

"It feels that way because it *is* high stakes," she says. "Why don't you let him tell you what he thinks is best? Make him name the first number. He's a businessman, right? He'll understand that."

"He's a corporate attorney," I say.

"So what? He's going to screw you with your pants on and leave you on a conference table?"

"CLAUDIA."

"You're around little people too much," she says. "You've lost your edge. *Screw* isn't even a dirty word."

"It was a dirty metaphor." The mental picture makes me uncomfortable, but I'm afraid saying so will give Claudia the wrong idea. I'm already paranoid that people are getting the wrong idea, from Aunt Lila to Miss Leslie.

"I'm cranky," Claudia says. "You won't let me go back to bed."

"I should probably see what he's going to say before I ask for anything."

"He has more money than God," she says. "He won't agree to anything he can't handle. And he can't expect you not to have feelings, so just keep talking until he hears you, even if it's through tears. He won't know what you need unless you tell him."

"You're right, you're right," I say. "Thank you for talking to me. Go back to whatever man you left in your bed."

"How'd you know?" She laughs.

"Grinding coffee beans before noon? Please," I say.

"I'll have to tell Mom she raised a bunch of sluts," Claudia says. "Good-bye, defender of mallards everywhere. Love you."

"Love you."

I hang up, feeling somewhat better. And I think about how lucky I am to be able to talk to my sisters whenever I want, and the feeling morphs into something strange and a little bit hollow.

A short while later, Scotty and I are on our way to lunch.

"Who's George playing with today?" Scotty asks.

"Sarai," I say.

"Where does she live?"

"Sarai is a boy. They live further up on Park."

We sit at a table in the back of an Indian restaurant that looks like it could have once been a cathedral. It's cavernous, and the walls are made of stone. I feel like I have to whisper so my voice doesn't catapult in a thousand different directions when I speak. I didn't even realize they had restaurants this big at this end of town, down below the numbers.

"Do you have any preferences?" he asks, looking at the menu.

"Um . . . chicken?" I say. There have been so many gluten-free fish sticks in my recent meal history that I've forgotten how to order Indian food.

The waiter comes, and Scotty orders a bunch of stuff that I've never heard of, plus a gin and tonic. For a minute I am worried, and then I dismiss the thought. Not my job.

"Perfect," says the waiter. "A glass of wine for your wife?"

"No, thank you," I say. "I'm not—" I'm not his wife? I'm his babysitter? There is nothing to be said that won't make it worse for Scotty. "I'm not drinking," I finish lamely, and Scotty is amused, although I'm not sure how I know this since he doesn't laugh or really even smile.

"You sure?" he says.

"I'm good with water," I say.

"Very good," says the waiter. He leaves the wine list anyway and heads off to put in our order.

"I take it you got Matt to school," Scotty says, and I'm surprised he realized that there was a minor battle going on this morning.

"Yeah," I say. I don't tell him about the moment when Matthew literally dug his heels into the sidewalk outside North-Mad, and I had to pick him up, deposit him into the elevator, and then blockade the elevator door with my body in order to prevent his escape. George giggled the entire time, which I take to mean he'll be modeling his brother's antics sometime in the near future.

"Before I forget, Miss Leslie asked me for your cell phone number," I say. "She left a message at work for you, but she didn't, ah, hear anything."

"Did you give her yours?" Scotty asks, and I can tell he'd rather not discuss it.

"I did, for daytime stuff," I say. "But I think she wants to talk about something specific, so I told her I would mention it to you."

"Do you know what it is?" he asks.

"She didn't give me a lot of details," I say.

"Is Matt acting out?"

"I guess so," I say, and he knows I'm being careful, and I don't think he likes it.

"Is he belligerent with the teachers? Talking back? Punching kids on the playground?" The thought of Matt punching other kids, like some kind of tough guy, is relatively comical, but neither of us laughs.

"No punching," I say. "She didn't mention punching. I think he's kind of . . . harassing one of the girls."

"What, like mouthing off? Or trying to kiss her?"

"I really am not sure," I say, and it's a flat-out lie, which is unfortunate, as I'm a terrible liar. "I think that's why Miss Leslie wants to talk to you, though."

"Can she e-mail me? That would be easier," Scotty says. "Give her my work e-mail."

"Okay," I say.

Our food comes, and it's mostly red, yellow, and brown. I cut into something that looks like a pastry and find peas inside. I'm not a huge fan of peas, but I'm committed now, so I eat it. It's not horrible.

"So, Charlotte," Scotty says, and I have a terrible knot in my stomach, made of secret concerts and lives away from Park Avenue and sad little boys. "I haven't been thinking much about . . . much of anything besides getting through our day-to-day things."

"Of course," I say. "Me too, I guess."

"But Mae has been calling me every day since she left. I think she's really concerned about what's happening with the kids," he says. I'm not sure what he's getting at. "She wants us to move to Chicago." I can't help it; I raise my eyebrows.

"I know," he says. "That's how I feel. She thinks the firm could transfer me, and we could move close to her and Simon. She thinks that would be . . . good for them, for all of us, I guess."

"Okay," I say. "Are you thinking about that?"

"Lila thinks it's a terrible idea. She thinks we should move to Connecticut, and then I can commute into the city for work." Scotty passes me a basket of naan and spoons something in a red curry sauce onto my plate. Curry can mean nothing but trouble for the feeling in my gut, so I spend some time cutting the unknown meat into tiny pieces and pushing it around on my plate, hoping this will pass for eating, even though I'm never fooled when the boys engage in similar activities.

"Wow," I say. "I guess, well, I guess that's an option."

"Another option involves the boys going to stay with Mae and Simon for a while and me staying based in New York until I can get my act together."

"Did she actually say that to you, that you need to get your act together?" I ask, not sure whether that would be impressive or abominable or both.

"No, she's very understanding," Scotty says. "I'm the one who's thinking in terms of getting my act together. Mae always says things like 'weathering the aftershocks' and 'working through the grief' and 'testing the limits of my humanity.'"

"That's dramatic," I say. "I guess it's appropriate, though."

"Sure," he says. "Maybe. I haven't had the energy. I should probably see a therapist or throw some furniture around."

"Well, that *would* be energetic," I say. My sister Jane would yell at me right now for giving in to my instinct to deflect when things get serious.

"I want to be with them," he says. He picks up the wine list. I can't see his face behind it. "I don't want them to go anywhere. But." He swallows. "They look just like her. So. It's been hard." He lowers the menu, blinking a little, and if this is the first time he's going to cry, I'm not prepared. He doesn't, though; instead, he goes on. "Mae and I have been discussing options. But I'm not ready to send them away."

"Okay," I say. I don't know what my opinion is, but I'm surprised to hear that Scotty doesn't want to be rid of them for the time being. His recent actions suggest he barely notices that they're around. "Do you have ideas about what you might want to do?"

"I do," says Scotty, looking right at me. "I know you've been working crazy hours for me. Jesus, I probably owe you money."

"Don't worry about it," I say, but he's waving one hand and

writing a note to himself in his phone with the other. I take a few bites of my lunch while he does so. It's super spicy.

"Charlotte, if you don't give me a ballpark, you know I'm just going to make one up," he says, and something flutters a little in my chest, half resentment and half excitement. I don't understand people who can talk that casually about money.

"I haven't been counting the hours that they're both in school," I tell him, and I pick up my water glass and hold it to my face. The spice has caught up with me. I know that Scotty must be muddling through questions in his brain, like where have all the groceries come from? and who picks up my dry cleaning?

"When I add it up, I think it should be about twice what I've paid you so far. Is that right, or close to right?"

"But most of that time Gramma Mae was here." I stop talking when I see him rub a tired hand over his eyes. Matt makes that same gesture when he's feeling impatient with me. "That will be fine, more than fine. Thank you," I say, and I briefly wonder how I'm going to report my taxes this year.

"If you have time to come back to the office with me, Eliza can take care of this," Scotty says. "But I want to make sure we get some things decided before you have to leave and get George."

"I have a little time," I say.

"Here's what I want to do for now," Scotty says, and the way he says it, I sort of expect him to whip out some kind of presentational booklet. "I suppose I'll just tell you what I'm thinking, and then you'll have to be honest about what your thoughts are."

"Okay," I say.

He flags down the waiter and orders a glass of Cabernet. The waiter looks at me, and I'm tempted, but I shake my head.

"I want them here," Scotty says. "I'm going to start . . . looking for someone to see, professionally. I still think they should spend the weekends with family, maybe Lila, maybe their grandparents, or other family, other people who love them so they know they still have a big support network." He pushes his plate away, only half-eaten. "Even though it won't be quite the same as what they're used to."

"Okay," I say. "That sounds like a good idea."

"But another reason I don't want to send them away is because I think that taking *you* away from them on top of everything else would be too hard. Would be a . . . a mistake. Other than her and me"—he doesn't say her name, and I'm trying to remember if he's said it at all in the last six weeks—"you have been the most consistent person in their lives for the last two years, for probably as long as George can remember."

I'm at a complete loss for what to say. The acknowledgment makes my heart feel runny.

"But I don't want things to be too hard on you. I can certainly get a housekeeper to come and live with us full-time, but I'd rather have you, if you'll come. I'd rather have you move in, primarily to take care of the boys, and I can figure out how to make all the rest of the stuff, the running of the house stuff, work. And I would like to know, from you, if you think that might be possible, and what you would need, financially, for that to happen."

I think of what my sister said about letting him make the first offer. I wish I weren't so uncomfortable around money. I suspect it has a little to do with pride and a lot to do with my upbringing. I was raised by parents who are meticulous about money, responsible with it and respectful of it. I was taught that if you need something, you earn it, and if someone gives it to you, then they have earned it and are being purposefully generous. Nothing Scotty has done since Gretchen died has seemed purposeful, and taking his money, however much or little it means to him, makes me feel like Scrooge McDuck. Or some kind of mercenary.

On the other hand, a job is a job, even if our situation is unique. I think again of how I'll have to maneuver things to get away for even a few hours for Everett's concert. If I am living in his house, how can I possibly keep these things from Scotty? If

I am living in his house, in what ways am I accountable to him that I have never been before?

"I—I really have no frame of reference for what the appropriate arrangement is, financially," I say. "And, you know, the parameters of living in your house. I might have to think about it."

"But are you open to the idea, honestly?" he probes, not seeming to want to let me off the hook, and that is the Scotty I know, the Scotty that Gretchen always spoke of. Once he acknowledges that something exists, he doesn't stop until he has mined to the bottom of it, and right now, his target is somewhere on my person. "Can you even consider it, or are you thinking that I sound crazy, and you need a way to let me down easy? Because like I said, if you're not able to do the whole thing, I still want you to take care of the boys part-time. If you can. If it's not too much. I know it has been. A lot."

I want some time to think before I play all my aces, but Scotty has folded his hands on the table in front of him, waiting for my answer.

"I don't think you sound crazy," I say. "I am thinking about it. I want to think carefully though, so I don't say anything I can't, ah, take back."

"Understood," he says.

"Did you have a number in mind?" I ask.

He writes it down, and there's no hesitation when he does so. He must have been thinking about it. Or maybe he hasn't thought about it at all, and the lack of hesitation is a business strategy. Maybe he's expecting me to ask for more. I look at the number, and I want to react, but I don't. I can't imagine asking for more, even if he is buying my life from me for the foreseeable future.

"This is generous," I say, and I mean it. Now is the time to tell him about the concert—now, so he can make any adjustments he wants, so he knows, so it's not an issue later—"I would also want to keep my apartment." That's the end of the sentence. I don't say any of the other things I should say.

"Yes, of course, I will add that on at the end of each month." He's not blinking at all now, not even at normal intervals. It seems possible at this moment, though the transaction is small, that I'm getting a glimpse of the head lion, the great global deal maker, that shrewd focus he must maintain in business. Or maybe I'm making that up too. If I am, my imaginings are getting the better of me.

"Okay," I say, trying to replace this image with the faces of the kids I love.

"Okay, as in yes?"

"Yes," I say. There isn't another answer that I can think of. Scotty looks relieved, and I have the urge to add "for now" to the end of the statement, but the moment has already passed us by, and he is asking for the check.

Valentine's Day

When we get back to the apartment from the hospital, getting the kids into bed without waking them up is a stressful production, involving lots of miming and other forms of silent communication with Patrick.

I am terrified of waking them, terrified of their questions, terrified of irrevocably damaging their little minds if I say the wrong thing to them. But they're both excellent sleepers once they're down. We are able to get them into bed, and I even manage to get Georgie into pajama pants. He's incredibly particular about not having zippers and buttons dig into his skin while he's trying to sleep, and I don't want him to wake up and complain, or worse, call for his mom. On my way back down the hallway from his room, I almost bite it on a Matchbox car, catch myself on the washer, remember that my sweaters are in the dryer, retrieve them, and then start weeping for the loss of normalcy.

I collect myself before I come back out to the living room. The TV screen is blue. Wall-E and Eve have long since pledged eternity to each other, and the beanbag chairs are where I left them, with George- and Matt-shaped imprints in them. There is a partial chocolate cupcake overturned on the Oriental rug. I grab a stain remover and an old towel from the kitchen and get to work on the smudge before I notice Patrick on the couch, turning a glass around and around in his hands. He looks pale, and his eyes are bloodshot. He's looking at his glass, or maybe his knees, and it's not that I didn't think he had feelings; it's just that I never considered the possibility that I'd witness them.

I finish up with the stain, aware that the wrong move will make me responsible for dealing with his emotional state. He seems almost desperate to conceal how much he is hurting, and for a minute I wonder if he was a little bit in love with Gretchen, pining a little bit for her all these years. Gretchen's light was so bright. Probably most people who met her were a little bit in love with her.

"Patrick, have you eaten anything tonight?" I say, standing up.

"I honestly can't remember."

"Are you hungry?" I press him. He's giving me a look that's similar to one Georgie gives me when he's afraid of something and doesn't want to admit it but wants me to read his mind and hold his hand. I want to do something for Patrick because I feel so sad, but something other than hold him and inhale his stupid pheromones. Those jackass pheromones cause too much trouble, and I hate them. Pheromones are the worst.

"I don't know. Not really," he says.

"Me either," I say. "But I make pretty good kid food. I was going to make an English muffin pizza for myself. Do you want one?"

"My mom used to make those," he says, in a voice I can barely hear.

"Mine too," I say. "I'll make an extra one, and you can eat it if you want to. Or not." He gets up to pour himself another drink.

"Scotty never drinks the good stuff," he says, maybe to keep himself from crying in front of me again. "I don't think he can even tell what the good stuff is. He probably gets it from clients."

"Sure, probably," I say, as I assemble the little pizzas and put them in the toaster oven.

"Have a drink with me," he says, and for a minute I entertain this as a prelude to the thought of going home with him tonight, instead of alone to my apartment. I immediately hate myself and curse the circumstances that brought our paths together. The predictability of my pattern with men is laughable. First comes a moment where I'm off my game, then comes booze, then comes the shameful hunt for my underpants in the darkness of early morning.

"I can't hold my liquor," I tell him.

"If I were talking to you at a bar right now, that would be music to my ears," he says, and the gall of it is amazing, but I laugh anyway.

"You would never talk to *me* at a bar," I say.

"Probably not," he says.

"Anyway, I'm more of a wine drinker." I raise the setting on the toaster oven, hoping the cheese will melt faster and also that I won't wreck them.

"Perfect," he says, and without batting an eye uncorks what I'm sure is a great bottle of some vintage that would be orgasmic to a sommelier and will probably mean nothing more than a buzz to me.

He pours me a glass, and I bring the little pizzas to the table. We eat and drink without speaking, and I feel like my chest is bruised on the inside. I try to distract myself by thinking of other things. Massive school shootings. Humanitarian aid held up on its way to Syria. Exploited children in Indian mines.

None of these things, however, can work me into a turmoil equal to what I'm feeling now.

I finish, take our dishes into the kitchen, and suddenly feel like my eyeballs are made of shards of ice. Gretchen's coffee mug is on the counter, a partial errand list in her handwriting is on the refrigerator, a compact from her purse is in the mail basket. The calendar has pictures taped to it, pictures of a woman who is immortal in them.

It's as I'm about to drop a pile of mail with her name all over it into the recycle bin that I catch myself. What am I going to do, erase her existence from this apartment before the rest of the family gets home? Impossible. I put the mail back in the basket, under her compact. There is nothing to be done.

There is nothing I can do.

I load the dishwasher and wash the kids' cupcake plates by hand. I may have been standing in front of the dishwasher for more than five minutes, having trouble deciding whether or not to run it three-quarters of the way full, when I hear a key in the latch, and I know that Patrick's and my brief hiatus from dealing with reality is about to be over.

Scotty comes in first, and he looks shell-shocked. Those are the only words I can think of to describe how he appears when he walks through the door. Mae and Simon come in after him, and Simon is carrying both of their overnight bags and Scotty's briefcase. He looks subdued, like maybe he is all cried out and needs to replenish the water supply in his body before he can live through any more emotions. Somehow, I wish Mae looked more like that.

Simon sets down his load and joins Patrick at the table. No one speaks for a while. Everyone stands where they are.

Finally, Scotty asks, "Did they wake up at all?" He is not looking at me, but who else would he be talking to?

"No," I say. "I don't think they will."

Silence again. It is so silent right now, more silent than I could ever have imagined. This is a home where I have rarely heard silence, but now it is screaming at us.

"Are you going to send them to school tomorrow?" I ask, and my voice sounds harsh, not at all gentle, as I'd intended. Probably a by-product of the huge lump in my throat. But I have to ask because it seems that no one will be instructing me on how to proceed.

"No," he says. "No, we probably won't send them back to school until after, after her—" and here his voice breaks a little, a side effect of unshed tears.

"Until after her funeral, probably," says Mae. It's irrational, but the way she's holding it together is making me crazy. "We'll call to let you know when the services are, Charlotte. I'm sure the boys will want to spend time with you after this weekend. Simon and I can take care of them until we figure out . . . what's next."

"I have to go to bed now," Scotty says abruptly. "I'm sorry. I need to go to bed. Whichever guest room you like is fine with me, Mae. Patrick, will you please walk Charlotte down and get her a cab?" He starts to reach for his wallet, but Patrick stops him.

"Don't worry about it, Scott," he says, and I don't know if I've ever heard anyone call him Scott, except Gretchen when she was purposely being obnoxious. Patrick puts his hands on both sides of Scotty's face. "I'll be back first thing in the morning. Call me tonight if you're up." Scotty walks away without saying anything. I wonder if he'll actually sleep.

It takes me a minute to make sure all my stuff is gathered and the boys' things are put away. Patrick waits by the door.

The moment we get outside, he flags down a taxi, displaying a similar talent to his brother's for calling one up out of thin air. He looks at me as he holds the door open.

"Are we going to your place or mine?"

April, the year before

Gretchen and Scotty are out on a date night, and I have gotten the boys ready and into bed with no fuss. I'm mentally patting myself on the back for my babysitting genius as I dish out a pile of the Mediterranean food that Gretchen ordered for me onto a plate. I'm about halfway through the stack of *Newsweek*s I've been neglecting for the last month when I hear noises coming from the foyer.

My heartbeat speeds up. It's too early for the grown-ups to be home, and if it were a kid, they would have called for me (Matthew) or banged on the wall (George) by now. Whatever is making the noise is between me and the sleeping kids, so I have to go and see what it is. I'm tempted to call out "Hello?" just to see what would happen, but I'm either not brave enough or unwilling to admit my fear if it turns out no one is there.

I step around the corner, and there stands Patrick, shaking out an umbrella, looking too confused about the dripping to figure out how to close it.

"Oh Lord, shit, holy shit, it's you." My heart is pounding so hard I think he can probably see it through my T-shirt, but at least I remember to whisper. "How did you get in here?"

"Shel gave me the key," he says, referring to the doorman, and I take the umbrella from him and close it. His Burberry raincoat is dripping; his hair is dripping. The weather must have taken quite a dive since I picked up Matt this afternoon.

"You scared me," I say, and I put my hand on my chest where I can still feel my heart, and the post-adrenaline shakes start to ripple through me. "Scotty's not here. He, they, they're out. They didn't tell me I should expect you."

"Where are they?" he asks, and I reach for his raincoat, on autopilot, watching my hands shake as they go. He notices, of course, and grabs them before I know what's happening. "Oh, Jesus. I really did scare you. I'm sorry. Jesus, your pulse, I can feel it." He drops one of my hands and puts his own on my chest, over my heart, where mine was a moment ago.

I step back. He smells like bourbon.

"They went to a gallery opening in the village," I say. "And then dinner with a bunch of people, or something. They won't be home for a while." If he weren't completely shit-housed, he'd get the message.

"Sienna dumped me," he says, looking me full in the face so that I can't possibly miss the effect of his watery, bloodshot eyes.

"I don't know who that is," I say. I walk back into the kitchen and grab a couple of dish towels. When I come back out, he's still standing there with his coat on, dripping all over the floor.

"She was my, my—" he says.

"Your girlfriend?" I hand him one of the towels and toss the other to the floor, mopping up the water with my foot.

"I guess so. She hated that word," he says, and to myself I think, perfect, perfect that he would find THAT girl, but I don't say that. He is standing there, with his wet coat on, holding the towel, red-nosed, red-eyed, not seeming to have any idea what he should do. "Are you, do you, can I stay?" he asks.

"Yeah," I say and take his coat as he shrugs it off. I look at the tag and decide it will be fine in the dryer.

"Does anything else need to go in the dryer?" I ask, and he says yes and proceeds to take off almost all of his clothes, down to his T-shirt and boxer briefs. He pats his face with the dish towel, then says, "The neck of this is wet." He starts to pull the T-shirt up over his head.

I take the dish towel that dangles from his hand. "You can leave your shirt in the pile and go put on some of Scotty's clothes or something. Geez, man, the boys could wake up."

"Charlotte, you're such a good friend, a good girl, woman," he says, and before I can pick up his discarded clothes, he has his arms around me, and his head is on my shoulder. I freeze with my hands out, like they can ward off the advance that's already come upon me. He doesn't do anything else though, nothing improper, unless of course you count pressing his almost-naked body up against the body of his brother's kids' babysitter.

I pat his back while holding my arms away from his sides, lightly a few times, then harder in what I hope is a clear send-off gesture.

"Go get a sweatshirt or something; you're going to freeze," I say, and he does.

I toss his clothes into the dryer and turn it on low, and it occurs to me that I ought to text Gretchen so she knows what awaits her at home, so there's no possibility that this could be misconstrued. My phone is in the living room, though (stupid—what if it really had been someone breaking in?), and I can't do it right away. On my way back out, I reevaluate. They won't be home for at least three hours. Maybe I can get him to leave, and no one ever has to know he was here. That option is the most appealing; then no one will have any seeds of anything in their brains, and Patrick won't have to explain himself. Patrick won't have to explain himself? Apparently, I give a shit, don't want him to be embarrassed or something. Curse my bleeding heart.

By the time I check on the boys, go to put the teakettle on, and come back out, Patrick is sitting on the couch in the family room, wearing a Harvard Law T-shirt and a pair of Northwestern sweatpants, a combination that I never would have expected to come from Scotty's closet. He has poured himself something clear that is too viscous to be water, and is balancing it on his open palm.

"Don't drink that. Seriously. Where did you even get it?"

"I know all his stashes, my bro. All my bro's stashes, hidden around my bro's house. I know where they are," he says. I put out my hand, patiently, the way I do when one of the boys steals something from the other.

"Come on, dude. Aren't you pretty lit already?"

"Lit! Sure, I guess I'm *lit*, Charlotte, I guess you could call it that." He relinquishes the glass, and I dump it down the drain in the kitchen and wash the glass. I have no idea where this particular glass came from, but I'll deal with that later.

"I'm making tea," I say. "You can drink some of that, how about."

He groans. "What the fuck, Charlotte! I'm such a fucking fuckup. Scotty is going to be so pissed at me."

I am now officially dying to know what he's talking about, but it's probably better if I stay out of whatever it is. "Well, it's up to you if you want to tell him, I guess," I say. The teakettle whistles in the other room, and I take my time fixing a tray. When I bring the tea out, Patrick is holding his phone, stabbing at the keyboard.

"What a fucking bitch," he mutters. "Look at this! They're all bitches, not you, Charlotte, every one of *them*, such goddamn bitches. Goddamn it!" He throws his phone across the room, and I'm surprised it doesn't break. "Are you going to look? Look at it!"

I am still for a minute, deciding whether it's best to indulge him or to simply not participate, and after a moment, I get up, making no sound, as I did when I thought he was possibly a murderer, and I retrieve his phone.

"It needs a password," I say, and I hand it to him. He types in the password and hands it back. The text message screen is up, and the text bubbles come from Patrick first.

"Hey. What's up?" Then, "Where are you?" Then, "I'll meet you. But you have to tell me where you are."

One text bubble comes back. "Don't text me."

Patrick does anyway, apparently. "You miss me?" Then, "Did you miss me when you woke up this morning?"

Another comes back. "I really mean it. Not a good idea."

Patrick ignores her. "I have a lot of good ideas." Then, "Want to see one?" Then a somewhat graphic picture of himself in the mirror. I hand the phone back to him as if it has lice.

"I don't know why you showed that to me," I say.

"I didn't actually mean to traumatize you with that one," he says, switching the shot. "Here, look at this," he says, handing the phone back to me. I don't take it.

"Those weren't even to Sienna. That was to someone named Eliza," I say, sitting down on the opposite end of the couch.

"I know!"

I hold out the mug of tea I made for him, but he doesn't take it. I rest both of them against my knees, hoping he'll calm down once he gets this agitation off his chest.

"I'm showing you the ones from Sienna." He waves the phone at me. I trade it for his mug and take a look. The conversation is basically Patrick saying he's sorry, and it was meaningless, and Sienna telling him to go do something explicit with his mother.

"You cheated on her," I say, handing it back.

"Technically," he mutters.

"Did you sleep with someone else?"

"Yes."

"So, technically, actually, any way you put it, you cheated."

"With Scotty's assistant, I know."

"Wait. Wait. Eliza is Scotty's secretary? That's who you cheated on your girlfriend with?" Now I can make sense of it, can see even more of a need for candor. "Oh man. Patrick."

"Don't judge me," he says.

"It's hard not to." I sip my tea, but it's still too hot to drink properly. Patrick doesn't seem to notice; he's a third of the way through his.

"Compatibility-wise, I'm with Sienna, like, all the way. I think she might be the one, *the girl*, but fuck, I've always wanted to bang Eliza. And she just showed up; she made it so easy. Jesus," he says.

"You can stop now," I say. "You're making it worse."

"Charlotte, thank God," he says, and he crawls across the space between us. "Thank God, you're not beautiful. Scotty had to go and hire a beautiful secretary. Christ, what was he even thinking? Claims he tried to keep me from meeting her, but of course I met her. It's a good thing you're not, you know, that you don't look like Eliza, because if you did, man oh man. It's like toys, when we were kids, you know? He wanted mine. I always want his."

I don't say anything. What is there to say to that? I get him to drink some more tea, then a glass of water, and then his clothes are dry, so I have the doorman call him a cab, and he goes.

When Gretchen texts to let me know they are on their way home, I remember the liquor glass. I look around, but I can't figure out where it came from, so I drop it into the bottom of my purse, and when I leave to go to my apartment, it comes with me, erasing the last of the evidence that he was ever there, that we ever talked, that he ever said those words. If I forget about it, it will be as if it never happened.

On the way into my building, I toss the phantom glass into the dumpster.

April, six weeks after

"And what is it that *you* do?" asks the nondescript, tuxedo-clad older gentleman as I sip my tequila on ice, pretending it's water, counting the minutes until I can blow this popsicle stand. It's 9:30, and I'm at Everett's postshow reception, but Everett is nowhere to be found.

"I'm a marine biologist," I tell the well-mannered stranger. "I'm usually, you know, down below. Sea level, I mean. Underwater. In a submarine. But I had to come up for this. Everett and I go way back. I couldn't miss it."

He nods at me, the picture of polite interest. I can't tell whether he believes me or simply can't come up with a follow-up question for an answer like that. He begs off soon enough, and I chastise myself for wearing the dress with the sparkly beads instead of something more suited for blending in with walls.

"More water?" says Colleen from behind me, handing me another glass of tequila over my shoulder. "Or have you seen enough lately, you know, being a marine biologist and all? We could switch you to something brown, if you'd rather."

"Just don't give me another crab puff," I say, pouring my current drink into my new one and handing the empty glass to Colleen's husband, Roger. "Poor things. One minute, they're scuttling around on the ocean floor, minding their own business, the next, boom. Hors d'oeuvres."

"Must be a lonely life down there, with only the crabs for company," says Roger, as our friend Snyder joins us, carrying three glasses of wine. "Is it a giant relief to be up here among the humans, even if only for a day?"

"Oh, the giantest," I say. "Who is all that wine for?"

"I hate spending every minute of my time at these things in line for the bar," Snyder says, sitting down on the floor and setting the glasses down next to him. He's wearing sneakers with his tux, and I wonder if that's an L.A. thing or if he really thinks he has to have a gimmick. "Wait, Charlotte, I thought you were a foreign correspondent tonight. Isn't that what you told that couple?"

"I was a foreign correspondent," I say. "And then I got bored. Now I'm a marine biologist. Where the hell is Everett? I need to say good-bye."

"Probably out smoking," says Colleen. "You're not leaving. Just settle down."

Across the room, there's a burst of laughter. I know without looking that it's Jess. She is standing with a large group of admirers, in front of a small stagelike platform at the front of the room that holds a microphone, and there's a baby grand piano to the left of her. I haven't spoken to her, but I have known where she is at all times, and I wonder if she knows the same about me. On the other side of the platform is an even larger group, gathered around two little kids in tiny formal wear. A man, most likely their father, stands slightly apart, holding up his phone, videotaping. Who in their right mind would bring little kids to an event like this?

I nod toward the platform and nudge Colleen. "I know. How about you get up there and entertain the crowd until the man of the hour gets back? You could sing 'Begin the Beguine.'"

"Ha-ha," says Colleen, crouching to try to find a way to sit down next to Snyder on the floor without giving the bystanders a show. She is unsuccessful, and she stands back up. "I hate being a girl. Dresses are terrible."

"I disagree. Dresses are awesome," says Roger. "Go ahead, baby. Sit down. No one's watching."

Colleen makes a face at him. "Baby. You would think he'd mind if his wife flashed the entire musical elite of New York City, but apparently he doesn't give a shit."

"I agree with Charlotte, Col," says Snyder. "Why don't you just manic-pixie your way up onto that stage and get a little intimate with the microphone?"

"Come on," I say. "Snyder will accompany you. You can lie down on the piano."

"Roger paid you to say that," says Colleen, laughing.

"She's onto us." Roger puts one arm around Colleen's waist and pulls me to his side with the other. How did he end up a conductor and not a quarterback? "But you're going to have to be the one to settle up, babe, because I didn't bring my wallet."

"Hey, you think Jess will ever deign to come and say hello to her former students?" says Snyder. He's super mood-driven.

"She will." Roger releases me and takes Colleen's empty glass, setting it on a nearby windowsill with his own finished drink. "But I'll give a hundred bucks to whoever's name she remembers."

"You're going to give all our money away." Colleen finally finds a way to sit down with her knees bent out to one side. Lord knows how she'll get up. "Of course she'll remember Charlotte. Charlotte was her favorite."

"That's right," says Roger. "We have Jess's prodigy in our midst."

"It'll be a shame if she doesn't remember *your* name," I say to Roger. "You're the one who slept with her."

"You slept with her?" Snyder slaps the side of Roger's calf a few times, with admiration or indignation; it's hard to tell which. "Damn. I tried really hard to sleep with her."

"I didn't *sleep* with her," says Roger. He stands over Colleen, with his feet on either side of her feet, nudging her ankles with his. "There may have been some touching, after a particularly intense work session, but there was never any sex."

"Get your facts straight. It was just a little groping," says Colleen.

"Oh man," grumbles Snyder. "On the piano? Piano groping is my favorite, you know."

"Yeah, we know." I step on the toe of Snyder's sneaker. I'm preoccupied with it because it's coming untied. "Maybe you should have tried wearing some dress shoes. Show a lady she's worth your best. Didn't Jess give you a reference for that commercial you did? She must know your name. I'd say there's still hope. Maybe take your shot tonight."

"I'm glad to see our conversational skills haven't evolved at all in the last few years," says Colleen. "Remember how much time we used to spend obsessing about Jess and the rest of our teachers? And now we're in Boston, and the cathedral almost couldn't spare me for these two days, and Roger is directing the majority of this season at the opera, and Snyder has seen Peter Jackson's hobbit basement, and Everett is at Carnegie Hall—"

And Charlotte is a replacement housewife.

"And Charlotte is here in New York, and still, all we can do is talk about Jess."

"No one is as cool as Jess, baby," says Roger. I finish my drink. I should not have another. I can feel the two I've had, rappelling up and down my thighs, urging me toward the floor.

"I'm going outside to find Everett." I leave them to speculate on Jess's coolness.

On my way through the lobby, I spot a private handicapped bathroom and step inside. I stare at myself in the mirror. I swear I used to know how to get ready for these things; how to get it up socially, how to approach a night with energy and enthusiasm, how to make myself look as good as I can look. I spent years figuring out how to do all of that, knowing that if I wanted a career in music, there was a certain level of socializing that I would have to get used to. But the last six weeks—and the two years before that—have undone all my work. The only things I'm currently used to are negotiating breakfasts and temper tantrums and reciting Captain America's vital statistics.

I make my way back out into the lobby and toward the side door that Everett pointed out earlier. The door opens directly onto the loading dock. I'm exhausted, and I've had too much to drink. Should I attribute the exhaustion to this throng of artistic temperaments, where priorities are all over the map and status is immediately assessed? Is my unsteadiness heightened by the adrenaline coursing through me from being on high alert for unwanted small talk and glimpses of Jess? Or could it simply be that having a night out with adults, with whom it seems I can no longer converse without rising to epic levels of snark, is wiping me out?

I find Everett leaning against a dumpster full of construction materials and lighting a new cigarette with the end of his old one.

"That conductor was bullshit," he says, as soon as he sees me coming.

"That conductor is world-renowned." I lean into his side and wrap both of my arms around his waist.

"His timing was erratic. It was like he picked the tempo based on his pulse or something."

"Maybe you ought to suggest he see a doctor, then."

"Your sarcasm is not becoming," he says, looking like he wants to smile but can't quite get there.

"I know," I say. "But neither is your self-deprecation. The audience loved your piece. It's some of your best work, my friend. You should come back in and celebrate. If you're bored with the rest of the room, you can always hang out in the corner with your old college pals. We've formed a little subgroup of introverts and misfits."

Everett hands me his cigarette. He lights another one for himself, inhales, and exhales with a sigh that could knock me over in my current state. "Colleen and Roger are gregarious misfits. They ought to be able to hold the conversation, should anyone try to infiltrate your subgroup."

We smoke for a while. There is an abandoned, half-loaded truck full of technical equipment right across from the dumpster that we're leaning on, and I wonder when the crew will come back out for it. I consider sitting down in the back of it to relieve the pressure in my feet but decide there's too much of a risk that I'll end up with streaks of dirt across my backside. Tomorrow when I wake up I'm really going to regret this night, but for now, it feels good to let my head spin. I'm shivering, and Everett wraps his scarf around my shoulders. It's very soft.

"Nice," I say. "Armani?"

"Ralph Lauren," he says.

"Chinese women with tiny hands?"

"Charlotte, you wound me."

"Come back inside with me," I say, and I let him hold my hand as we go, even though I know it's for all the wrong reasons.

When we step back inside the door, I come up short, flinching away from Everett. The two little kids I saw in the reception hall are here in the lobby, standing next to their parents. Now I am close enough to recognize them, and the collision of my two worlds cannot be successfully avoided. Ainsley, the little girl that Matty's been haranguing at recess, her twin brother, Aaron, their father, who hasn't been significant enough in the land of drop-offs and stroller parking for me to commit his name to memory, and Jillian, the Class Mommy.

There is no opportunity to hide. I pull on my hemline to make sure it's at a decent length and walk in their direction, forgetting about Everett for a moment, hoping it will be so out of context that they won't even notice. But alas, being perfect, Jillian's manners and perception are right on point. The fact that she brought her twin five-year-olds to Carnegie Hall, sporting little prom outfits and holding organic juice boxes, is incredible to me. And also, right in line with what I know of her personality.

"Charlotte?"

"Hey," I say. "Hi, guys. How are you?"

"How funny to see you here! You two remember Matt's babysitter, right? Honey?"

"Is that man getting the taxi?" says Aaron, pulling on Jillian's hand. "Are we going to miss it?"

"We're number fifteen in line," says their dad, extending his hand to me. I have to cross a few steps to reach him, as he's been rendered momentarily immobile by Ainsley, who is standing on his feet. "We've got a few minutes to wait, and it's very cold outside. Nice to see you, Charlotte. We saw you at the funeral, but you seemed very busy. I'm sure that life has been unbelievable for you in the last few weeks."

"We're so sorry about Gretchen," says Jillian, wrapping both of her hands around my forearm. "It's the worst thing I can imagine. Please let us know if there's anything we can do for you or the boys." Aaron and Ainsley are both staring at the floor, Ainsley at her miniature bedazzled shoes on top of her dad's impeccable Italian leather, and Aaron at a pull in the rug he's been nudging with his foot. I almost laugh, recognizing the postures as similar to those George and Matt adopt when they're listening very intently but trying to pretend they're not.

I nod at Jillian and her husband, not sure what I should say.

"Well. Thank you." I'm so preoccupied with their sympathetic gazes that I find myself startled to see Everett in my peripheral vision, standing next to me as if he'd like to be introduced. I try to remember Jillian's husband's name, but nothing comes. "This is my friend Everett. We went to graduate school, ah, together."

"Yes, of course!" says Jillian, taking her hands off me in order to clasp Everett's hand in both of hers. She is a physical communicator. "The composer. The piece was wonderful. We all loved it! I'm Jillian."

"Nice to meet you," says Everett, raising his eyebrows at me, in serious need of some semblance of context, which I decide not to help him with. "And thank you."

"Is Matt here?" Ainsley asks me.

"No," I tell her, unsure if she'll be disappointed or reassured.

"Well, you have very talented friends, Charlotte," says Jillian. "I didn't know you went to school for music. My husband works in the music industry too."

"Casey Donohue," says the twins' father to my relief, shaking Everett's hand. "Makes sense that she's musical, though, right, honey? Remember Matt's birthday, at the museum? Charlotte led the kids in quite the performance."

"She did?" says Everett, unable to contain a wolflike leer, which would probably traumatize the kids, if they were paying attention. "Please tell me the ukulele was involved. She's a wizard on that thing."

"A ukulele wizard. That's not something you hear of every day," says Casey, and he and Everett laugh, and Everett's laugh sounds the way it has all night at this event, which is different from his normal laugh.

"We come to a lot of these," says Jillian to me, while the two men continue to talk. "We support the New Voices program. This one's a little shorter, so it was a nice opportunity to bring the kids. We were debating L-E-A-V-I-N-G at intermission, but this one really wanted to stay." Aaron has begun hanging off of his mother's hands with all his body weight, trying to see if he can make her teeter on her heels, but so far, she hasn't budged. It's very impressive. I suspect pilates. The only mental image I can call up for Aaron is his using a full-sized soccer ball to peg kids in the knees while yelling "DODGE BALL!" in his Optimus Prime voice, which is incongruous with the picture of him being enraptured with orchestral music. Maybe I haven't yet been privy to his artistic side?

I tune back into Everett and Casey's side conversation as Everett says, "Of course, yeah. I thought A&R guys were a dying breed. But I did get to meet your engineers. They came in to record the dress rehearsal. I don't know whose idea that was, maybe the director, but I certainly appreciate it. I didn't think to have someone record it. I was writing up to the very last minute, and I couldn't think about anything else. But do you think the label would even release something like that?"

"There's a market for it. We can talk about it, if you want to, or I can put you in touch with someone who'll be better equipped to give you the specifics. The label is Atlanta-based," says Casey. "But we're in New York and L.A. too. This is not really my field, but I oversee the departments that deal with it. I'll give you my card, and we can make sure you talk to someone and decide what you want to do. We usually start out with an EP, anyway, and it's probably the right length for that."

Everett puts his arm around me. It's possessive, like he owns everything, which I'm sure he thinks he does.

"Mom, can we *go*?" says Ainsley. She has a sweet, high voice that makes her sound angelic, even though she's talking in that way little kids do when they're not the center of attention and are having trouble handling it.

"Not yet, sweet pea. It's not our turn," says Jillian, and Ainsley groans theatrically.

"Did you guys stay up to watch the whole concert?" I ask.

Aaron and Ainsley nod, proud of themselves. "Wow. I'm very impressed. Whenever I try to play something classical for Matt, he covers his ears and sings 'Call Me Maybe' at the top of his lungs." Everyone laughs, and Everett hooks his thumb under the back of one of my shoulder straps, which I hope that no one else can see.

"Well, it might be more the idea of coming out with the grown-ups and having a late bedtime that they like," says Casey.

"Charlotte, maybe one day we'll hear you play," says Jillian. "Wouldn't that be fun, guys?"

"It's more fun if you do regular songs," says Ainsley.

"Oh, yeah?" I say. "Give me some ideas. I'll write them down."

"Uhhhh, I don't *know*," says Ainsley.

"Okay. Well, just think about it, and tell Matt in school, and he'll tell me. Okay?"

"Okay."

I have the sudden, horrifying thought then that Scotty might hear about this night from a third party. That I will be caught, cheating on them. Cheating? Is that what I'm doing? I shrug Everett's arm off me.

"So, you play? Or, what's your field?" asks Jillian, polite as the day is long.

"Not really," I say, picking up one uncomfortably shoed foot and wrapping it around my other ankle, like a flamingo. "Well, the ukulele. Some piano. My master's was in composition."

The doorman comes in then to let Casey know he has a cab. Everett and I wave good-bye, and I march him back toward the reception room before he has the opportunity to comment.

The minute we're through the door, I regret it. They've gotten back on their feet, my old friends, and there's only one thing that could have gotten them there.

I have played this out so many times in my mind, but I don't react to this first clear sighting of Jess in the strong, courageously aloof way that I always imagined I should. What I feel is something close to longing. All I want, the minute that I see her face, is for her to bless me with her attention, to think of something witty to say so that she'll laugh, to be singled out as worthy of a meaningful conversation.

She is holding court without even trying to, as if her gravitational field is stronger than those around her. Such is Jess's magnetism, and it has not diminished over the years. The whole group spots us the minute we walk in the door, and they clap and exclaim and make a scene over Everett, and Jess throws her arms around him, murmuring into his neck about how wonderful, how insightful he is. Before the waves of nostalgia have released me from their grip, she has her arms around me. "I looked everywhere for you earlier," she says. "I am so glad to see you! It's been a minute, hasn't it."

I was never able to find the words to explain what had happened with Jess to any of my friends, not even Everett. It was possible that I had made too much of the situation. Sometimes I told myself that I couldn't say anything to anyone besides Jane and Claudia because I didn't want to put those who knew her in a position where they had to choose, Jess or me. But standing a few years outside of it, I can admit to myself that it probably had more to do with putting myself in a position where I might not be chosen.

I pull back from her, and she is holding on to the back of my dress strap—what is it with these dress straps; are they preternaturally shiny or something?—and I remember what Everett said. Her feelings are so huge. His assessment was exactly right, as usual.

"Hey," I say, but she doesn't give me time to not say anything else, to freeze her out, like I planned to before I saw her. She is pulling me in another direction, away from the safety of my protective cluster, and calling over her shoulder to them.

"We'll be right back!" she says, linking her arm through mine. "I promised someone I'd introduce him to Charlotte."

"Don't you want to introduce him to Everett?" I ask.

"I'm sure he's met Everett. Everett is the man of the hour," she says.

I let her drag me along, trying not to view it as symbolic, and from behind me, I hear a burst of laughter from my friends, and I wonder which one of them made the Jess-and-Charlotte-in-a-tree joke. I had indulged them in school, letting them make all the fun they wanted of how obviously Jess favored me, laughing right along with them. In my most honest heart of hearts, I was glad that everyone could see it. Jess was a genius, internationally recognized as brilliant, and she chose me. I was her wunderkind.

Now I'm standing with her in front of the man I just finished telling the tale of my ocean adventures to, listening to her rave about the downtown series he just produced, which featured students in their final year at Juilliard. I watch with a kind of awed detachment as they laugh together, and I find him giving me an "oh, you" kind of look, as if he's in on the sophisticated witticism of our earlier conversation, and I know the way he feels about me forthwith is all because of Jess's prestige. I accept his business card on her credit, and she tells him she'll connect us via e-mail. The words fellowship and observership and internship are thrown around, but I can't hang on to any of them in my churning consciousness.

Jess and I make our way back to the old familiar group, and it's not hard for me to say very little for the rest of our time there, to find excuses to move away from the group and toward the bar, or the bathroom, or the lobby to check my phone, or anywhere else outside the orbit of my past life. It's not hard, and so I do those things until I can finally escape, claiming too much tequila and an early morning, both of which are true. Before anyone can suggest we move the party somewhere else, or Everett can try to get in a cab with me, or Jess can comment on anything besides her recent travels or the weather, I gather my coat and my things and fold myself into the taxi line.

The taxi driver pulls up in front of my apartment twenty minutes later, and I step onto the sidewalk. I wait until he's pulled away down the block, and then I lean over the curb and throw up in the street.

The next morning I wake up, feeling properly spanked by the tequila, with a new e-mail winking at me from my in-box.

The e-mail is straightforward, and expected; it's from Jess, and she would really like to see me when we have time and space to talk, and could I come and visit her in her Brooklyn loft sometime next week. I can hear the last sentence in her voice, as if she's standing right next to me in my apartment, speaking out loud: "I can't wait to hear what you've been working on."

June, the year before

Matthew turned five amid much pomp and circumstance. There had been a rash of spring birthdays among his classmates, and it seemed like every party had tried its damnedest to outdo the last. As a result, Gretchen had spent the previous month grumbling about zoo animals and karate workshops, feeling misunderstood by Scotty, who went back and forth between disdainful mockery and straight laughter. I find the Manhattan kid-party culture baffling. I suggested giving the kids a refrigerator box and some chalk, and then letting them eat frosting out of a can, but I don't think anyone took me seriously.

Gretchen finally decided on the Museum of Natural History, and if I thought that I'd gotten used to the whole money thing, made my peace with it, and even come to a point where I barely noticed it, the fact that they've shut down the Hall of Ocean Life (known to lay folk as the Whale Room) to everyone except Matt's guests gives me a whack on the head to remind me.

"Charlotte, you're our guest," Gretchen keeps saying as she whizzes by me, back and forth, this time to greet Jillian and her husband, who might as well be David and Victoria Beckham.

Aaron and Ainsley are dressed in coordinated, nautically themed outfits.

"I'm having fun," I call back to her, as I pry a metal skewer, formerly bearing teriyaki chicken, out of George's hand. He didn't eat the chicken, of course—he flung it off the skewer in an impressive trajectory, and now it's hanging out in some dark corner, where it will likely attract vermin or be consumed by another toddler.

"Awfully dark in here," says a voice from behind me, as I am approaching the buffet. I find a utensil and start forking the chicken off the skewers and into the chafing dish. Who brings metal skewers to a five-year-old's birthday party?

"Hey, she's hot. What's her deal?" Patrick points to Jillian.

"That's her husband—the guy who looks like Colin Farrell—and those are her twins, the J. Crew baby models," I say. "You literally, *literally*, asked me the same question at Matt's party last year."

"I know," he says. "I wanted you to turn around."

"Didn't you bring a date to keep you occupied? She might appreciate the dark," I check underneath all the serving dishes to make sure no open flames are peeking out.

"Maybe," he says. "Were you asking about me?"

"If I angled my body a little to the left, I'm sure I could stab you in the arm with one of these skewers and make it look like an accident," I say.

"Aha. Open hostility. I guess I really did hurt your feelings last time we saw each other."

"There is nothing you could do that would hurt my feelings, Patrick," I say, and I'm pretty sure I mean it. "But showing up drunk at your brother's house, where young children are asleep in the other room, and refusing to leave, even though your brother is out and the babysitter is there, that's kind of high on my list of creepy things to do."

"You didn't tell him, though."

"You asked me not to!"

"If you thought it was that creepy, you probably should have told them."

"I didn't see the point." I move the silverware back a few inches from the edge of the table. "They would have felt bad about it, even though it wasn't any fault of theirs, and then things would have been uncomfortable. They don't need that on them."

"So you decided to keep it for yourself?"

I frown at him with my full attention. "That's a weird way to put it, dude."

"I was in a bad place," he says.

"Because you cheated on your girlfriend."

"Once! Well, three times if you're counting the instances. But it was only one night." Patrick stacks up a bunch of used clear plastic cups and tosses them into the trash bin at the end of the table.

"With your brother's secretary."

"Charlotte, you do have a head for details."

"Gross," I say.

"What?"

"Nothing. Belatedly from the three-times thing," I say. I'm tempted to pile the mini corn muffins into a pyramid.

"If you quit, Scotty will kill me."

"I would never quit over you," I say, with as much scorn as I can muster. "I really didn't give it a second thought." I did give it a second thought, actually, but only a second. I refused to give it a third or fourth or anything beyond. "You can put it out of your head. We never had that conversation." I feel two little hands encircling my knee, and I reach down to ruffle George's hair. "Hi, buddy."

"Tahr-lette, you bring your guitar?"

"I brought my ukulele," I say.

George leans against my leg. He looks like he's reached his wilding limit for the day and would like to go home. We've got at least another hour to go. "You bring that widdle guitar?"

"Yes, the little one. It's called a ukulele."

"Me hold that widdle guitar?" Things I bring from my house are like catnip to him. It doesn't matter what it is—a library card, a flashlight, a ponytail holder—if it comes from my house, it's special.

"I know you know how to be gentle," I say to George. "But if I let *you* hold it, then everyone will want a turn, and it might get broken."

"You sing a song with that?"

"Sure," I say. "I guess so. Which song?"

"That hammer song?"

I lead George over next to the sea otter diorama to sit down, and I notice that Patrick has migrated with us. "If you're joining us, you'll have to lend your voice. George will be Peter. I'll be Paul. You can be Mary." I start to strum up the intro, keeping it on the quiet side, and I'm surprised and kind of laughing through the whole song, because Patrick knows all the words and can hold his part against my harmony, even in the high falsetto he has adopted in his interpretation of Mary.

"Mary's voice is much lower than that," I say to Patrick. "You ought to get up to scratch on your fight-the-man protest songs."

"Make me a playlist," he says. I start to segue into "We Shall Overcome" on my ukulele, and he smacks the floor between us. "I could harmonize this one six different ways. I heard it coming out of Zuccotti Park every time I opened my office window last year." By the time I get into the second verse, Matt's little buddy Sahina has approached and is kneeling very close, with her hands on my knee, joining in at the top of her lungs when I get to the closing phrase. After I finish with all the words I know of that one (I might have made up a few of them), I go into "This Little Light of Mine," and by that time Matt has run up, with Ainsley, Little L, three boys whose names I can't remember, and a bunch of toddlers in tow.

"I know all the words because we sing this one in my Sunday school," says Little L, in a not-cute-but-prissy way. I feel sorry for her. Her life is going to be hard, in the emotional sense.

We finish the song, and I'd like to be done because several of the adults have started to hover on the perimeter of our little cluster, but the birthday boy has a request.

"That one about the flower," Matt says, referring to a song that I like to butcher the lyrics to, Weird Al–style, every time it comes on our Pandora station.

"The geranium?" I say. The majority of the party is looking on now, but I don't want to refuse a birthday request.

"Yeah! I teached that one on the playground," he says.

"You *taught* it," I correct him automatically. "Does that mean that you guys all know the words?"

"Yeah!" say several little voices, the first and most emphatic being Little L.

"Well, okay then. Here we go," I say. Patrick sits up straighter, like he's ready for more. Gretchen is standing to one side, poking Scotty in the ribs while he holds up his phone to record this for what I'm sure will be many instances of future Charlotte humiliation at McLean family gatherings. Electronic pop is tricky on a ukulele, but I manage, and when we get to the chorus, all the kids join in. We finish up to laughter and applause, and Matt is grinning as he runs away with his friends, still singing at the top of his lungs, which I'm sure must be thrilling to the museum-party leaders.

"You're their babysitter, right? Or did they hire you for the party?"

I look up, and it's Jillian's husband standing in front of me with Aaron, Ainsley's twin brother. I get to my feet and hand the ukulele to George, who gives me a very smug I-knew-I-could-bend-you-to-my-will look.

"No. Yes, I'm the babysitter, I mean," I say. "Matt's brother was getting antsy, so we decided to improvise a little. I'm Charlotte."

"Casey," he says, shaking my hand. "Interesting material. I'll bet you have to have a lot of that stuff in your arsenal, huh?"

"It's just messing around. The boys and I do it together." I want to dismiss this topic of conversation before it can go anywhere near my musical background.

"Well, with two little boys running you around all the time, I'm sure you need to sit down and catch a break, sing a song every once in a while," he says. "I get my cardio in and then some, and we only have one boy. Luckily, Ainsley would rather sit me down in front of Barbie's dream house, so Dad gets a break. But I would love it if Aaron took up a hobby that required him to stand still for a few minutes. I tried to get him started on *World of Warcraft*, but Jill wouldn't hear of it."

"What's *World of Warcraft*?" Aaron asks at the top of his lungs.

"Shh, buddy. Never mention it around Mommy, and maybe I'll let you in on the secret." Aaron pulls on his father's hand, clearly inspired by all this talk of running. "Nice to meet you guys," he says, letting his son drag him off in the direction of the dessert table.

"Nice to meet you too." George is wielding my instrument as if it were a croquet mallet. There are traces of bile in the back of my throat, as if I've been punched in the stomach instead of barely engaged in a conversation about how pleasant it is that I make music for the kids.

I snap out of it when I see Gretchen giving me the thumbs-up from across the room and pointing to Scotty's phone, where my antics have been immortalized.

"I didn't know you had an entire arsenal," Patrick says. He and George are still sitting on the floor. George pulls the ukulele closer to him.

"Do you want to go ahead and get my autograph now, before I decide to go international?" I say, sitting down next to him.

George picks at the ukulele strings, at his most careful since he sees that he has my full attention back and knows the instrument will disappear with one wrong move.

"It's nice that you play with them," says Patrick after a while, as we sit there on the floor with our backs to the otters. Georgie puts down the instrument and crawls into my lap, and I let him dissolve there, my little balm of Gilead. "Scotty would play with me sometimes, but Max was too old, and my parents never did. Do you feel sorry for me?"

"Do you feel sorry for yourself?" I say.

"Never," he says, and I'm sure he means it. "I don't blame them. Playing with kids is B-O-R-I-N-G."

"Sometimes," I say. "Even if you really, really like the kid." I tighten my arms around George.

"You know, today's my birthday," says Patrick, and I'm surprised. It affects me, this declaration that today is his birthday, even though I'm not sure why. But I have an instinct that he hasn't told many other people, and this, of all the things he's ever said, makes me think, *Bless your heart*, as my grandmother would say. "My birthday is the second, four days before Matt's. It's been fun, sharing my birthday with a little kid. It makes the family celebrations more interesting."

"I know," I say. "Holidays are better with kids around. They get so excited. Fourth of July, St. Patrick's Day . . ."

"Halloween," he says.

"Martin Luther King, Jr. Day," I say.

"Celebrated with civil disobedience by children everywhere," he says.

"Well," I say and kiss him on the cheek, then wonder what would possess me to kiss him on the cheek. "Happy Birthday, Patrick."

George is mostly in my lap, but his feet are stretched out into Patrick's lap, and Patrick's shoulder is warm against my shoulder.

We sit there together on the floor for a while longer, side by side, listening to the unique ambient noise of the Whale Room combine with the dull roar of little voices.

April, seven weeks after

I'm not sure how I expected things to change after our conversation in the Indian cathedral, but I did, and they don't. Scotty still comes home well after the kids are in bed. He's still a zombie in the morning. The kids are still having their own personal difficulties, daily. The only difference is that now I live there, in a sea of hearts that have not even begun to find their way back to unbroken.

Scotty and I had our conversation last Wednesday. I moved a few things in over the weekend, and now it's a week after the decision was made—the decision that I thought would change everything—and I am wondering when I'm going to start to feel less exhausted, like I'm fighting fewer battles.

The apartment is large and incredibly old New York. The moldings and the baseboards and the archways in the living room have history visibly embedded in them, even though Gretchen's taste was modern and a little on the delicate side. I've always been amazed at the number of glass tables and painted porcelain bowls that have managed to survive the occupancy of two little boys.

To say that the apartment has wings makes it seem larger than it is, but by Manhattan standards, it's huge. There is a formal area in the middle, which reminds me of a Victorian parlor, with archways on two sides, and it is surrounded by a living room and a large kitchen that wrap around it and into each other. It's a bizarre setup that makes me think the architect was envisioning a spiral, with all the other rooms as offshoots. To the left and right of the central area are two long hallways with additional rooms, and that is where I got the idea of "wings"; off on the left, there is a smaller kitchen, family room, and guest bedroom, bathroom, and small office suite on one side (Gretchen and I had always joked that it was the maid's quarters, which now I'm not so quick to laugh at, since I'll be living in it), and a master suite with a bedroom and bathroom, closets, and a larger office, which Gretchen had ironically referred to as her "sewing room." Off to the right are four bedrooms, and one and a half bathrooms. The kids are in the right wing, but Scotty suggested I take the maid's quarters in the left so I'd have my own bathroom. I never thought I would live on Park Avenue, let alone in an apartment like this.

Georgie is asleep in the stroller as we walk to get Matt. When I transferred him from his bed, I hadn't had the heart to pry Chickie out of his grip, even though we have always made it a policy not to take the animals out of the boys' rooms. I make a mental note to do a Chickie check at several points along our journey. I still have Pup's blood on my hands, after all, and I don't want a repeat of that situation. I don't know if either of our little hearts could take it.

I leave Georgie sleeping in the lobby, under the watchful eyes of one of the assistant teachers, and walk into the kindergarten classroom to retrieve Matt. He sees me, but he sits there at his table anyway. What used to be transitional wrath has turned into flat-out refusal, and I'm not surprised that he doesn't have the desire to summon the energy to stand up and get his stuff together. We're all so tired, every one of us.

"Matt," I say. "It's getting kind of empty in here. George is sleeping, so you get to decide what we're doing today if you hurry up and get your stuff on." He scoots his chair back but doesn't get up. I don't want to fight with him, but deal making is getting us into a dangerous pattern, so I wait.

A boy named Yuri pokes Matt as he passes by on his way to join his nanny and several other nanny–little boy pairs. "Matt, are you going to the playground?" he asks, then adds, "We're not going," in a voice that makes me feel sure that they *are* going. I wonder why the kid is deliberately being tricky.

"I don't know," says Matt, glaring at him, and then stands up to get his stuff.

When we make it back to the lobby, George is awake and crying. The assistant teacher is squatting down next to him, trying to comfort him, and when he spots me and Matt coming out of the classroom, he cries even harder and presses against the stroller restraints. The assistant teacher is trying desperately to unhook them, but the extra pressure George is exerting is making it impossible.

"Maaaaaatttt," he is wailing. "Matty, Matty, Matt, Maaaaaaatttt."

I bend down to relieve the poor teacher. If George doesn't calm down, he'll never get out of this bear trap of a vehicle. "Lovebug," I say. "Matt's right here. See him?" Matt might as well be filing his nails, for all the interest he is displaying.

"Want to get oooooouuuuut," George wails.

"Ok, little bear, I'm gonna get you out. But I need you to sit still for one minute while I undo the straps. Okay?"

He is too upset though. There is no hearing me in his state. We have attracted a bit of that attention where you know people are watching but politely turning their eyes away, and I'm sure no one feels the non-eyes more intensely than George.

I finally get one of the straps undone, and he wiggles his way out the side and runs to where Matt is standing. Matt stands there, unmoved, as George throws his arms around him. I need to get them both out the door before this melts down any further.

"Come on, guys, let's take the stairs," I say. I walk out the door. I carry the stroller down to the bottom, and once we're all there, George is much quieter but still hanging on to Matt, who might as well be made of stone.

"What do you guys feel like doing today?" I ask once we're safely on the sidewalk.

"I want to go home," says Matt.

"We go to that tore with candles?" George suggests. "And we can sah-mell the candles? And remember, it have the cards? They play music—the cards," he adds, as if I need convincing.

"Why don't we stop and get a snack on the way to that store?" I say.

"I don't want to go to that store," says Matt.

"Well, why don't we get a snack and then decide?" I say. "That coffee shop up the block has good snacks."

"We can get a treat?" asks Matt. He's suspicious of an afternoon treat.

"Maybe," I say. "Let's see what they have."

He doesn't exactly agree, but we start to head in that direction. George has opted to walk instead of ride. He can probably keep better tabs on Matt's and my whereabouts if he's independently mobile.

"Mommy let us get that juice," says George. "That pink juice. Remember, and we got the juice, we got pink and Mommy got green? Remember, Matt?"

"I don't remember that," says Matt.

"We ask Mommy if we can have that pink juice, Tahr-lette?"

"How about we ask the person at the counter if they have the pink juice," I say.

"We call Mommy on the phone and ask her?"

"I'm sorry, honey," I say, hating myself as much as Georgie probably hates this repeated message. "I can't call Mommy on the phone. I bet we can find it, though, if we ask someone at the coffee shop."

"Me call Mommy?" George asks. "And I can use your phone?"

I steel myself to give the same unacceptable answer, but Matt beats me to the punch. "Mommy is dead. She doesn't live on earth, so you can't call her on the phone, Georgie."

"Matty," I say, but what am I going to scold him for? His harsh tone?

"Where Mommy lives now?" Georgie asks, trying not to cry.

"She lives with God. She likes God's house better, so that's where she lives now," says Matt, as if he's already explained this concept a million times to a crowd full of imbeciles.

"Where did you hear that?" I ask.

"Gramma."

I am at a loss. I didn't hear this conversation firsthand, and while I'm certain that's not how Mae explained it, I have no idea what she *did* say. What can I possibly tell them? If there's one thing that I don't get to decide here, it's what these two kids think about God.

"We call her and ask her to come back?" says George, and I am completely, totally, one-hundred percent inadequate as a guardian right at this moment.

"Here we are," I say. "Those brownies look great. Anybody want one?"

February, four days after

In the days leading up to Gretchen's funeral, there is a frustrating lack of information coming my way as I sit alone in my apartment and fret. It's hard to figure out what to do with myself. I mostly wake up late, watch TV, order takeout, and find as many excuses as I can not to leave my apartment. If I'd had the wherewithal to put Patrick's number in my phone, I'd stoop to texting him, but as it stands, the only numbers I have saved are Eliza's and Gretchen's.

What would happen if I called Gretchen's phone or sent a text? Was anyone thinking about what to do with her phone? Was anyone going to be able to check her voice mail, go through her contacts and notify them, get the pictures off of it?

I call my family members. My mom tells me I should come home for a few days, or that she could come and stay with me, but I decline both. The last thing I need is to feel like I have to entertain someone, even though I know her intention is to take care of me, and besides, I would have to work up the energy to clean my apartment if she were going to see it. My dad calls, my grandmother calls, Jane calls, and Claudia calls, and I know that my mom is behind the relentless display of support. I tell them to leave me alone. They all ignore me and call anyway, and I'm grateful.

The weekend passes, and on Monday I get a call from Mae. "We're holding services on Wednesday," she tells me. "There will be a viewing in the morning with a mass to follow and then a sunset graveside memorial. I'll understand if you're busy, Charlotte, but we thought it might be good for the boys to have someone be consistently responsible for them, in case . . ." I look around my apartment. There is a pile of takeout containers in the sink, and the entire contents of my pajama drawer are strewn around the floor, in varying states of cleanliness. I wonder what it looks like in their apartment. "In case Scotty is having a hard time. There will be a lot of family around. There has been a lot of family here, but the boys have been asking for you."

"Of course I'll be there," I say. "I'm glad you called. How are they? I mean, how have they been? Do they understand what's . . . what's happening?"

"They know that Mom is gone, and people are sad. I think Matthew has a handle on what it means, but it may take George a little longer to adjust. He thinks that she'll be back as soon as the doctor fixes her." My heart is breaking, breaking.

"I'll meet you at the apartment on Wednesday." I am standing up in the middle of the room, between the piano and the kitchen island, poised to move if she says the word. "What time should I be there?"

"Bless you, Charlotte," Mae says. "This will be a nice bit of good news to tell them, that they can play with you on Wednesday. Is eight o'clock too early?"

"No, that's fine," I say. "See you then."

Hanging up that phone call is like catapulting myself out of

Siberia. I straighten the couch cushions and get myself into the shower. I get dressed and use a blow dryer. I do the dishes, vacuum the floors, send my laundry out, and make my bed. After those things are accomplished, I text Eliza, asking her to meet me for a drink after work. She suggests a bar on Amsterdam, and I get the impression from the immediacy of her reply that she'd really like to see me too.

That, I get. Family and friends are great. Everyone wants to be there for you, to help you get through the difficult time. But there is no substitute for someone who sat in a room with you, waiting for the end of the world.

A few hours and drinks later, Eliza and I are old friends. "I resisted him for a long time," she says, swallowing the first bit of her third Manhattan. "Even now that I'm engaged, I go out of my way to avoid him. I'm kind of afraid of what I might do around him! He has something, some kind of, like, power, some kind of animal thing going on. Otherwise, there's no way so many women would sleep with him. He's such an asshole."

I nurse my second Jack and Diet and don't say anything.

"I couldn't even believe myself when I agreed to go home with him. I knew he had a girlfriend; she was like a model or something, with a model-y name. Sierra?"

Sienna. But it's not worth correcting Eliza.

"Something," she continues. "It felt so dangerous, like if my boss found out it could wreck everything—his brother, for goodness' sake—and he was kind of a dirty talker. I felt like—I don't know—like a different person. With a different life. Like the darker side of myself. Totally stupid, right? Anyway, I learned my lesson. Is that only your second drink? Catch up!"

"But Scotty's not like that, right? I mean, he and Patrick seem like polar opposites," I say, and I feel bad for prying, but not that bad. "Scotty doesn't really dick around. Right? It always seemed like he went out of his way to . . . I don't know. To be present, I guess."

"No way would he ever have cheated." Eliza fishes the cherry out of the bottom of her cocktail by the stem and eats it. "He was totally obsessed with Gretchen, texted her all day long, on his way to meetings, illegally from airplanes, everything. I rarely went on trips with him; he always took some junior associate from our department, for propriety's sake. But not in a gross way, like he thought he couldn't control himself. In a classy way. You know? He was, like, a class act." I wish she would stop talking about Scotty in the past tense. I know that she means the Scotty of before, the Scotty who existed before this altering event occurred. I want to hold on to my certainty that he'll eventually come back.

I order my third Jack and Diet and another Manhattan for Eliza. She starts to protest, but I wave her off. "Maybe your fiancé will meet us here and take you home. He'll understand. It's a rough week." She laughs like this is a bad, bad thing that she knows she shouldn't do, and maybe she's right. Maybe we shouldn't be here, exchanging stories this way. I don't know why I feel the need, except that there are all these nerves creeping up on me, the anxiety of knowing that Gretchen's whole world, her entire life, will be showing up in the next few days. I feel like I need to arm myself to be in the middle of that, have everything I can at my disposal in order to prove my value, should the need arise. I don't want to feel that way. I don't want to be part of that competition, but Mae's making comments about how much the boys "like playing with me" has gotten under my skin. I can't afford to think of myself as the insignificant thing she seems to want to reduce me to. That wasn't our relationship.

"Not that he hasn't had the opportunity," Eliza continues, without any prompting from me. Hooray for alcohol. "There are girls at work, girls who are younger than me, who are constantly throwing themselves at him. And they're not even—what's the word—detracted? No. Deterred? Yes, they're not even *deterred* by the pictures of Gretchen and Matt and baby George all over the office. If anything, they seem, like, spurred on by them. Like the fact that he's a family man would make him a better guy to have an affair with." She rolls her eyes and almost falls off her stool. I hope she remembered to text her fiancé.

"Younger than you?" I say. "What are you? Twenty-six?"

"Twenty-eight, like you," she says.

"I'm twenty-nine," I say, like it makes a huge difference.

"There's this one woman, this mom from Matt's class, who calls all the time. Like, who do you think you're fooling, lady? There's no reason she should call to 'keep him posted' on what's happening at school. I think she said she was a class mom or something. He never wants to talk to her. She had the nerve to call yesterday, like she thought he'd be at work? I didn't even bother to take the message."

"What's her name?" I ask. "I've probably met her."

"It's so disgusting," Eliza says, slurring a little. "Ooh! I'm pretty drunk. She has an odd name. I've never heard it before on a real person. Melody?"

"Ellerie," I say, and I feel a spike in my chest, a sharp surge of anger.

"Yes! Have you met her?"

"She's not my favorite person to have a playdate with," I say, and we both laugh, maybe a little too loudly. Not that you could hear it over the bar's stereo system, blasting the Velvet Underground.

"Water," Eliza says to the bartender, and I know we're getting close to the end of this. I don't want her to go.

"Eliza, I'm seriously so glad to see you. No one else really knows . . . you know?"

"I know!" she says. "I'm glad you called. It's so unreal. He's been calling in for his messages every day, and he sounds normal even though things must be totally crazy. It's so sad. I'm sad." He's been calling for his messages every day?

"I hear you," I say, and the bartender slides another Jack and Diet my way. "I didn't order that."

The bartender points to a guy at the other end of the bar who can't possibly be older than twenty-two.

"Did that guy order that for you? Ugh, Charlotte, I miss being single!" When I hear people in relationships say things like that, it's kind of a blow to their authenticity, but I try not to hold it against her. Her fiancé walks in the door then and spots her. "Baby, this is Charlotte."

"Nice to meet you, Baby," I say, and he tells me his name is Mike.

"I was just telling Charlotte how much I miss being single," Eliza says. "Babe, no one ever buys me drinks anymore."

"I'll buy you a drink," he says, "as long as you promise to go home with me."

"I don't think I need any more drinks," she says as she slides off her stool, unsteady. "I'll go home with you anyway." I say good-bye to them, and Eliza hugs me because—I don't know—she feels like we're the same, and I hug her because she's the only one that I can hug right now who *knows*.

Almost as soon as she vacates her stool, the guy from the other end of the bar comes in for a landing. "Hi," he says, "I'm Mike."

"That's such a coincidence," I say. "I just met another guy named Mike," and he laughs, bless him, because if he didn't, I probably wouldn't have ended up going home with him. But he does, so I do. Because I'm sad, and I don't have anyone to hug.

April, seven weeks after

"I'm gonna stomp on your head, and then I'll throw you out the window," says Matt.

"I poop on your mouth, and I kick you on the face," says George.

"Boys, that's really gross talk. Please stop," I say, but I'm in the kitchen trying to unearth the takeout menus, and they're halfway down the hall to their bedrooms. Proximity is a make-or-break with these kids.

"I'm gonna punch your tummy, and knock you on the floor, and sit on you until all the air comes out," says Matt.

"Matty," I call. "Please stop. When you get going, George gets—"

"I punch you on the face; then I hit you!" George says. He's getting riled up, and Matt is enjoying getting him that way. It makes me want to lock them both in their rooms.

After we ate brownies, no amount of coaxing, threatening, or bribing could get Matt to the candle store, so here we are at home, going stir-crazy. We'll all be lucky to survive the evening.

I find the menu for a home-style southern chicken restaurant and wonder how it got in there among the vegan bistros, organic pizzerias, and sushi restaurants. I consider it a sign from the universe and call in an order for fried chicken strips, mashed potatoes, biscuits, and macaroni salad. If I'm really, really lucky, we'll get through the meal with no complaints.

"I'll throw you on the ground and pee all over you!" I hear Matt say, and just as I'm about to decide to give up and let them exhaust their ugly talk on each other, all becomes quiet for a few minutes. I should know better than to think it's because they're done because the very next moment I hear Matt whine "owww!" loudly, and a few seconds later, George starts to scream. I step over the pile of coats and lunch boxes in the doorway to the kitchen and hurry down the hall to find George smacking the crap out of a cowering Matt.

"Ow! Stop! George is hitting me. He won't stop hitting me! OWWWW!"

I pick Georgie up. What am I going to do when he gets too big for me to physically remove him from the situation? He screams in my face as I take him to his room and shut him in there. I don't lock it, but he knows better than to try and come out. I can hear him sobbing as I go back into Matt's room. Matt seems to have recovered in an instant, as if nothing happened, and is dragging out a bucket of Legos into the center of the room. I'm speechless as I watch him dump them out, because the only word to describe his demeanor is satisfied. Like he's done what he came to do.

"Matt," I say, trying hard to control my temper. "What did you do? George is screaming like a banshee. What did you do before he started hitting you?"

"Nothing," he says. "I didn't do anything to him."

"Okay, then, what did you say?" He doesn't answer me. "Matt," I say. "Please tell me what you said to make him so upset." I expect him to start making some kind of excuse for whatever it is he did, and it's usually easy enough for me to extract the vital information as to what occurred from the content of the excuse. It's also how I can tell he feels guilty and knows that he has something to feel guilty about.

But he is just sitting there, building an L-shaped base for what looks like it might become an epic tower. He doesn't look at me but not because he's ashamed. It's more like he doesn't care. He might even be bored as he informs me, "George said he was going to kick me off a bridge and shoot lasers at me in the water. And I told him that I would push him in front of a car and he would die like Mommy."

I can't say anything to him right now. Whatever I say will be completely out of rage, and unproductive and potentially scarring. I'm totally out of my league, for the second time today.

So I walk away. And a greater person than I would walk into Georgie's room and say something to soothe him.

But I walk out of the room, down the hallway, into the living room, open my laptop, and reply to Jess's e-mail with my availability for next week.

A few hours later, Georgie is listless in his high chair, refusing to feed himself. I am cutting the fried chicken into tiny bites and trying to get him to eat it. Both of us are distracted by the nasty, full-throated yelling that is coming from Matt's room. He has refused to curb his horrible talk. It has gone on all day long, toward me, toward George, toward inanimate objects. He's in a black hole of crankiness. No five-year-old on the planet can think abstractly enough to know that he shouldn't be around people until he gets it together; as smart as he is, he's no exception. So I have set him up with his dinner at the little art table in his room and told him he can come out when he has nice things to say to the other people in this house. And he has screamed, called me every awful name he can think of, pounded on the door with open palms for a solid fifteen minutes, and thrown his dinner plate across the room. The door is not locked, but I'm contemplating it for everyone's safety if this goes on much longer.

"This chicken is delicious," I say to George. He takes a bite in resignation but doesn't chew it once it's in his mouth. I have a feeling that someone will be going to bed hungry, and another someone will be eating her feelings after the first someone is in bed.

"CHAAAARRRRLOTTE!" Matt screams. "I WANT TO COME OUT! LET ME OUT CHARLOTTE! LET ME OOOOUUUUUUT!"

"How about some mashed potatoes?" I say to George. He opens his mouth and uses the potatoes to wash down the bite of chicken. Maybe I should put in a feeding tube and save us all a lot of trouble.

"CHARLOTTE! CHARLOTTE! I WANT TO COME OUT RIGHT NOW!"

"Hey, George," I say. "What if we skip this whole farce of a dinner and have a milkshake instead?" He wags his head from side to side, looking exhausted, and while it's not exactly a nod, I take it for assent and click on the TV for him to watch while I scrounge up a drinkable dinner in the kitchen.

I mix up vanilla ice cream, whole milk, a scoop of protein powder, chocolate syrup, and peanut butter in the blender and am impressed with my own genius as I stick a straw in it and take it back to George.

"CHARLOTTE?" Pause. "CHARLOTTE?" Longer pause. "CHARLOTTE? CHARLOTTE? ARE YOU STILL HERE? I WANT TO COME OUT PLEASE! IS ANYONE HERE?"

I hand the cup to George and walk across the living room and down the hallway to Matt's room. I open the door, then close it again and count to ten. Then I open it back up.

Matt's dinner hit the wall when he threw it, and the mashed potatoes, gravy, and macaroni salad have slid down the wall into a hamper of stuffed animals. God knows where the little cut-up bites of chicken have landed—I see a few sticking out from under his dresser. His biscuit is still on the table, half-eaten. He has pulled many of his board games (mostly the ones with tiny pieces) out of his closet and dumped them out, and every object formerly in the toy chest has been thrown against the wall. They lie in a telltale pile. And when I get closer, I see where the paint has chipped, under assault from some of the things composed of harder materials, like wood or plastic. It's like a postapocalyptic toy-factory wasteland in here, as if someone came and kidnapped Santa, causing the elves to flee in a blind panic. I feel tears rush up behind my eyes, so I press on either side of my nose and will them back. Matt is staring at me, possibly looking at the room through my eyes, and his face, red from screaming, starts to regain its normal color. His breathing calms down, and he tries to wipe at the tears he can't seem to control.

"Matty," I say. "I think it would be a good idea for you to eat some dinner. George is watching TV out in the living room. Why don't I make you a plate? You can sit on a towel in front of the TV and eat something. Okay?"

He nods.

"But, bug. There can't be any screaming, or mean talk, or throwing or anything else you know you're not supposed to do. Okay?"

He agrees, and we go out to the living room, and that's where Scotty finds us when he comes home early for the first time in almost two months. George scrambles off the couch and runs to him as soon as he's in the door, but Matt looks at me like he needs some instruction. I don't blame him for being confused, so I say, "You want to go and kiss your Dad hello?" He shakes his head, and I'm glad I didn't say it loud enough for Scotty to hear.

"What's going on, guys?" Scotty comes into the living room with Georgie attached to his leg. Matt looks at me. Am I going to tell on him?

I look back at him. Of course I am. I have to. Why do I feel so guilty?

"We had a little delay with dinner tonight, so when Matt finishes up, we're going back to get ready for bed. It's almost time," I say, nudging Matt so he'll keep eating. "George, can you come finish your drink?"

George clings to Scotty's leg.

"Georgie, you haven't had enough to eat, honey," I say, and Scotty kind of shakes him loose, so George goes for the next best thing. He sits down next to Matt, practically in his lap, and I hand him the milkshake. When I'm satisfied that he's sipping it, I get up and go into the kitchen, where Scotty is sitting at the table, contemplating the macaroni salad.

"Do you want me to make you a plate? Or do you just want a fork?" I say.

"A plate would be good. Thank you."

I'll have an easier time telling him about Matt's meltdown if I'm busy doing something else while I talk, so I start organizing a fried chicken dinner on a plate for Scotty.

"So when we picked up Matt from school, he was in a really bad mood, and it got worse and worse through the afternoon. He was being really mean to George, saying things he knows he's not supposed to, hitting, kicking, pushing, the works. I finally had to tell him that he needed to stay in his room until he was ready to, you know, act right." I finish my monologue and set Scotty's plate down in front of him.

He laughs a little, and I realize that I have cut his chicken into kid-size bites, in an obvious fit of autopilot. "Oops," I say. "Sorry. I'm programmed, clearly."

"That's okay. Their mom does that too." We both stop laughing, because he so rarely mentions her and because this time he used the wrong tense. "I mean," he says, clearing his throat, "she did, from time to time."

I start to make a plate for myself. "You did the right thing," says Scotty. "Matt's not allowed to talk like that. Dr. O'Neill says we need to keep the routine the same and not make a lot of exceptions. He's allowed to be angry about his mother, but he's not allowed to take it out on other people, that kind of thing."

I need to step carefully through this minefield. "I'm not sure it was completely about that today. It seemed like it started with some boys at school."

"But you don't think he's upset about his mother?"

"No, I do think he's upset about that. Of course. I just mean that there are times that I think he is upset about other things, like kid things, and since people have been excusing him for so much, he thinks he can act however he wants. No matter what the actual problem is."

Scotty looks at me, and I can't tell if he thinks I've crossed the line. The trouble is, the line has relocated, and I have yet to discover where it is since our world came into its present state. "Well," he says, "maybe you should talk to Dr. O'Neill next time you take him, and ask what he thinks. Maybe he can figure out the motivation, or tell you what he thinks we should do. For now, I think you handled it the only way you could. I'm sorry that he's been so nasty. I'm sure it's not pleasant for you."

"I think you should probably take a look," I tell him, and I feel guilt and nervousness sitting on top of my stomach as we walk back through the hallway to Matt's room. Scotty's eyes bug out as he surveys the damage, and before I can say anything to justify what he is seeing, he is back out of the hallway like thunder.

"Matthew," he calls in his dad-voice, and I'm surprised, because I haven't heard that voice recently, and it's kind of nostalgic.

Matt comes out and stands in the doorway to the living room like a dead man walking. He has come out of the confessional; his soul is unburdened. There is no shame left to hide. He walks with Scotty back to his bedroom. A minute later, George realizes he is alone and comes running after us.

"Son, did you do this to your room?"

Matt nods solemnly.

"This room is unlivable. You've made it so that no one can sleep or play or do anything in here. Why did you do this?"

Matt shrugs, not because he's ambivalent but because he doesn't want to say anything that could incriminate him further.

"This is not an acceptable thing that's happened, Matthew. Do you understand? You need to make it right. Tomorrow you will clean this up, and you will need to do it on your own. Tonight you can sleep in one of the other rooms."

"Georgie's?" Matt asks, with tears in his eyes, hoping that the answer will be yes.

"No, son. You can sleep in one of the guest rooms, and tomorrow, if you do a good job cleaning this up, you can move back into your room," Scotty says. Matt nods and blinks the tears back.

"Let's get some pj's out of your dresser," I say, picking my way through the rubble.

"I'll take them to get their teeth brushed," Scotty says, and neither of the boys puts up a fight or causes any kind of delay, which freaks me out a little.

When the boys are tucked in, and Scotty has gone back out to the living room to finish dinner—I think I hear him watching infomercials—I go into Matt's room with a roll of paper towels, carpet cleaner, and a water-and-dish-soap solution that I hope won't eat the paint off the walls. I pull all the affected animals out of their hamper and take them to the bathroom sink for a sponge bath, gather up all the excess macaroni, chicken, and potato into a paper towel, wash the wall, and spot treat the rug, and then run the Dustbuster. I finish and gather up my supplies, and when I turn around, there's Scotty, watching me from the doorway.

"Holy C-R-A-P, you scared me," I say. "I didn't want his room to smell like gravy. I don't think he would really know how to clean up the food effectively, so I figured I should do it now. Don't be mad."

"I'm not mad," he says. He doesn't move out of the doorway, so I can't get out either. We both stand there, amid the wreckage.

"You're home early tonight," I say.

"There was no more work. I literally ran out of work," he says. "There was nothing to keep me away from home."

"It's nice," I say. "We—the boys—were so glad to see you."

"You don't think they thought it was strange?" he asks.

"No, I *do* think that. I just—I think it was in a good way." Since I may have already crossed the line, I add, "They want you, Scotty. They want to see you."

I think he's going to step out of the doorway, so I move toward him, wanting out of the havoc. But he doesn't move. We're standing really close together. He presses his hands to both sides of the doorway, as if there's a danger it will close in on him.

"It's funny that you spell *crap*," he says.

"I used to spell both of their names when I was talking about one of them to someone else, but Matt's onto that now. I spelled B-A-D-A-S-S the other day, and he figured that one out too. Stupid phonetics," I say. Scotty steps out of the way, and we make our way to the family room, where infomercials are blaring. I clear his plate and the boys' stuff and sit down to finish my dinner.

He clicks off the TV. "I think I'm going to bed early," he says. "And by going to bed, I really mean have a *Game of Thrones* marathon. My workday put me in the mood to watch people put their money where their mouth is when it comes to evisceration," he says, and it has the essence but not the inflection of his former banter. "Good night, Charlotte. Thank you for dealing with Matt. See you in the morning."

"Good night," I say. I finish dinner and watch the news for a while, but by the time nine o'clock rolls around, bed is sounding pretty good to me too.

I have finished in the bathroom, put on my pajamas, and am about to get in bed with *Vanity Fair* when I hear a small voice from the doorway to my room. "Charlotte?"

It's Matt. He's clutching a blanket and pillow, and his hair is all messed up. All of a sudden I feel so sad for him, and the sadness is walking around in my gut with footsteps that echo.

"What's up, love?" I say.

"Can I sleep in here with you?"

I pull down the covers and put his blanket on the other side of the bed while he crawls in. He pulls the blanket all the way up, almost over his head, so his voice is muffled and tentative as he says, "Will you sing to me before I fall asleep?"

I smooth the baby hairs off his forehead. "What would you like me to sing?"

"Something I've never heard before," he says.

I sing to him, making it up as I go along so that there's no way any memory can attach itself to the song and permeate the fragile safety of this bed.

January, the year before

After a year of pleading, manipulation, and bribery, I still haven't come up with an effective strategy for getting Matt moving in a timely manner. Today, as we wait in the lobby of North-Mad for Gretchen, I have resorted to shaking his coat at him like a bag of dog treats *and* threatening to take away *all* future snacks.

Matt has allowed me to get each of his arms into a sleeve of his coat, and he is kicking his toe against the wall and occasionally sighing loudly while, through a glass wall, we watch Gretchen chatting with Miss Annabelle, George's lead teacher.

George has let me bundle him within an inch of his life. The only piece of him that is visible is his left eye. The rest of him is swaddled like an arctic explorer, strapped into the stroller and ready to go. George, with his one exposed eye, watches his brother pace the lobby with an aggressive set to his jaw.

If I'm not imagining things, the look on Gretchen's face is similar to Matt's expression, and I'm beginning to wonder what Gretchen and Miss Annabelle are talking about. Gretchen's arms are folded, and she is interrupting Miss Annabelle every now and then—a very un-Gretchen-like thing to do—and as she starts to leave the classroom, she turns back toward Miss Annabelle and says something that makes the younger woman's eyes widen. She comes out and squats in front of Matt, zipping up his jacket before he knows what's happening. I'm dying to ask her a bunch of nosy questions. I restrain myself.

No one says anything as we get into the elevator, and Gretchen puts her phone to her ear. Apparently, there is no answer, because the next thing she does is start stabbing at the keyboard, sending a vehement text to an unfortunate recipient.

We walk a block and a half, all of us sensitive to her mood, before she decides to clue me in. "It took me so long to convince them to let G-E-O-R-G-E start there," she says, and her voice is wobbling, like she's about to cry. I can't tell whether or not she wants to talk about it, and I definitely don't want her to cry. Matt's backpack is hanging off the handle of the stroller by one strap, swinging into her knees as she walks. I take the backpack and sling it over my shoulders, on top of my own. Matt notices the backpack-on-backpack action and laughs. Gretchen presses her phone to her ear again.

"I wish S-C-O-T-T-Y would answer his D-A-M-N phone," she

mutters. She is pushing the stroller one-handed and pressing the fingers of her other hand to her forehead, right above the bridge of her nose.

"Daddy?" asks Matt.

"Yes, Daddy, smart boy," she says. Tears are starting to leak out the corners.

"Matty, did you have fun at school?" I ask. He shrugs. "Come on," I press him, nudging his arm with mine. "What's the most fun thing you did today?"

"We read a book about a bunch of stuff that got stuck in a tree."

"Did you like it?"

"I liked it until the end."

"What happened?"

Matt frowns. "He got one thing down out of the tree. Everything else was still up there. But everyone went to sleep anyway. Even though there was a whale in the tree outside."

"You don't think that could really happen?"

"No," he says. He does seem genuinely perplexed. I look at Gretchen and make an I-want-to-laugh-at-his-cuteness face at her, but she is staring at her phone, miserable and trying to remain inaudibly so.

When we get in the door, Matt leaves his foul weather gear in a pile in the hallway and runs into the kitchen. Upon his liberation, Georgie follows suit. Gretchen and I wade through the mayhem.

"This time, they're concerned," says Gretchen, as if we are picking up a conversation only recently abandoned, "about George's lack of response to the other kids. Or rather, that he won't *say* anything to them. 'Concerned for his safety and well-being' is how Miss Annabelle put it. She says he sits there and lets kids take his toys or push him or stand in his way or take his turn . . ." She turns the fleece lining from Matt's coat right side out and zips it back into the shell. "He just sits there. He doesn't do anything to defend himself, or 'defend his personal space,' says the teacher."

"I can't believe she would admit that the other kids are pushing and taking his toys in her classroom," I say. I am extracting the art projects from Matt's lunch box, which are mostly done on hot pink paper with varying hues of glitter glue.

"It's just another way for them to tell me they think there's something wrong because he doesn't speak," she says. The more upset she appears, the quieter her voice gets. "The thing is," says Gretchen, "he does communicate. You know, of course. He has his own way of saying what he needs, but it's not assertive or loud or territorial most of the time. Unless, I don't know, he's overtired or it's really escalated. And I know that's not common in two-year-olds." She's getting teary again, and I grasp for the right thing to say, but I can't catch the appropriate words.

"And Scotty," she says, and I can see that set to her jaw starting to re-emerge. "He's so freaking optimistic about everything. He says the same things over and over, affirms me so often that it's like he doesn't even have an opinion."

From our position in the hallway, I can see into the kitchen. There Matt stands in front of the open refrigerator. George points at something on a shelf that is too high for him. Matt holds up a carton of strawberries. George shakes his head no.

"We thought he might have hearing problems. Did I ever tell you that? He went through all these tests as a baby," says Gretchen.

"I think I remember a few of them," I say, stepping on the peg to fold the stroller.

"One of the doctors we saw said something that stuck with me. He was Israeli, formerly a medic in their army. I don't know why that's relevant, but I guess it felt significant at the time," she says. "Anyway, this doctor said that there were probably a lot of doctors in New York City that would send us to other doctors, to child specialists, and if the problem wasn't physical, they would go to great lengths to prove it was mental. Miss Annabelle thinks I ought to have him tested. Again."

"For what?"

"Who knows? It obviously makes her uncomfortable, that he isn't talking. She wants to classify him in some way, so she can make a plan for what to do, and I guess I can try to understand that. But that Israeli doctor said he thought George would start speaking as soon as he felt like he had no other option. Whenever things come up where I can see potential for words to be needed urgently, I try to see how long I can let it go. Even when it gets hard to watch. But of course, she's known him for less than a month."

"Do you and, I mean, does Scotty think that's a good idea . . . also? More testing?"

"I wish I knew," says Gretchen, pulling a tissue out of her purse and dabbing her eyes every few seconds, letting no tear escape. "He says he trusts my instincts. It's like he's left me alone to deal with this thing, and it's so fucking *isolating.* You know what I mean?" She wipes her eyes and inhales sharply. "Oh God, Charlotte, I'm so sorry. I don't mean to dump this on you."

"Well, shame on Miss Annabelle," I say. "It doesn't seem appropriate to casually mention to a mom on her way out of the classroom that she thinks she hasn't done enough for her child."

"Exactly. Thank you," she says, then gives me a small smile. "Yikes, I swore at her. The teacher. Scotty's going to kill me. We'll probably have to buy the school new terrace equipment or something."

I laugh in surprise and turn back to watch the boys. Matt looks impatient, but he continues to hold up snacks for George to examine, until George settles on green grapes. George carries the grapes carefully to the table and climbs up into a chair that doesn't afford him much of a view over the table.

"You know what? He told me to have faith, that doctor—the Israeli guy," says Gretchen. "Not like the way my mother would say it. He just said, 'Have faith,' and that was that. I guess I was hoping that I could surround George, and myself, with people who would keep the faith with us." She pats my hand, like I'm the one who needs to be comforted.

We walk together into the kitchen. Gretchen's phone buzzes. She looks down at the text, presumably from Scotty. "Now he's super worried about the missed calls from me, and I've forgotten all about calling him. Because we have our Charlotte to help us get through the day, don't we, boys?"

"Our Pahr-lette," says Matt. Georgie points to Matt's portion of grapes and then to his own empty bowl. He puts out his hand, hopefully. Matt sighs but breaks off a stem and puts it in front of his brother.

"Our Schmar-lette," I say.

"Try not to think I'm too much of a basket case, won't you, Schmar-lette?" Gretchen says.

"I think you're kind of B-A-D-A-S-S," I say.

"Can we keep you forever?" Gretchen asks, and I know she is mostly joking, but I know, too, that at the heart of every joke is the truth, and the thought is satisfying and worrisome.

April, seven weeks after

The morning after Matt's epic tantrum, I wake up when my alarm goes off, startled, feeling like I haven't slept at all. Matt is next to me, with his head on my pillow and his feet hanging off the edge of the bed. It was one of those nights that felt like fever dreaming and waking up every half hour with some new, urgent thought, which fled the moment I tried to wrap my mind around it. Matt is still sleeping. He looks peaceful. I hate to wake him up.

The night was long, but it's morning now, despite my fear that it might never come again.

PART THREE

Scotty

April, eight weeks after

Stick to yoga pants," says Claudia. I had turned my laptop the other direction so we could continue to video chat while I changed, so I'm not sure how she's onto me, but I stop in the act of pulling a skirt up over my hips and come back around to face her.

"Really?"

"Those aren't your normal clothes. You always look uncomfortable when you wear something that's meant to impress someone."

"What I would normally wear has crumbs all over it, and tiny holes that George manages to find and stick his fingers through. I need at least a slight upgrade."

"But it's Jess," she says, and I'm jealous of the amount of disdain she's able to inject into that one syllable. "We don't care what she thinks."

"After I see her, I'm meeting with their doctor, their psychologist," I say. I finish pulling up the skirt and then put on a jacket that may or may not match. "Matt's having trouble in school. And trouble adjusting in general."

"Shouldn't their father be meeting with the doctor?"

"He's coming too," I say, before I can stop myself.

"So the kids are in Connecticut, and you and Scotty are going in to meet with the psychologist? Oh Lord. You'd better be grateful you've got me on the line and not Jane."

"Why?" I put my coffee mug into the microwave, to reheat what's left of it. "What would Jane say?"

"She would tell you to stop being so easy. And then she would try to soften the blow with a follow-up statement, like, ah, you're being ridiculously generous, and what if one day, they're not equally generous to you, and then you get hurt?"

"Geez," I say. "Jane really knows how to poke at the heart of things."

"She sure does."

I pull the collar out from under my jacket and use my image on the computer as a mirror to adjust it. "Hey, what would Oprah say to me, do you think?"

"She would say you have to teach people how to treat you."

"What about Jay Carney? What would he say?"

"He would tell you to keep up the good work and then casually segue into an anecdote about how the president captured Osama bin Laden with his bare hands."

"Ha! And what would Claudia have to say, if she weren't so busy being on my side?"

"Claudia would tell you to watch yourself. You don't want to find yourself acting like a stand-in."

"A stand-in. Ouch." I have to find my way to Brooklyn and try to remember how to be *me*—not the flipper of pancakes, the master of stroller folding, the mender of scraped elbows, the enforcer of bedtimes—just me, Charlotte. "I love you very much, Claud-monster," I say, holding one finger up to the screen.

She puts her finger up too, against mine on the screen. "As much as you love Jay Carney?"

"No. Not that much," I say. She sticks out her tongue at me, and that's how she is frozen as I close out the chat screen.

February, six days after

I wake up before the sun on the morning of Gretchen's funeral. I spent an hour the night before agonizing over what to wear, only to find that when I get out of bed, I no longer want to wear it. Twenty minutes pass. I sit on the edge of my bed in the dark. I want the boys to be able to feel their emotions. I want them to know that I will be here for them. I don't want the emotions of everyone around them to scare them. And very little of that is within the bounds of my control.

At the last minute, I decide on an outfit that's not really in season but feels appropriate. I grab my winter coat and flat boots and scoot out of the apartment.

When I get to the McLeans' building, Shel, the doorman, is engulfed in a sea of people, all dressed in black, all talking. No one seems to know which apartment number they're going to. I see Aunt Lila's daughter and deduce they must be members of Gretchen's family. Shel looks relieved to see me, like maybe I can help sort this out. I wonder why no one mentioned to him that a whole lot of people would be descending on the apartment.

"Good morning, Miss Charlotte," he says.

"Good morning, Shel. I think it's okay if these folks come up with me, as long as it's okay with you," I say.

"Everyone going to a wake with Mr. and Mrs. McLean?" Shel asks, and I am horrified. I haven't yet had to bear the news of the tragedy in person to anyone.

"Yes," I say. "We *are* going to a wake, Shel. I'm so sorry no one told you. Gretchen—Mrs. McLean—was hit by a car last week. And she died."

Shel takes off his hat slowly and puts it on his chest. After a moment, he crosses himself and says "Amen. God rest her."

"Can you buzz Mr. McLean and let him know we're on our way?" I say. And I shepherd the wavering mass of sad people into the elevator. As the doors close, Shel picks up the phone to call Scotty.

When we get to the top floor, Patrick is standing there with the door open. He hugs and murmurs his way through the shuffling crowd, and as soon as they're all in, but before I can get in, he steps outside of the apartment, into the foyer. He leans over, and I think he's going to kiss my cheek, but really he kisses the corner of my mouth and only separates his face from mine about an inch before asking, "How are you?"

"I'm fine," I say, stepping back.

"George has been asking for you."

"Not Matt?"

"Matt hasn't said much of anything."

My eyes tear up, and I can't really see. I feel Patrick take my hands. "That is. I don't know what that is. It's so far past sad. I don't know."

"I know," he says, and I would do anything, anything, to be able to stay here, even with Patrick, anything other than walking through those doors and into the house of motherless children.

I harden my resolve and drop his hands. "We should go in," I say, and he holds the door open for me.

The first person on the other side of the door is Mae, and today her eyes are teary, and I'm relieved. She hugs me, and I hear her catch her breath in my ear, and she's speaking, but I'm not listening, because over her shoulder, I can see Matthew.

He has on jeans and a little suit jacket, with a button-up shirt underneath. He's sitting on the edge of the couch, holding his tie in his hands, twisting it around and around. Vaguely, I register that Mae is saying something about his suit pants and shoes being put on right before we leave so they don't get messed up, and I try to tune in for the information about where we need to be and when. George, I see, is wearing his full suit already. We all know how meticulous he is about not getting messy. He is sitting on the floor at Matt's feet, playing with his trucks, trying to see how high he can stack them before they fall over.

"It's up to you, Charlotte. Use your discretion. There's a vestibule outside the door to the sanctuary, and you can always take them out there, or even outside on the lawn if it's not too windy. Whatever you think best."

"Is it . . ." I don't know how to ask this. "Will they, I mean, are we going to be able to see her?"

"No, the casket will be closed." Mae seems short of breath, and she has a hand on her chest, as if to measure the air in and out. "Her face is too—too swollen, really, and a little discolored. She doesn't really, not really—she doesn't really look like herself."

"Are there calling hours?"

"This morning. They are not terribly formal. Father Gregory will be there, and people can come in and say prayers over the casket and offer condolences to Scotty and the family. There won't be any time for that after the service—I thought it best we get right over to the cemetery. Scotty's not in . . . great shape. Father Gregory has offered to stay by his side."

"I've never met Father Gregory," I say, like it matters.

"He flew in from Chicago. We attended his parish when Gretchen was growing up, and he married the two of them," says Mae. "The cars are coming at nine, so we should probably be outside at eight forty-five."

"If it's okay with you," I say, "I might walk with them. Georgie can ride in the stroller. I think it's only six or seven blocks from here."

She hesitates for a moment, and I wonder if she wants to ask me how many streets we have to cross between here and the church. "Sure, it might be good for them to have a walk."

"Great," I say. "We can leave when you guys go outside to the cars. How many people are going with you?"

"I think this is it," Mae says. I should have been more specific. I can't tell how many people are in the apartment. There are six who came in with me. Mae and Simon. Scotty and the boys. Patrick. Are Scotty and Patrick's parents here? I've never met Jeanne and George McLean, but as I walk further into the living room, I spot a couple who are older than the rest of the crowd but younger than I would have guessed for Scotty's parents, sitting across from Matt and George. Grampa George occasionally zooms a car or truck back toward his little namesake after a particularly disastrous tower collapse, but other than that, they don't seem to be speaking to anyone or moving much. They look frigid, stately. Old money. Not at all like they've ever engaged in an act that would have spawned Scotty, let alone Patrick or Uncle Max, the older one.

"Hi, little boys," I say, as Matt glances up and spots me. "What are you doing with those trucks, George? Trying to send someone flying?"

"Noooo Tahr-lette," George says, like I am so silly. "We building a tower." Every once in a while, I see Matt nudge the tower with his foot, trying to see if he can surreptitiously collapse it.

I squat down in front of Matt. I don't normally get in his face because he hates it. But I want to see what's in his eyes today. It's impossible to be well-dressed around little kids—too much squatting and kneeling for Isaac Mizrahi designs. "How are you doing?" I ask him, like he's an adult.

"I wish I could see Mommy," he says, and his eyes tear up.

"I know, love. I'm so sorry," I say, and he lets me hug him but not for long.

Neither of the grandparents says anything to me. "Hi, I'm Charlotte," I say. "Are you Sc—Mr. and Mrs. McLean?"

"George," says Scotty's father, in a voice that's disturbingly similar to Patrick's. He shakes my hand.

"Jeanne," says Scotty's mother. She does not offer her hand. I feel like I should still call them Mr. and Mrs. McLean, even though they both said their first names. There isn't anyone else consistently in the room, which I take to mean that Scotty's parents are currently on grandkid duty, although they don't appear particularly engaged. Every once in a while, I see another little kid whose name I can't remember pass through, and I wonder how many kids Uncle Max has now. Normally, I would ask Matt, but he is so occupied with his stillness that I don't mind staying in the dark.

The way people are moving in and out of the room reminds me of chickens in a coop yard. I have yet to spot Scotty. Is he pulling a Howard Hughes back in his bedroom? I wish I couldn't picture it so clearly.

"Would you like something to eat before we go, Charlotte?" asks Mae, appearing from nowhere.

"No, thank you," I say. "Except, do you have coffee?"

"Sure. How do you take it?"

"Intravenously," I say. It takes her a minute to figure out that I'm joking. I'm such an inappropriate joker.

"How about with a little Irish in it?" Patrick suggests.

"Patrick." This is his mother's voice, and a whole sentence is contained in the way she says his name. Patrick, don't you dare joke around on a day like today? Patrick, maintain the proper decorum? Patrick, don't speak to the help in familiar terms? Growing up in her house must have been character building, as my own grandmother would put it.

Mae brings my coffee, and I slip into the smaller kitchen and transfer it into a travel mug. I grab a few snacks for the boys and stuff them into a freezer bag, and I am back out in the living room in less than forty-five seconds. The time has come for us to be on our way. I strap George into the stroller, and we are off, waving good-bye to Mae and ignoring everyone else. When we are safely alone in the elevator, Matt lets out a sigh, and it sounds like relief.

Georgie chatters the whole six blocks. "We going to cool, Tahr-lette?"

"No, bug," I say. "We're not going to school. We're going to a church."

"When we going back to cool?"

"Maybe next week?"

"Why we going to a turch?"

"Well," I say, "there's going to be a special service to say goodbye to your mommy."

"Mommy going to be there?" he asks, like he would ask if we could play a game of *Go Fish* later.

"I don't think we'll be able to see her," I say. "It's a time where people can get together and talk about how much they loved your mom, and all their favorite things about her."

"Where Mommy going to be?"

"She—" I have no idea what to say. No idea, no idea, no idea. I want to cry.

"She died, Georgie," Matt finally pipes in, and I wonder what he thinks that means. "A taxicab hit her, and she got broken, and she died. We can't see her anymore, ever again."

Georgie looks down and starts playing with his fingers.

When we get to the church, the first thing we see in the aforementioned vestibule, sitting atop an easel, is a large picture of Gretchen. As soon as Matt spots it, he bursts into tears, great gulping sobs that sound like words but that I can't understand. I don't say anything, because what will comfort him? I unstrap George and point him through the church doors, and then I pick up Matt and sit down with him in the back pew. I rock him back and forth until the volume decreases a little bit, and I finally understand that he's saying, "I want Mommy, I want Mommy!" over and over.

"I know," I say, and George climbs up next to me and kneels down with his forehead on Matt's back. "I'm sorry. I'm so, so sorry." And there we sit for the next fifteen minutes, until people start trickling in, and Matt no longer feels he has permission to live with his emotions.

Family members walk by, giving me looks ranging from concern to sympathy to thank-God-you're-dealing-with-this, and then I see Scotty. He walks in with a priest, presumably Father Gregory, and stops when he sees us sitting there in a pile. He is looking in our direction, seeing us without really catching the contact of our eyes, and I think of a prisoner, just out of solitary, being reintegrated to the general population, whether he likes it or not. Scotty is surrounded, trapped even, by people who care so deeply for him, and yet he has the look of a man who has been condemned to be alone forever. He closes his eyes, like he's blinded by the sight of us, and when he opens them again, he is walking forward, past us, without a word, without even a silent word.

I don't think it would be exaggerating to say that I watch somewhere between five hundred and a thousand people come and go in the next three hours. Some I recognize; most I don't. Father Gregory seems to be fielding much of it, and he doesn't seem to want to let anyone touch Scotty. He effectively body blocks anyone who seems to want to go in for a hug or handshake. I feel a bit of camaraderie with him; we are human shields.

No one seems to know what to say to the boys, so people pretty much leave us alone. I download a bunch of games onto my phone to keep Matt occupied, and George runs around in the back of the church with his cousins, Uncle Max's kids. It goes on like this until calling hours are over, and by the time the last few people are leaving, I am filled with a righteous assurance. The boys cannot sit through a long lunch and a funeral service. The graveside service later tonight will have to be enough. Making them suffer through this afternoon will be like a handful of gravel to a skinned knee.

I approach Scotty from behind so as not to be waylaid by Father Gregory. "Scotty." I don't want to ask Mae about this. "Can I talk to you for a second?"

Like he's seeing me for the first time today, he zeroes in. "Of course," he says. "Thank you for coming, Charlotte. Are you okay?"

"Well. Not really," I say. "I know you must feel like you're in a nightmare. God, Scotty. I am so sorry."

The muscles in his face twitch, and I have to move on because I cannot stand it. Scotty's face will suck me into his suffering if I let it collapse, so I have to move on.

"I don't—I don't know if they should go to the service," I say, with no appropriate preamble. "Matt and George, I mean. Maybe I could take them home for lunch and a little rest time. And then we can meet you at the cemetery? They're really having a difficult time here. I mean, in this environment."

Scotty looks up, appearing to study one of the many stained-glass windows. The light coming in through those windows casts a pattern on his skin, making it impossible for me to make any inferences from his expression. "Okay," he says. "If you think so, then that's what you should do. I want them to . . . I want to do what's best for them. It's okay, Charlotte; it's probably the best idea anyone's had in days."

"Thank you," I say. "We'll get a cab to the memorial later."

"Call a car service," he says, pulling out his wallet and handing me a couple hundred dollars. "Do—do whatever they want this afternoon. Okay?"

Uncle Max comes now to give Scotty a gentle push in the direction he's supposed to go. I have met Uncle Max on one prior occasion, a family visit when his wife was pregnant with their fifth child. I was left with the impression that Scotty's mother must have had an affair with a lobster trapper or some other burly blue-collar worker up in Maine, where they live, and that's how Uncle Max came into being. He's massive, able to move furniture around the living room that I have never seen anyone else move, and he looks and sounds nothing like Scotty or Patrick or their father. When Scotty and Uncle Max had conversations, from the sounds of them, many cigars and slaps on the back and exclamations of "You don't say, old boy!" were involved. Now I feel grateful for his comforting density. I head back to collect the kids, keeping my eyes in a straight line, not allowing any Maes or Jeannes or Aunt Lilas or Uncle Patricks into my periphery.

At home, where it's blessedly quiet, we have lunch. We take a nap. (Two of us do—one of us watches three consecutive episodes of the *Berenstain Bears.*) We change our clothes and then walk through the park, looking for Pale Male on the edge of Fifth Avenue. Eventually, we make our way to the Museum of Natural History, where we spend the majority of our time in the early-man exhibit. ("Tahr-lette, where their wee-wees are?" asks George, repeatedly pointing to the wee-wee-less female models.) By the time we are done, I make the executive decision not to change them back into their suits. They are wearing matching plaid flannel shirts that Gretchen loved, and they will fare better in a cemetery wearing sneakers. I call the car to pick us up on the Columbus Avenue side of the museum, and while we are waiting, I catch Matt eyeing a flower vendor.

"Mommy said it was crazy that those daisies were orange and red," Matt says. "She only liked white."

"Daddy got the purple ones," says George. "Remember? And Mommy say, not the crazy daisy!"

"Would you like to bring her a funny color?" I say. "You can pick out the craziest one, if you want."

"And we give the flower to Mommy, Tahr-lette? She see what colors we pick?" I nod because it's the easiest thing to do.

Matt gets a red one, and George picks purple, and our car pulls up then to take us out to the cemetery. I feel irrationally afraid that the sun will set early, and it will be too dark to see when we get there, that we'll have a hard time finding our way through to the right site, that Father Gregory will have trouble reading from his prayer book, that we won't be able to see the return of dust to dust. That Gretchen won't be able to see what color daisies her boys picked out to make her laugh.

But the sun stays up. We find our way. Father Gregory knows the prayers by heart, and we can all see clearly as Gretchen's casket is lowered into the ground. And I'm pretty sure that when George throws his daisy in after Matt's that he understands that he is giving the flower to his mom.

April, eight weeks after

Jess is living in a huge loft-style penthouse on the top floor of a glorified warehouse in one of the most up-and-coming sections of Brooklyn. The elevator I take opens into her kitchen, and to my left, past all of the appliances, a huge window is part of a clock face. To my right is a wall made of windows overlooking the East River. Train tracks, buildings, people the size of pinheads, sidewalks laid out in a grid, taxis, and bridges are bisected by extreme angles of light in every direction. The view from her living room window could be a painting, could sell for millions, could be studied in modern art classes.

The light comes through the clock in a way that casts long shadows of Roman numerals on Jess's kitchen table. The table is made of reclaimed wood, and she seems to regard it as some kind of postmodern conference area. She gestures to it while smiling and setting out mugs.

"I'm so glad to have you here, finally," she says, as if she's been chasing me down all these years. "Would you like coffee or tea?"

"Sure. Coffee, please."

She pours it, without offering cream or sugar. I guess they take it black in this part of town. I am keyed up, trying to concentrate, to take it all in with a shred of perspective. I remind myself that the more important meeting—the meeting with the boys' psychologist—comes after this one. I don't want to let her do what I always let her do, swing me along in the dreamy logic of her ambitions. I grip my too-hot mug with both hands, to let the burning sensation on my palms keep me on point. On the way back into Manhattan, I can try to document things about Matt's behavior for Dr. O'Neill, all the little patterns I can see developing. I want to make sure the doctor hears it all. I should have made the list last night.

"What part of the city do you live in now?" Jess asks, like she had known the answer at one time.

"The Upper East Side," I say.

"What, Park Avenue?"

"Far east, by the river." I notice the shadow of a Roman numeral seven on my chest. Who is she, to judge Park Avenue?

"You're out of school for a few years now, yes?"

I sit back in my chair and then worry it might fall apart. It looks like it's made of tree branches, strung together with twine. "Yes."

"Why New York, by the way?"

I ordinarily have a great answer to the why New York question, involving a successful avoidance of the career-goal discussion, by using generic phrases like "so much to learn" and "stretching my wings in the professional world" and "listening to the advice of mentors who are further along." I've given it to everyone in my life, from my mother, to Gretchen when she first hired me, to other musicians I've met along the way. I can't summon it today, though.

"This is where people go to be composers," I say. "Writing music is kind of an elusive career. I'm sure you understand that, even though you've had some great successes and you live in a clock tower."

"You should have seen my first apartment," says Jess. "I had to name the mice in order to help myself sleep at night. Like, oh,

Byron is too shy to run over my face in the middle of the night. Gussie is afraid of heights—he would never climb up my sheets and hide, waiting to nip at my toes."

"That's horrifying." I stand up from the rickety chair to take off my jacket and lay it over the back, noticing that the edge of twine right beneath my fingers could be pulled on just slightly, and the whole top part may well come crashing down.

"There was always the option to stay in academia, until it branched off into a clearer professional path," she says.

"Everett did," I say. "Academia was not for me."

"I was surprised to hear that Everett was accepted into that doctoral program," she says. "Makes me think they've relaxed their admissions standards." If Everett had been saying these words, they would have been full of arrogance, a degree of rivalry. But the way Jess says them sounds completely objective, and that makes them much harsher. "Maybe it was just a fluke. They haven't had a trumpet player in a while."

"Not since you?" I say.

She smiles. "I don't have a DMA. Only an MFA. You can't call me Dr. Fairchild."

"That's funny. You let us call you that all the way through the semester at school."

"Not you, Charlotte," she says. "You always called me Jess, didn't you?"

"Only behind your back."

"You talked about me behind my back?"

"Constantly," I say. "We all did."

She pulls the tea bag out of her mug and wraps it around her spoon, squeezing the water out. I can tell she is happy with that answer. "I'm not much of a trumpet player, anyway," she says. I have heard her play the trumpet. The sound is aggressive, raw, heartbreaking. Beautiful, in a way that feels unholy. There aren't many people, if any, on the planet who can sound that way on the *trumpet*. Yet she isn't being modest. Of all her musical strengths and talents, trumpet skills are not the thing she would choose to highlight.

"Well, that's not Everett's only instrument," I say, feeling like I need to defend him, which he would hate. "He's got like six or eight other . . . proficiencies."

"So does your average high school band teacher," says Jess, and it's the first thing she's said that really sounds like an on-purpose insult.

"He wants to compose symphonies. It's not like his instrumental concert skills matter all that much." I sound hostile to my own ears and wonder if she hears it.

"They used to, for that program," Jess replies. "If you looked in every corner of the earth, you could find yourself a colony of people that could design a competent symphony. You know what you would have trouble finding?" She gets up and retrieves a notebook full of staffed papers from the piano bench in the living room and puts it down in front of me at the table. "This."

"You wrote this?"

"Yes."

"I'm sure it's lovely."

"It could be. I want you to tell me what's wrong with it, though. There's something missing. I can't make it work. I have the sense that it would tie my whole new piece together if I got it right, but I'm having trouble getting there. So, how can I fix it, do you think?"

"It's the wrong time signature," I say, without thinking, "for a start. But you might also try reversing some of this phrasing." I start to mark it up, remember where I am, and put the pencil down on the table. "You constructed it strangely. You . . . you, like, stacked everything on top of each other. These two sections should switch places." I fold my hands in my lap and squeeze them together so hard that the knuckles crack.

"Will you come to the piano?"

I stand up and follow her, and I think of what Eliza said to me, about Patrick and the darker side of herself. There's a way of living in the present that Jess has mastered, and being with her feels euphoric, careless, light-headed. We work on her piece for so long that when I glance outside, I can see that the light has completely changed over the river water. How long have I been here?

I'm about to stand up, and then she says, "The world should hear you, Charlotte. You're keeping it all to yourself."

"I'm not keeping it to myself on purpose," I say. "But Jess. Holy shit. The *rat race*. Everybody scrambling, all the time. Living hand to mouth. People lying and cheating and stealing." I think of the way Everett was laughing the night of his concert. Not his real laugh. "That's been my experience of the lifestyle in the land of musicians, and I'm not cut out for it."

"I would have helped you," she says. "If I knew that you were having trouble figuring out where the work is, I would have made a connection for you. Or brought you onto some of my projects."

"If I knew where to find you," I say. "If you hadn't disappeared all of a sudden, maybe I would have asked."

She doesn't say anything. Personal accountability is not a thing she does, and I hear it as her fatal flaw in the lack of response. I haven't made much of an accusation, but to her, I might as well have requested that she recalculate the speed of sound. How could she run all over the globe being famous and brilliant if she had to answer to someone?

Something in her living room catches my eye. It's folded neatly, cashmere, straight out of a Ralph Lauren ad. Everett's scarf.

"You should think about switching those two sections in the piece." I gather the loose sheets of music on the piano, stacking them into a neat pile and sliding them back into her notebook. Jess still handwrites the majority of her work. She probably has an army of copyists inputting the music she scrawls into composition software for her.

"You can come and work for me whenever you want," Jess says. "I'd hire you in a heartbeat."

My phone buzzes in my pocket, making my heart race with an adrenaline surge. Scotty, Matt, George—which one?

I read the text—"Dr. O'Neill office called, moved us up 3/4 hour, can you make it?"—and relax. No one is in a state of peril or meltdown. I realize that I am standing up and have done so in a way that must have seemed abrupt.

"Is that clock right?" I ask.

"Yes," she says. "I had it set. What do you think of it?"

"I'm sorry," I say. "I didn't realize that it was so late. I have to get going." If I find a taxi immediately, I'll make it to the appointment on time.

She walks with me to the kitchen. "I'll be here for a few weeks. Maybe you and Everett and I can get together."

"I'm sure Everett will want to come back for his scarf."

"I'm playing a salon, of sorts, at the Park Avenue Armory," Jess says. She doesn't recognize sarcasm as a valid form of communication, never has. "A fundraiser for my foundation. I'll reserve tickets for the two of you. You'll get to hear the whole piece, complete with your revisions."

"Great. So I guess I'll see my name in the program, then."

"If that's what you want," she says, "I'm sure it can be arranged."

The option to have it out with her is right in front of me, but now I'm in a hurry, and I'm suddenly distracted by the possibility that maybe I forgot to pack sweatpants for George to nap in this weekend at Aunt Lila's.

I hurry across the kitchen to the elevator and push the button. Of course it isn't there right away. I press it seven or eight times, even though I've told Matt over and over that pressing the button a bunch of times won't make the elevator come any faster.

It comes, finally. "I forgot to ask, Charlotte, what is it you're doing with your time these days?" Jess asks, as I'm about to step inside.

"Babysitting," I say. As if that one word could sum it all up.

February, six days after

After Gretchen's graveside service, I somehow end up in a large black car with the boys, Patrick, and Jeanne and George McLean. The silence in the car for much of the ride is pregnant with regret, but I get the feeling that it's an old regret. George the Younger tries once or twice to rope us all into a discussion about which two animals combined would make the best villain in a story he is making up about chickens, but so far, no one will engage with him past a halfhearted smile in his direction.

"Maybe the chicken could be the villain," I say to him. "Like a mutant, featherless chicken. The chicken who ate New York City."

"That not the *real* tory, Tahr-lette. Chicken is the hero."

"Okay, I see. Does he have a cape?"

"No."

"Can he fly?"

"No. Chickens don't fly. Them not have long wings enough. Long enough wings," he corrects himself, before I can.

"Well, what are his powers, then?"

I'm not doing a good enough job of taking Georgie seriously, I suppose, because he narrows his eyes and doesn't say anything for a while. Then, "He doesn't HAVE to fly to be the hero," he says. He turns his head away, and it's not long before he falls, still scowling, into sleep. I don't know how to assess the emotional toll that the day has taken on him because, unlike Matt, he hasn't cried or screamed or had any meltdowns. It's been almost like a normal day in the life of Georgie. That thought fills my chest like a balloon. I wish with all my might to release the air without upsetting the balance in the car. Who knows what poking a hole in this tension could do?

Across from me and the boys, Patrick sits next to his parents. Dull-eyed, vacant Matt is in the middle, leaning against me, and Georgie has gone to sleep with his head against the window. I feel Patrick's foot stir against mine, so slightly that I wonder if he did it on purpose. When I look at him, I know that he did. George the Elder seems to have noticed as well, while Jeanne wears much the same expression as Matt, staring straight ahead. I'm disconcerted to see both fully grown McLean men looking right at me, but no one says a single word until, just as we're pulling up to the building, without ever changing the direction of her straight-ahead gaze, Jeanne says, "Not this, Patrick. Think of your brother."

Matt holds on so tightly to my leg that I couldn't get free of him if I tried as we take the elevator to the top floor in silence. "Can you put him in with Matt, please?" I say to Patrick, who is carrying Georgie.

We pass through the entryway to the apartment, and I can see that the side table is covered with food, piled artfully, a sculpture of helplessness rendered by people who don't know what else to do besides send food. I am preparing to concede to Matt that yes, he may have one pastry and maybe a small cookie, but he passes right by the overflowing trays of treats without a sideways glance.

"Are you ready for bed, buddy?" I ask him as Patrick disappears off down the hallway with George's prone body.

Matt's eyes are rimmed in pink, and splotches of the same color are visible through the translucent skin at the tops of his cheekbones. All of a sudden he seems to really take me in, zeroing in on my waterless eyes, without knowing what a struggle it's been for me to keep them that way. "Not *you*," he says. "Daddy."

George Senior comes to my rescue. "Come along, grandson. I'll walk you to your room, and you can put yourself to bed. There's a young man. Come, now." And, poor thing, Matt doesn't seem to know his grandfather well enough to throw a tantrum, so he follows, his footsteps soundless, as Grampa George leads the way to his bedroom. Jeanne remains taciturn, standing in the foyer like she's waiting for someone to take her coat and direct her to the ballroom.

Uncle Max's wife, Ashley Lynn, passes them in the hallway as they go, on her way back from putting her own five children to bed, all of them crowded into George's room. As she passes, she reaches out and touches Matt's head briefly, but he leans into it for a moment longer, and I think to myself that certain women are simply born with a maternal energy, and that the McLean men seem to be drawn to them, and that maybe it has something to do with their own mother's lack of warmth.

I see my chance for escape then, the opportunity to walk home through the punishing cold, daring my ears to be frostbitten. I am rifling through my purse to make sure I have everything while anticipating drowning my sorrows in a large glass of wine and the White House press briefing, set to play over and over in a loop while I fall asleep, when I become aware that Ashley Lynn has gotten very close and is addressing me.

The way she speaks is breathy, lilting. Kind of romantic. "Oh Charlotte, do stay through the cocktail hour and tell us all about being a composer. Won't you?" It's past eight, at least, but apparently Gretchen's funeral will not be usurping the daily rituals.

I miss the beat where I can make an excuse. Scotty and Gretchen have never referred to me as a *composer*, at least not to my face. I'm surprised to hear it come out of the mouth of a member of their extended family.

I follow Ashley Lynn into the formal living room, where Scotty is sitting with his brother Max. Both men stand when we enter, probably due to a long-ingrained habit, and Max scoots his chair up so that it's adjacent to Ashley Lynn's. He puts his hand on her knee when she sits down. Actually, his hand is more on the inside of her thigh, but I'm pretending it's on her knee. Patrick comes in with his father, and Jeanne hands each of them a drink. Scotty gets up again when his father enters the room, automatically, like he's forgotten something and only just now remembered. I watch as George Senior sits down in the chair occupied only moments ago by Scotty, and Scotty takes a seat farther away, next to the windows. I don't sit down. There is nowhere in this room that I want to sit.

"Did you know that Charlotte has a master's degree in music?" Ashley Lynn addresses the room at large, but really, her energy is focused on George Senior.

"Composition." Patrick corrects her, but he is facing his father.

"Is music just something you're doing until you decide to have a family?" George asks me. "Or will composition be your life's work?" His eyes are piercing, without any of the cloudiness usually found in a man his age.

"That's not a very feminist way to put it, Dad," says Patrick.

"Well, I'm not a feminist, so that's all right," says George.

"Oh, heavens, George. Who isn't a feminist in this day and age?" says Ashley Lynn.

"Me," says George, clapping Patrick on the shoulder, hard, like Patrick has set him up for an amazing punch line.

"I was hoping to convince her to play something for us." Ashley Lynn lets Max take her hand in his and put all three hands in his lap. "It's such a beautiful piano, don't you think? You have wonderful taste, Scotty." She doesn't mention Gretchen's taste, which is all over this apartment, staring us down. I cast around, trying to come up with the proper tense for "Gretchen and Scotty," realizing that that's probably why Ashley Lynn left her out.

"It was a wedding present," says Jeanne. "George and I found it through Sotheby's." From the way she says it, they might have been wandering around lost on the Upper East Side, until a kind soul from the auction house noticed and took pity on them, gave them a hot cup of coffee, sold them a piano, and then called a taxi to take them home.

"I'm not much of a pianist," I say. "I had to learn competency for my master's, but that's about it."

"So you can play," says Max. His voice is too loud for the parlor. "Know any Gershwin?"

"Let's not get too crazy," says Patrick. "Unless you want seven kids to wake up and demand bedtime snacks."

"Nonsense. These old walls are made of brick," says George.

"I think I need to call it a night," I say, certain that if I stay any longer I'll be auctioned off in some way to the highest bidder. Maybe through Sotheby's.

Scotty stands up, making it look hard. I'd almost forgotten he was in the room. "I'll call the doorman and let him know."

"No, thank you," I say. "I'm going to walk. It's not very late. I'll call in a few days to see, ah, what's what. I—" *I love you* is what I want to say. *And tell the boys I love them, that I loved* her. "Would you tell the boys I'll see them soon?"

I head into the foyer and grab my things quickly, thinking that I'd rather walk out into the freezing night and then get my clothing situated than be detained here for a minute longer. Patrick catches me in the hallway as I'm waiting for the elevator, trying to turn my gloves into a hat.

"Are you really going to walk?" he asks me.

"Yeah," I say. "It's less than a mile."

"Do you want me to walk you?"

"No, thank you."

"*May* I walk you?" It must be the proximity of his parents encouraging this display of manners and propriety, but I don't want it. I miss the guessing game of his borderline comments.

"No. It's super close, Patrick; there's no need."

"I remember where it is. Here," he says, reaching into his jacket pocket for a beanie. "Take my hat. It's too cold not to have something on your head."

The hat I left hanging next to my apartment door is the hat she gave me. I left it there on purpose earlier today. It's the guilt-hat, the hat she bought me on the same shopping trip that she bought a skinny tie for Scotty, which I'm sure he'll never wear. I couldn't bring myself to put that hat on my head this morning. Before I can start crying about it, like I suddenly feel like doing, Patrick adds, "And then when you get home, you'll smell like me."

The sound of my laugh is loud and startling, so I clap my hands over my mouth. "Okay. Give it."

As I'm getting in the elevator, he says, "You can drop it off for me anytime this week. After nine, preferably." The doors close before I have to decide to agree or disagree and, thankfully, before any of Patrick's family members decide to come out looking for him.

April, eight weeks after

I am standing on the sidewalk outside Dr. O'Neill's office, which is in a lovely brownstone between Madison and Park that I wish I lived in. I am watching Scotty type an e-mail on his phone. He hasn't said much of anything since we left the office, and I'm not sure if he wants me to wait until he's finished so we can talk. Dr. O'Neill just gave us a whole load of buzzwords to ponder concerning Matt's psyche, as well as a full report on both boys' "grief progression." Apparently, moving in and out of periods of intense emotion is more common than sustaining one long heightened state of emotion. In essence, both boys are moving along quite naturally, and we need to "create enough space" to let them "feel what they feel." It makes a lot of sense, in the abstract. Unfortunately, the practical strategies are difficult to determine. I thought he would lay some out for us. But if he did, I totally missed them. Maybe Scotty got one or two?

An expression somewhere between weary to the very bones and daunted by a complex question has become more common on Scotty's face than any other. He wears it right now as he types, and when he finally looks up at me, I feel like I'm supposed to answer some question that he never asked in words.

"I'm hungry," he says. "I was working all morning, and I forgot to eat. Are you hungry? Serafina has truffle pizza."

I hesitate for a moment, thinking of my conversation with Claudia. "Yes," I say, turning off my phone. "The boys never let me get anything exotic on my pizza, so that sounds great."

"Strictly pepperoni guys," he says, as we walk around the corner. It's pretty early, so they seat us right away. Scotty orders two gin and tonics, and neither he nor the waiter ask me what I want, but I'm sort of wondering if he means them both for himself.

"I think we need to figure out what to do with Matt," he says, interrupting the nonsense in my head. "I just got an e-mail from the attorney who's representing that guy. You know, the cab driver. Sorry about the wait. I thought I should respond before I had a chance to think of reasons to put it off. Do you think squash would be good in a salad? I didn't think it was in season, but I guess we're into April now. Maybe squash is plentiful in South America or something."

"I'm not a fan of squash," I say. "Don't tell Georgie. Spinach is okay though, if that one looks good to you."

"And you like truffle pizza, right?" he says, closing his menu.

"Right," I say. "Do you mean the, the driver who, the driver who hit her? His attorney e-mailed you?"

"Yes," Scotty says. "We've been communicating."

"But the trial, or whatever, that shouldn't have anything to do with you," I say. "I mean, it's not you pressing charges, right? Isn't it, like, the people?"

"It's complicated," he says. "Both sides need more from me than I thought they would. I think this attorney wants to know if I'll speak to him. The driver. He's been asking to talk to me, and I've been avoiding it. I suppose they think it's possible that the prosecutor might want some kind of a statement from me, and they want to know what I'm going to say. He's smart to ask.

I would, if I were his attorney." The waiter is heading our way with the drink order.

Scotty pushes one of the drinks toward me and then tells the waiter what we're eating. "I don't know how to answer him any better than I already have," he continues, as the waiter retreats. "What else can I say?"

"Wow. That's a lot."

"What would you say?"

"I don't know," I say. "I kind of feel like no punishment could ever be enough. If I did decide to go, I'd have to muster up the part of me that wanted to see him rot in prison."

"I thought that part of me would be the loudest," says Scotty, and we might as well be discussing the electric bill. "But now I have Mae's voice stuck in my head. 'Vengeance is mine, sayeth The Lord,' and all that shit."

His voice is so low that I've been leaning forward, with my forearms resting on the table, to be sure I can hear what he's saying. Now I lean back, taking the lime off the edge of my drink and stirring it into the gin and tonic. Scotty watches me do this, then takes the lime off of his own and squeezes it into my drink before discarding it onto a bread plate.

"To be completely honest, I don't want to think about it," says Scotty. "I don't have much energy, and that man doesn't deserve a single bit of it."

I think about the trouble he is having addressing the subject in his actual life, with his bewildered children in his house of precarious silence. How could he walk into a courtroom or even a law office and talk about this? And what would happen if I left the boys there, on the inside of that, with no mother and an echo of a father? Imagining this feels so bad that I have to force the idea from my mind.

"I had my first session of therapy this past week," Scotty is saying, "and most of the time we talked about work." He is all the way through his gin and tonic, and it feels more like he is thinking out loud than talking to me, especially since I can't come up with anything to add to the conversation. "But I have to do something about Matt. That much is clear."

Our salad arrives, and it looks like the waiter is expecting us to eat with two forks out of the same bowl. "We need a couple of plates," I tell him.

"I'm so sorry about how he was with you the other night," Scotty continues. "It must have been awful."

"It was the worst it's been," I say, "although there are some moments that have come close. The school thing with Ainsley sounded really bad." Now would be a good time to tell him about running into Ainsley's family at Carnegie Hall, but I don't.

"How is George doing, do you think?" Scotty hands our empty glasses to the server who drops off the salad plates, and orders two more gin and tonics.

"I can't really even tell." I push the yellow tomatoes all to one side in the salad bowl, preparing to distribute it onto our plates "He's just so *sad*. He's clingy with Matt, and with me, and with you, when he sees you." Scotty spoons the tomatoes out onto his own salad plate, seeming to understand that I need them out of the way. "He knows that he can't see her, but I don't think he knows what 'dead' means. He asked me if we could call her on the phone."

The waiter delivers our new drinks, and Scotty hands his lime over immediately. "What do you say to him, when he asks about her?"

"Sometimes I avoid the question." I unfold my napkin and put it into my lap. My grandmother would scold me for the delay of this gesture. "But mostly, I try and tell the truth. You know, as gently as I can."

Our waiter comes back and delivers the food. Scotty hasn't eaten much of his salad, and he doesn't seem interested in the pizza. I am, though, if only for the diversion it provides while I take it apart and put it onto our plates. It's hot, and I have to cut it up and use a fork to eat the first few bites. If Matt were here, he'd be mad at me for allowing the pizza to come out too hot to eat right away.

"I used to get jealous," Scotty says. "I never thought of myself as a possessive person, but on the day I married her, I was so self-satisfied. I thought, this is mine; *she* is mine. We used to wake up two or three hours before I had to leave for work so that we could just *be* together. And then when the kids were born, I was jealous. I was jealous of the time they took up. That makes me sound awful, I know."

"It makes you sound like you really loved her," I say.

"I love the boys too, so much, much more than I thought I was capable of loving anyone, and the fact that she gave them to me made me love her more." Scotty stirs his drink, watching intently as the ice cubes make a little funnel. "We never let them sleep in our bed. We always went in with them to their own rooms if they were having some kind of issue. But never overnight, because we would miss each other. It sounds pretty crazy when I say it, but there it is. That was us." He stops stirring and puts down the straw, and it seems to take him a lot of effort.

"You sound sad, not crazy," I say. "Maybe . . . maybe you can be sad *with* them, you know?" And I have the urge to reach across the table and put my hands around his hands, which are now holding on tightly to his tumbler. Just as the urge is about to overwhelm me, he says, "This pizza is sort of awesome."

"Agreed," I say.

"I thought that Dr. O'Neill would give us a few strategies for dealing with Matt, but he really didn't. He basically said what you just said, only in elaborate terminology," says Scotty.

"Me too," I say. "I mean, I thought so too." I feel solidarity with him, even though it's a purposeless, foolish kind of solidarity. It's surreal, the way life moves on, even if you feel like you're not moving with it.

"Do you need another drink?" Scotty asks and signals to the

waiter before I can translate *I don't think it's a great idea for us to get drunk together* into acceptable words.

But then I think to myself, we might as well drink. Neither one of us will be driving, because neither one of us knows where we're going.

July, the year before

"Why did you say you'd deal with the cupboards later?" Matt seems to be standing behind whichever kitchen cabinet I happen to be opening, putting his cute head at risk of getting smacked with a panel of beautifully carved wood.

"Because we need to get some stuff to put in them, and there's no sense in reorganizing until we have everything."

"Why don't we have everything?"

"Um, I guess we ate it all."

"But why can't we go get it now?"

"Buddy, we're almost out of time for the day."

"Why can't you stay longer?"

"Matty, you're driving me bananas. The day is over. I'm going home, kid."

"But why—"

"You're doing it on purpose!" I grab him and throw him over my shoulder, and he laughs as I deposit him on the couch. George launches himself up from the books he's been looking at and tackles Matt the minute he lands.

"Charlotte, do a sarcastic," Matt says, his voice muffled from the weight of George's conquering stance.

I once asked my father for the meaning of the word *sarcastic*, and he said something that was so hilarious to my young sensibilities that I begged him to come up with more. His examples had turned into a game, something we would do back and forth to make each other laugh, and I taught the game to Matt one day when we were bored on the train.

"Okay," I say. "Matt, I'm so happy that you threw that water balloon in my face just then. It was really, really fun for me."

He laughs, and then it's his turn. "Charlotte, it was so cute when you threw up all over my shoes. It smells really great."

"Eww," I say, laughing, which pretty much ensures that George and Matt will both be making vomit jokes for the foreseeable future. "Matty, you know what would be great? If you climbed into that dumpster and rolled around in it. That would be so precious."

"Pweh-suss, pweh-shush," George shrieks, trying to wrap his mouth around the word, and he is laughing so hard that he slides off Matt and onto the floor, which makes Matt laugh, which makes me laugh. Like a physically disconnected game of chuckle-belly.

Gretchen and Scotty come in the door together then, just in time to hear us all making crazy hyena noises. Gretchen goes for the window right away, and Scotty walks back toward their bedroom, stripping off his tie as he goes.

"Guess who I just saw outside?" Gretchen says. She picks up the binoculars then, and I am onto her, but the boys make a different assumption. Matt starts for the window, but George is faster, so Matt climbs up on the windowsill to wait.

"Me see Pale Male, Mommy?"

"Yes, yes, you can look—careful, Matt; here, why don't you stand behind George. That's right; make sure he doesn't fall, and in a minute it will be your turn." She motions to me, and when I join them at the window, she points to the line of people congregating outside the building across the street.

"You saw him?" I ask.

"Better," she says. "I saw his wife and kids. We talked about a playdate!"

"Oh man," I say. "You'd better warn me in advance so I can at least wear jeans or something."

"Not you too," says Scotty, walking out in shorts and a T-shirt, a very un-Scotty-like ensemble.

"Okay, George, Matt's turn, please," says Gretchen. "Honey, you're not going running in this heat."

"I won't be long."

"Go to the gym. Please? I don't need you stroking out."

"You'd have your new friend across the street to keep you company," he says, and he doesn't kiss her on the cheek like he normally would to accompany a remark like that. I feel awkward, so I move over to monitor the boys' progress in tracking the elusive Pale Male, and out of the corner of my eye, I see Gretchen follow Scotty into the kitchen. I can hear them in fragments, and I'm consciously trying not to listen. But my subconscious is a jackass, and it overrules my consciousness.

"Babe, that's kind of upsetting."

"What?" Scotty says as the water turns on. Maybe he's filling up a water bottle.

"You had a bad day. Don't take it out on me."

"A bad day? The firm is in danger of losing the client. If that happens, I'll have to fire people. That makes it the worst day."

"Do you want me to call—"

"Don't say your father. Do not say your father."

"Okay, you're right. I'm sorry. I want to help. Honey, I don't like it when you let these things destroy your normal shields, is all."

"My normal shields? What is that, some pop-psychology bullsh—"

"You come home and do something you know will make me worry. You act jealous."

"Don't be stupid. I'm not jealous of that—"

"You call me stupid."

"Not stupid. Starstruck."

"What are you doing?" says Gretchen, and I've never heard her voice so sharp. I want to pull out some toy maracas and shake them in the boys' ears so they won't hear. "Are you *trying* to piss me off?"

"The *minute* I get home from *this day*, and you're all over some guy from across the street—"

"Are you kidding me? I'm running your house over here, I'm raising your children, I *met you at the front door* today for God's sake, and you think I'm all over some guy from across the street?"

"This day is not the day to screw around. I have already told you what my day was like—" Scotty is shouting now. Both boys turn to look in the direction of the kitchen, and I try to look unfazed for their sakes. "And you just can't help yourself or something; you have to push my buttons—"

"Because you take yourself so seriously! I told you I could call my father, and he could talk you through this mess with the clients—"

"ARE YOU KIDDING ME—"

"But of course your ego—"

"Mommy," says Matt, jumping down from the window. I make a halfhearted attempt to catch him when he goes for the kitchen, but am glad I don't succeed. What instructions could I give him? This is not for me to solve. "What are you talking about in here?"

There's a silence, and then I hear Gretchen say, "It's just adult stuff, baby. Mommy and Daddy are sorry. Daddy had a bad day at work, and Mommy did something insensitive, so we just need to work it out. But we'll do it later, okay? Don't worry."

Scotty says nothing. George is sliding his hand into mine. He looks thoughtful, as if he's considering his mother's explanation.

"Will you come look in the binoculars? I can't find him," says Matt, and Gretchen lets herself be pulled back into the living room. She doesn't acknowledge what she knows I must have heard, and I'd prefer that she keep up that charade until I leave for the day.

"There he is! Mommy, he's bringing something into the nest—Mommy, look! Look! There's another one, that must be the girlfriend-bird—!"

George yanks his hand out of mine and commands, "ME SEE!" He goes barreling off for the window, and Scotty comes out of the kitchen, his face dripping like maybe he splashed some water on it. Or Gretchen threw it at him?

"Okay, okay, yikes, Georgie, I was just giving them to you," says Matt as he lets George pry the binoculars out of his hands.

"DADDY, ME SEE IT, ME SEE PALE MALE AND PALE MALE GIRLFRIEND-BIRD!" George is so excited that he's bouncing. Gretchen steadies him.

"That's great, son. Can Daddy have a turn? I don't think I've seen him before." George hands the binoculars to Scotty. "Oh yeah. You're right; he's right there. Amazing."

"Good bird spotting, boys," says Gretchen.

Scotty kisses the tops of both boys' heads, then puts his hand on top of Gretchen's hand. She pulls it away, in a casual way that I'm sure is meant to send different messages to the boys and to Scotty.

"I'm going to the gym," Scotty says, with an edge in his voice. "Back in half an hour."

Gretchen watches him go out the door and then looks back out the window. There's a little more hustle to the line of people outside the building across the street, and we watch as people start to stream out the front doors.

"Quick! Boys," says Gretchen. "Give Charlotte a turn with the binoculars. Charlotte wants to see Pale Male!"

April, eight weeks after

Aunt Lila has brought the kids back from Connecticut later than normal on Sunday evening, and George is drooping in the doorway, too tired to move across the threshold. Matt looks sullen, and I wonder what the report will be this time, not that I expect to hear it from Aunt Lila. Of all the people who seem to be uncomfortable about our current living arrangement, Aunt Lila is the most skeptical and the most vocal about it. She prefers to speak to anyone except me about how the kids are faring over weekends spent at her house.

"Hello, Charlotte," she says. There is resentment on her face. She resents that she doesn't have a key to this apartment. She resents Scotty for not taking her suggestion and moving the kids to Connecticut. She resents Gretchen for dying.

"Hi, Lila. Hi, pals," I say, and Matt leaves all of his stuff in a pile on the floor in the hallway and walks into the apartment with his shoes on. I let him go; I don't want to have a battle in front of Aunt Lila, and Scotty is not here to run interference. I don't know where he is, in fact. He could be at work. He could be out at a monster-truck rally.

"Georgie, can you come through the door so Aunt Lila can get in?" I say. "Thanks, buddy." He comes in about six inches and then sits down on the floor with his hand on his foot, like he is trying to muster up the strength to take off his shoe. I kneel down to help him.

"Is Scotty here?" Aunt Lila asks.

"No," I say. I focus on helping George with his coat. She can think whatever she wants to, but I won't help her along.

"Do you know when he'll be back?"

Oh wait. Actually, he is here! Let me just run back to our mangled bed and tell him to throw on some pants. "No. I'm sorry. George, can you go and pick out which pj's you'd like to wear tonight? I'll bring your stuff back in a minute."

"Have to wash hands," he says, and his voice is scratchy, like maybe he fell asleep in the car. I hope he doesn't get a second wind.

"Okay," I say. "You can wash your hands first."

"Matt have to wash hands too."

"I know, bug." Why is Lila still standing in the doorway? "Matt will wash his hands in a minute, but you don't need to worry about him, okay?"

Georgie doesn't stand up but kind of pulls himself across the floor with his hands and scoots his knees along behind him.

Aunt Lila is pressing her lips together and texting. Probably mean, sordid things, about me, to Mae.

"Do you want me to write Scotty a note to call you when he gets back?" I don't ask about the kids. I know she won't tell me.

"Sure, sure, that would be fine," she says. "See you next weekend," she calls. Neither boy responds.

"Boys, can you say good-bye to Aunt Lila?" I call after her.

"Byeeeee," moans George. Matt mumbles something from the TV room. Aunt Lila is back out the door before I can ask them to say good-bye properly.

"Matt, did something happen at Aunt Lila's?" I walk into the family room and click off the TV, which he has turned on without permission.

"I was just trying to help with the pie," Matt says, looking a little teary.

"What pie?" I sit down next to him. "Aunt Lila didn't mention anything, so maybe you can tell me what happened? That way I'll know what to say to your dad when he hears about it."

"Georgie accidentally got knocked over," Matt says. "But he didn't get burned! The stove was on. I didn't see him!"

"You were trying to help with the pie, and you accidentally ran into Georgie, and you knocked him toward the oven, but he didn't touch it? Just almost?"

"Yeah," says Matt, and I'm either a sucker for his tears, or he's telling the truth.

"Did you get in trouble?"

"I had a time-out until we were coming back. I want to watch TV, Charlotte."

"Did you have dinner?"

"I didn't like it." He looks defeated and sad.

"Was it something *really* awful, like mung beans and tofu?"

He doesn't laugh. "No. It was chicken that Mary made, and

Aunt Lila said I was hurting her feelings. But it was yucky. Can I please watch a show?"

"In a minute," I say. "Sometimes, when you don't like something, there's a more polite way to say you don't want any. Like, no thank you, or I don't really care for chicken, but could I have an extra roll please?" He smiles a little. "I'll make you something. But let me get George in bed first, okay?" I say, and he nods. "George ate dinner, right?" He nods again. I click the TV back on for him.

George is on the floor of his room with no pants or underwear or socks on and his shirt kind of stuck all bunched up around his neck. I help him get the shirt off and put on his pajamas; then we brush teeth and get into bed.

"You want a story, little buggie?"

"No tory. Mine tummy feels full," he says.

"Does it hurt?" I put my hand on his forehead. He doesn't seem warm, but I check the back of his neck too. He is nodding. "Would you rather go right to sleep?" He nods again. This is very unlike him. More than anything, he loves his routine. "Okay, love. You can go to sleep. Good night, honey, I'll see you in the morning. I'll send Daddy in to kiss you when he comes home." I say this every night, and it never happens, but the boys are sleeping, so I prefer to think that *they* think it's happening. I turn out the light, head back to the kitchen, and slap together a turkey sandwich for Matt, with some steamed Brussels sprouts on the side. The silly kid loves Brussels sprouts but won't touch certain types of cheese. This is a Gretchen triumph, for sure.

After his dinner, I let Matt play in the bathtub for half an hour, so by the time he gets in bed, it's almost twenty minutes past his normal bedtime. As I'm tucking him in, he reaches up and holds me around the neck. He doesn't seem to want to let go, so I stand there, half hunched over, ignoring the pull in my back muscles, until he is ready to release me.

"I had a dream I was Pale Male's friend," Matt says.

"Oh yeah? Could you fly?"

"Yes, but I lived in the park, and I couldn't land on his building because there were pigeon spikes."

"Was it fun to fly?" I ask him.

"Yes," he says. "But I was scared."

"I think I'd be scared too, that high up," I say.

"I wasn't scared to fly, I was only scared because I didn't know anyone. I couldn't talk to George or Daddy or Gramma. Or you or anybody. I was just a bird. I couldn't talk at all," he says. "And I couldn't chirp to Pale Male because I couldn't get on the building."

"Were there any other birds you could chirp to?" I ask him.

"No," he says. "There weren't any other birds. I was alone."

"Well, I'm glad it was just a dream," I say, "cause I like talking to you." I kiss him on the forehead. "Goodnight, love bug." I click off the light. I shut his door and stand in the hallway for a minute before I go back out to the living room to pick up and do the dishes.

Half an hour later, I have cued up a trashy TV marathon for myself and am about to place a food order online when sudden, hysterical crying comes from down the hall. At first I think it's Matt, and I hurry to his room, but when I open the door, Matt is asleep with his covers up over his head. The cries are coming from George. In his room, I can make out his silhouette sitting up in bed, and something smells disgusting.

"I'm sorry, buddy. I'm turning on the light," I say, and when I flip on his bedside lamp, I can see he's covered in vomit, sitting in a pool of it, all over his pillows and sheets and Chickie and the rest of his unfortunate comrades. He must have thrown up multiple times before he was even able to cry.

"Oh George, oh buddy, oh no," I say. "It's okay, Georgie. We'll clean you up, okay? I'm sorry, pal."

"Tummy huuurrrrrrt," he wails, and I pick him up and run

to the bathroom, holding him out in front of me with my arms almost all the way extended.

I sit him down on the floor when we get there, pull back the shower curtain, and start running the water into the tub, trying to get it to a gentle temperature, willing it to get there quickly.

"If you feel like you have to throw up again, lean over the potty, okay?"

"Want Puuuup," he sobs. I pull the neck of his pajama top wide so that it won't touch his face as I pull it off over his head. "Don't like it, don't liiiiiiike it!"

"I know, Georgie. We're going to clean you up," I say, and I pull off his pants and underpants and his little fuzzy sleep socks. As soon as he is naked, he kneels in front of the toilet and manages to get all the vomit in the bowl. Unfortunately, it is now coming out the other end too, all over the floor.

I want to cuss like a sailor. Georgie is weak and weepy, literally sitting in a pile of shit. I take off my own socks and roll up my pants, then take off my shirt so that I'm only wearing a tank top. I lift him up and set him in the tub. All he can do is sit there and cry as I run the water over him, wipe his face, wipe his bum, and try not to kneel in the diarrhea on the floor. When he is clean, I plug the tub until it fills up about six inches; then I let him lie back with his head on a towel pillow as I run out to the hall and root through the closet for something to clean up the floor. I leave the bathroom door open so I can see him, and I grab an old towel, a bottle of bleach tile cleaner, a roll of paper towels, and a plastic bag for garbage. I run back toward the bathroom. The chicken! The chicken that Lila's teenage daughter made, probably undercooked, and then force-fed to the boys. I want to call Lila up and take my foul mouth out on her. Just as I decide that's a productive course of action, George sits up and vomits again, right into the tub.

"Holy shit," I whisper. "Shit, shit, shit, shitty shit!" I press my fingertips to both sides of my nose and suck the tears back up into my eye sockets. George is crying and splashing at the water, trying to keep all the yucky stuff away from his body. I throw the old towel down over the stain on the floor and pet his head while trying to avoid the little splashes.

"Honey, please don't do that. Let me drain the water, and we'll wash you off again," I say. I don't hear the key in the latch or footsteps in the hallway, but before I can stand up to retrieve the shower head, Scotty walks into the bathroom. He detaches the nozzle and holds it out to me.

"Daddyyyyy," George wails, and I'm about to suggest that Scotty roll up his sleeves, but he is already doing it. He kneels down next to me as I rinse George yet again. Then Scotty helps George lie back against the towel.

"Hi, baby George," says Scotty. "Are you not feeling good?"

"Tummy hurrrrrt," George moans.

"Food poisoning," I say, trying to keep a tone in my voice that won't alarm Georgie. "Undercooked chicken, I think. Mary made dinner, Matt said."

"Is Matt sick?" asks Scotty.

"No," I say, and I laugh at the irony. "Matt refused to eat it. He said it tasted yucky. He got in trouble."

Scotty looks amused also, thank God, or I'd be such a horrible jackass. "Did you call Lila to see if she was sick?"

"No." Lila doesn't want to talk to me.

Scotty pulls out his phone and sends her a text. A minute later, he gets one back.

"Yep, they're all sick," he says. "Mary hasn't stopped throwing up in the last hour, so they're taking her to the ER to get a hydrating IV, Lila tells me." I shouldn't feel vindicated, or satisfied, but I do. I feel both of those things. They poisoned George.

"Do you think we need to take him?" I ask, and I hope he's not having the same horrid ER flashbacks that I am, but he probably is.

"Let's wait a little bit and see how bad it gets," Scotty says. "He might work it out earlier, since he's littler and probably ate less."

"Maybe we should just leave him in the tub then." George's eyes are drooping, and it looks like he's about to go to sleep. I hand Scotty a towel, and he covers George with it.

"Don't move that towel in front of the toilet." I stand up on painful knees. "There's a mess under it. I was about to clean it up. I need to throw his bedding in the wash too."

"Oh man, Charlotte, I can do that. It's really awful," Scotty says. "You stay here with him. I can clean up."

"I think he wants you," I say. "He calmed down once you got here. He's so sick. You stay. I don't mind." Scotty shifts off his knees to sit on the floor, with one hand in the tub, stroking Georgie's forehead.

Back out in the hall, I plow through the closet until I find some rubber gloves, and I snap them on. I strip George's bed and put the bedding in the washer, along with Chickie and the other animals.

"I can't believe Matt didn't wake up," Scotty says, after I throw the clothes in and start the laundry and then return to deal with the bathroom floor. There's absolutely no way to look graceful and effortlessly competent when you're scrubbing crap off the bathroom floor, so I don't even try.

"He's a heavy sleeper. They both are." I start stuffing all the rags into the trash bag. "Okay if I ditch this towel?"

"Please," he says.

"I don't know if I'll ever eat chicken again," I say, sitting down against the base of the toilet. And there we stay for the rest of the night, jumping every time George tosses or turns. In the wee hours of the morning, when I wake up with my head on the toilet, I see a sleeping Scotty holding a sleeping George's hand over the rim of the tub, and I decide that it's perfectly okay to let them sleep it off in the bathroom.

February, twelve days after

Georgie sits on the floor, his lower lip jutting out. We are forty-five minutes into naptime, and no one is sleeping. The way he keeps listing to one side with droopy eyes is cute and funny and mildly exasperating, but he will not admit he's tired and get into bed. Every time I suggest it, all he says is "Pup," and then he returns to the serious business of holding a Lego in one hand and barely moving.

"You can be with Pup if you get in bed," I say. "But Pup needs to stay put, you know that."

"Pup not in my bed," he says.

"Did you leave him in another room?"

"Pup not here."

"Well, he has to be here somewhere." I pull back the bedspread. "Please get in bed, George. I'll look for Pup while you're having your rest time."

"Pup going on an adventure."

"Where did you put him, honey? In Matt's room?"

"We missing Pup."

I pick through the pillows, animals, covers, and glance between the wall and the bed, but he is right. Pup is not in his bed. I look underneath the furniture, in the animal hamper, in the closet, and in the multiple bins of toys, but I don't see even a wink of golden fur.

George finally gives up and topples over sideways. I pick him up off the floor. He gets a few good shin kicks in before I get him to his bed, but once he is there, he stays put.

"I'm going out to look around while you rest, buddy. When you wake up, I bet I will have located that tricky little doggy."

"Tahr-lette, Pup gone." I don't answer George this time because I'm sure he's projecting Pup onto Gretchen, or something else heartbreaking and deeply psychological.

An hour later, I'm not so convinced. I have been through

Matt's room, the bathrooms, looked under all the guest beds, and opened every drawer, cupboard, and bin, which is no small feat in this apartment.

Mae is in the living room, watching a cooking show with no sound and knitting something that looks like it will one day become a large poncho.

"Mae," I say, "do you have any idea where George's little dog got to? That stuffed golden retriever? Pup? Did he maybe take it somewhere, like on an outing?"

"I haven't seen it," says Mae. "He's been asking for it since the morning after, the morning we were home from the hospital. But I haven't seen it anywhere."

"I thought we brought him home from the hospital," I say. "But maybe we didn't."

I call the hospital, and they pass me around to multiple departments. No one has seen Pup. They all seem sympathetic though, like they want to help, so I believe that they are looking. I thank the last person I speak to and tell her I'll come by and look around at some point.

On a whim, I call the NYC taxi authority. I'm on hold for almost twenty minutes, and when I finally speak to someone, he tells me they don't have anything like that in their facility. Like he could have looked all the way through their inventory in the five seconds of silence that elapsed after I asked.

George wakes up soon after, and he doesn't ask me about Pup, doesn't seem at all surprised that I haven't found him. But I spend the rest of the day, the week, the month opening doors I think I haven't checked around yet, and then holding back tears when it turns out that neither Pup nor Gretchen is hiding behind them.

April, eight weeks after

Poisoned little George wakes up one more time, around 4 a.m. in order to dry heave and let go of the rest of his meal out the other end. I am asleep on top of the bed in the guest room closest to the bathroom when I hear him and Scotty moving around. I spring out of bed, my heart pounding like it always does when I wake up suddenly. At the end of the hall, I can see Scotty kneeling on the bathroom floor, with his knees on either side of the toilet, holding George's tired body upright while he finishes up on the potty. I go into Georgie's room and unearth some clean clothes and a pull-up diaper that is left over from six or seven months ago to give to Scotty.

"We probably need to keep him home from school," I say, as Scotty helps half-sleeping Georgie into the new pajamas. "I'll have to take him with me when I drop off Matt though."

"I can be a little late to work," says Scotty. "I'll stay until you get back."

"Are you sure?" I say.

"I think I need the sleep, anyway," he says.

I'm glad he wants to sleep. It seems like it's been a while since he did anything other than stay up late in some corner of the house. "I'm going to pull out the trundle and sleep in George's room," I say. "Just in case he's got anything, you know, left in there."

"Thank you, Charlotte. God, that was . . . kind of *harrowing*, wasn't it? Watching him get so sick."

"Yeah," I say. Scotty picks up Georgie. I go in to kiss his sickly little cheek, and Scotty hugs me around George. I guess maybe it looked like I was leaning in for that reason? I'd rather pretend that there's nothing awkward about this moment, so I kiss the side of George's head a few times and hug Scotty back, then let him carry Georgie in and deposit him on his bed.

After the animals have been liberated from the dryer, I throw in the stuff from the washer and turn it on, feeling a pang in my chest that George has obviously been missing Pup without mentioning it. I pull out the trundle in George's room and am reminding myself just to doze and not to fall asleep, when all of a sudden, Matt is calling me.

"Charlotte?"

I sit up. It feels like no time has passed, but the sun is super bright all of a sudden.

"Did you sleep in here?"

"Yeah," I say, and I rub my eyes. The sun is so bright. The sun. Is so. Bright? "Oh no!" I say, and I sit up. "Matt, what time is it; do you know?"

He's unconcerned with the time. "Why did you sleep in George's room?"

"George got sick. The chicken made him sick. We were up very late." I look at the clock. 8:17—no way will I make it to school with Matt by 8:30. Crap.

"Chicken made him sick?" Matt looks worried.

"Not all chicken. Just *that* chicken. You were right; it was yucky," I say as I run down the hall, into the kitchen, and start throwing things into his lunch box. "Matt, do you want these tiny oranges in your lunch?"

"Can you peel them?"

"I will peel them if you run back right now and put some clothes on, as fast as you can."

"Are we late?"

"Yes, but we'll only be a little bit late if we do this really, really fast. Okay? Help me out, pal."

"But what about Georgie?"

"He has to stay home, Matt. He threw up a lot last night."

"Because of that yucky chicken?" Matt, like me, may have lost his taste for chicken forever.

"Yes. Can you please put on your clothes?"

To my surprise, he runs back into the hallway. I peel three little oranges and then have just enough time to run back to my own room and change my shirt before he's back out.

We both put on our shoes, and I tell him we can stop for a bagel on the way to school. Matt suggests that we get one for Georgie too, for when he's feeling better, which melts me a little, so I agree. Gretchen would totally kill me. She would understand our being late, and the finger-food lunch, and even the fact that Matt had to be the one to wake *me* up. But a bagel, made from refined sugar and processed flour—*that*, she would rip me a new one for.

When I get back to the apartment, Scotty is dressed for work, sitting on the couch with a pale, mostly sleeping Georgie. He is holding the newspaper in one hand and one of Georgie's little feet in the other, and for a moment, I'm convinced from the look on his face that there's no way he'll be going to work, no way he'll be leaving his son. But the minute he spots me, the look changes to one of relief, and he stands up to leave. He is out the door a few minutes later, and I'm left with an odd feeling, wondering what might have happened if I hadn't walked through the door.

Valentine's Day

Patrick holds the taxi door open. "Are we going to your place or mine?" Then he slides in next to me as I give the cab driver my address.

The thing is, it would be so easy. So easy to make him feel better for a little while, so easy to let him make *me* feel better. Patrick puts my bags down in the space between us.

When we arrive at my apartment, we both get out, and he pays the driver. We stand on the sidewalk for a minute, and I don't want to be the first one to speak, but someone has to, or this charade will go too far. We're both waiting for the other to cry uncle.

"I thought you were, you know, making an inappropriate joke," I say. "But here you are. Did you want to grab a cup of tea or something?"

"Matthew made a sarcastic comment to me the last time I saw him," says Patrick. "At the time, I wondered where he learned it. Scotty and Gretchen can be—could be—funny, but they're not sarcastic. Now I get it."

"He's a funny kid," I say. "Some might even call him hilarious."

"I'm coming upstairs," says Patrick. "And when you want me to leave, all you need to do is say so." I want to protest. I don't want to be alone. I settle for not saying anything, turning toward my apartment and letting us both in the front door.

I don't turn on the light right away when we get in because I can't remember if I washed my breakfast dishes or hung underwear to dry in the bathroom. Then I think about how petty those things are, so I flip on the hall lights and dump my stuff under the coatrack.

"There are wineglasses in the cupboard above the sink." I take out the warmest clothes I can possibly sleep in and go into the bathroom. I shut the door, taking off most of my clothes. Everything I'm wearing is damp, and I feel cold down into the bottom of my lungs. I come back out to the living room to find Patrick swilling vodka out of the cheap bottle on my counter, and a very full goblet of wine waiting for me.

We drink, and my mind plays the events of the day in repeated fragments, like a cable box in a windstorm. Patrick is restless, not seeming to want to be still. He walks around the perimeter of my tiny living room with his bottle, stopping next to the piano. He pushes one of the keys down, so slowly that it doesn't make a sound. "You know those horrible days, the ones where someone shoots up a school, or a bunch of kids die in a bus crash, or somebody sets off a couple of car bombs?"

"Yeah." I open the cupboard I keep my dishes in. I want to find a glass to pour his vodka into, to make sure we have a way to measure how much he's actually drinking.

"And you know the days that follow it, the media circus, the vigils, all the sad people on the news, the way you feel when you think about doing something normal in the face of such heartbreak?"

"Yeah." I have to approach him to take the bottle away. He gives it to me without an argument. I pour him a glass and put the vodka away in the cupboard above the refrigerator.

"I always felt like I never knew the appropriate way to mourn those things. What's the right thing to do? Embrace love as the enemy of hate? Live your life like there might not be a tomorrow? Wallow? Is there a *right way* to do it, do you think?"

"Probably not."

Patrick sets his glass on the counter, and I feel like I can hear all the blood rushing to my face. He sits down, finally, on the piano bench. "This tragedy, this personal tragedy, that's not at all national, that nobody knows about but us—will I be able to use it as an excuse for as long as it is actually affecting me? I don't know how to do this. I can't imagine how I'll ever get over her. And I'm only thinking about me here. No Scotty, no Matthew, no George, and no Gretchen's family in the mix. Just me. How will I ever get over this?"

"I don't know," I say. And I mean it with my whole heart.

"Do you want to go to bed?" he says, and I do.

He gets undressed, and we get under the covers. Then we close our eyes on the worst day we've ever known, and we sleep.

May, ten weeks after

The boys spend one more weekend with Aunt Lila, but by two weeks past the food-poisoning incident, we stop shipping them off to Connecticut on Friday nights. I suspect it's due to some chicken-related trust issue. I'm now on duty seven days a week. No one ever asked me if I was okay with that, but neither did I give any indication that I might not be. I'm still pretty pissed at Lila for the whole ordeal. It has been two and a half months since we lost

Gretchen, and the multiple therapists this family employs have all said pretty much the same thing—that this first year, with its many milestones, is going to be one of the most difficult that these three guys will ever live through. The first birthday without her. The first Fourth of July without her. The first new school year without her. The first Christmas, the first time we walk by her favorite restaurant, the first time we visit all the places we've been with her. Those things will happen, and we will anticipate them and agonize about them, and then we will live through them. And the next birthday won't ever have to be the first one without her again.

We seem to have come to a mutual agreement in this house not to mention Gretchen in front of Scotty. Even Matt is on board. For the life of me, I can't think of the last time I heard someone say her name, and I'm starting to feel paranoid about what will happen when someone finally does. We've fallen into a routine that covers all the loose ends, that neatly constructs the allegation that maybe she never existed at all. Denial holds the walls up here.

"Mom wants to know if you need money, but she doesn't want to insult you," says Jane in my ear as I'm walking to my own apartment, after dropping the boys at school. I haven't seen my apartment in a few weeks. "She wanted me to do some reconnaissance, but I thought it would be easier just to ask you."

"I don't need money," I say. "I've never needed money less."

"When you stop calling her, it's usually because you're ashamed of something, like a lack of money. Are you? Ashamed of yourself for some reason?"

"What?"

"Her words, her words, my little chicken pot pie. Hey, you're not doing Scotty's laundry are you? That might be cause for a little bit of shame."

"It's just part of my job."

"What a weird job."

"Well," I say, "I guess we can't all be stable and traditional like you."

"It's still laundry. It's not exactly unbridled freedom. You've been in a holding pattern with these people for more than two years now. Maybe, and I'm not saying tomorrow, but maybe someday soon, you'll go and find a different job."

"You're right," I say. "Probably not tomorrow." I cross York Avenue and consider ducking into my usual coffee place, but I'm already running a few minutes behind. "I have to go now, Janie Doodle McPoodle. Tell Mom I'm rich, will you?"

"She'll never believe me."

"Rude! Hey, here's a cliffhanger for you. Everett's scarf was at Jess's apartment the day I was there, and she left it out for me to see."

"Ew. Oh god. Ew. What does it even mean?"

"I'm going to find out right now. He's sitting on my doorstep."

"Intrigue. Scandal. The plot—"

"I have to go now."

"Bye, love-goose."

"Bye, love-pony." I hang up. I climb my front steps. Everett stands up to greet me. "You got here fast," I say, brushing past him so he can't do anything to throw me off my game, like kiss me or say something to make me want to have sex with him.

"I borrowed a car. Which sister was that on the phone?"

"Who says it was a sister?"

"You're calling someone else love-pony?"

"It was Jane," I say, unlocking my apartment door and letting us both in. "Ugh, it kind of stinks in here. You know what I should do? Clean out the refrigerator."

"While we're here, you want to clean out the refrigerator? That's what you want to do?"

"Yes. I didn't even think of that when I was packing up. I hope there's nothing disgusting in there."

Everett opens the window next to the piano and drags the bench closer. "Can you hand me an ashtray?"

I hand him a chipped ice cream dish and open the fridge. "Yikes. I think there used to be a head of lettuce in the bottom drawer, but it seems to have passed on. Into, like, a different material state."

"How are you here right now?" he asks, attempting to exhale through the screen. The wind blows the cloud of smoke back at him, and he waves his hand around to disperse it.

"The kids are in school."

"And the dad is at work?"

"Yeah."

"What did you tell him?" Everett asks. "I mean, I'm curious what you tell him when you're going out, or if you tell him that you're not coming home, or whatever."

"I didn't tell him."

"Charlotte." Everett's face can change so quickly. He has put out his cigarette, stood up, and made it halfway across my living room before I've even looked up from the fridge. "You fucking snuck out of the house? Like you're seventeen or something? That is so fucked up." He is laughing, but the way he says it makes me feel responsible and guilty. "But I get it. It's kind of hot." He pulls on the waistband of my leggings. He doesn't look into my eyes or try to hold my face, but he does spread his hand on the small of my back underneath my shirt.

"Hold your horses," I say.

"Hold my love-ponies?"

"I called to ask you about something."

"You had to ask me in person?"

"I wanted to see your face."

"You could have said you trapped a roach or something, needed me to come and kill it for you."

"Did you go home with Jess? The night of your concert, I mean."

"No, I didn't. But I like it that you think I'm that smooth."

I open the fridge again so that the door is between us, and I start pulling out all the condiments to check the expiration dates. "I don't know if I believe you."

"Why would I lie?"

"She has your scarf."

"Yes, she does. I gave it to her."

I pitch a six-month-old bottle of thousand-island dressing into the garbage can. "Did you offer it to her? Or did she ask for it?"

"I don't remember. I might have been a little preoccupied that night."

"Can you please just try?"

"I think she said she had to walk a few blocks, and would I mind letting her borrow it, and that she would return it or send it back. Or something like that. Did you think I was sleeping with her?"

"I mean, I wondered. It wasn't as accusatory in my mind as all that."

"But you thought I might sleep with her? While I was sleeping with you?"

"You're not sleeping with me."

"Well, not right now, I'm not."

"But I mean. You know what I mean. You can sleep with whoever you want."

"Shit," he says, and I'm relieved to realize that the worry in his eyes makes me feel like laughing. "Do we need to have a talk?"

"God. No." I hear a buzzing noise, and I jump a little. "Hold on a minute." Scotty McLean, says the readout on my phone. "I have to answer this," I say and move away from the refrigerator to stand in front of the window. "Hello?"

"Simon is here," says Scotty, and I try not to mind that he doesn't say hello back to me, because he sounds distressed. "I didn't know he was coming. He came alone. Mae's still in Chicago."

"Did he show up at your office?"

"No, I'm at the courthouse."

Everett bends down to put his ear right next to my phone. I move away from him. "Is the trial today?"

"It's not really a trial. He pleaded guilty; his attorneys have already entered the plea. But now he has to be sentenced, and Simon came to hear the proceedings. He's restless. I don't know what he's here for, what he wants to do."

This is beyond the call of a babysitter, and even though no question has been asked, I feel like whatever I say will be the equivalent of signing my name to a new contract or tearing up the old one.

"What do you want me to do?" I say.

"When you pick up George from school, could you come down here with him? Maybe seeing his grandson will make Simon forget whatever retaliatory agenda he came to push," he says.

"It could add more fuel to the fire," I say.

"I'm not saying it's not a risk," Scotty says. "But it's the only thing I can think of. Will you come?"

"Text me the address," I say, and he says thank you with more relief in his voice than I can handle emotionally. I hang up the phone. The last thing I need is to start bawling and have Everett think it has anything to do with the fact that I suspected him of sleeping with Jess.

"You have to go?" he asks.

"I do. Please believe me when I say I had no idea that phone call was coming though." I grab my jacket and keys and start tying up the trash bag with all the rotten food in it. It would be very unfortunate to have it come undone halfway down the stairs.

"I'll wait for you," says Everett.

"There is no way that I will make it back here tonight," I say. "I'm sorry."

"You know," he says, "I believe that you really are. I wish that it made me less pissed at you."

I open the door and wait for him to walk through it. He

doesn't offer to take the heavy garbage bag from me, so I haul it out into the hallway and lock the door behind me. We walk down the stairs without saying anything, our out-of-sync footsteps the only noise.

He watches me struggle to open the dumpster with one hand, and after I've dumped the trash bag in and gotten the lid closed, he's still standing on the sidewalk, looking at me.

"Some things are more important than money," I say.

"I know."

"Some things are more important than my art, than art in general."

"I know that." Everett pulls a set of car keys out of his pocket. I wonder how long it took him to find a parking spot in this neighborhood.

"Okay."

"Now are you going to tell me that some things are more important than friendship? Is that what's next?"

I reach for his hand, and he takes a step back. I step forward and grab it anyway, even though he doesn't want me to. "Love is not a limited resource, like oil. There's an infinite amount. Okay?"

Eventually, I have to let go of him and catch a cab if I'm going to get to Georgie on time.

"ME RIDE IN the troller?" George and I are on the sidewalk outside the courthouse, and neither one of us is in a good mood.

"I didn't bring the stroller. You walked today, remember?"

"You hold me?"

"I have a lot of stuff, Georgie. Can you please try to walk a little bit? Just to those big doors."

"Want somebody to hold me!" George says, and when I don't say anything, he is insistent. "Tahr-lette, you hold me? I want you to hold me! Tahr-lette! TAHR-LETTE!" My resolve not to let him get what he wants by throwing a tantrum is wavering in the face of my need to get him where I want him to go. He starts to make a loud, tearless cry-noise and cry-face as I dump our things onto the ground and squat down to concentrate on their consolidation. George stamps his foot once and then again.

"Please don't get so angry with me, George. I need you to wait a second so I can get organized, and then I will see if I can carry you. But not if you're going to yell at me. That hurts my feelings, and I don't like it."

He stops making the noise but stamps his foot again. "I'm sorry that you're frustrated, love. When we get inside, we'll find your dad and your grampa, and we'll figure out a snack for you."

I finally manage to shove everything into one bag, pick up George with the other arm, and secure my hands under his bottom. It works until we get to security and have to wait in line to pass through. I keep trying to put George down, but he is clinging to my neck and refusing to let go, which makes dismantling our bag much more strenuous.

We find the court we're looking for at the end of an empty hallway. It reminds me of a middle school classroom, which is not at all how I pictured such a fate-deciding room. Simon Edgerly is sitting outside the door on a long wooden bench, next to another man. They are both wearing expensively cut suits, and as I release George, and he starts to run down the hall in their direction, I realize that the other man is Scotty.

He is different, but I can't put my finger on why. It's like all the calm, all the dullness that had settled in, has dissolved. In this person I can see a stirring, a motion under the surface. A digital image with a higher pixelation. A man who is no longer comfortable blocking out his consciousness. Georgie can see it too, this awakening of sorts, and he runs to him as if he knows his real dad has come back to obliterate the impostor. It takes me longer to identify him than it took George though, as if they are on the outside of a cloud I'm still stuck in. It should feel like a return to the Scotty of yore, and it should overwhelm me with joy, but there's an edge I can see now that I've never seen in his face before. So instead of recognition, I have this feeling of foreboding. If we are out of denial, where are we headed?

Simon, on the other hand, is in a familiar posture, a posture I am comfortable with. He looks heavy, like a rebel who has won his war and has no idea what to do next, and therefore sits immersed in his memories, his grief, his deflated passion. He doesn't move a muscle as Georgie reaches the end of the hall and flings himself into his father's lap, not even a tiny flinch. There is no acknowledgment of me or of his grandson, no trace of Mae's courageous faith, and as I approach, I am desperate for a clue to what's been happening between Scotty's phone call and now.

Scotty looks at me with burning eyes and says, "It's over. They just read out the sentence. He's getting pretty close to the maximum, but he'll have the possibility of parole. I think that was part of the plea bargain. He wasn't drunk. He wasn't on drugs. He wasn't texting. He just didn't pay attention. He wasn't paying attention, and her life is over."

For a moment, all I can think is, it's not real. That can't be the end of her life, a moment of inattention.

"Are they still inside?" I say.

"Yes," he says. I don't have to ask what we're waiting for.

When the door opens, several men walk out, one in handcuffs, with a teary-eyed woman and a uniformed officer trailing them. As they pass, Simon speaks for the first time since we got there.

"That's the man who killed your mother," he says.

George's eyes track the handcuffed man down the hallway, and for a moment, I think I see compassion flash across his little face.

SIMON STAYS WITH us for a week, and for the life of me, I can't figure out why he is hanging around. He doesn't help with the kids. He doesn't eat dinner with the family. He doesn't even hang around the house. As far as I can tell, he goes out and walks around all day, not downtown or to any of the tourist attractions, but from east to west through the park and all around our neighborhood. He doesn't say it, but it's almost as if he is looking for Gretchen, taking in her old haunts and trying to reconstruct her trajectory.

Scotty is gentle with him. I keep waiting for him to call Mae so she can organize a retrieval, but he doesn't. Eventually, something shifts, because Simon tells us he'll be leaving the next day. But whatever the change, it is invisible to my eyes, as if it's happening underground, and I try not to worry that there'll be an earthquake or some kind of volcanic eruption somewhere down the line.

George is in his room, alternately pleading and demanding to come out, having been punished for picking a tulip from someone's window box after being told not to. I try my best not to be one of those adults who punishes a kid because I'm embarrassed by their behavior, but this incident pushed all of my shame buttons, particularly when I was being ripped a new asshole in the middle of the sidewalk by the woman who lived there for not "SUPERVISING MY CHILDREN" properly. George refused to apologize to her, and when we got home, I told him he could come out when he was ready to say he was sorry to me for having to endure the consequences of *his* actions.

That was forty-five minutes ago. Every time I go to check on him, he wants to show me something or play a game, but he refuses to acknowledge why he's being punished. I am so frustrated that I can't even laugh with Scotty when he gets home from work, hears the story, and then dubs the tulip the "shame flower" and puts it in a vase in the kitchen.

"Does that mean you think I should let him out?" I say.

"No. But I don't want this beautiful, hard-won tulip to go to waste." Scotty dips a piece of ancient-grained bread into the spaghetti sauce I'm stirring. "This is great. What are we eating it on?"

"Brown rice rotini with eggplant and turkey meatballs," I say. "Maybe you should talk to George. I'm spectacularly ineffective right now. He's looking at me like I'm making the honking noise from Charlie Brown every time I say something. And then he asks me if I want to see Chickie wear a diaper."

"You're upset about this," Scotty says, in his even-keeled lawyer tone, leaning his hip on the counter. I want to fling spaghetti sauce at him off my spoon.

"Well. Yes. Mostly about what that woman said. She was kind of right. George has ignored everything I've said, all afternoon," I say.

"That's just kids," says Scotty. I'm not sure he could have picked a more infuriating phrase. "Do you want me to try? Not that I think I'll get different results. But I want him to know we're together on this, and it's not just mean Sheriff Charlotte raining down the law on the cowboys."

Before I can answer, Grampa Simon appears in the doorway, holding George by the hand. George looks solemn.

"Tahr-lette," he says, and I sigh, because his eyes are shiny, and I'm a sucker.

"Yeah, bug?"

"Tahr-lette, sow-ee I picked that flower, sow-ee you're mad," he says, and I don't know what the version of events in his head looks like, or why he thinks I'm mad, but I can tell that he's sincere.

"Okay, buddy, I forgive you. Where's Chickie's diaper?"

"He fell out of my bed," he says and runs back down the hall, ostensibly to retrieve the diaper-bottomed Chickie. Scotty hands me an oven mitt, and I take the sauce pot off the burner.

"Thank you," I say to Simon. "How did you get him to do that?"

"I told him it's important to make sure that the people you love know that you love them, and when their feelings are hurt, you have to make it right while you can." I have a flash of understanding, right then and there. This man will never get over losing his daughter. The rest of us will be changed, for sure. We will always be different, even after we move on—Lila, Mae, the kids, Scotty. But her father has shown no sign that he will ever move on.

"Well, thank you," I say. There's not a lot of point in saying anything else. Scotty is setting out bowls and forks, offering no indication as to whether he is taking in this conversation or not. As to whether George will now live his life in the constant fear that everyone he loves will die, I suppose that will have to be dealt with later. Simon putters off to the living room to watch TV with Matt.

"George and I will have to find a way back into your good graces," says Scotty, sliding plates underneath each of the bowls he has set the table with.

"I'm not mad at you," I say.

"Maybe you're not mad, but you're not over it," says Scotty. "I'm determined though. You will be by the end of the night, no matter what I have to do."

All through dinner, Scotty is on. Teasing the boys, deferring to me on small decisions, telling stories about Grampa Simon's business days and how Uncle Patrick and Uncle Max both tried to get Simon to hire them when they heard Scotty and Gretchen were engaged—this is a pre-tragedy side of Scotty. By the end of the meal, I am laughing, mostly because the boys are laughing, and we are all having fun together. There is a moment where Scotty looks at me to assess whether or not he has gotten back to the right side of my graces. He knows he has. Maybe I'm too easy, as Jane and Claudia repeatedly suggest.

After dinner is over, Scotty and the boys bring me dishes to load into the dishwasher, and I can't help thinking that now, three and a half months later, when Gretchen no longer occupies our every waking thought, the time has arrived when our postmortem relationships with her will get more difficult. The memories attached to her will be less black and white, will start to run together into a messy, muddy puddle. Wading out into the middle of a mess and living there until the silt settles around me isn't something I've ever been particularly good at, and the thought keeps me up late that night, questioning whether or not I've ever really seen to the bottom of anything.

PART FOUR

Charlotte

May, eleven weeks after

Scotty, sitting on the couch in sweats, stares at a news anchor reporting on a tornado somewhere in the Midwest. I bring his reheated plate out and hand it to him, and he takes it without looking away from the television. The anchor is a young man, and he is speaking loudly, standing too close for comfort to the disastrous weather as the wind dislodges lawn ornaments from the ground behind him. Scotty is horrified and enraptured, the look on his face similar to those on Matt's and George's every time they watch the dad lion fall off the cliff in their favorite animated movie. I hid that DVD after Gretchen died, though no one has asked for it since then anyway.

"We don't have to watch this," I say. "I was listening to them comment on a statement from the White House while I made dinner, and I never turned it off."

"What do you feel like watching?" Scotty pulls up the channel menu on the screen. He came home just in time to say good night to the boys as they were getting into bed, as he does on most nights, and he and I have fallen into our routine of staring at the same things on the TV screen for the rest of the evening. There have been very few inconsistencies with how we've conducted ourselves as April turned into May. We've gotten along without many disruptions since Simon left, and the feeling that we're working together toward something stable is strange but welcome.

My phone rings, and the number on the caller ID makes my stomach drop: Everett. It feels like I'm getting a call from another lifetime.

I hang up after speaking briefly, trying to make sense of the date and time of the concert Jess invited us to, but I can't make the details work together in my head. Scotty is looking at me for an explanation. Neither of us answers our phones very often, preferring to behave like agoraphobes and text back the answers to voice mails, so I understand why he would succumb to the urge to pry once he's overheard my plans.

"What's at the Park Avenue Armory?" He turns the television volume down a few notches.

"Something I have to dress up for," I say. "I'm not sure I can walk there in heels though, so maybe I just won't go."

"You don't have to walk. Call a car."

"It's not *that* far." I sit down next to him, careful not to disturb the balance of his dinner plate.

"We have an account. That's what it's for."

"Okay, but I was sort of kidding."

"Charlotte."

"I said okay. I'll call a car."

"What's at the armory that requires heels?" he asks.

"Paintings of dudes with sashes. Ladies wearing stoles," I say. "It's very fancy." I know Scotty wants to pry further but won't, and I'm relieved that the manners he was brought up with are working to my advantage. There are other parts of my life, parts that don't involve action figures and green plastic utensils and creative wheedling, but telling Scotty something that doesn't pertain to this household feels like betrayal, and betrayal is not a suitable action item for the benign agenda we have worked so hard to craft for our evenings.

"It's . . . this thing," I say. "This guy. I've known him for a while. We have a mutual friend in town, and she's performing at the armory."

"Is this a guy you're, ah, seeing?"

"No," I say. "It's not, no. Not, like, a guy. Well, a guy. An old friend. But the one who's playing, she's a girl."

"An old friend? From your music program?"

"Yes." I dig my hands down between the couch cushions and come up with three pennies and two puzzle pieces. George will be relieved to see those pieces; he hates incomplete puzzles.

"She plays?"

"Yes, she plays her own work. She's a composer."

"I didn't even realize that was a job anymore," Scotty says, and either my imagination is projecting, or there is scorn in his voice.

"Well. It is."

"And that's what you do," he says. I can't tell if it's a question or a fuzzy memory.

"Play?"

"Yes, play." Scotty looks at me like I'm a witness for opposing council, trying to evade him. "And write music. I'm not sure what to call it because you never talk about it."

"I went to school for composition," I say. "So I play. Although I'd never dare to play that thing you have here. It looks like a museum piece."

"No one uses it." Scotty gets up and goes to the kitchen, returning with a glass of something that could be either bourbon or organic apple cider on ice. "My mother thought we should have it because civilized households have pianos."

"Or some kind of harpsichord, at the very least."

"You should use the piano," he says. There's this strange sense of melancholy welling up in me as he speaks, almost like nostalgia, a wish that all I was waiting for before sitting down at that magnificent instrument was permission.

"I remember some of the songs you made up with the boys." Scotty sets his drink down in front of him. I'm happy to see him pick his dinner plate back up and continue to eat. "She, she used to sing me some of the ones that I didn't get to hear firsthand. She thought they were so funny." We're no longer talking about his mother.

"Mostly with my ukulele," I say. "But yes, I play the piano. Not well. I can play some things. Just not, like, late Rachmaninoff."

"I don't know what that is," he says.

"Well, your mother would be appalled to hear that," I say, with a strong urge to distract him, as I do with his sons, from the sense of Gretchen that has just snuck up on us. "Hey. Want to see what's on the DVR?"

"How about the next episode of *Walking Dead*?"

"Only if you skip through the biting parts," I say.

Scotty clicks away from the channel menu and cues up the DVR. "The boys are making you soft," he says. "Zombies are one of Matt's top five greatest fears."

"It's the way they *move*," I say. "So weird and erratic." Scotty is scrolling through the recorded programs, and in the corner of the screen, the program on the current channel begins. Familiar music plays out over the sophisticated speaker system in the family room, and the sound of it is fierce, coming at me from all sides. My stomach twists with pride and regret and all the other emotions that bristle me when I encounter this particular forty-five seconds of sound. It's never come upon me in this place before, and my sense of insulation, of being able to block it out forever if I stay inside my fortress, dissolves into the suede couch.

I take the remote from him and turn the volume all the way

down before he can find our next episode. "Can I ask you a question?"

"Maybe I should put on some pants first," he says.

"Those pants are fine," I say. He's wearing the Northwestern sweatpants that I first saw on Patrick.

"You prefaced the question with 'can I ask you a question?' It seems like daytime pants might be required."

"Stop it. *Daytime* pants. Ha."

Scotty slides his finished plate off his lap and onto the coffee table. "Ask."

"Did you ever study intellectual property? In law school?"

Scotty puts his elbows on his knees and steeples his fingers in front of his face. Even in sweatpants, he looks like he should be addressed as Counsel.

"This is a serious question," he says.

"Mostly hypothetical, maybe."

"Intellectual property as it pertains to artists? Composers, for example?"

I pull one of my legs up over the other in a half lotus and straighten my spine. "Yes. Was that part of your, ah, training, ever?"

"We protect intellectual property for a handful of companies at my firm," he says. "I know a thing or two about that kind of law. I can probably be much more helpful if you give me the specifics of the situation though, and try not to generalize it too much."

What I can't figure out, what I've never been able to figure out, is how to open. What is the right way to start this story?

"The nice thing," says Scotty, like he can read my mind, "is that you can say anything to me, anything that you want. We've cleaned up vomit together, so pretty much any barrier between us is gone."

I click the sound back on the television and hit rewind on the current program. I let him listen to the theme, the last thing I've composed up to this point, and then I tell him the story. And I'm surprised at my detachment, surprised that I feel so far removed, surprised by the steadiness of my voice. When I finish, Scotty is looking at me with interest, not sympathy, and I'm grateful that he's also able to maintain that emotional detachment. Too many of my emotions have already run down Jess's drain. I don't want her to have anything else of mine.

"I understand why it's been so gray for you," says Scotty. "In my opinion, it's not a legal issue. It's a question of ethics. Someone in a position of authority, like a teacher, ought to be clear about the boundaries of the work you're doing. When doctors publish in medical journals, for example, they publish under their own names, even though they have research assistants and interns working with them. But the interns know the game going in. They have a certain amount of responsibility to opt in or opt out. I'm assuming it was never put forth in that seminar that any of the work you were doing might be used for outside entities?"

"I don't think so." The circulation in my legs starts to cease, so I uncross them.

"As I thought. My guess is that she never considered that one of her students would come up with something worthy of being appropriated for her own purposes. But once she had it, instead of bothering with the proper ethical channels, she decided to bank on what she knew of you, of your inexperience, rather, and take what she needed."

"So there isn't anything to be done, really. I thought so, but it's always been in the back of my mind that I should ask a lawyer about it."

"I don't think you need a lawyer," says Scotty. The ice in his drink has melted, turning the liquid a light yellow.

"It's really only curiosity at this point," I say. "I haven't written anything since then. I don't need protecting. I'm not going to go after her."

Scotty studies me. I have trouble withstanding his full attention. I look at the TV, my hands, the space between our knees.

"You have no culpability here," he says. "There were no parameters, no expectations set up. Nothing that could have prepared you. You were not naive. What she did was an abuse of power. A breach of ethics."

"No parameters," I say. "That's the terrible part. That lack of boundaries. If she could do it, it must be part of that whole world, you know?"

"I don't think you should let her have this one, Charlotte," he says. "Don't let her decide that this project was your last move as a composer. She played you, but you're onto her now. If she needs to steal from you in order to keep her career moving forward, then it's only a matter of time before she's finished. But you don't need to be finished. This is not your shame. It's hers, and you should let that weigh her down. The further you go, the more it will pull on her. Don't you think?"

"I'm not doing it on purpose." I feel shaky, and I don't want him to notice. A drink will help, so I reach for his, and he lets me finish it. "It's not like I have this spectacular symphony sitting in my head, waiting to explode out of me, and I'm too scared to let it. There just isn't anything in me to write."

"You have been writing a little," Scotty says. "With the boys and all."

"I guess they're the only ones I can be sure won't steal my stuff."

"George won't. You might have to watch out for Matt though."

"He's a stinker, it's true."

"Will you play me something?" Scotty says. "Something you play with them? You should sit down at that museum piece, before you lose your nerve, and play right now."

"I don't know."

"It's only me. I wouldn't know an E-sharp from a hole in the ground."

"There's no such thing as E-sharp. E-sharp is just F."

"See? You're safe."

We make our way into the living room, and I sit down. Scotty sits in a chair to one side of me, visible from my periphery, and my mind jumps to his father. He's sitting in the master-of-the-house chair, the one George the Elder had assumed when he was here for the funeral—the one, I realize, Scotty usually sits in but had abdicated for those few days when his parents were here. I'm surprised he's sitting there now, with no one in the room but him and me.

There's very little space on this piano bench, on any piano bench. But it would be better for him to be this close than as far away as that chair puts him. I scoot to one side and pat the bench beside me.

"They sit next to you?"

"Actually, they usually sit *on* me in some way."

He joins me at the piano. I put my hands on the keys, and the feeling in my chest makes me think of one of those toys, available at museums and in educational catalogues, the ones that take an impression of your hand or arm or face (if you dare) in a bed of pins. It's as though I'm pressing against one with my entire torso and then taking a step back and letting the pins slap into the front of me, hoping that if I move the right way, they'll stay lifted, suspended, instead of coming back down to knock the wind out of me.

"We wrote this song the first time I took them to the pediatrician's office. Mae was here, and we'd never really met before. Maybe we'd seen each other on video chat or something. But this was her first visit since you guys hired me, and I remember feeling terrible, thinking she would hate me forever because George wanted me to hold him, instead of her, while he got his shots that day." I push the keys down into chords under my fingers, moving up and down chromatically until I find the right key. "I also remember thinking that a one-to-one ratio should have been easier with the kids, but instead, it seemed to add an element of, like, competition to the whole outing. Matt was being such a smart aleck, and Georgie had this terrible, short fuse. It was really hot, much hotter than I thought was appropriate for early June, and I didn't blame them for being listless and draggy, but you know how it is when you have a witness to your child-care skills, right? My rapport is not the same as when I have them on my own. I promised that we could stop for some kind of cold treat if we could make it through the appointment without incident, and then thought, great, Mae's probably thinking I'm the worst, resorting to bribing them with treats."

"We bribe them with treats all the time," says Scotty. I think back to the first time I heard that from Gretchen, but I don't mention it. "Mae is superwoman, but I'm also pretty sure she invented bribery via treat."

"Well, I know that now, I guess." There is sheet music on the piano in front of me, Beethoven's Thirteenth Sonata. I have never thought to ask who decided that this was the music that should be displayed in the parlor, or how they came to that decision. "Anyway, we got into the waiting room of the doctor's office, and I expected it to be a relief with the air-conditioning on full blast, but instead it felt damp and sweaty. There was this miserable-looking baby with bright red fever spots on her cheeks sitting on the lap of her Jamaican nanny and wailing into the woman's stomach. Another little boy, with this like *absurd* amount of energy propelling him around the room, was barking out a cough every fifteen seconds and putting his hands all over every toy in sight. His mother sounded like she had the same ailment. And the lights in those offices, they're green, and they buzz. No matter how nice the office is, you know?"

"It has that universal smell too," Scotty says. "Like antibacterial soap and tongue depressors."

"The boys didn't want to go in," I say. "So we sat on the floor in the hallway outside the suite until the doctor was ready to see us, and Matt and I talked about all the things we'd rather be doing instead of getting shots. George wasn't talking yet. Somehow we turned the conversation into a song, kind of a bluesy-folksy tune. I saw it as an opportunity to educate them about Johnny Cash, but Matt kept singing over me, at the top of his lungs. He was totally hilarious. I couldn't be strict at all. I couldn't keep it together because he kept making me laugh. And I thought, wow, their grandmother must think I'm the most irresponsible, irreverent influence on these kids. I figured she'd probably say something to—to you guys, and you'd never trust me to take them to an appointment again."

"She's not like that," says Scotty.

"Nope. She was gracious and saintly about our antics. Even as the song got increasingly crude and ended up with the title 'I Can't Take Another Shot,' she was smiling away."

"I Can't Take Another Shot," he says. "It does sound like Johnny Cash. Are you sure you need the piano? I can see if we have a banjo in one of these closets."

"There are no banjos in this house," I say. I play through the song for him before I can come up with another excuse for delay. Scotty starts to join in when he catches on to the refrain, and I wish the boys were awake.

We are interrupted by a horrible sound, terrified screams coming from the right wing of the apartment.

"It's Matt." I look at Scotty, searching for affirmation that what I'm hearing is real. "It sounds like Matt, right?" I'm standing, about to reach for his arm, wanting to pull him to his feet and then push him until he takes off running, the way I think he should have, the way I want to.

"He'll calm down." Scotty's voice is measured, detached. Like his mother's.

I leave the parlor quickly and go for Matt's room, not sure what I expected of Scotty. When I get there, I see that Matty has gotten out of bed, taking most of the covers with him. He is trying to claw his way free in the middle of the room. It's not clear whether he is awake or asleep or somewhere in between, but he is so distressed that I can't stand it. I charge into the fray. I take a couple of whacks to the pelvis, kneel down to try to disentangle him, and take an elbow to the side of the head.

"Matt," I say, trying to be calm and not too loud. "Matty, Matt, Matt, it's Charlotte. You were sleeping, okay? Just having a dream. Wake up, honey, it's okay; it's me, Charlotte."

"He's here, Charlotte! He's in here; he's in here!" Matt sobs. "He'll put me back in the hole, pleeeeeease—"

"Shh, shh, there's no one here but me and you." I clamp my arms around him and hold his arms to his sides until he stops flailing, and I end up in a pile of blankets on the floor, holding him while I try to get his hysterics under control.

"Noooo, the fooooooxxx," he wails.

"There's no fox, love bug. Shhh. We can turn on the light if you want, and you'll see," I say. "Do you want to turn it on?"

"There was a fox." Matt tries to catch his breath. "He was in here, and he took me to his hole and put me down there. I don't want to go in that hole!"

"It's okay now," I say. "It was just a dream. No fox is getting in here, babe, and nobody will put you in a hole."

"I don't want to be alone! Mommy is alone. I don't want to. I don't want to!" Matt dissolves into sobs again. I hold him against the front of me. I want to sob too, because I have no good answer.

After what feels like hours, he cries it out and goes back to sleep in my arms. I am afraid to move for fear I'll wake him up again. More than once, I think about shifting him off me so I can pick up his bedclothes, but each time I start, I can't get over the paranoia that he'll wake up if I move. I don't know how long I sit there, in a deep void of uncertainty, before Scotty appears in the doorway. He lifts Matt off me, and I scoop up the sheets and blanket and spread them out over the end of Matt's bed. Scotty puts him back in bed and tucks him in, and when I stand up, parts of my body have gone to pins and needles.

"Was it a night terror?" He is whispering even though there's no longer a need. We head back out to the kitchen.

"He definitely couldn't get out of it," I say. "But he was speaking in sentences. Maybe it was just a bad dream."

"He used to have them, when he was younger," Scotty says. "What happened to your face?" He puts his hand up next to where Matt hit me, on the edge of my right eye socket. He doesn't touch me, but I can feel his hand there.

"He thought someone, maybe something, was after him. He was trying to get untangled from the sheets." I wince, which is uncalled for because he's not touching me.

"Do you want some frozen peas?" he asks. "It looks like it's going to be a thing. A bruise."

I don't want frozen peas. My head feels heavy, and what I want is to put the side of it down into Scotty's hand and have him hold me up for a minute. I straighten up at the thought.

"It's okay for now," I say. "I'll get a bag of ice before I go to bed."

I move to the opposite side of the kitchen island. I am close to emotional overload. I need to let myself feel helpless for a minute with no one watching. Scotty follows me, standing really close in order to inspect my face. Is it written all over me, this need for consolation? Our unspoken boundaries have been holding us just exactly the right amount of together and apart in this house, but right now I am overwhelmed with the feeling that they may have been redrawn tonight, without premeditation. There is one person on the planet who knows the ins and outs of my daily life. There is one person who comes close enough to know what my daily joys and trials are. It used to be Gretchen, and now it's Scotty. And this kind of communion isn't the same with Scotty as it was with Gretchen, because it just isn't. I tried to make it that way, but it's impossible.

"Charlotte." He's still whispering. "You can tell me."

Scotty no longer has that expression, the one that had emerged briefly before he collected himself and came to help me. I have seen him wrestling for the last few weeks against the impermeable place that he goes to, and I want him to win. I want him to beat it, for the boys' sake, and so I keep still as he focuses intently on my face. He's looking for something, and I don't know if I want him to find it.

"It was a nightmare." I do my own intent focusing, on the five feet of space on the floor between us. I don't step back, but neither does he step forward. "I guess I don't think it was, you know, *overly* psychologically complex. It was something about a fox."

"The fox who wants to eat his face off? Or the fox with the loud voice?"

I want to laugh, but we don't do that here, and I'm suddenly conscious of all the rules I'm breaking. "I didn't realize there was more than one fox."

His face is so serious, and his eyes could be burning a hole right through me. The muscles above my stomach feel tight in an emotional way I don't recognize. Is it possible there's an emotion that exists that I haven't yet experienced? I feel like if I move, I'll give myself a hernia, so I am rooted to my spot. A flush is creeping across my face, and as I meet Scotty's eyes, I almost wish for shell-shocked to return. Because what I see there is sharp, like a million kinds of pain, and all of them acute.

"There are two foxes. Three, if you count the 'mean Swiper.'" His voice is so quiet. Searching my face. What does he want to see?

There's a wild drop in my stomach, and I want to cry, but it's not my tragedy; crying would be unfair. "I must have missed that episode."

"I think mean Swiper was in one of the books," he says. I cast around in my mind for something else to report on. He wants to keep talking to me, and I want to let him because there isn't anything else I can do. And maybe I want him to talk because I want to talk too.

"We went to the playground today, the far one, on the west side of the park," I say. "The Mariners' Playground. We walked there, even Georgie. I wanted to wear him out so he would sleep better. It seems to have worked."

"Baby George," Scotty says.

"I think there are things," I say, "that neither one of the boys knows how to express, things they aren't telling Dr. O'Neill or me or you. Matt was truly terrified when I went in to get him. He is terrified that he might end up alone because he thinks that Gretchen is alone wherever she is."

When I realize I've used her name, I'm horrified. I don't know how to get myself out of this unbearable moment.

Scotty closes his eyes, and when he opens them, it's there again, his scrutiny of my face, and all of a sudden I know.

I know he's thinking, what if my hair were a shade or two blonder? What if I were a few inches taller, smaller through the hips? I already hold his kids, protect them, feed them, talk them out of their nightmares. I'm in the room across the hall. And most importantly, I was there, on that day, in this life, in the middle of this family.

Maybe this is a logical option, this attempt to will my eyes to turn from brown to blue. If I tried to turn him into Gretchen, it's only fair that he should try to turn *me* into her. Maybe this will make him feel better, at least for an hour?

Now he does take a step forward.

I'm working so hard to keep my breathing silent that I end up holding most of it and then having to work twice as hard at it when I realize I need to let it go. Scotty's eyes are glassy, and the rims are a beautiful translucent red. He *would* have to be a pretty crier, like a movie star, just to make this moment, the first release of tears, more difficult. But the tears won't spill. He won't let them out. He's waiting to see what I'm going to do.

Maybe this action will provoke Gretchen's wrath, and she'll walk through the door to make it stop?

He takes another step, and I haven't moved, I haven't shaken my head or laughed uncomfortably or done anything proper or decent that could possibly shatter his fragile spirit. He is so close to me that I could chart a course through his five-o'clock shadow.

He can tell that I am holding my breath now, so I let it out in a rush that touches the side of his neck. His mouth is right next to mine for a second that feels like an hour, and then I feel his cheek scrape down the side of my face until his head has dropped onto my shoulder.

I can't help it. I cry. I cry and he cries, and I let him hold me around the waist. I let him pull my hips in against his own. I wrap my arms up underneath his shoulders and hold him like I've just held Matt, like I held Georgie earlier.

I'm not Gretchen, but I have strong arms.

HOURS LATER, I wake up, disoriented because the lights are still on, and everything is as we left it in the living room, only it's close to two in the morning. I shift Scotty's head so that he is sitting fully upright with the side of his head on the back of the couch instead of the half-sitting position we've been sleeping in. There is a warm red blotch in the middle of my chest below my collarbone where his temple left its mark, and the corner of my eye socket is throbbing.

I am engrossed in trying not to wake him as I shift out from underneath him, so I don't notice Matt until I am standing fully upright, pulling the neck of my T-shirt to rights. When I do, I start and almost gasp, and he jumps a little in response.

"Is Daddy sleeping on the couch tonight?"

"I think so, maybe. Why aren't *you* sleeping?"

"My bed's all wet. I think I spilled my water. Why is he gonna sleep on the couch?"

"He was really tired." I arrange a bunch of throw pillows on the opposite end of the couch from where Scotty sleeps, noticing that the covers are dingy. Historically, the pillows have been in pristine condition, and I'm trying to pinpoint the moment that changed. "And kind of sad."

"Did he have a nightmare?"

"Yes, I think maybe he did."

"Are you gonna sleep out here with him?"

"Let's go change your sheets."

"Can I have some more water?" Matt starts to move in Scotty's direction, and I step between him and his sleeping father.

"Not if you peed in your bed, sweetie."

"I didn't pee in my bed! I spilled my water! I need more!"

"Okay," I say, herding him back through the hall to his bedroom. I turn on a dim lamp and strip his bed, which he definitely peed, but may also have dumped his water on in order to mislead me.

"Daddy should go in his bed."

"Your dad is very tired. I think we'd better let him sleep until he feels better."

"He had a nightmare?"

"Yeah." The mattress pad is soaked through, so I take that off too.

"About Mommy?"

"I think dreaming about Mommy would be a good dream, not a nightmare, so maybe it was something else. You can ask him in the morning."

"Were you giving him a hug?"

"Yes." I dump the sheets into a pile on the floor and grab another set from his closet.

"I don't want to go back to bed. I want to play."

"I'll read you a book before you go back to bed."

"I don't want a book." Matt's volume is increasing. "I want to play."

"What do you want to play?"

"I don't want to go to bed!"

"I heard you say that. I'm asking, what do you want to do instead?"

"I want to play with Daddy."

I shake his pillow out of the case. "Matty, you can't. Daddy is sleeping."

"I want to give him a hug."

"How about in the morning?"

"NOW."

I don't say anything as I finish making up his bed. He is watching me, waiting for my response.

"I want to give Daddy a hug NOW."

"I hear you, Matt."

He watches me check all the stuffed animals for wetness. "I want to—"

"Matt, I heard you the first time. I said no already, and I know you heard me. I'm not changing my mind, so there's no need to keep talking about it."

For a second I think he's going to start screaming, but instead he furrows his brow and climbs up onto his bed. He turns over to face the wall and puts his nose in the pillow so I can't kiss him. I turn off his lamp and stand there for a minute, wondering whether to respect his five-year-old boundaries or ignore his wishes and kiss him anyway. While I mull it over, I hear a muffled voice in the darkness.

"I don't want to dream about Mommy."

I lean my knee on the edge of his bed. "Why not, pal?"

"Because then I want to sleep forever."

I ignore his boundaries and kiss the back of his head. "See you in the morning."

I hear him sigh and flip over as I close the door.

I tiptoe into the kitchen and try not to make too much noise while I get out a pan to grill myself a cheese sandwich. I'm wide awake, but I want Scotty to sleep—because he needs it and because I don't want to face him awake yet. I need some time to convince myself that I was mistaken in my earlier impression, that he just needed to cry, and I happened to be there when it came out.

There's a voice in my brain that is insisting I pay attention to my own well-being, a nasty little nagger of a voice that says it's okay to hold, to be held, to receive a little comfort in exchange for what I'm giving out. This is the part of me that wants to defend myself, that wants to deny impropriety, that wants to ignore the connotations of our actions because this is an unusual situation. There's nothing *usual* about finding our way through this much suffering. Scotty's crying on my shoulder doesn't mean what it might usually mean, I want to say to Lila and Everett and all the other skeptics. I flip my grilled cheese and think to myself, it's fine. It's fine, it's fine, it's all fine.

The couch creaks as Scotty gets up, and I force myself to keep moving at a regular pace. He appears in the doorway to the kitchen, rubbing his eyes like a little kid, and I reach for normalcy with every faculty I possess.

"Want a sandwich?" I ask.

"Yes. Thanks." He starts to pull his shirt off, which is stained with sweat and probably tears, and I keep my eyes on the frying pan. I know that taking off his shirt is a natural gesture, devoid of connotation, but the part of me that isn't ruled by logic is afraid of what his next move will be, or won't be, so I hold out a hand for the shirt without looking.

"I'll throw it in with Matt's sheets. He wet the bed."

Scotty lets me take the shirt. "A horrible nightmare, and now a wet bed?"

I take my sandwich off the pan and put it on a plate, cut it in half, and hand it to him. "He came out here and told me he spilled his water."

"That's not what happened?"

"It smelled like pee."

He eats for a minute while I put cheese on the new sandwich. "Did he see us?"

I mush down the top piece of bread until my sandwich looks more like a cheese pancake. "What?"

"Did he come out while we were sleeping?"

I have to look at him this time, or I won't be able to make him understand what I mean. "I told him you had a nightmare, and I gave you a hug." I take my sandwich to the table.

He sits down with me a moment later. "Hey, you. I'm sorry."

"Please don't apologize. It's really okay."

"You've been unbelievable with the kids. I don't know what we would do without you right now." What he means to say is please don't leave, and what I want to say back is I promise that I will not. We have just been so close, and now no one knows what to say, especially not me.

"I want to help." I get up to dig through the freezer, and I find some ice cream buried underneath two plastic bags containing frozen chicken breasts, labeled with the date in Gretchen's precise handwriting. I'm not sure that chicken will ever get eaten. "I want to be there for you. For them." Scotty and I slide the ice cream container back and forth, not bothering with bowls. I'll have to get groceries right after I drop them at school in the morning. George will have a fit if he realizes that someone ate all his ice cream.

"Do you want to go to bed?" I'm not sure how Scotty means that, and it must show on my face, because he clarifies. "I think I'll probably stay up for a while, but don't feel like you have to stay up with me. It's fine if you want to go to bed." I sort of think he didn't know how he meant the question either, until he heard it out loud.

"Pretty soon." I put our spoons in the dishwasher. "Did you see the flier that Matt's teachers sent home?"

"I think I saw it on the counter. A green half sheet?"

"Yes, that one. You didn't read it?"

"No."

"The kids are about to start their Mother's Day projects. They need to bring in some materials from home. One shoebox. As many egg cartons, mason jars, or glass bottles as they can find.

I think they're going to convert them into planters and build seed gardens, or something to that effect."

"Do you need me to pick up some eggs?" Scotty pulls the empty ice cream container toward him and compresses it until it's folded into the smallest version of itself. He gets up to put it in the recycling bin, which is already too full.

"No." I sit back down at the table, thinking he'll sit with me to have this discussion, but he remains standing. "I can help him get the materials together. I think we can get through enough pickles in the next week to make a worthwhile jar contribution."

"What are you asking me?" Scotty tries to push the ice cream container farther down into the bin, but it won't budge. He pulls a plastic bag out from underneath the sink and empties the recycling into it.

"I think we should decide who Matt will make his present for." My face feels too hot on one side, the side that was pressed against the arm of the couch while we slept. "Miss Leslie hinted that they would like that information so that she and his other teachers can be, ah, prepared."

"What do you think the options are?"

I want him to stop letting me make all the decisions. He's their father, and I don't want to be the one with the responsibility for their entire states of being, even though I know that's the way he prefers it.

"Well. He could still make it for her, I guess. He could make it for Mae, or you."

"Or you."

I look at the clock above the stove. It's 2:47. Tomorrow is going to be unbearable. "We could keep him out of school for a few days."

"If you think that would be easiest, then that's what we should do," he says.

"I don't know what I think is easiest. I just—I don't know."

"Would his teachers have any insights?"

"Maybe."

"Will you copy me on your communication with them?"

I stand up. "I can ask them at pickup or drop-off if they have any suggestions. I don't usually communicate formally with them." Because they want to hear from parents, not babysitters.

"Thank you, Charlotte. Good night," he says, and I'm confused by the dismissal, when only a few minutes earlier I'd been alarmed at the possibility of an invitation. I have to walk away before I can start to fixate on Scotty's mental state, because I've just seen him retreat, right before my eyes, watched him go back to a place that I can't imagine, with walls made of paper and no door to be found. All I can do is hope that it's not possible I have anything to do with sending him back there.

I HAVE A long succession of dreams that night, the kind that make the night feel arduous, like I'm having another daytime within my unconscious mind. First, there is Gretchen. We push two strollers side by side. I never think to look around at the front of either stroller to make sure Matt and George are really there. I trust that they are because their mother is here, and she takes care of everything. In the next dream, Gretchen and I are on a balcony overlooking the reservoir, and Patrick is with us. We smoke cigarettes together, and I pay close attention to the chemistry between them, to the chemistry between Patrick and me, but it is impossible to discern either energy. Another dream comes. I am in Scotty and Gretchen's apartment. Scotty is away on business. I'm not sure how I know that. It's one of those dream-givens, a fact established not in words over the course of the dream but rather a known circumstance. Gretchen is in the kitchen making dinner. I am in the bathtub, and I don't want to get out. I want dinner, of course, but getting up and out of the bath, drying off, putting on clothes, and wringing out my hair—these things all seem like too much effort.

I dream that my arms and legs are made of beanbags, and I can't move them of my own volition. I call for Scotty and he comes to me, and I tell him how to move my arms, where I want my legs to go, and he moves them for me. I dream that I am lying underneath a lead blanket in the park, and I can't move it off me because I'm not sure whether or not I have clothes on. I watch Scotty in the distance. He trips over something that I can't see and goes down hard. I can feel the stinging in his palms as he scrapes the ground. I dream of terrible struggles for Scotty, over and over; the boys asking him unanswerable questions, the train he rides to work derailing, buildings collapsing and leaving him the only survivor in a pile of rubble.

"BERLIN?" I SAY to Scotty. A few days have passed since we discussed Matt's Mother's Day project, with no further mention of how the problem might be resolved. I hold the phone between my ear and my shoulder while I attempt to unfold the stroller. I want to do this quickly, before Miss Leslie spots me, but it's an illogical process. Whoever designs these things must be a sadistic bastard. "When are you leaving?"

"First it's D.C., then Istanbul, then Berlin for nine days," Scotty says. The stroller unsnaps, and the kickback makes me drop my phone.

"C-R-A-P," I mutter. Georgie scrambles over and picks up my phone. "Sorry, I dropped my phone," I call as George puts the phone to his ear and says, "Daddy?"

"Hi, baby George," Scotty's faint, tinny voice says from the phone. "How are you?"

"Tahr-lette not unhook the troller," George says. He'd like to inform anyone who will listen of my delightful incompetence. "She drop her phone."

"Are you still at school?"

"Not leave until the troller unhook."

"Okay. What are you and Charlotte getting up to today?"

"We going to the party tore, and Matt and me going to the widdle playground. We gonna play Batman versus pie-derman."

"Sounds like fun, honey. May I speak to Charlotte when she gets the stroller unfolded?"

"She all done." George hands the phone to me, plopping himself into the stroller, which straightens it out the rest of the way.

"Hi," I say. "So how long will you go for? Two weeks?"

"Twelve days. I have one meeting in D.C., and from there I'll take the red-eye and meet the clients in Istanbul, and we'll go to Berlin together," Scotty says.

"When are you leaving?" I strap George in and stuff my purse underneath his seat.

"I'm flying out two weeks from Saturday. Early in the morning."

"Will you be back in time for Matt's birthday?" I push the stroller into the elevator.

"If all goes well, I should be back the day before, the morning of June fifth," says Scotty. "Is that why you're going to the party store?"

"Yes," I say. "It kind of snuck up on me. I think it would be cool to do it outside, like maybe at the boat basin? But I'm afraid it will rain."

"Maybe you can put a rain plan on the bottom of the invitation. I think I've seen that," he says.

"We can make a plan tonight when you get home, if you want to." I push backward through the front doors of North-Mad and pull the stroller out. "I can do a lot of the shopping and stuff."

"We also need to talk about what you want to do while I'm gone," he says. "I can call my parents and see if they can come for a few weeks. Or Mae, if you want. Lila can probably check in once in a while."

I stop in front of Dean and Deluca. "Let's talk about it when you get home."

"Sure. See you later. Say good-bye to George for me."

I hang up. "Georgie, Dad says bye." No response. I look around the front of the stroller, and he is sleeping. Not exactly time for a nap yet, but I'll take it.

I wander into Dean and Deluca and pick out several things that Gretchen would never want the boys to see me eating. It's a beautiful day outside, so I find a spot on the edge of the park to sit and eat, and I dial up Claudia.

"Hello?" she says, but it's hard to hear her through the techno music blaring in the background.

"Claudine. Claudabell. Claudelia."

"Hold on a second," says Claudia.

"Where are you, a disco?" The music stops.

"Pal, nobody calls them discos. My friend DQ is spinning at a downtown bar. I told him I'd weed out the loser beats."

"Do you think he was born in the parking lot of a Dairy Queen? Is that how his parents came to give him such an enchanting moniker?"

"It's short for Daiquiri," says Claudia, and we both laugh. "I'm serious though; that's really his name."

"I believe you," I say. "Hey, want to come down and visit me in two weeks? I'll buy you a ticket."

"I do want to visit you. But I'm shooting a film that week, so I have to stay in Boston," she says.

"A *film*?"

"Yeah! I got picked to be an extra in these crazy pre-Revolutionary War crowd scenes. I have to get fitted for, like, bonnets and lace-up boots and shit. Isn't that awesome?"

"That *is* awesome," I say. I open the container of cut strawberries that I just paid $10.95 for. "Did you tell Mom? Maybe it will be your claim to fame."

"I don't really think that's how it works," says Claudia.

"Scotty's going out of town," I say.

"Why? Did something happen?"

For a minute, I panic and wonder what she knows. "What do you mean?"

"Is everyone okay? I don't think that man could take anything else," she says.

"Oh. It's just for work." I pull the shade on top of the stroller all the way out to shield Georgie from the sun. "He's been trying to take only day trips for work, but now he has to go to Berlin, and if I can't come up with another alternative, I'll be stuck with Mae the whole time," I say.

"Mae's not so bad," says Claudia. "I like her."

"You've never met Mae," I say.

"Yes, but everything you've ever said about her makes her sound amazing," she says. "*You* don't like her because she makes you feel insecure."

"The alternative isn't too appealing either," I say. "Jeanne and George."

"Right, George. Patrick the first."

"I don't know if I could make it through two weeks of cocktail hours with Jeanne and George the Elder," I say.

"Well, what about Uncle Patrick?" she asks, and her voice takes on a quality I don't like. "He's around, right? Maybe he can come over and check in after work or something." I wish I hadn't broken down and told Claudia anything about Patrick, but there was no one else to confide in who wouldn't judge me. I'm sure she's told Jane by now. I'm not looking forward to that discussion.

"I will not be suggesting that course of action," I say.

"Scotty will come to it on his own," Claudia predicts. "It's pretty logical. Uncle Patrick is right here in town. And he's been insistent about helping."

"Have I been drunk dialing you or something?" I pull out a pastry bag the wrong way and drop crumbs all over my lap. "How do you infer these things?"

"You're literally the most transparent person on the planet. You're the worst at keeping things close to the vest."

"You're the worst at everything!"

"Ha. Hey, what are you eating?"

"A croissant."

"Two croissants?"

"Yes. And a scone."

"Nice." DQ must be getting impatient. I hear his muffled voice in the background. "I'll come and visit you soon, honey bunny," says Claudia. "I promise. Maybe we can even convince Janie to get on a plane."

"Yeah, right," I say. "Love you, Claud."

"Love you too."

"Claudia?"

"Yeah?"

"Am I crazy? I mean, Scotty should just stay put, right? We shouldn't even be having this conversation."

"Yeah. I know."

"Okay. Bye, pigeon."

"Bye, squirrel."

May, fourteen weeks after

"Are you my mom now?" Matt asks me one morning a few weeks later, after Scotty has left for his business trip. His tone is casual as he steps into his jeans. If it were the first time he was asking me this question, I'd be freaking out. Unfortunately, it's not.

"Love bug, of course not," I say. "Your mom will always be your mom, whether she's here or not."

"Then why do you get to tell me what to do?" It's going to be one of those days.

"Other kids in your class have babysitters too," I say. "Babysitters are around to help when parents can't be, because they have to work or do something else that's important."

"Or because they died."

"There are lots of reasons that babysitters help out."

"But you live here now."

"Yes."

"Only families live together. Like I'm going to live with Ainsley when we get married. Are you going to marry Daddy?"

"No, sweetheart." He is struggling with the button on his jeans, but he bats my hands away when I attempt to help him fasten it.

"Then why do you live with us?"

"Don't you know any other babysitters who live with the families they help?" I ask. I hold up a polo shirt, and he shakes his head. I hold up a pin-striped button-down and he vetoes that one too.

"The white one," he says, and visions of bleaching out marker and lunch stains dance before my eyes. "Babysitters have their own houses," he goes on as I button up his short-sleeved little man shirt.

"I have my own house."

"But you're here at night."

I stand up. "Matt, honey, we could talk about this for hours. You know that things have been hard around here without your mom, right? You know that. Everybody misses her. I'm around to help out for a while because your dad still has to go to work, and you still have to go to school."

"And Georgie still has to go to school."

"That's right."

"But are you leaving?"

"What? No."

"But you said a while." He ignores the plain white socks that I hold out to him and instead picks a pair with tiny whales on them out of his drawer. Those socks make me think of the massive clothing orders that Gretchen used to put in from Lands' End. "What's a while? You're not going to leave, are you?"

"No, pal, not now."

"When?"

"I'm not sure. But not anytime soon."

"When you die?"

"Matt." I am out of patience. "We need to eat breakfast. I bet George is already done. Would you like a waffle?"

"Can I have pancakes?"

"We don't have time, love," I say, as we walk into the kitchen.

"Actually, Charlotte," says Mae, holding a spatula and beaming at me. "That's exactly what I made for breakfast." Matt looks at me triumphantly, like he's so satisfied by this outcome. It's such a Scotty look.

"Me hold it, Gramma?" says George, reaching for the spatula. She gives it to him, and he starts banging on the side of his booster seat.

"If you don't mind, Gramma," I say over the noise, "I'm going to run back and make their beds really quickly."

"Of course," she says.

I'm terrible at making beds (Gretchen was perfect), but I attempt it every day anyway, maybe in tribute, maybe because my own mother would want me to, maybe because it just seems like something that should be done. I finish making George's, tucking the oddly angled flap of the top sheet in under the bedspread, where no one will know it's out of order. I arrange his pillows and animals on top of the bed, with Chickie in the middle, the king of them all. When I get into Matt's room, I have to reassemble his bed. The sheets and blankets are all untucked at one end, indicating the tossing and turning that have become the standard for him all through the night.

I retrieve several fallen stuffed compatriots from the pit between the bed and the wall, and pull the fitted sheet all the way off the mattress. I untwist the sheet and spread it out, tucking it back in around the edges. I notice a lump between the mattress and the box spring and think that it must be some unfortunate stuffed soul, a victim of the maelstrom formerly known as Matt. I reach in to rescue the little guy, and when I pull it back up, I can't believe what I'm holding in my hand.

Pup.

A few days earlier

Once the dreams descend, there is no stopping them. They've become more vicious since they first started a few weeks ago, in the sense that the details are only just to one side of what could actually be real.

I have a dream that my mother dies, and I miss her funeral. I come home three months later to find her gone and my father sitting in a recliner, watching the news and commenting on the reports. Jane and Claudia are arguing about different pieces in my mother's jewelry box as I stand there, crying with confusion. This isn't who they are. I don't know what's happening. I'm on the other side of the looking glass. I want to ask why, why, why didn't anyone think to tell me that my mother was dead?

I have a dream that Claudia doesn't exist. Jane is far away on the other coast, and I can never get her on the phone. Every time I call, her husband answers and tells me she is busy, to call someone else. But Claudia is not an option, because she is not my sister. I don't have another sister, only Jane. I don't know how I can even think the name *Claudia*, because she isn't real. Claudia was never born.

May, fourteen weeks after

Staring at Pup, clutched in my adrenaline-riddled fist—after having laid him to rest, after having made my peace with his departure—seeing him just *there*, as if maybe he's been there all along, is like seeing an apparition. It's a sudden lightness of mind and body that comes upon me; I feel untethered, like I'm floating, a balloon that a toddler just couldn't hang on to.

I asked Matt. I asked Matt more than once. And he looked me right in the face and said he had no idea. Yet here it is, George's security blanket, wedged deeply, *intentionally* between the mattress and the box spring.

I sit on the edge of Matt's bed and let all my baser impulses bounce around in my brain. It doesn't take me long, however, to come to the conclusion that I don't have any of the options I'm considering. I may not check out. I may not run away. I may not cease speaking to this grief-stricken five-year-old.

No. I have to *parent* him. Scotty is in the air somewhere between Istanbul and Berlin. I am the only parent available. Right now, I'm a single parent.

Passing this matter off to Mae is not on the table. It would take too much to get her to understand the significance. I wonder if even Scotty would truly understand.

Somehow, I get them where they need to be. I arrange a playdate for George that he only halfheartedly protests, and after I drop him off, I head back to the apartment. When I get there, I stand in the foyer, stand and stand, not knowing which direction to move. Finally, paranoia that Mae will catch me out here acting catatonic overtakes me, and I walk down the hall to Matt's bedroom and sit on the floor. I pull Pup out from his hiding spot and stare at him, and I'm thrown back in time. It's a feeling of immediacy, like coming out of a dreamless sleep or out from under anesthesia. Wasn't I just counting backward from ten? Did Gretchen know, when she started counting, that she would never come back to consciousness? Did she feel herself slide into oblivion, hear her soul leave her body, see the faces of George and Matt and Scotty as she went? Or was she unconscious from the moment she was struck by a few thousand pounds of metal, remaining in that state until it was all,

all over? It's both morbid and satisfying, the contemplation of these things.

Next to the contemplation of mortality, the issue with Matt seems dramatic, like I've created something huge and crazy out of something that will sound meaningless when I say it out loud. Dimly, I recognize this as a sign that I am trying to detach, as is my instinct when I'm in danger of being powerless. Move on to the next thing.

I don't know what to do, so I call Jane, and when she says hello, all I can do is shake my head, which is not an effective strategy for phone communication.

"Are you there?"

"I'm here," I say.

"Is everything okay?"

Pup's fur is all matted in one direction from his tenure under the mattress. He looks misshapen, a side effect of being constantly smushed. I do my best to ruffle his fur up with my fingers. I want him to look normal.

"Charlotte?"

"I don't know if I can do this anymore."

She doesn't ask me what I'm talking about because she already knows. If the situation were less dire, I'm sure she'd be saying she told me so, but she knows that I know she told me so. She doesn't need to say it.

"Where are you?"

"Sitting on the floor of Matt's bedroom."

"Something happened?"

"It's hard to explain."

"Scotty?"

"No, Scotty's in Europe. It's the kids. Matt, I guess. Both of them. I just—I don't know what I'm doing. They need someone who *isn't me*. They need Gretchen. I mean, Jane, what the fuck. Seriously, what the fuck? You know?"

"Yes, love bug, I know." I forgot that I got *love bug* from Jane.

"I have to go now."

"I'll be worried if you hang up," she says.

"No, it's fine. I'm fine. I think I need to call Scotty. I'll call you back later. Everything will be, well, not fine, but you know, everything will just, just *be*. I really will; I'll call you later."

"No, don't hang—"

"Love you," I say and hang up.

I text Scotty and ask him to call me, and he does, right away. "Is something wrong?"

"Yeah," I say. "Yeah, something's wrong. I found Pup. Remember, George's little dog? I looked everywhere for it, all over the apartment. And now, three months later, I find it in Matt's room. Hidden underneath his mattress."

Scotty doesn't say anything.

"I haven't said anything to him yet. He doesn't know that I know."

Silence.

"Scotty, you're still there, right?"

"Yes," he says. "I'm, God, I'm relieved. I thought maybe something—"

"You're relieved?"

"I'm glad that no one is in the hospital, is all I meant."

"Well, Matt might be, when I'm through with him." I shouldn't have said that. You can't say things like that about a child that's not your own.

"I'm so sorry that you have to deal with this," he says. I don't even feel frustrated with him when he says it, only mildly confused, because I am certain in my current frame of mind that I will *not* be dealing with this. "I wish I were home with you guys."

"Me too," I say.

"Maybe you should take the dog and put it away," says Scotty. "I think he should have a chance to realize that it's gone. He should know that the hammer's about to drop, be afraid it's going to come down hard."

"How do we know he won't just forget about him until you get here?" I say.

"Should we call Dr. O'Neill?" He means me.

"I can look up the number for you," I say.

"I have to think about this," he says. By that, I know he means he wants his wife to do this for him. And so do I.

Someone, probably my sister, is beeping in on my other line, and I'm thrilled for the excuse.

"Okay," I say.

"Okay. Talk later." He hangs up. I could answer Claudia's call, but I hit ignore, knowing that she's acting as Jane's proxy.

My phone dings with her voice mail. I dial in to listen to the message, and her voice is hard, like it can sometimes be, full of scorn. "You know I'm going to get you one of these days, and you're going to have to apologize for ignoring me and hanging up on Jane." I hold the phone away from me, like I can hold her off forever that way. "I will stalk you. I bet you wish you could turn off your phone, but I know you can't. So get ready to see my name every five minutes." She hangs up.

I group text them: "Please don't worry. Everything ok!!! Had a moment. Working it out with them. Will fill you in when there's something to tell."

Ten seconds later, I get two replies, two beeps, one right after the other. "Liar," says Jane, and "Throne of lies!!!" says Claudia. I want to make that wordless whine noise that Matt makes.

"Charlotte," says Mae from the doorway, startling me. I forgot she was here. "I thought I heard you back here." She doesn't ask me why I'm sitting on the floor, probably because she's such an empath that she's invented a reason that's far more legitimate than the actual reason. "I'm so sorry to have to do this. I'm really . . . Well, I'm needed at home, and I wondered if perhaps you could get along without me for a few days. I hate to do this, really—"

"It's fine," I say, interrupting her and then feeling like a jerk.

"I mean, of course, you should go if you need to, Mae. Is it Simon? Is he okay?"

"He's fine, physically. He wanted to come out here, in fact, but I wasn't sure it was the best—well. I think it would be better if I went back home to him. Unless you think you'll have too much trouble on your own."

"No, you should go if he needs you. We'll be okay here."

Mae steps out of the doorway, all the way into Matt's room to join me. "I . . . I didn't mean to eavesdrop . . ."

I fill her in on Pup. She's caught me in one of my increasingly frequent moments of weakness. I'm too worn down to try and censor myself, so I tell her, and I try not to worry too much that I'm influencing her feelings about the situation with my own.

"Well," she says. She pats me on the back. "Well, Charlotte. Of course that would make you uncomfortable. And with Scotty away, my, my. It seems rather sinister, doesn't it? Like he has no feelings."

I'm holding Pup between my knees, petting his stuffed golden head.

"You know," says Mae. "A friend of mine, a child psychologist, once told me that children have no idea that minds are separate. They are dismissive when you ask them how school was, or what they ate for lunch, or what they've been up to, because they think you already know. And if they're doing something naughty, they'll think you know about it too. I imagine that's why Georgie always tells us right away if he thinks he's done something we might not like, and why Matt can be withholding. Perhaps he thought you already knew and were okay with it. They believe in a, a collective consciousness, I suppose."

"Maybe," I say. "I mean, it makes sense."

"Regardless," says Mae, sitting down on the edge of Matt's bed noiselessly, without squeaking the bed frame, as I would. "I'm sure that even if he was keeping the secret on purpose, there are lots of deeper reasons that he would do so. It's been much easier for George to endure the loss than it has been for Matt. Oh, he misses her. They both do. But somehow, George has had an easier time accepting this world, this place here on the other side of Gretchen's . . . ah, existence. Matt is holding on to whatever he can. As I recall, Pup was quite a presence in this family. Maybe Matt couldn't bear to give up another one."

There was a time, not so long ago, when I wasn't so emotionally naked. I have this thought as tears run down my face, tears that I resent, tears that don't feel like they are allowed to belong to me.

"Thank God you care so much," says Mae, like she's just read the scrolling banner that's thrumming through my brain, *I wish, I wish, I wish I didn't care so much.* "Thank God you're here, that it's you right now, even though I know it can't be you forever. You know, people are moving away from God, from religion, because it's—I guess it's *trendy* and much, much easier to serve your own needs than the needs of others, as God calls us to do. I don't know if you believe in God or a higher power. But even if you don't, I have seen you be compelled to act in a way that puts the needs of others before your own. There are many people who could have done all the wrong things in your position, and here you are, trying to do what's right, reaching out, like the hand of God. I want you to know that I see that. I know that. The world has been so dark, but I am grateful that your light has been here to shine on us."

All I can do is stare at her through my inappropriate tears, stare and stare, as every hateful thought I've had, every horrible urge I've had to squash in the last few months, bubbles up. If she can't see what's in front of her, see the me who's actually standing there, then she's delusional. She and her God, they're both beyond reason.

Mae leaves the next day, holding me tightly as she hugs me good-bye. Scotty calls, and the sound on the line is faraway and staticky, even though I know, in theory, that overseas calls aren't supposed to be that way anymore. This time there is no mention of Pup, or Matt specifically, of phone calls to Dr. O'Neill, or sleepless nights, or eagerness to get home. He offers again to send family members over to help me, this time mentioning that Ashley Lynn is willing to bring her three youngest kids and stay with me while he is away. I promptly decline, horrified at the thought of having three extra kids hanging around, vulnerable to the damage I might accidentally inflict on them while we're eating breakfast or making sticker pictures.

"What about Patrick?" says Scotty.

"You mean, to stay?"

"Maybe just to check in and see what he can help out with. Take some of the pressure off."

"It's up to you."

"You're the one who will be most affected. I'd rather it be up to you."

"It's fine, I guess."

He says good-bye and hangs up. He probably feels that he's done his best by sending in a ringer. But I wonder what it is in Berlin that could be so important to pull him away, or if it's actually something here in this house, pushing him.

When the boys get home from school, I stick them in front of the TV and talk myself out of all the wicked things I am imagining. Methodically, like a list: I will not feed the kids Pizza Hut every night until Scotty gets home. I will not wait until they go to bed and then drink myself to sleep every night until he gets home. I will not send them off to Lila's. I will not set up playdates for them every day. I will not let them eat cake in place of breakfast until he gets home.

My phone rings, snapping me out of it, and I'm about to push the ignore button. I've been doing this automatically for the last thirty-six hours as Jane and Claudia bombarded me with calls and texts. This time, I happen to look, and it's Everett calling. I pick it up, in the most pathetic bid for freedom ever, as there is no one here to witness it. He barely bothers with a greeting, which I take to mean he's still pissed at me for that day I ditched him for Scotty. He's describing which door to use as the entrance and coordinating the timing of something. I feel like he's tracking footprints through the mud in my brain until I remember Jess and the armory.

"You're sure you can make it?"

"Well," I say, "I'm not sure. I'm so sorry. I have the boys—their dad is in—he's overseas."

"Can't you get them a babysitter?"

"Everett. I am their babysitter."

Everett always has something to say, even if it's mean and quippy, so his lack of response upsets me. I hear a thud from the TV room and hope it's not George falling off the couch.

"Let me see if I can work something out for Saturday," I say. "I really want to try and go with you."

"All right."

"I will. I'll work something out."

"Okay," he says and hangs up.

I look at the clock and try to calculate the number of hours I have until Saturday at 5 p.m. It's less than forty-eight. I have only a minute to think strategically about the things I'll need to do to prepare; to think of what to say to Everett, let alone Jess, or find some armory-appropriate attire, or get a haircut, or do anything at all that is mine, that just belongs to me, seems out of the realm of possibility. Because here I am in an apartment that isn't mine, with two kids who don't have anyone but me, and it feels a lot like we're playing a high-stakes game of house in which none of the characters are named Charlotte.

"YOU KNOW, SUNDAY's my birthday," Patrick says the following evening, sitting at the table and watching me clean up the kitchen.

"Oh, right. I guess I remembered that. Did you get your invitation to Matt's party next weekend?" I ask.

"Yes, I did. I'll be there."

"Are you going out for your birthday?"

"I have to work most of the day."

"On a Sunday? That's so silly," I say. "Can you move your arms?"

He lifts his arm, and I wipe the table. "I'll come by that evening, after work, to check in," he says. "You can cook for me, if you want."

"I'm not sure you'll want to eat what I can cook."

"Kid food? Always," he says. I'm surprised he remembers that conversation, considering all the other memorable things about that night.

"Tiny hamburgers it is." I sit down across from him at the table. "I have to ask you something, okay?"

"Finally," he says, leaning forward. "I was wondering how long you'd hold out."

I throw the rag at him, but he has quick reflexes, and he catches it. "Something serious, jackass."

"I can't wait to hear it."

"I need to go somewhere tomorrow in the late afternoon. Do you think you could take the boys for a little while? It will only be, like, two hours, tops."

"Sure, I think I can handle it," he says. "What, you mean you have a life outside these walls?"

"Ha. Not really."

There's a crashing sound from another room, which causes both of us to jump, and I run halfway down the hallway before Patrick has a chance to speak. "It was our marble run," he calls after me. I turn around and run right into him. He's followed me down the hallway. "The one I built with the boys after dinner. It was ill-proportioned, and it collapsed. It was only a matter of time."

"Oh," I say. "Oh. Thank God. Okay."

"That freaked you out, huh?" he says. "You're pretty fast. Like a bunny."

"The kids have been having trouble sleeping," I say. "We've kind of been on high alert here at night."

"Right. The black eye."

"Exactly." I turn my head to face down the hallway, listening for any sounds of distress or urgent calls for a drink of water, but nothing comes. I can't seem to shake the jumpy feeling, like I'm being startled over and over, like I'm not only unsure of what's coming next but if anything is coming at all. A minute passes, and I decide that they are fine. So far tonight, they are resting undisturbed.

We're standing close to Matt's door, and Patrick is on the side that leads back to the rest of the apartment. There's not enough space for me to get around him. He isn't moving. He looks like he's listening down the hall, as I am.

"I'm pretty sure they're getting ready to arm the Syrian rebels." I say it in a whisper, nervous about Matt and his singular ability to hear only those things that no one wants him to hear.

"Who is? I thought the president said no to that last year," says Patrick.

"I think he's going to change his mind," I say. "Just the way I think the wind is blowing."

Patrick grasps my arms, above the elbows. "Are you lightheaded?"

"I don't know how I feel about it." I consider leaning back while he grips my arms, to see how long he can hold me up without letting me pull him over. "Nobody wants another Vietnam, of course, but those pictures. Have you seen those pictures? The nine-year-old, holding a rifle and smoking a cigarette? God, I just—I look at them and I weep."

"I agree. It's very sad."

"I mean, it's part of our responsibility, I guess. As a superpower. He's not the kind of man who can sit back and pretend that genocide isn't happening. The president, you know? He's just not that man." My sisters would mock me right now for paraphrasing Jay Carney, and I miss them and wish that I could answer their phone calls. But I'm afraid of their empathy, so here I am alone in my petri dish.

"I think we should sit down," says Patrick, and I let him walk me back to the kitchen. He pulls out a chair. I use it as a step stool and lever myself up onto the table. He pushes the chair back a few inches and sits in it, and I think he's worried about my apparent unsteadiness, worried that I might keel over. But my head doesn't feel light at all. It feels very, very heavy.

"The thing is," I say, "he has to draw the line somewhere. He has to have boundaries. And he has to respect the historical boundaries, the boundaries of the office, you know?"

"He has to be careful of precedent too. The boundaries of the future," Patrick says. I turn to face him, swinging my legs around to the end of the table. I expect him to push back further and give me some room, but he doesn't.

"I found George's little stuffed dog, the one we thought we lost. Matt had it. He's *had* it. He's had it all along. He's been hiding it. I want to go nuclear on his ass."

Patrick starts to laugh.

"You can't, you, no, you don't understand. I made this apartment my *bitch* trying to find that dog. It meant so much to him, to George, that little dog; it was like another member of the family. He loved that freaking thing. We brought it to the hospital that night, and it didn't come back, just like, you know, just—"

"I know what you mean," he says.

"And Matt, *he took it*. Didn't care that George was heartbroken without it. Didn't care that I spent hours trying to find it. Lied to me over and over, with a straight face, like a little sociopath."

"Did you tell Scotty?" Patrick stretches his legs out in front of him, like the chair is too small.

"Yeah, I told him."

"What did he have to say?"

"He said he was relieved that it wasn't an emergency."

"That sounds like him."

"You want to know the worst part?" I say, kicking my legs back and forth, noticing how far they are from the floor and how close they are to his knees. "I can't even give him back to George. I can't resurrect Pup for him, because—"

"How could you not be able to resurrect his mother?" he says.

"Exactly," I say.

"Kids are self-centered," he says, reaching out to steady my legs, to stop the back and forth. Without the motion, a nervous energy builds, concentrating itself right where Patrick is holding my ankles. When he lets go, I have to focus really hard not to start swinging my legs again. "Empathy isn't a thing they're capable of, right? He wasn't thinking about George, or you, or anyone else. Just himself. Kids, they want what they want."

"Maybe sociopath was too strong of a word choice," I say.

"It's nicer than what I would have come up with if I were in your position."

I have the urge to keep talking, to spill my guts in the hope that it will loosen the knots on my insides. I want to tell him everything that's happened since she died, everything about the boys, about Scotty, about me. I want to. I want to.

"Can I say something to you?" he asks, before I can do any of that, and I don't know if I'm disappointed or relieved. He's making a face that looks like Matt's when he's searching for the best words to communicate. I want to hold him, wrap my arms and legs around him, feel the weight of his whole body.

"What?" I ask.

"I have this thing. All of a sudden. There's this part of me that wasn't there before. Like an extra organ. A lump. And it's harder than the rest of my organs, and sometimes it moves around, gets into my throat or my chest, but most of the time it sits in my stomach. It's a thing that wasn't there before Gretchen died, but I . . . I don't know. I woke up one day, and it was there, and I can't get rid of it." I nudge him with my toes, right above his knees. He covers my feet with his hands, trapping them there. "I thought it was grief—intense, physically painful grief—but now I think it might be fear. I think I might be walking around with a constant knot of fear."

"What are you afraid of?" I ask.

"The end of the world. The end of my world, my life."

"You're afraid of dying?"

"It's the most asshole cliché you've ever heard, right? But yes, that's it. I have this fear that I'll die and be . . . nothing."

"You were nothing before you were born. And you didn't mind then," I say.

"Yes. But now I have been alive. I know what life is like, and I'm afraid of the nothing."

"I hear you," I say. "Sometimes I worry about being nothing while I'm still alive. Mae and her people would probably call it purgatory, but I think it can happen to you while you're living."

"Ha," Patrick says. He is moving his thumbs over the arches of my bare feet. "Mae and her *people*."

"It's late." I slide down off the table. "Are you sure you don't mind babysitting tomorrow? I can text you the exact time."

He doesn't get up right away. He sits in front of where I'm standing, his head right next to my stomach, looking up at me. I don't know what I'll do if he does anything other than answer my question.

Finally, he stands. "Yes, it should be fine. Happy to do it. I'll call in the morning and see how things are going."

"Okay," I say.

He goes.

I walk back to my room, turn off all the lights, and get in bed.

I dream again about Scotty, and it's graphic.

I keep my eyes open while he kisses me. Sometimes I kiss him back, and sometimes I just watch him kiss me.

Scotty's eyes are closed, the eyelids resting against his eyes so lightly they appear to be fluttering, and the way he's gripping the collar of my shirt as we kiss suggests that he has no idea what to do with his hands. He starts to undress, only himself, as if it's a given that we will have sex but not that he has permission to be the one to make me naked. I stare at his body, his chest an upside-down triangle, the bones protruding at his shoulders, elbows, the bottom of his ribcage. I've never imagined what his body might look like underneath his clothes, but now I know. He is pale, inconsistently so, and on his skin there are bumps, dots, lines, patches.

I take my clothes off in a rush. My zipper doesn't come down very far, and it causes my pants to catch on my hips. I have to move back and forth to get them past, and something roars behind his eyes when I do it. He reaches forward, suddenly in the same rush that I'm in, and helps with the last of my clothes. I am naked, he is naked, and now I want to close my eyes, but his are open, so I can't.

He pulls me down into a chair, on his lap, and adjusts until he is pushing up inside me. I am in control, but there is no escaping. I start to move, pushing myself against him as close as I can get, and he says, "Charlotte, Charlotte, Charlotte," over and over, along with some other noises that I've never heard, never imagined. I like them, and they make me feel powerful, and I forget myself and think of him, every part of him. I'm not me. He is not him. We are we. I put my forehead against his. His eyes are closed again, so I open them with my thumbs, and we look at each other.

Suddenly Scotty has a strength I don't know. He picks us up and moves us to the floor, he on his knees and me on my back. He moves until he is all the way in, until there is no space left that's only mine, and says, "Gretchen."

And then it's nothing but a frenzy, and I really do close my eyes as it escalates. It's angry. I made it that way when I forced him to look at me. It goes on, and there are hands and mouths and sounds and shouting, and then I come, hard, my stomach contracting, and he pulls out of me, but it's too late. He came inside, and he continues on the outside. It's a mess. We're a mess.

I watch Scotty, collapsed at my feet, breathing hard. I think of his need, the way he raced me to the finish. The clawing, the pulling, the selfishness, the abandonment of ego in favor of id. I'm not used to being wanted that way.

"We've got to clean up," says Scotty. "The boys will be awake."

"Sure, that's practical."

"I don't know what to say." Scotty walks naked into the kitchen and pulls a bunch of paper towels down, many more than he actually needs. He tears one off, not seeming to mind that it doesn't stay within its perforation, and hands it to me. He wipes himself and then uses the same one to scrub at the floor. I think he needs water, bleach, paint thinner, acid. Something to eat the finish off the floorboards.

AT 4:07 ON Saturday afternoon, I glare at my phone, willing the text message in my hand to transform itself into something else. "Got sucked into a meeting. Can't get out. I'm so sorry." I need to make a decision in the next three minutes, or I will once again be letting my inability to control things become my reality. The thought of being powerless makes me furious, furious at Patrick, furious at Scotty, irrationally furious at the boys, at Everett, at strangers on the street who look at me and dare to make assessments about my life, that I am only a babysitter, a girl with two kids. I'm furious at myself for putting my arms into this strait-jacket and at Gretchen for zipping it up.

Before the boys know what is happening, I've stuffed a bag full of activity books and crayons and wrangled us out the door, hoping they don't figure out that we're running an errand of mine instead of one of theirs until they're trapped in their seats for the concert. There isn't enough time to think about what any of us should wear or what we'll do when we get there. We'll have to improvise, and I soothe myself with Claudia's words in my head. *It's Jess. We don't care what she thinks.*

In the elevator, I bend down to fasten George's shoes more securely, and Matt whines, "I don't want to go anywhere. I want to stay home! I don't want to go outside—"

"Matthew, stop it," I say, in a voice I regret the minute it's out there. I do my best to take it down a notch. "Something came up at work for Uncle Patrick. I can't leave you guys alone in the apartment. You have to come with me to this thing. I'm sorry."

"But where are we going?"

"We're going on a crazy adventure. To a fancy building down the street."

"What are we doing there?"

"Listening to some music."

Matt is still suspicious, as he should be.

When we pull up in front of the armory, Everett is standing outside, dressed all in dark gray, smoking a cigarette. He looks very similar to one of those tiny storm clouds that follows Eeyore around in Winnie-the-Pooh stories. I can only imagine the field day he's going to have, after witnessing my arrival with two kids via town car.

I let Matt out of the car first and tell him to wait on the sidewalk while I gather up George and all of our belongings. By the time we've joined him, Matt has already initiated a conversation with Everett.

"Smoking is not good for your body," he is saying.

"That may be," says Everett. "But I like it very much."

"If they took an x-ray of your lungs, they might be gray. And fuzzy."

"Well then, they would match the rest of me, wouldn't they?"

"Poisoning your body is not the right thing to do. It's the only one you'll ever have," says Matt. This is a direct quote from his mother.

"Haven't you ever had an ice cream cone, kid?"

"Yes."

"And you liked it, right?"

"Yes."

"It's the same thing."

"No, it's not!"

"Yes, kid, it is."

"I tried to make other arrangements," I interrupt, "but they fell through, so I hope they'll sell me a couple of extra tickets in there."

"They're expensive," says Everett. "It's a fund-raiser for the foundation she's working on."

"That's fine," I say. The mean part of me feels satisfied that I can do something active to take out my aggression on Scotty, like put a couple of expensive concert tickets on his credit card. "Matt, George, this is my friend Everett."

Everett offers his hand formally to Matt, who gives him the stink eye and doesn't take it. George slaps it, like a sideways high five.

Everett looks surprised. "Which one are you, Matt or George?"

"George," says George.

"I'm very happy to meet you, George. Charlotte's told me a lot about you," says Everett. Matt knows he's been outdone, and he doesn't like it.

"Let's go in," I say, wanting to head off a smart-aleck remark from Matt. Everett grinds out his cigarette on the bottom of his shoe and then leads the way to the doors. He holds open the heavy door for me and the boys and starts to walk straight back. I stop him.

"I thought it was in the Veterans Room."

"No, the Drill Hall."

"She called it a salon."

"It got too big for that room once word got out. She told them she was happy to play amid whatever installation was currently in the larger room. She said she thought it would be inspiring."

"For who?" I have to stop and pick up George, who has begun pulling on my hand, needing me to slow the pace a bit. Matt's head has been tilted all the way back against his neck since we entered the building, as he takes in the huge space and daunting architecture. "Matty, babe, please watch where you're walking. I don't want you to accidentally run into something, like a suit of armor or a cannon."

Everett looks from Matt to George to me and then says, "For the few hundred or so people coming to hear her, I suppose. Or maybe for herself. Who knows?"

"You think they have cannons in here?" asks Matt. "Like, real ones?"

"Maybe not cannons. But probably an old torpedo or two."

"What pedo?" George asks, tightening his grip around my neck.

"Ouch, G, that's too tight," I say. "Can you hold my shoulder instead of my neck?"

"What is that, that pedo?"

"It's called a *tor*pedo, honey. It's like a little rocket that submarines used to fire at each other during big fights."

"Why the submarines fighting?"

"Um," I say, searching for the words that will preoccupy him the least. "Like, when a superhero needs to defeat a bunch of villains, all at once. He could maybe get in a submarine and fire his torpedo and take down their headquarters. Or their boat."

"The villains' boat?"

"Yeah."

"Torpedo," says George. "And they shoot the villains all at once."

"That's right. Hey, can you and Matt hang out here for a

minute? You can walk around, but don't go through any doors. I need to talk to this lady about tickets for the show."

I set George down next to Matt, and Everett joins me at will call.

"God. That conversation. I'm never having children," he says.

"You probably shouldn't, if an easy one like that freaked you out," I say.

"Hi," says Everett, and the woman in charge of the tickets glowers at us, maybe because I'm wearing tights and a wool skirt instead of a ball gown. "Jess Fairchild reserved our tickets." The woman's face twists a bit, and I take that to be her version of a smile, indulging us because we're acquainted with Jess. Everett gives her his name, and I press my lips together so I won't say anything to her that I'll regret, because I need her to do me a favor.

"Is the seating general admission?" I ask.

"It is."

"Can I purchase two additional tickets, please?"

The woman gives me a jaw-dropping total, and I give her the credit card. She gives us the same twisty face as she hands over our tickets, and I beckon to Matt and George to follow me into the hall, ignoring the incredulous looks from the ushers as we find some aisle seats and get situated.

"Are there programs?" I ask the nearest usher as I pull out a number-activity book for Matt and hand him a red colored pencil.

"Not today," he says. "She'll be announcing the sets as she goes. It's meant to be informal, in the style of a—"

"A *salon*, yes, I know," I say. "Thank you."

When the house lights begin to dim, indicating the start of the show, Matt and George look up toward the ceiling automatically. The way the light filters into this space looks like magic, and I can see that magic on their faces. I find that I'm not sorry that I brought them here, even though I've never imagined a scenario with all of these elements in play. As Jess walks onstage to a rush of applause, I can tell that Matt has forgotten that it wasn't his choice to be here. He listens with rapt attention, at least for the time being.

Jess starts off solo on the saxophone. Everett catches my eye, and I imagine that he is also thinking back to our school days. Snyder would find some obscure venue in the Meatpacking District where some guy with a mustache was performing his new piece, "Seventeen Suites for Tambourine and Castanets," and we'd all get dragged along to watch. The evening would be warm, so we'd decide to walk back to school, and Roger would be stumbling drunk and overly friendly. Snyder would get moody because the guy with the mustache had beaten him to the punch. We'd all make fun of Colleen for wearing inappropriate shoes *again*, and we'd wonder out loud, for at least fifteen minutes, what Jess would have thought of castanet-guy's performance.

Now, she's joined onstage by a brass quartet, and she surrenders her saxophone in favor of the piano, which she plays well. By this time, Matt has decided he needs to copy the numbers in his activity book in the colors according to the order of the rainbow, so he has worked out a silent system where he pokes my arm every time he needs the next color. George, on the other side of me, is sitting with his head sticking out into the aisle and his hands between his knees. Every time something in the music strikes his fancy, he looks at me to see whether or not I've noticed, and more often than not, I've been struck too.

Jess follows the dramatic movement with a piece I recognize, a piece that I've seen on paper, the one I deconstructed for her. She turns around on the piano bench and pulls out an acoustic guitar, singing the song herself, a simple melody. A quiet moment. It's beautiful, and I'm so lost in the music that I almost miss what she says to the audience after the long bout of applause is over.

She's talking about teaching, and what a humbling, edifying experience it can be if you let it in the right way. She doesn't mention me by name, but I wonder if this is meant to appease me, as close as she can bring herself to putting my name in the program.

"My students inspire me every day, and I'm grateful for the opportunity to work with such insightful and talented young people," she says, wrapping up, and I look around at the faces in the audience, so appreciative of her, not only because she makes humanity better with her music but also because she acts as a mentor to the composers of tomorrow. I wish I was fighting the urge to stand up and expose her for a fraud, but I'm not. I almost admire the way she views the world, the way she's able to spin the tale of her own life. She is a composer *and* she is a performer, through and through, and I am not the things that she is. I am something else, something separate.

After the program, the audience is shepherded en masse to one of the reception rooms across the hall. Everett is chatting with the couple who sat behind us, who had also been to see him at Carnegie Hall those few months ago. The kids are not going to last much longer, so I hand their jackets and my backpack to Everett in his distraction, and then I bring the boys with me to say good-bye to Jess.

"They're adorable," she says, kissing me on both cheeks. "Thank you so much for coming to see me, boys. Did you enjoy the concert?"

Matt kind of shrugs, without ever taking his eyes from the table full of cookies and champagne to the left of us. George stares straight up at her, too occupied with whatever assessment he is making to say anything.

"Okay, guys," I say. "Two cookies each. Help your brother, please, Matty." They scamper off, and I call after them. "Don't put your hands on any of the ones you're not going to eat!"

"You got the tickets I left," says Jess.

"Yes. Thank you."

"I hope they didn't charge you admission for the kids."

"We didn't mind making the donation."

"Well," she says, "then I should say thank you to you. The generosity of donors is going to make the foundation possible."

I could explain where the money came from. I could ask what the foundation will benefit. I could compliment her work. But instead of any of that, I ask, "Is there anyone here to see you?"

She looks around at the packed reception room. "Charlotte, you're so funny."

"No, I mean, specifically to see *you*. Do you have, like, a boyfriend somewhere in here? Or, I don't know, a cousin?"

"The head of the chamber series at Lincoln Center is here. And some folks from the festival in Prague. The executive producer over at BAM. I can introduce you, if you'd like."

"No, thank you," I say. "I've got to get going. These two aren't going to be adorable for very much longer." I look over at George and Matt, who are now standing with Everett. George has his jacket on and is holding on to Everett's pant leg, waiting patiently. His cookies are gone, with not a crumb left in sight. Matt is licking chocolate off his fingers and ignoring Everett, who is holding his hoodie out to him on the end of one finger, looking perplexed.

"I'm surprised," says Jess. "You can't stay for five more minutes and meet a few people, make a few connections? It's so important."

"Well, so is dinner, to these guys. Somehow I can't picture the man who runs BAM throwing himself on the floor and moaning about his dire need for mashed potatoes." I take a few steps toward the door. I'm about to reach back, to squeeze her arm and tell her what a nice job she did, to part on peaceful terms and let go of her, gently, without her even knowing that it's happening. I'm about to.

"That's the difference between you and Everett, I think," she says. "I'm looking forward to the day when you get your priorities in order. I don't know how to make it any clearer that I think the world is missing out on you."

"It's funny you should bring that up again, Jess," I say. "It kind of feels like a dare, every time you say something like that to me."

"I'm not sure what you mean by that."

"A significant portion of the population has heard me, in fact. That theme you sold a few years back, the one we wrote together during my final for your seminar. No one knows who I am because my name is not on that piece. But as for depriving the world of my particular sound—I don't think we have to worry. You took care of it."

Jess is looking around. There are a bunch of people in close proximity. "I don't like what you're getting at."

I lower my voice. "It's not important though, what you did. It doesn't matter that there's this blurry, uncomfortable thing between us, because we don't have to see each other again. You taught me a lot, and now I'm done learning from you." I start to button up my sweater. "You know what is important?" I point to Matt, whose sweatshirt is now on the floor, being used as a picnic blanket by George. "Them. They're important. Their dinner, and everything else they need. That's George, over there on the floor. He hates to stand around for too long, and if I'm dawdling, I always find him sitting on the floor, looking resigned, by the time I'm ready to go. I know that about him, just like I know that if I crack a snarky joke to his brother, Matt, I can distract him from almost anything. I could fill a hundred volumes with all the things I know about them. What I'm doing for them is important. But you, and all the things you do to get what you want—that is not important, at all."

"Well, that can be your opinion. You're allowed to think whatever you need to think," she says, and I've never seen her face so red, never seen her struggle so hard for grace. I want to feel vindicated and smug, but instead I'm feeling something closer to pity.

"The larger world probably needs you, Jess, just the way you are," I say. "Maybe the world that needs me is smaller. But I don't think our worlds have to be static, only one way forever. It's probably better if we don't run into each other again, even though we might be part of the same circles in the future. Okay?"

I don't wait for her answer, and I don't look at her face before I turn around to go. I don't savor the moment the way I always imagined I would. I don't want to spend my energy thinking about it anymore. Everett is nowhere to be seen, and I don't bother trying to locate him. I help Georgie to his feet and take his hand, pick up Matt's jacket, and let him follow me out of the room. He comes with me reluctantly, not because he wants to but because he knows that that's the rule, and by now, we have a very good understanding of each other's boundaries.

WHEN WE WALK in the door to the apartment a few minutes later, the phone is ringing, so I drop our stuff in the hallway and run to grab it.

"Hello?"

"Charlotte? Is your cell phone off?" I can hear the tension in Scotty's voice.

"Oh. Yes, it is. I'm sorry. I had to go to this—"

"I just got off the phone with the bank."

"Um. Okay."

"They want to know why my credit cards are being used in Berlin and New York, which was easy enough to explain, but then they mentioned a charge for twelve hundred dollars. To something called the Fairchild Foundation."

"Oh. Yeah, that was me."

"The Fairchild Foundation?" It sounds a lot worse in Scotty's voice than it did in my head.

"Yes," I say. "I asked Patrick to babysit today, and he canceled. I had to take the boys with me to a benefit concert, and the tickets were six hundred dollars. I'm sorry. I didn't know what else to do."

Matt walks into the kitchen, where I'm standing with the phone, with his shoes untied but still on his feet. "I'm hungry."

"TUCK!" bellows George from the other room. I hope it means that his shoe is stuck and not his head.

"Matt, take your shoes off, please, pal. I'll get you something to eat in a minute."

"Why didn't you call me?" asks Scotty.

Matt opens the refrigerator door. "But what are we having for dinner?"

"Please take your shoes off, Matthew, and then we can talk about it."

"Charlotte," says Scotty.

"What?"

"Why didn't you call me about the tickets?"

"TAHR-LETTE! Can't get my foot out! Need someone to help me!" George yells.

Matt flings one of his shoes off the end of his foot, and it hits the wall. "Oops," he says and starts to laugh.

"I didn't have time to call you beforehand. I thought Patrick was coming until the very last minute," I say, gesturing at Matt not to do that with the other shoe. He ignores me. His left shoe flies upward, barely missing one of the blades of the ceiling fan. "Matt, do you understand that you could break something? Please, please, take your shoes out to the hall and put them away."

"I could have helped you figure out another alternative," says Scotty.

"OW!" yells George, and I look around the kitchen for Matt, who has disappeared. I walk out into the hallway to find him trying to pull off his brother's shoe, but wedging George's knee into an uncomfortable angle in the process.

"Hold on a second," I say, to both Matt and Scotty. I squat down to loosen the Velcro on George's shoes and pry them off his feet. The boys run into the kitchen, so I stay seated on the floor of the hallway. "I'm sorry about the money. I had to make a call, and I'm sorry if it was the wrong call."

"I don't care about the money," says Scotty. "Taking them to something like that, though—isn't Fairchild that woman who screwed you? You might have considered staying at home when Patrick canceled. Taking it as a sign or something."

I hold the phone away from my head, gripping it while I think of a response that doesn't involve curse words. I want to throw the phone across the room and let the sound of it smashing be my answer to him. "It was all I could think of at the time, so I did it. I don't know what else to say."

"Charlotte, I'm sorry that Mae left you there alone," he says.

"Mae is not the one who left me alone," I say. I glance through the kitchen door just in time to see Matt attempt to pull a Tupperware container out from under several others in the refrigerator. The squelching sounds as cucumbers, avocados and yogurt containers start hitting the floor take precedence over everything else.

"I have to go, Scotty," I say. "Matthew just caused some sort of refrigerator avalanche. I'm sorry. If you want to take the twelve hundred dollars out of my paycheck, I understand. We'll try to get you on video chat tomorrow, okay?" I hang up.

George and Matt are staring at me with wide eyes and frozen expressions as I survey the mess they made. Matt bends down and picks up one of the avocados with two fingers, holding it out for my inspection.

"We could still eat the top part of this," he says, cringing, like he expects me to smack him upside the head.

"You know what, boys? I'm gonna cut you a deal," I say. I take the avocado and set it on the counter. "We need to do something fun right now. Your babysitter needs to do something fun, and that means you guys get to come along. If you'll both go and get your shoes back on with no fussing, I will clean this up, and we'll go out. Okay?"

"Where are we going?" asks Matt, predictably.

"I don't know. Maybe we'll, we'll go down and kidnap Uncle Patrick from his office. We could surprise him and take him out to dinner. Tomorrow is his birthday."

"Okay!" These boys love surprises, getting them and giving them, and they race to put on their shoes, forgetting what a chore it was to take them off only moments ago.

I pick the vegetables up off the floor and pitch them all, wiping up the yogurt with a sponge and putting the tower of Tupperware to rights inside the fridge. I text the driver who just dropped us off to come back for us in five minutes, but it is less than that before we are down in the lobby waiting for him, shoes on our feet and snacks in hand.

We get in the car, roll down all the windows, and pretend we're on a roller coaster as the driver speeds downtown toward the financial district. The boys are giggling and have taken up the phrase "going to kidnap Uncle Patrick" into a singsongy chant, and I laugh with them and feel my stomach flipping between joy and worry that we'll never be this joyful again. The driver pulls up in front of Patrick's building, and I ask him to wait.

I have to convince the security guard at the front desk that we're not here for sinister reasons (at this point, the cries of "kidnap Uncle Patrick" are no longer helpful). Finally, though, we're allowed onto the elevator. When we get to the floor that Patrick's firm occupies, the place looks almost deserted.

The dark-haired, exotic-looking receptionist is wearing jeans and a loose ruffled blouse, along with Chanel flats and a Roberto Cavalli bracelet. The casual dress seems to suggest that she's been called in for a last-minute Saturday, and I notice that her purse is on the desk, like she's been packing up to leave.

"Hi," I say, grateful in a silly way that I've at least exchanged my usual yoga pants for a skirt today. I point to a spindly gray couch that looks like it might be made out of felt, with shiny chrome legs, and the boys bounce over and pull out their crayons and colored pencils. I'm glad I didn't pack markers. "We're looking for Patrick McLean. I'm . . . these are his nephews. We came down to surprise him, to take him out. For his birthday. So, is he still here?"

"He is," she says, smiling in such a brilliant way that I am a little bit in love with her. "He's got a few things to finish up, last I heard. I'm sure he'll be done soon. He told me I could go, that he would be done in about a half hour. But I wouldn't mind staying for a while." She raises her eyebrows, and it's a polite I'll-stay-if-you-want-me-to-because-I-have-Stockholm-Syndrome-for-this-company look.

"No, that's all right. We can wait on our own," I say.

"Wonderful," she says as she shoulders her bag. "His office is down that hallway, the last door on the left, if you get tired of waiting. There are all sorts of drinks and snacks in the refrigerator, through the second door on the right. That room also has an amazing city view. Nice to have met you." She flips a switch behind her desk, and the lights dim.

"You too," I say, and she smiles again as she glides out the glass doors. The elevator doors open for her as she approaches, either because it's Saturday evening and no one else is here, or because she's Queen of the Elves.

Twenty minutes pass, and I start to get nervous that there's some secret door Patrick will leave from, that I'll have to disappoint the boys with no actual surprise to fulfill all the buildup. I decide to go looking for him. I'll let him know I'm here, and he can pretend to be surprised when he comes out later and sees the boys in the lobby.

"Matty," I say, "I need to go to the bathroom. Can I ask you a favor? Since you're the oldest?"

If he were a peacock, he'd spread his tail. "Yes," he says, sitting up straighter, or maybe it just looks like it, since George is drooping over to one side. This whirlwind of a day I've been dragging them around on is starting to catch up with him.

"Can you be in charge of your brother? I don't want either one of you to move from that couch until I get back. You might have to—I don't know—help him color his Smurf or something. I won't be long."

"Okay," he says and flips the page of the coloring book. I'm pretty sure he'll take the responsibility for keeping George occupied seriously, so I leave them to their crayons on the spindly couch and walk down the hall toward the door the receptionist pointed out earlier. It's only half-lit, like the lobby after she flipped the switch, the way I imagine most buildings are at night. As I get nearer to his door, it only gets darker. The outer office door is open, the room is empty, and I almost decide right then that Patrick isn't here. Maybe I should try calling his phone. But his office door is only a few feet away. I might as well knock.

The inner door is closed but not latched, and I raise my fist to make my presence known. I hesitate as I hear a noise that I recognize immediately and then almost as quickly try to talk myself out of admitting I heard. I don't know what streak of perversity compels me to open the door at that point, but I do, and what I find is so inevitable that I'm not even surprised.

Her back is toward me as I stand there holding the door open. It's a little too dark to see one hundred percent clearly, but I do catch the occasional glint off her blondish hair, a color close to my own. From the back, I muse, amazed at my own objectivity, she could actually *be* me, except I'd bet the farm, as my grandmother would say, that she's been to a yoga class more recently than I have. She is mostly clothed, but her skirt is bunched up around her stomach, and her legs are slung over his shoulders even though she is sitting pretty much upright on his desk. Yoga, for sure. His hands grasp her waist as he buries himself inside her, rhythmically but not frantically, as if he has all kinds of time to get her off. Each time his hips meet hers, her breath hitches, and she has to brace herself more firmly on her post.

I have maintained such a wild silence since I opened the door that it could go either way, whether I walk away unnoticed or not, but I don't leave. I don't go right away, because I'm fascinated by the silhouette. It could be us, me and him.

He must hear the door creak as I lean against it because he looks up and meets my eyes. He wraps an arm around her back to pull her in and keep her from noticing me in the doorway, but he doesn't stop, and he doesn't drop my gaze. He's not going to stop, and that's okay because I want to watch. So I stand there and watch, and he watches me watching, until finally her legs start to shake, and she says, "Oh God!" He finishes without ever taking his eyes from mine. She lets her legs slide down the sides of his arms, and he locks his other arm around her back to keep her from turning, and casually waves me away as he does so.

My legs feel like jelly as I walk back down the hall, as if I were the one who just came with Patrick.

The boys are coloring nicely, or rather, Matt is coloring nicely, and George is holding three crayons and having trouble sitting upright, his eyes are so droopy. I pull George onto my lap and try to pry the crayons out of his fingers, but he insists, "Me hold it!" and goes to sleep with his head on my shoulder and his legs to one side of my lap. Matt is lying on the floor on his stomach, and it's not long before he quits holding his own head up and goes to sleep face-down on a picture of Smurfette with pink hair. I don't know how much time passes before Patrick emerges from the half-lit hallway. There is no moving without disturbing the kids. It might be ten minutes, or it might be an hour. The blonde girl is nowhere to be seen, and I'd just as soon not know what her face looks like anyway, so I don't question it.

"You brought them here?" he asks.

"We thought maybe we'd surprise you and take you out to dinner for your birthday. It took a while to get downtown. I'm glad you're still here. They would have been really disappointed if, you know, if you weren't."

He looks at his watch. "I guess it's a little past their bedtime now."

"They had some Goldfish and banana on the way down to hold them over, so I guess that will have to do today."

Patrick looks down at his sleeping nephews. "I'll call a car to take us back uptown."

"No need. Ours is waiting." I don't ask him why he's coming uptown with us even though the birthday-surprise plan is already ruined. It seems like a given.

He carries Matt and I carry George, and we meet the town car downstairs. We load the kids in first and buckle their belts, and Patrick climbs in after them. I have a sudden flash of limbo, where I almost bolt up front to sit with the driver, but I don't make the decision quickly enough. Before I know it, Patrick has his finger and thumb around my wrist, guiding me into the car. The driver shuts the door, and I notice the screen is up. It must be standard procedure.

I roll down my window about three inches so that I can feel the air, as if I can expel the palpable communication between us into the night. I have to find a way to release what's in my belly, from my neck to my knees, and it has to be soon. I've been playing fox in the henhouse with him for so long that I don't even think I know who's the fox and who's the hen anymore. What I do know is that *he* knows what's going on inside me, that the perfect marriage of accident and design that happened this evening could produce no other result.

I am wedged between the door and his body. He has his eyes on me. I have my eyes on him.

The car is flying up toward Houston, and his hand is on my knee. I put my head back against the seat, and he is moving it, the hand, almost without me noticing, he is moving it slowly up and down my tights-clad thigh. I didn't think I had the capacity to clench any further, but I do. It's a hard left onto the Bowery, and I think we're going to get held up by Union Square. It's the button on my skirt now, and it doesn't make a sound, which is the only way it can be because the kids are right there next to him. All he needs is his hand really, and it's barely even touching me. There's a fabric barrier between his skin and my skin, but it almost doesn't matter what's there because I need this so badly, and I'm going to have it. As we lurch forward onto Park to speed uptown, it's his thumb, his knuckle, his hand, and I am straining and trying not to interrupt our silence, and he can tell that I'm about to fail because right when I get to the top, just before the fall, he puts his other hand over my mouth, and my fingers clutch his hair and the back of his head, and any sound I make is absorbed into him.

When he is sure that it's okay to let go, he does, and I shift to adjust my tights and button my skirt. His fingers are on the side of my face; he wants to turn my chin and look at me, but my eyes are watery, and I don't let him. The thing about release is that it's a slippery slope, and if I let him look at me, I might laugh or cry or moan or pee my pants, none of which are desirable actions in the moment. He seems to understand, and he settles his fingers on top of mine and lets me hold his really tightly for the rest of the ride.

The driver pulls around to the side entrance of our building, and we manage to get the kids up to the apartment. We work together, without saying a word, to get them de-shoed and into bed. Patrick motions me out into the living room, shutting the door to the hallway behind us.

The decorations for Matt's birthday party are laid out on the coffee table. I've been doing my best to sketch the section of Central Park we'll be setting up in for the party, and totaling up the number of trees that will need to be adorned.

Patrick examines the streamers. "Pink and yellow?"

"Matt picked a color, and he let Georgie pick the other color. It was sweet."

"Matt wanted pink?"

"Yeah. I talked him out of the glitter ones."

"I like glitter." He steps toward me.

"But you don't want him liking glitter, do you? Mae and Simon are staunchly opposed to his love of glitter."

"He can like glitter when he's old enough to know what that implies," says Patrick.

Six months ago, I wouldn't have liked that answer, but something about actually *doing* the parenting has watered down my liberal side when it comes to the kids and their preferences. I open my mouth to say that.

Instead, I say, "So. Who was she?"

"An assistant from down the hall."

"Aren't you worried she'll get you fired?" He takes another step. I stay on the opposite side of the coffee table, trying to keep it between us.

"You're not going to like my answer."

"Tell me anyway."

"That's the culture. It wasn't a big deal. It won't be a thing."

"Well," I say. "Well. That's . . . incredibly misogynistic."

Patrick is amused, and it seems like he should smile, but he doesn't. It's a different kind of amused, one I'm not sure I like. "What do you want to ask me?"

"I guess, maybe, I want to know what that was about. Just now. In the car."

"That's not what you wanted?" Patrick takes off his suit jacket and drops it on the floor.

"Did I say that's what I wanted?" I want to hang the jacket up for him, but I don't move. I think maybe he dropped it on purpose because he knew that would be my impulse.

"Jesus Christ. Who are you talking to? I know exactly what you came for, with Scotty out of town."

"Patrick!"

"I didn't hear you saying no," he says, and out loud, it sounds ruthless.

"What do you mean, with Scotty out of town?" I say.

He looks at me with something hard in his eyes. "It was going to be one or the other of us eventually, wasn't it?"

I haven't been so frustrated that all I wanted to do was smack someone since I was a kid, but I have a sudden appreciation for George's and Matt's temper tantrums. When there's nowhere for your feelings to go, your hands can almost seem like a logical outlet.

"What are we going to do about this?" he asks, moving forward like he's going to come to my side. My painful doubts and insecurity, my fury at Scotty, the wild elation of finally saying my piece to Jess—all of these are moving through me, and I let them. I let them course through my veins and distribute throughout my whole body until I feel like I'm humming with them, until all the things that are unrequited, the things I haven't felt I was allowed to say or feel are right at the surface and aimed at the target standing across the table from me.

There is so much energy building that I can't tell the difference between positive and negative, and I could swear that if either one of us moves, the air will crackle with electricity.

"Don't come over here," I say.

He is across the room in two seconds, taking it for granted that he knows what I want, anticipating my will. I watch him unknot his tie faster than I have ever seen anyone unknot a tie, and I want to hit him or, better yet, grab him and drag my hands all the way down his back until I have his skin under my fingernails. I am so angry, so angry.

"What do you want me to do?" he says. He doesn't put his hands on me but leans over and bites my neck, kind of hard.

"Not that." I turn my head. "Don't leave a mark. What am I supposed to say to the boys?"

"*What* do you want me to do?" He leans over again and kisses the spot he just bit. "What do you want me to do, Charlotte?"

"I don't know," I say. He does put his hands on me then,

because he thinks *he* knows. Maybe he does. His hands slide, not to my hips but to the spot right above them, that intimate spot right above hipbone and right below waist. I try not to react, but I can't help it. He doesn't rest his hands there; his hands are moving, and I am shivering. He settles me back onto the table, but I won't be putting my legs up onto his shoulders anytime soon. I haven't been to a yoga class in months.

He turns his face. His mouth comes in contact with mine, but I don't kiss him, and he doesn't kiss me. My skirt is down around my ankles now, and he pulls it off and kicks it away with his foot. I have a feeling he'll go for the tights next, and he does.

"Tell me what you want," he says, right against me.

What I want *least* of all right now is to be any more vulnerable than I have already allowed myself to be, but for a moment there is nothing but chemicals, and Patrick, and Patrick and his stupid man-chemicals. There is nothing but an immediate cure for loneliness, an outlet for rage, an impending action of mindless need. My willpower is rapidly being absorbed into my pounding, traitorous heart, and I struggle to hold on to my rational mind.

Patrick pushes me further back on the table, and in a minute, my indecision will become a decision, again, *again*, and I'll never be able to take it back. His fingers are inching up the sides of my ribcage, and I keep losing my train of thought. My legs are wrapped around his waist in a natural grip, like I can somehow have more control, slow things to the pace I need them. Without thinking about the implications, I lie back on the table, with the intention of putting more space between my senses and all the chemicals. Of course, that can't be what it looks like, and before I can say so, he is down to his briefs, crawling up over me on the kitchen table. Absurdly, I wonder for a moment if either of us will come back up with spots of mashed avocado in weird places, since I'm pretty sure I forgot to wipe down the table after feeding Georgie lunch. It's this thought that snaps me out of it.

"What was her name?" I ask, right against his face.

He lifts himself up off me abruptly, and I adjust my clothes and think about my heartbeat. I feel like it's slowed way down in the last fifteen seconds, and if I let it speed up again, I'll start blushing. He is standing there, appearing totally at home almost naked, whereas I am scanning the floor for my skirt with every fiber of my being.

"Are you going to tell me?"

"Why do you want to know?" Patrick looks dark and unsettled, like he could take off running at any minute.

"I don't know. Maybe so when I tell the story of this night, I'll be able to say something like, I saw him having sex with Bailey in his office, and it really turned me on, so I took him home with me."

"Bailey?"

"Or whatever her name actually is."

"Her name is Genevieve."

"Genevieve? You made that up. No adult is named Genevieve."

"You have to be kidding me right now."

"It sounds like one of those situations where the hippie parents let the kid name itself, like Matt's little classmate, Rainbow." There is no way to cover up my bare legs gracefully. My skirt is on the wrong side of Patrick, and putting on tights is not my stealthiest process.

"Who is it that you're planning on telling the story of this night to?"

"I don't know."

"Scotty?"

"You're the one who keeps bringing up Scotty."

He comes at me so fast that I take a few steps back on instinct, and then laugh, and then immediately regret my laughter. He looks like he wants to throttle me, and I honestly can't blame him.

"I'm sorry," I say.

"Jesus," he says, raking a hand through his hair and finally snatching his pants off the back of Georgie's booster chair. "What the fuck do you want from me?"

"I don't know. I really don't know. I'm sorry. I'm sorry."

Patrick steps into his pants and zips them up, and I hand him his undershirt. He takes it from me without saying anything and puts it on. The backs of my thighs are pushing into the table, because it's as far as I can physically get from him, but he isn't picking up on my need for space, or if he is, he isn't respecting it.

"No one in this family has been very good to you." He is standing with his knees on either side of my knees, and his shoulder is only inches from my face, which for now makes me feel better, since there's no way I could look him in the face. "Especially not when you consider what you've been to the boys. It's selfish, what we've all let you do, and I know Scotty was worried about it before he left—why he called Mae to come and help out. But I'm sure he doesn't plan on stopping anytime soon. He needs you." He puts his hands on the table, on either side of me. "We all seem to kind of need you."

If I were to lean forward even five degrees, I could rest my head against his collarbone, just for a minute.

"You're calling all the shots right now." I can feel the vibration of his words on my face, skating over the top of my head and all down my sides. "At some point, you're going to have to speak the fuck up if that isn't what you want."

"How could I have been in their lives for this long and just, just not have feelings about them?" I say, like he's demanding that I defend myself. "I'm not calling the shots. If I'm not here, what happens to these little boys?"

"People need to find their own way through grief," says Patrick. "You can't do it for them, no matter how much you love them and feel compelled to lift it off them."

"Maybe I can't," I say. "But I can keep my eyes on them."

He looks at me like I'm on a sinking lily pad, and I press

myself against him. I can't hold anyone above the water the way I wish I could, not Scotty, not the boys, not myself. All of my buoyancy is gone. And Patrick can't hold me up, either, but I cling to him anyway. If I'm going to sink, I don't want to be alone.

June, sixteen weeks after

A week later, it is the morning of Matt's birthday party, and Scotty is home, and Patrick is gone. I woke up to a screen on my cell phone reminding me that I have missed thirty-nine calls from Jane and Claudia, accumulating from the time I first discovered Matt's secret. My mind is functioning on brownout level, the same way it did when I found out about Jess's betrayal.

It's 5:30 a.m., and Scotty sits across from me. Between our two coffee mugs sits Pup. Scotty is speaking intermittently. We're both supposed to be thinking of what to do, but only one of us is actually trying to do that, and it's not me. I'm staring at Pup and imagining myself tossing him down the trash chute.

"I'm not sure," Scotty is saying, and I'm annoyed, because that's pretty much all he's been saying since we ran into this incident. He's been saying he's "not sure" from here to Istanbul. I don't open my mouth, for fear I'll accidentally say the words "It's your call" for the twenty-seventh time and hurl us right into the middle of a Beckett play. And there are tons of things left to do if I'm going to be ready to throw a birthday party this afternoon; my mental to-do list feels overwhelming enough without the added pressure of this decision.

I put my palms on the table and start to push back my chair. "S-H-I-T."

"What's wrong?"

"I forgot to get him a present," I say.

Scotty reaches across the table and rubs my forearm. "All the presents we give him later today will be from both of us."

"No," I say. The tags on Matt's presents cannot say "from

Daddy and Charlotte," even if Scotty's not thinking clearly enough to see that. "I mean, thank you, but no. I wanted to get him something from me."

"You still can," he says. "Please. Don't be worried."

It's at exactly this moment, when we've resorted to distracting ourselves from our crippling indecision by having a disagreement, that Matt comes walking out in his pajamas, rubbing his eyes, scratching his head, catching us red-handed.

He looks like he's about to say something, something normal for morning, like "Can I have a brownie for breakfast" or "I think I'll go outside without pants today," but the words stick in his throat when he sees Pup on the table between us. He stops moving. His eyes get wide, dart back and forth between me and Scotty. If he were an adult, this would be the moment where he tried his best to come up with an excuse. Being a kid, his brain doesn't work that way or that fast, so all he can do is stand there, like a caricature of combusting emotion.

Scotty says, "Son, why don't you sit down at the table with us," and Matt does it without an argument. The look on his face is so naked. He has nowhere to go. So though he'd rather be anywhere but here, he's going to take it like a man. I want to sob with pride or, at the very least, reach over and stroke his hair, but I know that if I do, he'll no longer have the courage to face what he knows is coming. There's a certain strength that comes upon you when you know you're on your own. I tighten my hands in my lap.

"Matthew, did you take this from George?" Scotty asks.

"Mmm," says Matt, not wanting to commit fully to yes.

"When did you take it?"

"At the doctor's. He fell asleep, so I was holding him."

"The night, ah, the night we were there with Mommy?"

I can tell by the way Matt breathes through his nose that he's about to cry.

"Did you know that Charlotte and George were looking for it?"

"I thought they knew I had him. I was just tricking them."

"Did you understand that they were looking for it later though? After that night at the hospital?"

He doesn't want to answer, which means the answer is yes. His chin lowers, and his eyes start to water. I dig my nails into my thighs, tighten my stomach muscles, and breathe in measure. Drag air in, push air out, as quietly as I can. Drag and push, drag and push.

"But you kept it anyway?" Scotty is struggling to make this a question and not an accusation, to give Matt room to respond, to exonerate himself.

Matt mumbles something, and Scotty and I both lean forward.

"Speak up, son," says Scotty sternly.

Matt starts to cry. "I said, I woke up, and he was in my bed."

"Patrick must have assumed it was his," I say.

"I came out in the morning to give it to Mommy," says Matt. "But she wasn't here. Gramma said she went to heaven. I'll give it to her when she came back."

Scotty sits back in his chair and grips the armrests, and I think I know how he feels. What to do? Set an example of stoicism for my child? Get angry and discipline him, to show him that we move on, that we don't get an excuse to stop doing what we know is right? Live in this emotional tar pit with him? Watching Scotty struggle is almost as bad as watching Matt flail around, but I can't be the one to throw them the life vest. Or is it that I can't wear it for them?

"But she didn't come back," I say.

"Yes," says Matt.

"Yes," says Scotty, right on Matt's heels. They're different yeses, but somehow they mean the same thing.

"Well, Matthew, I guess I don't know what to do," says Scotty. "I'm not happy that you kept this a secret, especially from George. But I know that things have been sad and scary without, without her." Without my wife, your mother, Mommy, Gretchen. He chooses *her,* still. "It's not black and white. Do you know what that means?"

"Mommy says that," says Matt.

"Yes. She did say that." The silence stretches out. Neither one of them can stand to walk any further into the memory of her.

It's that moment that another voice cuts through the racket. A voice that's clearer, possibly quieter, but much more distinct.

"Pup come back?"

George has somehow removed almost all of his clothing, probably in his sleep, the sweaty little mess, and he's just standing there in his underwear, with his belly sticking out like an old man who doesn't give a shit about clothes. Chickie is tucked into the back of his underpants, held fast by the waistband.

"He wasn't gone," says Matt. "He was living in my room, Georgie. Sorry you thought he was gone."

"It okay," says George. He puts Chickie on the table next to Pup and says, "Nice to meet you," in a high baby voice. Chickie's voice, I guess.

Scotty lifts George onto his lap. "Pup can come back and live in your room now."

"He can live in Matt's room. He like Matty," says George, and the way he says it is casual, almost flippant. But to me, it's the sound of a match strike in a dark, dark place.

IN THE EARLY evening, when the party has ended, we are all at home together, me and Scotty and the boys and Patrick. I am so tired I could lie down on the living room floor and pass out, but George and Matt are on fire from the success of the party. Or maybe it has more to do with the onslaught of endorphins ricocheting around in their little brains, due to the cupcake and brownie and doughnut consumption that mostly went unmonitored. They're getting ready to open a tremendous pile of gorgeously wrapped presents, and they are too excited to sit still.

A little over an hour later, we are nearing the end of the present pile. Scotty hands them out, Patrick reads the cards, and I take notes on who each one is from. We come to two identically wrapped packages, which I know are some sort of fancy new handheld gaming devices that Scotty picked up in Germany, and the boys start to open them, and Patrick reads the card over the sounds of tearing paper.

"For Matthew, with love on your sixth birthday, from Daddy, George, and Charlotte. And yours is for George, with love on Matt's sixth birthday, from Daddy, Matt, and Charlotte."

All the air in my lungs rushes away. Some kind of mass is cutting through my chest in free fall. Nothing to grab on to. A straight drop. Matt and George giggle at the funny tag on George's package. I start cleaning up abruptly, balling up wrapping paper as tightly as I can inside my fists.

"I asked you not to do this," I say to Scotty, ignoring the protests of the boys as I add the ribbons, even the fabric ones, to the trash pile.

"Do what?" Scotty says.

"Put my name—were you even *listening*—"

Patrick sweeps all the presents into a pile and runs off down the hall with them, and the boys laugh and run after him.

"Why is this so upsetting to you?" Scotty asks.

"Because you mentioned it earlier, and I said not to, and you didn't—"

"I don't know why it's even a conversation. I was trying to—"

"Why would you write that? It's, it's confusing—"

"It won't confuse anyone who matters," he says. I pick up as much of the trash pile as I can and walk to the kitchen with it, losing a few pieces of wrapping as I go.

When I turn around to retrieve the stray paper, Scotty has

followed me into the kitchen and is standing in the doorway with his hands pressing into his temples. The hair around that area is sticking straight out to either side, due to the repetition of this gesture, and if he were a little grayer, he'd look like a mad scientist from a public television show.

"Can you hand me that piece of foil?" I ask, pointing to a scrap with Ninja Turtle faces all over it.

He picks it up and brings it to the trash himself. "I didn't think it mattered that much, okay? I'm sorry."

"If you say so."

Scotty bangs his fist down on the counter, four or five times in a row. "I don't want to fight with you," he says, and his voice has increased in edge and resonance, a combination that spooks me, making it harder to hold my corner. "I left all the hashing out, all the details, all the employee stuff—"

"The *employee* stuff?"

"Jesus Christ! The *life* shit. I left it to my, my, to her."

"Gretchen," I say, but he ignores me.

"She had the talent for knowing what the right thing was to do, always. I don't have an ounce of that intuition."

"Well, me neither," I say.

He's giving me a look that makes me feel like a pillar of salt. I don't know how much longer I'll be able to hold out before I start to blow away. "Are you serious?"

"Yes," I say.

"I don't feel that way about you. I feel like you always know what you're doing, and it takes me ten fucking years to catch up," he says.

"Well, that's how I always felt around Gretchen. I had to take a cue from someone," I say. He actually winces at the sound of her name, and it seems to make him even angrier.

"So, what?" he says. "What do you want to do?"

"I don't know what's on the table."

"Well, you could quit."

"Okay."

"Or I could fire you."

"Okay."

"You could move into my bedroom with me."

"Oh, well, if that would keep you from *firing* me—"

"Seems like the next logical step, doesn't it?" He should be flipping tables, throwing vases, breaking dishes for all the energy that's trapped there underneath his voice; instead, the nastiness comes out through his words. "You? Me? The kids? Isn't that why you're still here?"

"Aunt Lila thinks it is, that's for sure."

"Cut the crap, Charlotte."

"I don't know! You asked me here. Is it what *you* want?"

He presses the heels of his hands into his eye sockets, but it can't stop the tears from starting to come down his face, and he lets out a noise that sounds like George when Matt snatches all the square Magna-Tiles from his pile.

"I know it's not," I say, and it would be much better, much more elegant, if my eyes and nose weren't streaming the same way his are. "I know what you want. You *want Gretchen*, and I'm not her; no one will be her, ever. So if you're mad about that, and you need to scream, then do it. *Do* it."

And I think that if things had gone differently, he might have. He might have screamed at me, sobbed with rage and fury, punched a wall, *something*. Something. But instead, a movement in the doorway to the kitchen catches our attention at the same time, and we both look, and we see Matt. And we don't know how long he's been standing there.

Nobody says anything for a long time, and I expect the silence to be thick and suffocating, but instead, I can hear all the noises of the house. The TV still on a low volume because Patrick insisted he be able to watch the NASDAQ while we opened presents. The dishwasher changing cycles. George chatting back in his room. The sound of plastic clicking against other plastic—

maybe the newest Lego set? Matt is looking from one to the other of us, waiting for an explanation that never comes. And so he nods a few times, like maybe he knew this was coming all along, and then he walks out of the room.

"No more," I say.

"What does that mean? You're leaving?"

"No, no more of *this*," I say. "No more 'her.' No more 'my wife.' No more 'she.' You have to be able to say her name! If you don't talk about her, then she'll be nothing. And George will never know her, and even Matt will start to forget what it was like when she was alive. You have to, *you*. Mae is telling them that she's in heaven, but they don't know what that means. I can tell them that she loved to dress Matt in green and George in orange, and I can tell them that she was staunchly opposed to spaghetti, or I can tell them about that time when Matt heard the story of Jonah and the Whale from Mae, and he was so scared that Gretchen had to look up pictures of cuddly whales to show him on the Internet—"

I can see that Scotty is starting to really come undone now. He's pulling at his collar like it's too small, like it's strangling him. His face is flushed. He has his hands flat on the kitchen island, like he doesn't trust himself to let them be anywhere else.

"But that is nothing." I am past the point you can come back from, so I'm going to have to try and find my way to the other side. "*Nothing* compared to what you could tell them! How it felt when George was getting older and older and still not speaking to you, and all the research she did, and how she struggled to keep the faith. How she was when you first met her, how she was when you got married—how those two versions of her were different, how she changed! What you did that made her crazy, what she wore, how fast she walked, all those moments that made up your life as a family. The outings she took with Matt when he was a baby, and what she did when she had two of them! That time when your brother Max and his family came to visit, and she got up at 4 a.m. to poach eggs and arrange flowers; that time she bought you all those belts from Brooks Brothers, more belts than you said you could possibly have use for; the time she let Matt take all those pictures with your digital camera, and he erased the vacation pictures by accident, and she covered for him and told you *she* did it; that time she made that horrible sesame seitan for dinner, and you and the boys rebelled and secretly ordered pizza; that time she made a Halloween costume for you out of *stainless steel*—"

"Stop, oh God, stop. Stop." Scotty looks at me. His expression is like a wound that will never close, on its way to a permanent scar. "I'll tell them, if you want me to. I'll tell them I made a mistake."

"What?"

"That I got the tag wrong, I'll tell Matt and George—"

"I can't be part of Daddy, Charlotte, George, and Matt. It has to be Daddy, George, and Matt. Just Daddy, George, and Matt."

Scotty walks out of the kitchen. I'm afraid he's going to leave. I follow him and find him sitting in the middle of the couch, as if he'd like to be swallowed by it. As if he'd prefer to be the smallest thing in the room. "I can't be that," he says. His head is resting on the back of the couch. His eyes are on the ceiling. "I can't do that."

"You don't have to let this decide for you," I say. "She had to leave them. You don't. You can still be their father."

"I'm too tired," he says. "So if you could just stay, stay here, I'll give you whatever you want. Just please stay here with me." *Not them, not us,* and then I know. I know it's not me he's talking to. "If I hadn't been away so much—"

"No," I say, and I cross the room to him quickly.

"If I had paid more attention, helped more, you wouldn't have felt like you needed to work, you wouldn't have gone to—" Scotty is gasping, like he can't pull enough air into his lungs.

"No," I say. "No. Calm down."

"We had such a stupid fight, the night before."

"I know." I kneel next to him on the couch.

"Do you think she died thinking I didn't value all the things she did to make our life together?"

"No, not even a little bit."

"It should have been me. It would be better for everyone. It should be me."

"Stop it," says Patrick, from the doorway, and I should have known he was coming. Matt has never been one to keep his mouth shut. "Don't try to bargain. It's bourgeois. McLeans don't bargain."

"You're such an asshole," says Scotty, but it looks like he can breathe again.

"I have to go now," I say, and I get up, and I leave them there. A short while later, when I get to the front door with my belongings, I look down the hall toward the boys' rooms. But I'm absolutely sure that I need to walk out of here before I see their faces, so that's what I do, even though it means I can't say good-bye.

I MAKE IT back to my apartment, which hasn't felt like mine in months, and climb the stairs. When I step into my living room, there are Jane and Claudia, sitting on my couch, looking at me through eyes that could be my own, knowing me. I walk across the room without acknowledging them, kick off my shoes, and crawl into my own bed. And a moment later, I feel the mattress depress as my sisters crawl in after me.

PART FIVE

George

July, five months after

The weeks go by, and as they pass, the days even out, and I'm no longer thinking of them every waking minute. They are alarmingly present in my subconscious, however. I've been sleeping terribly for the past month while my mind untangles itself, continuing to dream in a way that is so vivid that I often confuse it with reality.

Last night I dreamt alternately of Patrick and a disastrous kids' birthday party where everything that could go wrong did. First, I was in Patrick's bed, waiting for him, and then I was knee-deep in the water of the boat basin, searching for Pup, while Matt sat on the grassy bank wearing a tiara and screaming. Then I was back in Patrick's bed, and he opened the door and invited the receptionist from his company into bed with us. I was back at the boat basin after that, and George had somehow gotten himself into a rowboat and was drifting out into deeper water, crying for his mom. The worst one of the night started off with

Patrick cooking breakfast. When I came out to the kitchen, George was already in the booster seat being fed. A moment later, Matt came out fully dressed, ate his breakfast with no fuss, and we got off to school with barely a hiccup. When I got back from dropping them off, I expected to be alone, but Patrick was there, waiting for me, knowing that I wanted him to be. I walked in the door and said nothing. He picked me up with only one arm around my waist, and I buried my face between his shoulder and his neck. He carried me into the empty room across from Matt's, and he was devoted, even loving, and I took off all my clothes, and he took off all of his. We lay there, staring at each other, and all I could think was that I was glad we were in the guest room, and not in my apartment, or my room in Scotty's apartment, or on the kitchen table, or any other place that I'd have to look at on a regular basis, and Patrick said, "Let's see how long we can keep this up," and I had to sit up suddenly because I knew Scotty was out in the kitchen, waiting for me to be ready so we could leave for Matt's birthday party, and I was afraid if I didn't get out there *right then*, he'd see me naked, in bed with his brother.

It takes me a few minutes, sitting up in my own bed, to register that the clock says 11:06. I'm awake, and I'm in my home, not theirs. The longer I am away from Park Avenue, from them, the more I sleep. It has been hard to maintain any kind of schedule.

I get out of bed, not bothering with anything more elaborate than sweatpants and flip-flops, and venture outside to obtain the largest cup of coffee I can talk the barista into. I walk up the promenade in Carl Schurz Park, toward Gracie Mansion. When I get to a relatively isolated spot, I sit down on a bench and stare across the river to Roosevelt Island. I think to myself that I'm a good swimmer, that I could make it across the river if I had to, current be damned.

These past few weeks have felt like treading water in the River Styx, and I have had to set limits for myself. One of the limits has been to remain steadfast, not to call any of them until I feel ready, but today, staring out at the water, I can see that this river is just a river. It leads to the ocean and not to Hades. The expressionist element that had overtaken every action, every thought, every motive in my last few weeks at Scotty's has lost its grip on my mind, and I have the impulse to call up all of my demons and name them Legion. I wonder where that random thought came to me from, and so I dial my grandmother. She knows these things.

"Gramma, it's Charlotte."

"Hello, dear. I've been wondering how you are."

"It's rough not working," I say. "If I were any good at drawing, I'd sketch the inside of my apartment and title it 'Purgatory.'" I think of Patrick when I say it.

"Taking some time to sort things out before you move on, in one direction or another," she says. "I think that's a good idea, honey."

"It's harder than I thought it would be."

"I've lost my fair share of people who were close to me," says Gramma. "That happens more and more when you get to a certain age. But I suppose this kind of loss never really gets any easier, no matter how common it becomes. I never feel quite prepared; it's like opening up a floodgate that can never be closed again, and you have to find a way to redirect the water." Across the river, I can see the lighthouse in the park on the end of Roosevelt Island. To me, it's always seemed small, like a playground-sized lighthouse, meant for kids. But I have never been to Roosevelt Island, not once since I've lived in New York, and I realize that I have no idea how large or small that lighthouse actually is.

"I was wondering about something," I say. "Nothing serious, just a quote that popped into my head. I think it's left over from Sunday school, or something."

"What is it, Charlotte-love?"

"Something about naming your demons. Or the name of the demon was Legion, or that was the devil's name. Something like that. Do you know that one?"

"It's from the Gospel," says Gramma. "Two of the Gospels, in fact. Mark and Luke. There was something similar in Matthew but nothing about the name Legion. It's an exorcism story. The demons came out of the man and showed themselves to Jesus and said they were called Legion. Is that what you're thinking of?"

"Yes," I say. "It got in my head."

"Are you thinking of exorcising some demons?"

"I guess I was thinking I might try. I mean, if you give something a name, it loses power, right?" I say.

"In essence," says Gramma. "I've never found that I had a talent for naming the right things, though. I'll go along, thinking I'm so self-aware, thinking I know the right name to give the thing that ails me. And then I'm taken quite by surprise when it rears its ugly head again, and it turns out I haven't called it by the correct name. Like a whack-a-mole, always popping back up. Incidentally, I can never remember the right name for whack-a-mole when I need to, either."

"Do you find yourself referring to whack-a-mole in everyday conversation?"

"You'd be surprised. Saying it to you right now, it came out so naturally. But somehow, when I need to think of it urgently, the name always eludes me."

"It's the *mole* that always eludes me," I say. "I suck at whack-a-mole."

"You get that from your grandfather. He had the most difficult time multitasking. You have to be three moves ahead to get those little suckers," says Gramma.

"What happened to that demon? To Legion?" I ask.

"I believe it was a whole gaggle of demons, and together they were called Legion. They begged Jesus not to send them back to hell, and of course, being a man of compassion, he agreed to let them possess a herd of cows. Or pigs, actually. Swine. And when the demons entered into them, they ran down a large hill and drowned themselves."

"Poor pigs," I say. "Thanks, Gramma. You're better than Wikipedia."

"I must be absolutely glorious," she says. "Love you, dear heart."

We hang up. I have to shield my eyes from the glare off the river as I walk home, feeling sorry for the fictional pigs and thinking about how Jane and Claudia would mock my sensitivity if they knew. Before I can put so much thought into it that I end up paralyzed, I dial Scotty's cell phone, prepared to leave a message since I know he'll be at work. I run down the hill. I jump. I am suspended, over the water.

"Hi," he says, picking up after only a ring and a half. I can hear Georgie singing in the background, one of the *Star Wars* themes, at the top of his lungs.

"Hi," I say. "You're not at work."

"I took the week off," he says.

"You took the *week* off?"

Scotty's laugh sounds echoey, like he's switched me to speakerphone. "Yes."

"Okay," I say. "Well, wow. Is it totally weird if I ask you what you're wearing?"

"Is it totally weird if I tell you a cowbell G-string?"

"Ha! I have trouble picturing you in anything other than a suit, that's all."

"What's happening with you?" he asks.

"Not too much," I say.

"Are you busy?"

"Like, in my life?"

"I meant right now," he says. "Although I would also like to hear about how you're busy in your life."

"No, I'm not busy right now."

"I would love to see you. We all would. We'll be here for most of the day. If you can come, I'll send a car over to pick you up."

"I don't need—"

"I'm joking about the car."

"Well. Nobody thinks you're funny," I say, and I let the feeling stretch out over the line. There is a *thing* between Scotty and me that hasn't been named, and therefore hasn't been cast out, and furthermore, I can't force a name onto the thing, no matter how hard I try. I know what it's *not* called, and I know that I've never had it with anyone else. We've been carrying this fragile thing between us, and we don't know what to call it, and we're both afraid to drop it.

"I'll be glad to see you guys," I say, and I walk faster, turning away from the river and heading back up the road toward my apartment. "I miss you."

"We miss you, too."

June, four weeks earlier

For the better part of a week, I do nothing but lie in my bed and eat the food that Jane cooks for me. I have no energy, not even to cry. After a few days, my sisters force me out of bed and into the shower and make me put on real clothes for the first time since I left Scotty's house.

"Gross. No way," says Claudia.

I blow a raspberry at her, like I'm twelve, and turn to Jane. "Come on, Janie. You'd help me out, right?"

"Well, aw, I guess so, sure," says Jane. "I guess I would try to do something."

"Hell no," says Claudia. "If I opened the door one morning, and you had turned into a giant cockroach, I would *not* try to figure out what to feed you. I'd slam the door and buy a giant can of Raid."

"MEAN," I say. "You're the meanest, meanest, *meanest* girl I know." Claudia pours more seltzer into my glass. She and Jane are splitting one of my larger bottles of Yellowtail, but Jane has decreed that I have to stay sober.

"You're in danger of shutting off all of your feelings," she says. "Like you do when you don't know how to handle something. I guarantee that no one in that Pup situation was as attached to that stuffed animal as you were."

"Of all the things to make you come unglued." Claudia sits up straight and reaches behind her to stretch out her shoulders. "A stuffed animal."

"It's not the freaking animal itself," I say. "It's what he represents."

"Okay, fine, but what now?" says Jane. "You're never going back to that house? You can't work anything out with Scotty? You're never going to see Matt and George again?"

"It's like . . . it's like Gretchen died, and I'm not me anymore," I say. "I didn't try to be her, but somehow I lost me. And Scotty let me do it because he's in pain, and I was there. I didn't really have a choice, when it started."

"You did have a choice," says Claudia. "Getting into it with them in the first place was a choice."

Jane rearranges the pillows at the head of my bed into a more logical order as we finish our drinks. "But you only got halfway into it with Patrick."

"Patrick only got it halfway into you." Claudia thinks she's pretty hilarious.

"That thing with Patrick was the worst attempt at retaliation ever," I say.

"Retaliation?" says Jane. "It might be more than that."

"You don't know what you're talking about." Jane and Claudia look at each other. "What?" I ask. "What did you do?"

"We might have stolen your phone," says Claudia.

"One of us may have stolen your phone," corrects Jane.

"Give me my phone right now," I say. "You horrible, horrible sluts."

Two days later, they're getting ready to leave, but all of us are dawdling.

"When I die," says Claudia, "I want one thing."

"For everyone to use your death as an excuse to call off work for a week and party?" says Jane.

"Hmm. Not a bad idea. Two things, maybe."

"What's the first one?"

"I want everyone to fucking *mourn* me. None of this 'celebrate the good times, she'd want you to move on' bullshit. No. I mean, by all means, celebrate. But I want to be toasted at every holiday. I want people to cry. I want people to think of all the things they loved about me. Otherwise, why was I even here?"

"Okay," says Jane, really seriously. "I promise to be incredibly sad and never move on if you die, Claud-hopper."

"Me too," I say, and they hug me at the same time.

"I'm sad that you're sad," says Claudia. "I hope we feel better soon."

"Me too," I say again.

"So you'll make your list," says Jane. "And you'll text it to us. Right?" They have insisted, after hearing the story of how things ended with Jess, that I start moving again on my career, and making a list is the first step, according to Jane. Claudia threatened to stage a sit-in until I did so, but Jane convinced her to leave and catch their respective planes (after I insinuated that the mortar on Jane's backsplash might end up a slightly different shade if she let it sit too long without finishing). I'm sure Jane meant for me to find it later, but I've already uncovered the list of grief counselors within a twenty-block radius that she wrote out and left for me.

Three group hugs later, I put my sisters in a taxi and send them off to JFK, and there is suddenly nothing here to distract me, no kids, no sisters, no job. I sit in front of my crappy piano and put my hands on the keyboard, but I don't play. Not ten minutes have passed, but I dial Jane and have her put me on speaker in the taxi.

"I had a thought," I say.

"What?" says Jane.

"Patrick's shoe size?" says Claudia, and she sounds farther away.

"Shut up; she's serious," says Jane. "Charlotte?"

"Yeah. Part of it is a thought, and the rest of it is writing. Songs, I mean."

"Okay," says Jane.

"I thought I wasn't writing at all for the last few years. I never really had the desire. Then Scotty said something to me, and I didn't give much significance to it at the time. But now that I'm thinking about it, I realize I have been. I have been writing for the boys, and *with* the boys. I have all these songs stuck in my head that I only thought of when I was with them, out of necessity for some reason or another."

"You need to write them down," says Jane.

"Put it on the list," says Claudia.

July, five months after

I arrive at the McLeans' apartment later than promised that afternoon because I have gotten used to moving at a slower pace these days. I let myself in without knocking, then wonder if that was the right thing to do, or if it will freak the boys out. I don't find either of the boys there, though, or anyone for that matter. The apartment is without motion, and the sight of its silent, empty, kid-less state is unnerving.

"Hello?" I call out. No answer, so I move back toward the left wing. "Marco," I say, and then I think I hear something, so I walk back further. "Marcoooo—"

"Polo," comes Scotty's voice, and I walk back into his room to find him kneeling on the floor at the entrance to Gretchen's closet, surrounded by newspapers, wrapping up everything within reach and putting it in a box.

"I sent the boys out to a diner with Patrick," he says, as I stand there, not able to judge his state of mind, "because Matthew was kicking boxes around and acting like a maniac. I swear, I've had such a hard time recognizing that kid lately. I know what Dr. O'Neill says, but I keep wondering how long it will actually be. Or if this is just him being six years old and me missing the part where he got there." Scotty reaches for a pair of ballet flats and holds them up, as if he isn't sure that one matches the other. "Plus, I thought I might be a mess while I did this. So far I'm okay, I think."

"Is this her—what are you doing with all of this stuff?" I ask.

"I'm not sure," says Scotty. "Right now I'm just packing it up. I was thinking I should give most of it away. Maybe to a church?"

The thought of him giving a box full of Prada shoes to a church is concerning; I'm not sure they'd know what to do with them. "Lila doesn't want any of it?" I ask.

"She said she didn't," he says. "But, oh shit, Charlotte, I didn't even ask you. If you did. Do you? Want any of it?"

"No, thank you," I say. "It would be too weird. Also, she was six or eight sizes smaller than I am."

"I have all these newspapers," says Scotty, continuing his methodical wrapping of objects both fragile and non-fragile. "This great, huge pile of newspapers. I haven't read one since, since Gretchen died. I've been staring at them without reading, then piling them up in here. I always think I'll read them later. And all of a sudden, I have this pile." He pushes the box he's filled away from him and starts assembling an empty one. "I must look like a hoarder. I kept thinking I would get to it."

"I know what you mean," I say.

"And now, as I'm wrapping up her things, I'm looking at the headlines and stopping every few minutes to read pieces of articles. Catching up on things that went on in the last five months that I only half knew about." He finishes with the box and grabs another empty one. "All these things happened. I wasn't really aware of any of them. Like I've been living in a vacuum."

"Well, you sort of have been," I say.

"I don't think I know how to get myself out of it," he says. "Even as I acknowledge that I've been doing this, I still have no desire to sit down and read today's paper from front to back. It seems—I don't know—left over. From before."

I kneel down on the floor next to him and start separating each sheet of newsprint from the rest of its section. "I think I understand," I say. He takes each sheet that I hold out to him, wraps up part of Gretchen's existence, and puts it in the box. He does it again, and again, and again.

"You know what? I want to tell you something," says Scotty. "I haven't seen you in a long time—it feels like a long time to me—and things will be crazy around here for the next few weeks or who knows how long, and I just want to tell you while I'm thinking about it."

On the inside, I go still, like I'm bracing myself, but I continue to separate newspaper.

"You were—you *are*—you're my best friend," says Scotty. "Through all of this. I should have leaned on someone else, but I leaned on you, and you've been my best friend. And you've been *their* best friend. We're—well, really me, I suppose—I'm so far from over this. I have a long way to go before I'll feel any kind of relief. My therapist says there will be a time, in the days to come, when I won't want to get out of bed in the morning, and even the daily business of our life will exhaust me." I envy his ability to keep his tears in his eyes, making them look watery and tragic instead of messy. "Nothing I've done so far has felt like the right thing," he says. "Except you. It was right that you were here. At least, for us."

His hands are on his knees, maybe wedging him up for support, and I put mine over his. "You're right. It was right that I was here. And I'm still here," I say. "I mean, if you want me here. I will be. But you know. I don't think you should employ me. I don't think that's where we are anymore. You know?"

He grips my hands briefly, then reaches for another sheet of newspaper.

"Scotty," I say, "what are you going to do when you get to her bathrobe, her jewelry? What are you going to do with her wedding dress? You can't give that stuff to a church."

He sits back again on his heels. "Do you know what I should do with it?"

"I think we can figure something out," I say.

We sit there together for a long time, putting things in boxes and stacking them up, like a melancholy game of Tetris. Occasionally, the headline of a newspaper will cause us to comment, the Boston Marathon bombing, the antics of the tea party, the occasional op-ed. "The geniuses at the *Times* put the words *Buddhist* and *extremism* in the same headline," I say, and he laughs, and eventually we finish up. The closet floor is empty.

"I have something for you," I say. "Well, really it's for the boys. But it won't mean anything to them for a while, probably until they start reading. So for now, it's yours."

I hand him what I've constructed, a book of all the songs I made up for the kids. I've devoted much of the past month to excavating the memories attached to each of them, where we were, what we were doing, why they needed distraction, comfort, or entertainment. Some of them needed more lyrics or verses, or other forms of completion, and all of them needed to be translated out of my head and onto paper, and that's what I've done.

"This is beautiful, the way you've put it together," he says, turning the pages, and I see him pause to smile at one of the titles, the one I've decided to call "Rhymes by George McLean." "I don't read music. I would love it—only if you wouldn't mind—I would love if you would play through this for me."

We sit on the floor of Gretchen's closet, me and Scotty and my ukulele, and I play the songs. We get close to the end, and I tell him that this section is meant to be played on the piano.

"As soon as they get back," he says.

"Okay." I stand, anticipating all the noises and normalcy that the kids will bring back to this house with them, waiting for their faces, and wondering what will happen when they see mine.

June, two weeks earlier

Everett comes over to help me with that list of Jane and Claudia's. I'm surprised that he comes, after the way we left things at the armory, but he comes. The first thing he does is comment on the business card I have from Jess's contact, the one I met at Carnegie Hall.

"Jess is so great. Of course she knows this guy. Of *course* she does. This is perfect," says Everett, smacking the kitchen island to emphasize Jess's greatness.

"I have to tell you something," I say. "But you can't touch me while I do."

"*Dirty.*"

"I mean it. You can't be near me. You can't be touching me."

Everett walks to the other side of the counter so that there is a physical barrier between us. This is as respectful as he gets. While I have his full curiosity, I tell him the story of Jess and me. It is no longer the most important story of my life. Its power diminishes a little bit every time I tell it.

When I'm finished with the story, Everett reaches for the business card Jess gave me. "I have a better idea," he says. He pulls Jillian's husband's business card out of his wallet and hands it to me, tossing the other into the trash can under the sink. "He's a nice guy. I bet he'd have some good ideas for you. And that way, Jess is not involved at all."

I tape the card to the list. I don't kiss Everett. It's the closest I have ever felt to him. Everett leaves, and I sit down at the piano to play.

That night, I have a dream that I'm pregnant with my third child. I can picture the face of my husband very clearly, and it is no one I know. My brain has drawn him in great detail, down to the buttons on the side of his expensive Italian shoes.

I'm making eggs for Matt and George. They are my first two children with this man that I have conjured, and their younger sibling will be here in less than a month. The width of my stomach causes me to have to recalculate the distance I stand from the stove, and my arm aches as I stretch it out to stir the eggs. George will not eat them if they burn. I rotate my body so that I am standing sideways.

"Where's Daddy?" Matt asks, and I don't want to answer him. I'm not sure who he means, this dream-man or Scotty. And I don't want to make excuses for their father, whoever he is.

I sit down at the table with them to eat eggs, and Matt will not stop talking. I don't want to take my bad mood out on him, because my feelings are not his fault, but more than once I feel my jaw tense as I struggle against the urge to tell him to shut up and eat his breakfast.

We finish, and Matt takes his plate to the sink. "I need a lollipop," he says.

"Are you kidding me?" I push the eggs around on my plate. My tone is not nice.

He laughs, in kind of a nasty way. He probably learned to laugh like that from me. He runs away to some other part of our house, which has also been designed in my imagination. George is struggling in his chair, unable to figure out how to get down out of it, and I watch him struggle, taking great satisfaction in it, refusing to come to his aid until he decides he needs to ask me for help. Maybe I'll get up and leave him on his own, take away the option of help, teach him that there isn't always someone there to make it easier for you.

Matt comes running back into the kitchen, like he's finishing a lap around the house. "Daddy's here!" He makes the announcement smugly, like he knows where his father has been and fully condones it. The husband of my design walks in and takes my plate from me as if nothing is wrong. He eats my breakfast, as if it's perfectly normal to waltz in at this hour of the morning and do so. As if it's completely acceptable that he spent the night, away from me and our children, with Jess.

Each time I wake up, my stomach muscles sore from clenching all night long, the only conscious sense I can make of these dreams is that this is what grief looks like, my own grief, a grief I have deferred.

Jess hurt me, and the fall of my own expectations hurt me even more. But the situation is this: This space is not empty. (This "pace" is not empty, Georgie would say.)

I made a buffer for myself, and I crawled underneath and hid there, letting the space protect me. There wasn't supposed to be anything inside of it, but as it turns out, an empty space is an impossible thing to maintain. I have filled it with things that need to be thought of, contemplated, sorted, written—though instead of taking those actions, I pretended that the space was empty. Now there are boxes that need to be gone through, memorabilia in a childhood closet, winter clothes in spring. Objects that I put in to dodge and crouch behind, like the world's most elaborate game of hide-and-seek. But the limit has been reached. The space is at capacity.

You have to be able to say her name, I said to Scotty, and it's time for me to swallow the pill that I prescribed.

I sit at the piano each day, and I write out the songs, as Jane and Claudia suggested. I write the song I played for Scotty, the one from the doctor's office. I write the song from the museum on Matt's fifth birthday. I write the playground rhymes, the bored-in-the-stroller songs, the bathtub blues, the narrative songs I used to pull Matt out of grumpy moods. I write the songs that the kids laughed at and played to and then sang for their mother when she got home from work or errands.

Music is insidious, like sorrow, like genetics. It sneaks into the corners. It pushes open the doors that you worked so hard to keep shut. It has been there, waiting to be defined, just like everything else in the not-empty space.

I tried to squeeze them all in, the boys and Scotty and all of the rest of their world, to make myself full of them so that I wouldn't have to be full of me. But everything amplified on the day we lost her, and there isn't enough room. Things are spilling. I have to fit them in around what's already there, and I won't know what that is until I go through it.

So I go through it. As I go, I play. I sing. I remember. I cry. I write.

The first day of May, the year before

We are late to take the kids to their haircut the day George starts to speak. The prospect of running with the stroller over to Lexington and down into the sixties is making me cranky. I hate running. I hate sweating. And I especially hate being in a rush. But George woke up late from his nap, Matt apparently needs to have a fifteen-minute bowel movement, and Gretchen is on the phone with Scotty, who is in Beijing and only has a short window of opportunity to talk to the family. Matt takes his turn to say hello to his dad while sitting on the toilet.

George is already zipped into his windbreaker and has his shoes buckled. I am trying to talk Matt into his windbreaker, and Gretchen keeps popping her head out of the guest room and mouthing "sorry!" at me. I decide to abandon my efforts with Matt and put on my own shoes and sweater. Gretchen comes skidding out, still holding the phone to her ear—I could swear she's saying "No, *you* hang up!" (and seriously, he's in *Beijing*)—and George keeps reaching out with both hands as I strap him into the stroller, but I don't know what he wants. I don't know what he's reaching for. Matt is finally zipped and is grudgingly settling onto the floor to put on his sneakers, and George is practically grunting with the effort to get to what he wants, and finally Gretchen stops running around and looks like she's about to hang up, when all of a sudden, George says, "MOMMY!"

Everyone stops moving. Matt stops putting on his shoes. Gretchen stops talking in midsentence. My backpack never makes it to my shoulder.

Gretchen is the one to break the silence. "Oh my goodness, can you hang on a minute, Scotty? Seriously, hold on." She looks at George, and I can tell she's trying not to breathe the wrong way, because that's what I'm also trying not to do, and maybe even Matty. "Yes, honey?"

"Me have a turn to talk to Daddy?"

"Of course you can, sweetie. Hold on just for a minute." She puts the phone to her ear. "Honey, you will not believe this. Guess who wants to talk to you?"

Gretchen puts the phone on speaker and hands it to George.

"Hello?" Scotty says.

"Daddy, you bringing a tiger from China? He live with us?"

Scotty doesn't say anything for a moment, and then, "Yes, I'm bringing some tigers home from China, George. But they're not real tigers, honey. They're just tiger toys. Were you worried about that?"

"You bringing a toy tiger for Matt and for me?" George asks.

"Definitely, there will definitely be tigers for both of you," says Scotty, and he sounds choked up. When I look at Gretchen, she is brushing away her own tears, and I can't even begin to imagine what this means to them, even though my own heart feels more full than it ever has before.

"You bring a tiger for Mommy too?"

"Absolutely, baby George. You be sure and tell your mom that a tiger is coming for her," says Scotty. "I can't wait to see you all. I'll be home tomorrow."

George hands the phone back to Gretchen. "Do you want to say good-bye to Daddy, honey?"

"Bye, Daddy," says George.

"Bye, son. Bye, Matty. Gretch, I love you so much. Love you, boys," says Scotty.

"We love you too, so much," says Gretchen. "See you tomorrow." She hangs up. "I don't really feel like getting our hair cut today, do you?" she asks, looking at Matt, who agrees emphatically, as averse to change as ever. "What about you, George?"

"We have some pickles?" George asks, and I am so unused to the sound of his voice that I feel like laughing in surprise every time he speaks.

"Great idea," says Gretchen. "Let's get some pickles!"

In the hallway, the boys fight over who gets to push the button for the elevator. Georgie is using words. Neither Gretchen nor I do a thing to stop the squabble. I think to myself, thank you, thank you for this moment; thank you for making me a part of it. I don't know who I'm thanking, but there is no word for how I feel other than grateful.

July, five months after

An hour after Patrick and the boys found Scotty and me on the floor of Gretchen's closet, we are standing in front of a brownstone embedded in a row of similar brownstones on Riverside Drive, above the Hippo Playground. Matt and George run up the stairs like they own the place.

Which, I realize all in one moment, they do.

"You bought this house," I say to Scotty.

"Yes," he says.

"You bought this house . . . just, bought it?"

"It took a little while to close," says Patrick, turning the key in both locks.

We walk in the front door. I half turn to watch Scotty coming up the front steps through the little window beside the front door, and I have this fleeting moment when I expect to see Gretchen right behind him.

"What do you think?" asks Scotty as we all stand in the foyer and look around.

"It has nice bones," I say.

"You don't know what that means, do you?"

"Hey, I watch HGTV. I know things."

"I'm having it renovated. Maybe you can give the contractor some tips."

"I would definitely go with columns, of some sort. Maybe Roman, maybe, you know Corinthian."

"I'll tell him," Scotty says. "His next project is replacing the old windows with floor-to-ceiling, energy-efficient ones."

Matt finds this boring adult talk of windows a perfect opportunity to run up the stairs, followed by a more fastidious George, who is trying to move quickly while simultaneously squeezing the railing in a death grip. Patrick follows them, and I'm surprised by his supervisory instincts.

"The contractors don't have much more work to do here," Scotty continues, gesturing to the recently painted walls, the blue tape around the baseboards, the new finish on the hardwood floors. "They'll probably be done by the time we start back up with school in September. Their major undertaking is going to be next door."

"You also bought the house next door?" I say, this time with as much judgment as I can possibly impart in one sentence.

"Not the whole thing," says Scotty. "We're renting the top two floors, at least until I can convince the owner to sell it to me. I figured we'd put a little work into renovating it, and see how long they hold out. It's for Mae and Simon. They're moving to New York, to be close. To help. Simon is retired, after all, and he can consult from anywhere. But, we've discussed it at length. And it seems logical."

"You've been so busy," I say, and it comes out the way it would if I were inspecting a macaroni collage designed by one of the kids.

Matt and George are on the landing, and I watch Patrick waver between standing above them or below them, trying to assess where the greatest risk lies. "He's been a huge help," says Scotty. "He hasn't left me alone for a minute, which I thought I would hate, but I don't."

I think of George and Matt, Jane and Claudia, Scotty and Patrick, and then strangely, of Lila. I have no desire to see that woman again, though I probably won't be able to avoid it for my entire life. But there's a part of my heart that holds her and wishes that she, out of everyone, did not have to suffer the loss of her specific Gretchen.

Matt is running up to see what the highest number of stairs he can jump from is. George watches him, frowning, and I can't tell if he is afraid to try it himself and resents that Matt can fling himself off so freely, or if he genuinely thinks that Matt's an idiot and might seriously injure himself.

"You'll be official Upper West Siders," I say.

"Don't go spreading it around and ruining my downtown reputation," calls Patrick.

"There's nothing left to ruin." Scotty unbuttons his shirt near the collar. It's hot in here; no central air just yet.

"You're moving in too?" I say, as Patrick comes over to join us.

"Sounds like a sitcom minus the humor, if you ask me," Scotty says. He walks over to put the kibosh on the stair-flinging game, leaving me with Patrick. I think of parasailing, jumping out of planes, cliff diving. I think of that day I sat with Scotty in the Indian cathedral and chose this weird, nonmarital but somehow for-better-or-for-worse relationship with all of them, and what will happen to it if I follow my instincts with his brother.

"You've become quite the helicopter parent," I say. "These guys must be keeping you busy."

"Mostly with chase games. What is it with little kids and needing to be chased?"

"Those games are the worst," I say.

"I'll have my own entrance, you know," he says, and his eyes are not on my face anymore. "Through the basement. I promise to hide a key somewhere easy enough so that you're not discouraged but hard enough so that I can be sure you're not just acting out of convenience."

"I've been thinking about what you said to me, about her," I say. "The end was so . . . it was so hideously *mundane*." Stampeding feet pound through the ceiling directly above our heads. Patrick brushes the corners of my eyes with his thumbs. He knows I don't want the boys to see me crying. "What happened was so large, so planet altering to us. The universe is not the same. And the people who read it in the newspapers—they probably shook their heads and thought, what a shame. It's so sad she had two little kids. And then they ate their breakfasts, and got on the train, and went back to normal."

"I'm sure they did," he says.

"Nothing that we do will go unnoticed," I say, lowering my voice as I hear Georgie's little footsteps at the top of the stairs.

"We would have to be pretty sure," he whispers.

Scotty and the boys appear on the landing. "It's getting dark," Scotty says. "We should get going if we want to walk."

"Tars coming out," George says. Matt is quick to jump down his throat, of course.

"You can't really see stars in New York City, Georgie. The lights are too bright."

I don't want George to feel bad, even though Matt is right. I try to move us on quickly. "I wonder how many miles we would have to drive outside the city to see them?" I say.

"I don't know," says Scotty. "I think you can sometimes see them here, especially later at night when it's really dark."

A short while later, we have almost made our way through Central Park. We take turns carrying George and exchanging the hands we're holding, on our way back to the East Side.

Georgie, currently aided by the security of Scotty's hand, is doing little hops on the walking path. Matt runs up ahead of us, stopping every once in a while to let us catch up.

"This is what it takes for you to let me walk you home," says Patrick. "An entire entourage."

"I'm walking *you* home," I say.

"Do categories, Charlotte," says Matt, already bored with walking.

"I thought that was a drinking game," says Patrick.

"Okay," I say. "The category is planets."

"Plants?" Matt is not impressed.

"No, *planets*. Like Pluto."

"Pluto isn't a planet; it's a dwarf planet."

"Geez, the things they teach you in kindergarten," says Scotty.

"Okay, so, like Mercury," I say.

"That one's boring!"

"You're a stinker." I poke Matt. "How about things that creep you out?"

"Okay! Um, spiders."

George is frowning in concentration, and I know he's trying hard to keep up. "What you mean, that creepy?"

"Um, like, things that ick you out a little. Things you don't like."

"Quash?"

"No, baby, not squash," I say. "Things that are scary, that you stay away from."

"Eels?"

"Sure Georgie, like eels. Eels is a good one."

"Your turn, Charlotte," says Matt, like he's been waiting ten years.

"Hmm. Dogs whose eyes are the same color as their fur. Matty?"

"Like, when Mommy sticks her fingers in her eyes."

"You mean when she would put in her contacts?"

"Yeah. Gross."

"Yeah, you're right, gross," I say.

"Things that are creepy?" says Patrick. "How about that scene in romantic comedies where the girl teaches the guy to dip his French fries in a milkshake like it's some new special thing that no one's ever heard of."

"That *is* creepy," says Scotty. "I was going to say toys that talk by themselves."

I let them take over the game. Matt and George can't get a word in edgewise once Patrick and Scotty get started. The light lowers to the particular hue of dusk, and we walk each other home.

Acknowledgments

I'm blessed to have wonderful people in my corner, who have spent many hours reading drafts, giving advice, discussing the fictional lives of the people I invented, lending me their kitchen tables and bits of their lives, and most of all, loving and supporting me. Thank you to my generous family: Mom, Dad, Gramma, my stepparents, Glenn and Diane, and my sisters, Betsy and Emily. And thank you to my brilliant friends: Heidi Donohue, Roddy Flynn, Cara Gabriel, Erin Kaufman, Anais Koivisto, Carl Menninger, Janet Patton, Jessie Redden, Amal Saade, Heather Fain Schaefer, the Schneider family, Margo Seibert, Amanda Thickpenny, Monica Waldie Timmreck, and Justin Waldie.

Thank you to Allie Larkin. You got this ball rolling, and I'll never forget your help.

Thanks to everyone at my agency, Levine Greenberg Rostan, particularly Lindsey Edgecombe. Thank you times a million to my agent, Victoria Skurnick, a smart, honest, kind, and lion-hearted lady whom I feel lucky to be connected to.

Thanks to everyone at Henry Holt who had a hand in the

production of this book, especially Rita Quintas and Meryl Levavi. I am so grateful to my fantastic editor, Barbara Jones, whose insight, spirit, and sensitivity transformed the story. Thank you to Stella Tan for your input, and for the grace with which you handled all the details.

To the Truman family, the Warren-Fulcher family, and the Donohue family: Thank you for sharing your kiddos with me. This story is what it is because you let them sing with me and be silly with me and drive me bananas and inspire me. The world is better because of people who parent with their whole hearts, and you are among them.

About the Author

CAROLINE ANGELL grew up in Endwell, N.Y., the daughter of an electrical engineer and a public school music teacher. She has a B.A. in musical theater from American University, and currently lives and works in Manhattan. As a playwright and director, she has had her work performed at regional theaters in New York City and in the Washington, D.C., area. *All the Time in the World* is her first novel.